# SKIN SLAVE

'You have been spanked bare, Belle, and are initiate. Now it is time to invite you to *appreciate*.'

'You mean, take a caning.' Belle's voice was casual, yet trembled with reawakened desire.

Dr Cunliffe nodded. 'On the bare bottom,' she said.

'How many strokes?' said Belle.

'Twenty-one,' said Dr Cunliffe. 'I take it you have never had a bare-bottom caning before?'

'I have never been caned at all,' Belle replied faintly. Something in her said, scoop up your dress and get out of the door – but a stronger force rooted her to the spot. Her bottom tingled, longing to feel the bite of the cane, and Belle felt herself grow moist with arousal.

# SKIN SLAVE

*Yolanda Celbridge*

This book is a work of fiction.
In real life, make sure you practise safe sex.

First published in 2000 by
Nexus
Thames Wharf Studios
Rainville Road
London W6 9HA

Copyright © Yolanda Celbridge 2000

The right of Yolanda Celbridge to be identified as the
Author of this Work has been asserted by her in
accordance with the Copyright, Designs and Patents Act
1988.

www.nexus-books.co.uk

Typeset by TW Typesetting, Plymouth, Devon

Printed and bound by
Cox & Wyman Ltd, Reading, Berks

ISBN 0 352 33507 6

# Contents

# Memoir 1

*There was never a time when I wasn't fascinated by spanking, whipping, or anything that would make a bare bum squirm. That sounds funny, doesn't it, when at first, I imagined my vocation was healing. Then I realised what true healing is.*

*After a while, I realised that helping people to fulfil their deepest needs is a healing process. Yes, I'm talking about thrashing them. And the process is two-way – any doctor, or healer, enjoys the feeling of power that comes from doing good. Another person is grateful, improved – obligated, and in a sense at your mercy.*

*Even as a young girl, I was determined to work in bio-technology. Gene-splicing, cloning, eradicating old age and disease, body enhancement. When other girls were talking about boys and ponies, I was busy at my mother's computer, surfing the web. There was such a lot going on, at that time. But, suddenly there was all this fear about cloning, and moral dangers, and interfering with nature, and so on. The Americans got scared, and shut down so many interesting programmes. The British had been the first to clone – sheep, it was – but they got scared too and all the rumours about genetically enhanced food, and everything . . .*

*At college, I started on biochemistry, switched to microbiology and graduated. But when I wanted to proceed to a doctoral thesis, I was completely blown out. My choice was intra-species genetic enhancement, and at that time, it was a no-no. Everybody knew about implants, monkey glands and stuff, but that was as far as you could go. You couldn't do a doctorate in cosmetic surgery.*

*I did get my doctorate, eventually. I had to switch to an acceptable discipline, but related and in a way more interesting, because more practical. But I'll get to that.*

*Well, the spanking and everything that follows – I had a head start, as it were, because that was my mother's trade. Dad had disappeared way back, with some barmaid from Rottingdean – the true tales are always the corny ones, aren't they?*

*We lived in this pretty villa on the south coast, roses and honeysuckle and all, with the Downs on one side and the sea on the other. Brighton was a smudge in the distance. It was pretty romantic. I suppose living by the sea makes you long for faraway places.*

*My mum was a professional dominatrix! Yes, she would thrash fellows, and made a handsome living at it. We always had super holidays, all over the world, and a house in the south of France, and everything. Not a fancy house; an old farmhouse in the Landes, the pine forest by that fabulous 100 km length of dunes the Atlantic beach, all of it nudist.*

*Mum was a nudist, so I was, too. She said being naked was healing. I thought she thrashed men to get back at Dad, but no, she said she forgave him and thrashed men because she couldn't help liking the poor lambs and their need for an auntie to beat them. That was healing, too. There were a lot of nudists around; northern Europeans generally. I saw an occasional striped bottom – male or female. More healing.*

*From an early age, I was used to my mum's business. I had to keep away while she 'treated' her subjects, but I could hear the sounds of whopping – she used to cane, or birch them, on their bare bums – and it turned me on, especially when I would peek at the fellow walking down the road, with a big happy grin. So I equated whopping with happiness. I didn't know why, yet. She used to advertise in smutty magazines, but she gave that up for the Internet.*

*People would come from all over the country – the nice seaside setting was a turn-on and Mum called herself 'Auntie' and acted like a school matron; I mean, none of this* kinky leather stuff, whips and chains and dungeons. Just bare bottoms and the cane, or birch. When I was older, she showed me the whole set-up.

I went to a co-ed boarding school, a 'weekly boarder', in Buckinghamshire. It was pretty lax and of course, corporal punishment is against the law, but they used it anyway. I know they did, because I wangled my way into being matron's helper and these boys would come in to have their caned bottoms dressed. They had taken a dozen of the best. I don't know if it was on the bare, but I think it was. I wasn't allowed to see, as only matron dressed their bums. She looked a bit like Mum, handsome, you know, and always smiled after she'd treated them. The boys didn't look happy after caning, but they were all coy when matron had finished with them. I wondered why these boys hated caning, when men would pay Mum to do far worse?

The Head was a woman, you see, in her fifties, a good ten years older than Mum. Maybe she was getting something out of her system. They took it, bcause they wanted to stay at the school, which was one of the top schools in the UK, and that was why I was there. Girls never got caned; I guess the Head thought girls were incapable of naughtiness. She was an old-fashioned feminist.

Oh, yeah – at sixteen, I got Mum's facts of life talk, although I already knew the facts of bloody life. Sixteen years old, I mean! It was like a birthday present, or something. She was so . . . innocent, my mum. Mum was from the twentieth century and I guess they didn't have the facts of life, then. I mean, we were nudists, but in her day nudists were supposed to be sexless and play volleyball all day and stuff. Well, there were a lot of hunky boys on the beach in France and plenty of forest to get lost in, even old German bunkers from some war or other, and . . . well, I needn't go into details.

I remember one boy, and he said he got the talk from his dad, who said very solemnly, son, think it is time we had a talk about sex and the facts of life, and the cheeky bugger said, sure, Dad, what do you want to know?

Of course, with Mum, I pretended to be all coy. One of her facts of life was whopping, so she explained, a bit shyly,

3

that this paid for all our comforts. She showed me her slippers and canes and birches and explained what she did, and that it was a cleansing thing, to make guys feel happy. I hugged her! I couldn't tell her how thrilled I was, but I asked her to let me watch. Next day, she let me hide behind the curtains!

It was a youngish guy, maybe 30, and not bad-looking. They chatted for a while, on the sofa, then suddenly Mum said he was a naughty boy, and had better strip for punishment. He took all his clothes off except for his panties – it was a woman's G-string – and she made a show of pulling that down, to spank him bare-bum, saying he was a very naughty boy for wearing indecent things, and so on.

She spanked his bare bottom for about ten minutes, all the time telling him what a naughty, naughty, boy he was.

Then she started with a leather-soled slipper, which of course is more painful than the bare hand, and gave him 40 or 50 whops with that. His bum was reddening nicely, and I was getting more and more turned on, and I started to finger myself . . . down there.

After that, she ordered him to kneel over her wooden stool, for caning. I saw he had a hard-on – I couldn't not see – and I started to frot myself hard, hoping I wouldn't make the curtains move. Mum said angrily she would cane his erection away, and she did.

She fastened a dog leash round his neck, and wrapped the chain round his wrists, binding him to the stool's legs. He was whimpering 'Please, Mistress,' and stuff.

She gave him twenty with a short cane, then held a mirror up to his bottom, so he could see, just like at the hairdresser's. His bum was all welted and blotchy and I was wanking off for real.

Then, another twenty – another mirror inspection – then, the longer cane. Three sets of twenty, and he was really striped, and I was on the brink of coming. Another inspection. His hard-on was gone, but she said he hadn't been punished enough, and now she tied his ankles to the legs of the stool and picked up her birch. It was really fearsome, as she swished the air, just by his face.

4

'Please, Mistress, not the birch,' he was moaning, 'Haven't I been punished enough?'

'No!' she snapped, and started to birch him, really hard. I flicked my clitty just twice, and exploded. The birch!

Unless you've witnessed a real birching, you can't imagine how awesome it is. The noise is so soft and sweet and crackly, yet it makes a bare bum jerk like a puppet, when the vip! lands on the skin. And the twigs cover the whole bum, like the embrace of a black widow spider . . .

I was still all warm and wet from my come, as I watched Mum continue the birching. At each stroke, his bum leapt up and clenched and the weals laid by the birch were different to cane weals. Small and sharp, like a mosaic of broken black glass.

He took three sets of twenty with the birch, and she kept stroking and feeling his arse-cheeks, to make sure the welts wouldn't break, although she said afterwards that some subjects actually liked that.

Then she said it was over and untied him, and he knelt down and started to lick and kiss her shoes, babbling about how wonderful she was and how grateful he was and only she understood him, and stuff.

She let him lick her shoes and stockinged ankles for a couple of minutes, then picked up the short cane and told him to stop and get dressed. As he was getting to his knees, she reached over and gave him a dozen real stingers, in rapid fire – vip! vip! vip! – on the bare, and he squealed in delight. I think he was actually sobbing with gratitude.

I watched him leave, through a chink in the curtains. He was skipping down the road! I had never seen anyone so happy. Mum asked me what I thought, and I said the right things – healing, cleansing, and all – though she must have guessed from my flushed face what I had been up to, for she had a sly smile. She was happy that I approved of her!

I didn't say that I intended to follow in her footsteps, or arse-weals, one day. That wank was the best I had ever known, and I used to wank off a lot, believe me. A nudist lifestyle makes you extra sensual and frees you of inhibitions. We are all just flesh. And it is normal for a girl to emulate *her mother. Why not add to my academic career a sensual, healing role?*

*She said the birch was indeed the most beautiful tool of punishment, and you had to know what it was like at first hand, to appreciate its artistic effect.*

*There were a lot of dominas who were not artistic, who didn't really like men at all – slags, who really got a kick from hurting and humiliating men as slaves, with all the weird costumes and kinky dungeon paraphernalia. Men accepted that, because they longed to submit to a lady, however brutal. Most men were submissive . . .*

*I wondered if ladies were submissive – I'd seen their wealed bottoms at the beach. Mum said that yes, in the past, she had taken every treatment she now gave out, and willingly, but wouldn't say more. I knew I should have to find out for myself.*

*Mother is always right.*

# 1

# Spanked Naked

Normally, Belle Puget dozed through lectures, but this speaker's voice had an authority, a menace almost, that kept her alert. It was as though she addressed Belle herself, personally. It was her friend Geisha who had lured her to attend. Geisha was Japanese, like many of the exchange students, as the city was twinned with one in Japan. She spoke English with scarcely a trace of accent, but for a slight American twang. She had family in Hawaii and San Francisco. Geisha's real name was hard to pronounce and she took her nickname as a mark of affection.

'Social Darwinism?' said Belle. 'That's sociology! I'm a microbiologist.'

'Check it out,' said Geisha. 'Dr Cunliffe is hot! Her theories go way beyond the academic field. Even molecules have a social hierarchy, you know.'

So here Belle was, in the dusty lecture theatre, hanging on to every word of the handsome, russet-haired young female, in scholar's gown and an old-fashioned scholar's cap or mortarboard, who spoke with such grace and power.

'The principle of hierarchy, dominance and submission, of extinction and survival,' said Dr Cunliffe, 'extends throughout the world of living creatures. It is found in human society, where the strong survive and the weak go to the wall. Of course, in the twenty-first century, most civilised societies look after their weak and sick, but they survive only in half-life. They are losers, and know it. Only

7

power and dominance bring fulfilment. There are still tribes in the Amazon, or the Pacific islands, who eat the bodies of their enemies slain in battle – the brains, the heart, the genitals especially – to absorb their power.'

There was an uneasy ripple through the lecture theatre. The few males looked embarrassed – lectures were mainly attended by conscientious girl students – but the females crossed their legs, or unconsciously licked their lips.

'There are spiders, scorpions and certain vampire bats, whose females devour their males after mating. The male has delivered his seed and is henceforth useful only as nourishment.'

Some of the girls blushed, but their eyes were bright.

'Our Japanese friends come from a more . . . realistic culture, where our own values of compassion and mercy are less important,' Dr Cunliffe continued. 'Less important, that is, than power, cruelty and survival, pursued as ends in themselves. Worker ants and bees are sacrificed for the good of the horde and sacrifice themselves willingly, like Japanese soldiers of old who thought death in battle glorious, but capture most shameful. Japanese literature, cinema, even everyday comic books attest to this. They are full of images of pain and suffering, of submission to the strong, whose role in life is to devour the weak. The weak may achieve wisdom only by understanding that it is their duty in the world order to *be* devoured. To be punished, for daring to exist.'

Geisha smirked.

Dr Cunliffe looked at her watch.

'Come round for coffee,' whispered Geisha, 'I've some cute stuff to show you.'

Belle nodded, happily. Geisha was pretty well her best friend.

'In further lectures,' said Dr Cunliffe, 'we shall be examining human social structures, and the ways in which under the business suits, and academic robes' – there was a polite titter – 'of so-called civilisation, the laws of the jungle still prevail. Sometimes we dress these laws in social codes, or games; ritualised enactments of survival and extinction. A losing player is "beaten" – symbolically destroyed – and, of course, we talk about football teams, or boxers, "whipping" their opponents. I give you the example of social Darwinism at its most powerful and primitive: the fight for survival of a single human sperm to fertilise the female egg. The hundreds of thousands of sperm are obliged to swim upstream, *whipping* their tails in the waters of the female vagina, each knowing that he must escape drowning in the female's fluid and battle against his fellow-sperm to make them die and transmit his own genome. Any individual is the product of the cruellest and most powerful sperm. Take this young lady here.'

She pointed at Belle! The gesture was meant to seem casual, random, but Belle shivered, for she sensed it was not. She had been chosen.

'Her blonde hair, her full figure, designed for optimum attraction of the male of the species – the sperm, which has become *her*, was the best and strongest of its batch. Think how many plain sisters drowned – thrashed to extinction – on the way to create this beauty!'

Belle blushed furiously, yet could not take her eyes from the dark gaze of Dr Cunliffe.

'She blushes – but blushing, too, is one of nature's tricks, a reaction that is both defensive and aggressive. We shall examine this and other questions in due course,' she said crisply. 'To conclude: only the most powerful individual shall survive, to be born as a human being. So, ladies and gentlemen, ponder on this: just by being born, we are killers. Cruelty becomes us.'

Dr Cunliffe wiped her gleaming lips; the lecture was over.

The girls walked the short distance through the June sunshine, to Geisha's room in the hall of residence nicknamed 'Little Tokyo'.

'Such a beautiful day!' Belle cried. 'Makes me feel I'll live forever! But I thought I'd *die*, when Dr Cunliffe pointed me out!'

'No, you didn't,' said Geisha. 'You were pleased. I'd have been. Optimum attraction of the male of the species!'

She expertly mimicked Dr Cunliffe's fruity contralto.

Belle blushed again, unconsciously twirling her blonde tresses over the tan hillocks of her breasts that swung, bra-less, under the straps of her summer frock.

Geisha was the smaller girl: elfin and wiry, with a hard, boyish body, yet her slender female curves were made more piquant by her tomboy's allure. She had her hair cut short; bobbed and with a kiss curl, in harmony with her big eyes and rosebud lips.

She followed slightly behind Belle's long golden legs, her eyes on the swelling panty line that swayed beneath the light cotton. Her own thin dress clung to her porcelain body, making it clear she wore neither bra nor panties. The morning sun was already scorching, and both dresses were damp with sweat.

'What was that grin of yours?' said Belle, as they entered Geisha's room.

'Oh, just when she mentioned comic books. We love them in Japan. *Devour* them.'

Again, she mimicked Dr Cunliffe's voice, and Belle laughed.

'I've just got a package of them from a friend.'

At once, on entering Geisha's room, Belle saw the half-opened package, and the gaudy covers spilling out. She took one and smelled it.

'Nice paper,' she said.

'Do you always smell paper?' asked Geisha.

'Yes . . . I suppose I've a good sense of smell.'

'I told you Cunliffe would be interesting,' said Geisha. 'The hall was packed.'

'It's funny,' Belle said. 'That stuff about . . . well, you know . . . sperms thrashing, it kind of ties in with something I've been working on.'

'Don't expect me to understand,' said Geisha, 'I'm just a humble Eng. Lit. student.'

Her floor was strewn with volumes of seventeenth-century poetry; in particular, 'Paradise Lost' and other works by John Milton.

'Oh, it is to do with DNA. It is far more complicated than we thought. You know that a human genome, the

10

whole genetic being, is determined in advance by our DNA? There is a theory that DNA is not a fixed quantity, but evolves within itself. That is, every strand of the DNA double helix has, at first, the ability to become any animal at any stage of evolution. The human DNA must fight to be supreme in the DNA arena, as it were, otherwise there will be no cell nucleus.'

'Or women would give birth to cats, or fish,' said Geisha.

'No, because if the cat or fish DNA triumphed, within the double helix, the cell wouldn't form, because the carrier is human. That is why not all women are fertile, or not all the time. Cat DNA appears, the human womb says, "No thanks, I'll wait for a human." '

'Unless there was a way to overcome the womb's rejection,' said Geisha.

Belle said it was a huge 'unless' and began to leaf through the topmost comic book. The text was in Japanese, of course – what text there was. She swallowed, seeing the surreal images.

The first story was all about schoolgirls, with their skirts up and spectacles awry, being spanked on the bare bottom. The images grew stronger, until the girls were gagged with their own panties and caned with rods on the bare buttocks, whose several welts were depicted with cruel precision; their spectacles, broken, dangled halfway out of distended anal cavities.

Then, a sea-dragon devoured a naked girl and had eaten halfway through her pubis; a tiger-man with a giant, distorted, erect penis and four testicles, whipped a girl on the naked bottom with a switch of seaweed and barnacles. A girl was stretched nude on the rack, over a fire of red coals, and whipped by two Shinto priests with quirts of live scorpions. It went on . . .

All the illustrations were of photographic accuracy and glowed with colour.

'Then what happens to the disappointed cat DNA?' said Geisha, teasing.

She began to lift her sweat-soaked skirt over her haunches.

Belle glanced up and laid the book aside, delicately.

'What? Oh . . . No one is quite sure. It is either absorbed – eaten – by the human genome, or else neutralised in some way, in a kind of stasis. This is all at molecular level.'

'Yuk! I think I'll stick to Eng. Lit.,' said Geisha, her voice muffled by her dress.

'Or comics,' said Belle, opening another book.

Here, the naked girls were whipped by nude women with tails, while their bare breasts and pussies were eaten by masked nudes with spiny teeth. Or, girls were tethered in bondage of glowing hot chains, their thighs splayed wide and their toes pegged in their mouths, to take a whipping on the bare quim and anus.

Belle grimaced, but did not take her eyes away. The next page showed a nude, pale-skinned girl, on all fours with her buttocks, clitoris and quim lips grotesquely enlarged. The view was from the rear, so that the openings of her vagina and anus were in the forefront, yet her head was twisted, so that her face was visible, distorted in pain – or ecstacy. The face looked like Geisha's. This picture was not a coloured drawing, but an actual photograph. Belle assumed that computer enhancement produced the fantastic dimensions of both male and female genitals.

The girl had one male's cock deep in her throat, and her lips clung to the shaft. She straddled a male, lying on his back, whose massive penis poked her gash. A third male, positioned to the side, for better viewing of the girl's body (which, Belle reasoned, was the point of the erotic picture) had an equally massive cock plunged into her anus, so deep that only his swollen balls were visible. No male head was visible; their bodies were dark and muscular, almost black.

Because her pleasuring males were positioned beneath her and to one side, the girl's body was visible in its entirety. In particular, the stretched skin of her bare bum was shown completely. There was a fourth male: only his arm was visible, carrying a cane which was in motion – descending on the Japanese girl's buttocks. Her arse was already a lake of crimson.

She was sucking one male, while being buggered and poked by two others and, if this was not enough, she was taking a bare-bottom caning at the same time! Behind her, a lookalike – her twin sister? – also nude, with her feet bound and her mouth gagged with glistening wet panties, masturbated as she watched, evidently waiting her turn. The man with his cock in the fucked girl's mouth buggered her manually, with an electric vibrator in the anus. Belle focused on the fucked girl's arse-cheeks, the cock buried in the anal hole and the cane descending. Her throat was dry, but her clitoris began to tingle and her pussy seeped oil. Belle was aroused by this cruel picture. She imagined herself in the place of the pleasured and whipped girl.

*How can a girl want such things . . .?*

Geisha gasped, as her dress came free. She tossed it aside and opened the bathroom door.

'Cold shower for me,' she said. 'What are you staring at? Ah so, my friends Mikyo and Tana, the terrible twins. Typical fun-loving Japanese girls!'

Geisha laughed and slapped each of her bare buttocks.

'Oh,' said Belle. 'I don't . . . don't remember seeing you in the nude before.'

'Well, do you approve?' said Geisha, facing Belle with her hands on her hips and her thighs splayed. 'We are friends, aren't we? And this *is* the twenty-first century.'

She clasped her arms at the back of her neck, stretching her narrow belly. Belle stared at the Japanese girl's naked body. She felt her cheeks redden and pushed a strand of hair from her brow. There was not a single hair and no hint of down or stubble on Geisha's white bare skin. The hillock of the pubis was an alabaster mound, full and shiny with the pink quim lips delineated neatly below, like a brush stroke or razor slash. The legs and arms were the same silky smoothness – and the armpits as well.

Geisha's nude body was like a precision machine; smooth and in proportion, as though designed for maximum efficiency. Her hard little conic beasts had nipples that were disproportionately large, to give suck; her buttocks were hard as fists, but with just enough round ripeness to signal that their owner was female.

13

'I . . . I don't know if approve is the right word,' said Belle. 'You're so perfect.'

Now, Geisha laughed. She picked up the magazine Belle had perused and her eyes shone as she looked at the photograph. She sniffed the glossy paper, at her lookalike's arse.

'She looks like you,' Belle murmured, 'doesn't she?'

'She should,' said Geisha. 'I mean' – teasing Belle – 'all we Japanese look the same to you, don't we? But this photo is especially naughty. In Japan, we have a different attitude to nudity than you hairy-backs. We make love dressed, and bathe naked.'

'Oh, *I've* been to nude beaches,' Belle protested. 'In France. My family was French, though Puget wasn't the original name. It was my great-grandfather's false name in the Resistance, in the Second World War; when he came to London with General de Gaulle, he kept it. I'm a respectable English girl from Brighton!'

'Brighton? Respectable?'

Belle laughed.

'I still have family in the Bordeaux wine trade and on that Atlantic coast, all the beaches are nude. It's fabulous, you can run across the sand for miles, without a stitch, and the only people you see are as naked as you. There are all these old German bunkers, from the war, when they were expecting an invasion and they are supposed to be haunted. So . . . anyway.'

'So, I guess it's fun to *fuck* in them?' said Geisha.

Belle stared at her, reddened, and then nodded solemnly.

'Yes,' she said. 'I've done that. Braving the spooks. *And* in the open, on the dunes. It is so – *innocent*. You should try it.'

'So innocent,' Geisha repeated, smiling thinly.

*Optimum attraction of the male of the species* . . .

Dr Cunliffe's pronouncement had awakened, or *sharpened*, something in Belle Puget.

'Shall we, then?' said Geisha. 'Shower together, I mean. Actually, I insist – it's my water bill.'

'Well . . .'

Belle shrugged and smiled.

14

She stood and lifted her dress over her haunches, feeling the warm air current on her own pubic mound. The dress stuck at her nipples and she struggled with it, while Geisha laughed. Belle was perspiring heavily when she finally had the dress off, and stood as naked as her friend. She placed a hand at her pubic bush, in mock coyness.

'God, I feel like an ape! So hairy, compared to you!' she said.

She looked down at her thatch, which crept up across her flat, tan belly, almost to her navel and dangled in a jungle of golden wet fronds between her parted thighs. Her arms and legs glowed with fine golden down. Her gash was a wet pink slit set in a golden cornfield.

'But so *alive*,' Geisha murmured. 'Come, let's shower, ape woman.'

The shower stall was meant for one person and it was hard for Belle not to press against Geisha's bare body, as both girls tussled playfully for the soap. But she made no effort to shy away from body contact and the Japanese girl noticed. Soon, they were soaping each other and fingers lathered breasts and thighs, belly and buttocks.

'You're shy, for a nudist!' said Geisha.

'No, I'm not shy,' murmured Belle, her eyes sparkling bright.

Belle's hand rested at the small of Geisha's back. She felt a little nubbin under the skin, at the base of the spine, larger than normal.

'My kundalini point,' said Geisha, 'where all the *tao*, the life energy, flows from. You've got one, too.'

Her fingers stroked the base of Belle's spine, delving deep in her bum-cleft.

'See? There!'

Belle felt a delicious wave of pleasure that was unavoidably sexual, course up her spine, as energy flowed downwards towards her clitoris. Geisha rubbed and rubbed at the nubbin, making it seem to grow larger; and as she felt it grow and smelled the delicate perfume of Geisha's nudity, Belle felt her clitoris began to tingle, in tune with her spine.

She felt guilty, yet not guilty at all. Naughty, rather. Nude, with another nude girl, a porcelain Japanese ... deliciously naughty.

'That is the stump of the tails we used to have,' said Geisha.

'Yours is bigger than mine! I'm jealous!'

'Don't be,' said Geisha. 'We all evolved into humans, but some bits and pieces are left. Like your appendix, inside you.'

Belle *was* shy, now! She said she had had her appendix removed, when she was eleven, and Geisha knelt, suddenly, to look at her scar.

'So tiny and white, on your golden skin,' she murmured. 'Like a snowdrop opening . . .'

Geisha's lips brushed against Belle's appendectomy scar. Then her lips lingered and kissed. Belle cupped the Japanese girl's black cropped hair and pressed her head against her belly. Neither girl spoke. Belle shut her eyes, then opened them again. Geisha's sharp little nose was sniffing her wet jungle of pubic hair.

'I expect you use a lot of shampoo,' said Geisha.

'Oh! You!' said Belle, as though cross. 'How come you are so smooth? You must go through a lot of razors . . . or are you waxed?'

'Born this way,' murmured Geisha. 'No hair; just on my head, and that grows no longer than you see.'

Belle began to stroke the thick, wiry fibres.

'I don't buy shampoo,' said Geisha, her mouth on a tuft of Belle's pubic jungle.

'It . . . it doesn't matter,' said Belle, faintly.

Her pussy was wet.

'Yes, it does,' said Geisha. 'I'll shampoo you.'

She drew back, and spat on Belle's crotch forest. She spat again and again, until Belle's golden hair was specked white with foam. Coolly, Geisha spread her pussy lips with her thumb and forefinger and, with her other hand, began to flick her clitoris. Belle stared, fascinated and excited, as she felt her own pussy gush. Come juice flowed copiously from Geisha's slit, almost at the first touch to the clitoris, which stiffened abruptly. Geisha masturbated until her cupped palm brimmed with come. She rubbed her come onto Belle's pubic thatch, mixing it with her spittle. Geisha began to rub her face in the mound-hair, against Belle's hillock and pubic bone, so that the point of her chin brushed Belle's clitoris.

'Special Geisha shampoo,' she murmured.

Belle gasped, trying not to moan in her excitement, and swallowed hard.

'You aren't going to eat me, like the cat-women in your comic book?' she said, trying to sound light.

'Did that bother you?' said Geisha, her tongue now a hair's breadth from Belle's clitty.

'I liked it,' said Belle. 'It was different. I'd never thought . . .'

The tip of Geisha's tongue flicked on her nubbin and Belle gasped, as a wave of pure pleasure flooded her loins.

'Did you like the picture of my lookalike?' Geisha murmured. 'The girl caned, as she took three cocks? I watched you, as I stripped off.'

'Oh . . .' Belle gasped – what was the use of coyness? – 'you know I did. It turned me on. But such things only happen in dreams.'

'You've dreamed of being taken by three giant cocks? And caned on the bare?'

'Oh, Geisha,' Belle moaned, coy again.

*Here's my arse bare for you. Fuck my holes, whip me, make my flesh serve you.*

'Dreams are real,' said Geisha. 'We'll have a good look. After.'

'Oh . . . after what?' moaned Belle, clutching the Japanese girl's head to her pussy lips.

'No questions,' said Geisha, and plunged her mouth into Belle's open gash, which was now very oily from her come juice.

Belle let herself go, as Geisha's tonguing washed her in pleasure.

'I've . . . I've never done this before,' she said. 'Have you?'

'That was a question,' said Geisha, her voice muffled by Belle's cunt-hairs. 'I'll spank your bare bottom for disobedience.'

'Are you serious?' Belle said.

'That is two questions,' spat Geisha. 'Two questions, two spankings.'

'Oh . . . Oh . . . don't stop,' moaned Belle.

'Don't you want me to spank you?' said Geisha, her hands stroking Belle's wet bottom. 'You've lovely round globes. European globes. I'd love to spank them.'

A finger crept into the pucker of Belle's anus and toyed there, poking an inch inside her. Belle wriggled her bottom as new pleasure excited her clit. Her pussy flowed come.

'Yes . . . yes . . . anything . . . just don't stop. I want to be spanked, hard. Oh, I'm going to come. Please don't stop . . . bring me off. I never knew . . .!'

Geisha fastened her lips on Belle's clitoris and chewed.

'Oh! Oh! Oh!'

Belle clutched the girl's head for support. The orgasm that exploded within her seemed more powerful than any she had known.

Suddenly, Geisha was on her feet again, briskly rinsing Belle's shampooed bush. She licked her lips, which shone with Belle's come. When both girls gleamed clean, she turned off the shower. Belle blinked.

'Oh, Geisha! I can't believe . . .' she began.

'You asked me to spank you on the bare bottom,' said Geisha, in a businesslike tone, with wide, blank eyes.

'Did I?'

'A third question,' said Geisha, leading Belle, dripping, into the warm living room. 'The punishment for *that* is, you must spank me, too.'

Geisha fetched two mugs of coffee from the stove, then sat cross-legged, still in the nude, and opened all the comic books in an array before her. At the top of Geisha's open, swollen pussy, her clitoris stood like an elfin thumb.

'Sit on my lap, Belle and we'll read our books,' said Geisha.

She directed Belle's haunches, so that her anal pucker rested squarely on Geisha's clit. Geisha sighed and began to leaf through the books, writhing her hips all the time with the tip of her clit poking inside Belle's anus. She stopped at a two-page illustration.

'I'm working on my thesis,' said Geisha, her fingers stroking Belle's cunt-lips, as she would stroke a kitten. 'Paradise Lost – seen from a Japanese perspective. Satan gets kicked out of heaven, for rebelling against God. But he is still an angel, even though a fallen one, and is given his own domain to rule – hell. He keeps asking God to let him back to heaven, but is refused. In my view, Satan is only pretending to plead. He likes hell – it is our oriental version of heaven, a sensual paradise. It is God who is the loser. And in a fit of pique, he creates mankind, just to spite Satan. Satan has the last laugh, though, for as they say, the devil has all the best tunes . . .'

As she spoke, Geisha's buttocks writhed in Belle's lap. The girl's clitoris was poked to its full length, into the tip of Belle's anus. Belle felt the delicious tickling of the stiffened limb and her pussy began to wet again.

'I think I'll come now,' said Geisha, 'and then we can do your spanking. Ah! Ah! Ah!'

She spasmed briefly, grunting briefly, three times as though in pain. Then, without warning, she grasped Belle and laid her across her thighs with her bare buttocks thrust upwards. She made Belle part her thighs so that her wet pussy was visible amid the tangle of cunt-hairs. Geisha spanked Belle's bare bottom, very softly, for twenty slaps, at intervals of ten seconds. Belle let it happen. Her buttocks clenched at each slap.

'You haven't been spanked before, Belle? On the bare, I mean?'

'Not spanked at all. I never imagined being spanked on the bare bottom.'

'Like it?'

'I'm . . . I'm not sure.'

'You liked it when I made you come, didn't you?'

'Oh! More than *like*.'

'A good spank, on the bare buttocks, is more than coming. A *caning* is more, again.'

19

Twenty more, harder, at intervals of five seconds. Now, Belle's fesses clenched more tightly. The spanks really stung. But a bare-bum *caning* . . . her cunt flowed, at that thought.

'Was it a lie, Belle?' said Geisha. 'That you've never *imagined* your bare bottom spanked?'

Twenty more spanks, this time ferocious, one to a second. Belle's arse quivered, squirming to dissipate the stinging pain, but without success. It *hurt!* Tears came to her eyes, but she rubbed her moist pussy and clitoris against the Japanese girl's thigh and, as her bottom smarted more and more, she felt a second come welling in her belly.

'Yes,' she sobbed, 'It was a lie. I've imagined it.'

'Many times?'

'Yes?'

'And masturbated at the dream?'

'Yes! Oh, yes! Damn it, Geisha! Spank me . . .'

Geisha continued to spank her buttocks, now in an easy rhythm of two-second intervals, but the spanks still very sore and smarting. Some of the spanks took Belle in the open cunt, which made her gasp.

'God, it hurts!' she cried.

'Pain and pleasure are the same,' said Geisha, distantly. 'Didn't it hurt when you came, under my tonguing?'

'No! No! Not like this!'

'Then I didn't tongue you hard enough,' said Geisha. 'Next time, I'll bite your clit hard, like that picture.'

The picture showed a tailed female demon, with monstrously distended teats and clitty, erect like a male penis. She whipped a nude bound girl with her scaly, spiked tail while she ate the clitoris of a second nude, bound with legs apart over a blazing fire.

'I like this one,' teased Geisha. 'It reminds me of Dr Cunliffe.'

'Oh! Oh!' gasped Belle, under her spanking. 'My bum's raw!'

'Going to come again?'

'Yes! Damn you! Oh! Oh! Ahhh . . . yes! *Ahhh* . . .'

A longer, more subtle orgasm, flooded Belle's body.

'Two comes, and so quickly!' she moaned. 'I've never even masturbated so much!'

When her spanking was over, they had their coffee. Belle longed to cuddle Geisha, hold her and be warm with her; but Geisha was cold, distant, abstractedly turning the pages of her comic books while slowly flicking her swollen pink clitoris. Belle marvelled. It was scary, that Geisha could be so coolly in control of her body.

'How could that picture remind you of Dr Cunliffe, when you hadn't opened the books yet?' she demanded suddenly.

'Oh ... Oh, I've seen that one before,' said Geisha.

'I don't believe you.'

'Then spank me for my untruth,' said Geisha and, still masturbating, knelt to present her bare fesses to Belle's hand.

Geisha's bare buttocks jerked back and forth like a metronome, as Belle's palm reddened her skin with spanks. The buttocks clenched and opened to an unheard tune and the squirming of the tensed bare nates seemed military in its precision. Geisha said nothing at all, not even a gasp or a whimper. Her breathing was normal, though her bare bottom was flaming scarlet.

Belle had delivered over 800 spanks, and her palm ached. Suddenly, she felt angry and made her slaps faster. She wanted the Japanese girl to react and lose her cool. Yet Geisha passively accepted the force of her spanking. Suddenly, after over 1,000 spanks, Geisha took Belle's fingers, led them to her distended clitoris and made her pinch the organ hard, with her nails. Belle obeyed, knowing it must hurt. Geisha climaxed at once.

Now, she permitted the naked Belle to embrace her, folding the hard white body in her arms and kissing her damp hair. Belle's eyes were moist; Geisha, dry-eyed.

'Oh, you poor dear!' said Belle. *'Why ...?'*

Geisha switched on an electric fan and the two girls lay beside each other on their bellies, each with her buttocks in its cooling air. They sipped coffee, which was by now, to Belle's surprise, exactly hot enough.

'Control,' said Geisha. 'Dominance, and submission to pain.'

She smiled, for the first time in ages, and Belle smiled back, gratefully.

'You spanked me hard,' she said, casually, 'and it smarts like hell. But by taking the pain, I show that I own it and can give it to others a hundred times over. I didn't spank you all that hard, Belle, however it seemed. It was your initiation.'

'You mean, you do this all the time? With others?'

Belle instantly regretted her jealous tone.

Geisha smiled, coldly, this time.

'With many others,' she said. 'Female, and male, and . . .'

She pursed her lips.

'And?' Belle pressed her.

'And,' Geisha continued, but shifting ground, 'it is not just spanking. These picture books are real, Belle. Where I come from, there are demons and their language is pain. We must live with our demons, my sweet Belle. Hell exists . . . *and it's beautiful*. Like an orgasm that doesn't end.'

# 2

# Love Hurts

'Initiation . . .'

What had Geisha meant? Belle tried to concentrate on her studies in the week following Dr Cunliffe's lecture, but kept wondering if Geisha had further things planned for her. She hoped so. Had Geisha planned her spanking and their lesbian sex, from the very first? Belle was joyous that Geisha wanted her, even as a plaything.

*Especially as a plaything.*

She had no contact with Geisha until Dr Cunliffe's next lecture. There were practical things to attend to. Belle, as a second-year student, would not take her finals for two years, but already her tutor had her marked for a good First and postgraduate work would follow, leading to a lucrative career. She was in the fast track. That meant her course would be interrupted by a one-year sabbatical, to gain practical experience.

'You will shine, Belle,' said Dr Sawyer, her tutor. 'You can easily combine a career in industry – pharmaceutical, biotechnics, whatever you choose – while retaining a foot in the academic world, like Dr Cunliffe. Each world nourishes the other.'

Belle asked for, and was granted, as much time as she needed to decide. As she sat down to listen to Dr Cunliffe, a stack of glossy paperwork lay on her desk only half perused: personalised letters from foundations, institutes and chemical and pharmaceutical companies.

Most of the opportunities were abroad and located in large cities; all inland. Belle recognised that one day she might have to dwell in cities, but from her nearby seaside village, Brighton itself seemed city enough. Even London was scary.

One folder had caught her eye. It was in Japanese, with parallel English text, and mentioned a bio-research institute located on a Pacific island in Micronesia. Oddly, the English text seemed much shorter than the Japanese; like an afterthought. So maybe this was the challenge she had been waiting for: truly original research, with no other English-speakers to compete.

Dr Sawyer said she had no knowledge of such a place and the prospectus had not been included by her in Belle's folder. It must have slipped in by accident, from another hand. Never mind. Geisha would help her translate. Geisha . . .

Remembering the girl's hands on her body and the hard efficiency of her spanking, Belle rubbed her buttocks. She recalled the utter, piercing intensity of her orgasm from Geisha's tonguing of her clitoris; the smooth velvet of her climax under bare-bottom spanking. She had masturbated often during the past week, dreaming of their lesbian sex; but alone, her climax was not the same. The Japanese girl seemed to beckon her. The sea beckoned, too. Belle had never lived or spent long far from the ocean, with its salt tang; its smell of far away. Geisha smelled of the sea. Smiling, she put the folder in her bag and hurried to Dr Cunliffe's lecture.

Again, the hall was packed. Geisha met Belle as though according to plan, with a smile and businesslike nod. She took Belle's arm and led her to the remaining two vacant seats in the front row, just below Dr Cunliffe's podium.

Belle listened, spellbound, while the hour sped away.

'And so,' Dr Cunliffe concluded, 'the extinction of the unlucky neanderthals is a valuable field model of the principles of Social Darwinism. The race may be to the swift, and beauty may indeed be in the eye of the beholder, but the whip hand is always the whip hand.'

Belle realised she was clutching Geisha's hand, and that Dr Cunliffe was watching her. Dr Cunliffe swirled from the podium and approached them. Belle disengaged her hand from Geisha's and both girls stood up.

'One whip hand generally finds another,' said the Doctor.

Belle smiled, uncertainly. Seen close up, Dr Cunliffe was younger and prettier than Belle had assumed. Her eyes were dark pools beneath a sweep of lush russet tresses. Even swathed in her gown, the ripe fullness of her breasts and bottom stood out. Her legs were long, her shoes pointed; high and spiked with silver points. Dr Jolita Cunliffe, Belle thought, was a most attractive female. She wondered how she would look nude, on the dunes by the Atlantic. Or bent over Belle's knee, for a bare-bottom spanking. Better still, Belle's own fesses bared to the Doctor's spanking hand. Belle blushed; now, Dr Cunliffe smiled as though guessing her dream.

'You two ladies seemed my most attentive students,' she said. 'Why, I do believe I sent some of them to sleep!'

'Impossible!' Belle blurted. 'It was . . . *thrilling.*'

'You are too modest, Dr Cunliffe,' said Geisha, suddenly.

Belle saw their dark eyes lock.

'And you, too flattering,' said Dr Cunliffe. 'I am sure half an hour of my company will dissuade you, if you shall be kind enough to accept coffee in my set.'

Lecturers' rooms in college were known as a 'set'.

'I have so many questions,' Belle said. 'My own field, molecular biology –'

'Wait and get some java inside us, Belle,' said Dr Cunliffe. 'I may call you Belle?'

'Why, yes . . .'

*How does she know my name?*

'The nameplate on your bag,' said Dr Cunliffe, smoothly.

'Oh . . . yes.'

*She must have cat's eyes to read it.*

Dr Cunliffe occupied a compact set on the second floor. After climbing the musty stairs, Belle was surprised at the stark neatness of her rooms, painted all in white and

25

almost devoid of furniture or decoration. There was an airy living-room, a kitchenette and two doors, for bathroom and bedroom. One wall of the room was filled by a giant computer monitor, with a keyboard on the floor beside a vase of red, long-stemmed roses. Belle excused herself to go to the bathroom, tried a door and found it locked.

'My bedroom,' said Dr Cunliffe. 'I keep my computer and valuables there.'

The bathroom was stark, like the lounge, with none of the normal lotions or scents. Belle returned and was offered a seat on a huge bean-bag covered in a white, washable cover. Geisha was already lolling, and Belle did the same. It was almost impossible not to loll in the low, comfortable seats, so that Belle had to cross her legs to stop her undies from showing.

Just as Dr Cunliffe returned from the kitchen with mugs of coffee, Belle had given up the struggle and sprawled, with her panties open to view at her hillock mound. Geisha lolled too, and her light dress rode up. She wore no knickers and the porcelain hillock of her pubis was visible, with the faint pink slash of her quim and her extruded clitoris. Dr Cunliffe seemed not to notice. Suddenly, Belle felt awfully stuffy for wearing panties at all, on this hot day. She was a nudist, wasn't she?

Dr Cunliffe draped herself aslant, in a practised motion, so that her own modesty was preserved, while she could observe the two young women. Her pouffe was slightly higher. She wore a severe, schoolmistressy outfit, of long grey linen skirt, white blouse and black stockings. She kicked off her spiked shoes, revealing a hole in each stocking where her long, sharp toenails had punched through. Her fingernails were also artfully long, sharp and painted green.

The only decorations on her white walls were two life-size black and white photographs and a mirror. The mirror was built into one of the photographs. On the left was a female nude with head and body completely shaven. The bare buttocks were slightly splayed. The model's arms were demurely at her sides, but she stood on the balls of her feet, as though ready to spring.

The right wall, facing, had the same model, photographed simultaneously from the front. Her very full, naked breasts thrust proudly, with large, dark nipples and a pubic mound entirely bare, like her other limbs. In place of features, her face was a mirror. The model was obviously Dr Cunliffe herself, with the conceit of a shaven scalp and body.

Belle scrutinised her and concluded that she must be wearing a very tight, indeed painfully tight bra, to restrain those massive teats. The buttocks were demure under her wide grey skirt, but the peach still swelled against the fabric. Belle felt a little bit envious, even though the Doctor must be 28 or 29, at least. They sipped coffee.

'Questions?' said Dr Cunliffe, looking at Belle.

Geisha shifted, to partially but not totally hide her bare crotch, and the movement was shameless: she shifted not for modesty, but for comfort.

'If I understand correctly, the neanderthals became extinct because they were wiped out by homo sapiens?'

'Massacred,' said Dr Cunliffe, crisply. 'Ethnic cleansing: sacrificial piles of bones.'

'Yet, they had coexisted for over 50,000 years?'

'Correct.'

'Then, why, all of a sudden?'

'It was not all of a sudden,' said Dr Cunliffe. 'Cruelty never is. It needs time to grow, feeding on itself until it becomes its own end. Karl Marx, speaking of social revolution, said that the end justifies the means, but he got it the wrong way round. The means justify the end. The means become the end. In 1945, to terminate the Second World War, the Americans dropped atomic bombs on Hiroshima and Nagasaki. The Japanese got the message and promptly surrendered. But they would have equally surrendered if the Americans had dropped the bombs ten kilometres out to sea, killing no one. They had the technology, and they had to show it off.'

'Why pick on the neanderthals?'

'Because they were stupid. Any successful animal evolves to the form best suited to survival of the species, and not beyond. The neanderthals were perfectly evolved human beings. They had basic language, basic tools; all they needed. They got no further. Homo sapiens did. About 200,000 years ago, there was a massive and unexplained increase in *our* brain size, from 950cc to 1450cc. An increase of 50%; far too much for purposes of mere survival. Why should a cave man need art? Superior art meant superior weapons, and that is why the human killed the neanderthal: for sport, to show off his *power*. It was something to do.'

'So, brains mean art, art means power, and power means cruelty.'

'Yes. For example, man is the only animal that copulates face to face and practises cunnilingus. Animals kill and mate for survival, not pleasure. Only humans torture.'

Belle laughed, nervously; Geisha did not. Her eyes narrowed to slits and she opened her thighs so that her naked minge was in full view. Geisha's quim lips glistened.

'Cunnilingus is delicious torture,' she said. 'To watch a girl's face twist in pleasure . . .'

'What is cruel about making love face to face?' said Belle.

'Watch,' said Dr Cunliffe.

She punched a password into the keyboard on the floor beside her. Geisha watched Dr Cunliffe's fingers, as she typed. The giant monitor flashed into life.

The screen showed a naked man and woman, copulating. Both appeared to be Japanese. The man was ramming the woman very hard. His buttocks flashed like scissors, as he poked the woman's hole. Close-up shots showed a massively oversized penis, like a machine piston, thrusting in and out of the oily vagina. The woman groaned, wept and shrieked, though her thighs were parted wide and her legs wrapped around the man's mid-back, clinging to him and urging him to pierce her. The man stared at her face twisted in pain, with a malicious grin.

Suddenly, he withdrew. The huge penis was shown in close-up again and the woman's vulva and cleft spread wide open. The penis glistened with the woman's come, oiling its passage into her anus. The penis thrust savagely until it was buried in her anal cavity, right to the balls. Now, the camera panned to show the man buggering the woman, on top and facing her.

His grin was devilish. She did not groan now, but shrieked, repeatedly, as the penis rammed her anus. Tears coursed on her cheeks and her mouth gaped wide open. Her cries of agony were shrill and her face contorted in pain, like a demon's. Her legs clung to the man as though to crush him, and her feet beat the small of his back in time with his poking, urging him to fuck her bumhole harder.

Belle shifted, allowing her own knickers to show and aware that they were stained with a damp patch at her gash. She found herself excited, despite her repulsion. Yet, all the time, the woman shrieked; an inhuman ululation of pain. The man grinned, like a lion toying with its prey. Belle glanced at Geisha and saw that her finger was at her bare pussy. The extruded clitoris was stiffened. Geisha was masturbating.

Dr Cunliffe suddenly blanked the screen.

'Now, what does that teach us?' she said, briskly.

'Why was the lady screaming in pain, when she obviously wanted the male to penetrate her?' said Belle. 'And in both holes.'

'The lady's pain was simulated,' said Dr Cunliffe. 'Or perhaps not. She wanted her pleasure to hurt her. And the male copulated face to face, even during anal sex, because he wished to observe her discomfort.'

'Power,' said Geisha.

'Oriental males have penises markedly smaller than occidentals, who in turn are smaller than Africans,' said Dr Cunliffe. 'There is a compensating subtlety in their sex techniques. You will note that the close-up of the penis was always detached from the Japanese male's person. In fact, that was another male's penis, and another vulva – stunt doubles, as it were. The male derives pleasure from the female screams, because he is convinced that his penis is big enough to hurt her. Pain equals power. It is a short step from this form of copulation to a display of power, where intimacy is unnecessary.'

She touched the keyboard again. Another scene appeared, in glowing colour.

Japan, again. Lanterns, kimonos, futons. A man and his wife asleep, naked. A burglar bursts into the room, wearing a demon's mask and a monk's robe. Close-up of the left hand, whose little finger has been severed: he is a member of the feared *yakuza*, the Japanese criminal brotherhood. He does nothing more than show the terrified couple his sword and his mutilated hand. They are powerless to disobey a *yakuza*.

The husband binds his wife's wrists and ankles and she is splayed, nude, on the bed, with her bare bottom raised. Her nipples are clamped in a vice that stretches her breasts flat. Her vulva is forced open and the lips pinched and flattened by a similar clamp, which has a tickler knob pressing right against her clitoris. The *yakuza* hands the man his sword and instructs him to flog his wife. Using the flat of the sword, the husband weeps as he canes his wife on the bare buttocks, savagely, to over 100 strokes. He is ordered to masturbate while caning his wife.

At each stroke, the woman shrieks, her mouth opening wide and tongue flapping. Her face is puffy and red, streaming with tears. Her cries and the twitching of her flogged buttocks become unbroken. The camera shows us her squirming vulva, close up; her clitoris is distended, the jolt of her flogging rubbing it against the tickler. Her gash gleams with come. The intruder surveys the proceedings impassively with arms folded.

By the time his wife's bare bottom is a mass of black and purple bruises, the man's penis is fully erect. Again, on orders, he parts his wife's wealed fesses and places his penis at the entrance to her anal chamber. In close-up, we see his monstrously erect flesh press and penetrate the tight, resisting pucker of the anal hole. The camera pans: she shrieks louder than ever, as her husband's penis plunges to the root of her anus. He begins to bugger his wife, stroking hard. After two minutes of vigorous bum-fucking, the husband withdraws his penis from his wife's anus and twists her head towards him, pulling her hair, so that her throat is taut.

In close-up, we see the penis plunge to the back of her throat and her lips enveloping his balls. Still sobbing, she begins to suck, as he thrusts into her throat. At the moment of coming, he withdraws his penis, slimy from her saliva, and ejaculates his sperm over her eyes and nose.

In horror, the man releases his wife and prostrates himself, begging for forgiveness. She needs few orders to bind her husband in return, with a tight cord sheathing his genitals. He too is splayed nude for punishment, gagged with his wife's heavily stained panties.

Snarling, the shamed wife begins to flog him. The intruder retreats into the shadows. The wife flogs her husband's bare buttocks with the sword, masturbating as his weals turn purple, although no orders have been given. After 200 strokes, his buttocks are quite black. Her clamped vulva is seen close up, with the tickler flicking rapidly on her stiff clitoris and her gash oozing copious come. She ceases flogging and rams the handle of the sword into his anus, right to the hilt. As she continues to masturbate, she buggers her screaming husband. With a savage twist of the sword, which makes his voice shrill in agony, she heaves in orgasm. Dropping the sword and with belly still twitching, she squats over his face and pisses copiously.

The husband is released, sobbing; the wife freed from her nipple and gash clamps, and the *yakuza* wipes his sword handle on the woman's hair. He orders the nude couple to embrace, kiss each other on the lips and remain kissing, for five minutes after his departure. Bowing gracefully, he exits the scene. The naked husband and wife kiss full on the lips, as the camera fades, and the last shot is of eyes glistening with tears of hatred . . .

Belle was trembling. Her clitoris was stiff and her panties soaked in come. She looked at Geisha and saw her openly masturbating.

'So!' murmured Dr Cunliffe. 'A perfect exercise in power: the intruder has shamed the husband and wife to each other and their shame will haunt them forever. Or . . .?'

'Or,' said Geisha, flicking her clitoris, 'they will understand themselves, and pursue pleasure through the arts of pain. The demon intruder has awakened them from sleep.'

'Even the actors are no actors,' said Dr Cunliffe. 'Those welts were real. Imagine the power the intruder possessed, as a secret society member. Imagine such power, wielded purely through the mind, by a raising of the eyebrow, a flick of the finger, or even a computer codeword. The submission automatic, and entirely in the mind of the willing subject, obeying his or her subjugator anywhere in the world. There are women called dominatrixes, Belle, who possess such power. Women who whip and torture submissive males and females to the brink of existence, whose slaves are bound by invisible chains and can never be slaves enough.'

'Imagine if there were a society so secret that its adepts were unaware of it,' Geisha whispered, her eyes glinting as she caressed herself.

'I believe you are a nudist, Belle?' said Dr Cunliffe, suddenly.

'Oh . . .' Belle blushed.

'Geisha and I know each other,' said the academic. 'We share secrets. I am a nudist myself.'

She smiled, and Belle felt suddenly at her ease: she told of her frequent visits to the Atlantic nude beaches in France. Dr Cunliffe widened her eyes in apparent surprise and said she, too, was well acquainted with the area. They swapped place names and Belle was convinced of her sincerity. But how much else had Geisha told her? Could she trust either woman?

'I was very nervous about nudity at first,' said Dr Cunliffe.

She loosened her tie and undid the top two buttons of her blouse.

'I think we all are,' Belle ventured.

'You'll see,' said Dr Cunliffe. 'I take it we may all be at our ease . . .?'

Geisha stood, grinning, and pulled loose the shoulder straps that held her dress. She let her dress fall to the floor and stepped out of it. There were streaks of juice at her pussy and the tops of her thighs and her clitoris swelled like a bud. Dr Cunliffe rose, too, unfastening her belt. She unzipped her skirt and dropped it. The tails of her blouse dangled over her mound but did not conceal her garter belt, suspender straps and the floral pattern of her black stockings.

She wore no panties. Her pubic mound was thickly afforested with lush brown hair. Belle watched, mesmerised by her furry hillock, as the lecturer stripped.

'Geisha did tell me more, Belle,' said Dr Cunliffe, 'as I suppose you were wondering. She told me about your lesbian sex act, that you made love, that you spanked and were spanked. That you orgasmed under spanking. That you are *initiate*.'

She began to peel off her stockings, one by one, and slowly. Belle stared. The woman's legs were covered in a pelt of russet hairs, sleek, like a cat's.

'If you are shocked or upset, Belle, there is the door,' said Dr Cunliffe, as she shed her blouse and stood naked, beside the hairless, nude Geisha.

'I . . . I am neither,' said Belle, standing also and lifting her short dress over her head.

She stood nude, facing two other bare women.

'I'm just frightened I cannot match your perfection.'

'There is always the door,' Geisha whispered, 'until you close it on yourself, by choice.'

Dr Cunliffe's cunt-hairs did not stop at her swollen mound: they continued, thinning into the same sleek pelt, right up her belly and over the massive, jutting breasts, whose nipples were hard, like earthen pots. Her whole body was covered in delicate, russet fleece. Only on the arse and heavy breasts, did the fleece thin to down, leaving the teats and buttocks almost bare. The pubic jungle extended into her anal cleft and hung between her thighs, enlaced like ivy.

'I thought *I* was hairy!' gasped Belle. 'Oh, I'm sorry! I didn't mean . . .'

Dr Cunliffe laughed.

Suddenly, she stretched her arms. With a sinuous twisting of her back, she placed her head at each armpit in turn and licked herself clean. Then, she lifted one leg, so that her foot clasped her neck and her vaginal and anal areas were fully bared. Standing one-legged, she bent her back to a perfect curve and licked her pussy and anus. The whole ceremony had taken seconds: an automatic reflex, like scratching.

When she stood straight again, a cane had materialised in Dr Cunliffe's hand. Perhaps Geisha had put it there, or it had been hidden in the folds of the pouffe. It didn't matter, for the cane was in Dr Cunliffe's hand, trembling like an antenna. The cane was all that mattered . . .

'We shall treat your exclamation as a grave impoliteness, which must be punished.'

'Oh . . . I said I was sorry!'

Dr Cunliffe laughed again. Her melodious contralto voice acted on Belle like a flute, charming her. She never wanted to displease the furry russet woman, naked for her.

'Your apology is unnecessary, as your reaction to my genetic oddity was quite normal. But, for the purpose of your appreciation, we shall treat it as a fault. You have been spanked bare, Belle, and are initiate. Now, it is time to invite you to *appreciate*.'

'You mean, take a caning.'

Belle's voice was casual, yet trembled with reawakened desire.

Dr Cunliffe nodded.

'On the bare bottom,' she said.

In shadow, Geisha was quietly stroking her extruded clitoris.

'How . . . how many strokes?' said Belle.

'Twenty-one,' said Dr Cunliffe. 'I take it you have never had a bare-bottom caning before?'

'I have never been caned at all,' Belle replied, faintly.

Something in her said, *scoop up your dress and get out of the door* – but a stronger force rooted her to the spot. Her bottom tingled, longing to feel the bite of the cane, and Belle felt her quim wet with come.

'I marked you in my first lecture,' said Dr Cunliffe. 'Unlike the many – even the intelligent many – you, Belle, are *alive*. Now, I want to mark your bare bottom with my cane.'

Geisha masturbated openly, her pink pussy lips swollen to rose petals. Her thighs ran with glistening fluid.

'Life means the ability to feel discomfort,' said Dr Cunliffe, 'thus, to evolve the skills for its easing. There can be no such thing as a pure intelligence, without form, for such a being would not know pain and would be merely a computer; indifferent, even to its own survival.'

'So,' said Belle slowly, 'intelligent life means the ability to feel pain.'

'Worms can feel pain. Intelligent life means the ability to *appreciate* pain,' said Dr Cunliffe, 'and to profit from its infliction . . . on others, or on one's own person. I propose to begin your appreciation with a simple bare-bottom caning of twenty-one strokes, no more and no less, which you may take bending over and touching your toes.'

*Begin* appreciation . . .!

'Take your time,' said Dr Cunliffe.

Lazily, she took a long-stemmed rose from the vase and Geisha spread her glistening pink gash. Dr Cunliffe pushed the rose all the way inside the Japanese girl's vagina, until only the flower was showing, wreathed by the petals of Geisha's pussy. Geisha shut her eyes once, but betrayed no other sign of discomfort. Belle swallowed, and breathed deeply.

'I *want* to appreciate, Dr Cunliffe,' she said. 'I'll take your caning.'

# Memoir 2

After I first witnessed a beating, Mum let the subject drop.
I was at school weekdays, of course, and busy planning
ahead for college and career. I knew I'd score 'A's in biology
and all the sciences, though I wasn't much good at the arts.
I could natter in French, but not very grammatically. It
depends on what sort of brain you have. Genetics fascinated
me. The bio teacher said I had a male brain. I said that was
no compliment.

A few months later, I had my exams over with. I had
secured a place at the college which offered the best bio
courses and I wasn't worried about the exam results.
Off-handedly, Mum asked if I would care to watch another
thrashing. She proposed that I should actually witness it
beside her in the room. It was an appointment for the next
day; a young guy, 'very hunky', she said, as if that made a
difference. Well, I suppose it did, for I wanked off in bed that
night, fantasising about this male bum being thrashed. He
was young, had plenty of money, and would pay extra if she
had a 'friend' to inspect – a sort of nursy set-up. Males are
exhibitionists, just like females.

I should have the best part of a year to spend, between
leaving school and going up to college, and had to find work.
So, with my experience in the surgery at school, I figured I
could be a temporary nurse or something. I knew I would be a
low-paid skivvy, but if it was somewhere abroad and exotic, I
didn't mind. Arizona, or somewhere. Mum never pushed me,
but always listened attentively, even if I seemed far-fetched.

*The subject arrived for treatment, and it blew me away when I recognised him! He was only the head prefect of my school, that's what. He was a hunk, and snobbish with it; he ignored all us girls who had secret crushes on him. His family was seriously rich and his dad was some kind of plastic surgeon, literally in Harley Street. He was Jewish – Henry Stone was his name and he had a really handsome, brooding face; like a pirate or something. It is often powerful, privileged men who want to be thrashed and humiliated.*

*From what I knew, his dad ran this clinic for rich old bitches who wanted nips and tucks, bigger boobs and bums, harder thighs, tighter pussies – all that. They came from all over the world. It was snob value; they wanted to go to swinging London to lunch and shop, and shop some more. They didn't want a surgeon in Miami or whatever – I mean, they lived in Miami. Dr Stone had this health farm thing, in Buckinghamshire, where they could be pampered like English duchesses, after the rigours of shopping and boob expansion.*

*Of course, Henry recognised me too; but we played this po-faced game of not knowing each other, which added spice: school was over in a few weeks anyway and it didn't matter. But I was juicing up as I thought of seeing his bare bum thrashed, so that when I saw him squirm and whimper, I wouldn't have a crush on him any more. That's what I thought.*

*Mum welcomed Henry – it wasn't his first visit, obviously – and gave him some bullshit about my going to be a nurse and needing experience, and la-di-da. I was creaming; I wanted her to get his pants down and get on with it. But she took her time, teasing him – that is part of being a good domina. I sat demurely on the sofa, dressed sort of nursily: a tight white blouse and a navy bra underneath, scalloped and thrusting the titties well up; a navy skirt and stockings and sussies the same. I had no panties on, but I hadn't told Mum. And I had super spiky blue stilettos. I brushed against Henry's thigh a bit and I saw him stiffening. It was great, my power!*

*At last, he was ordered to strip for punishment.*

*'Remember, my daughter is to be a nurse,' said Mum, 'and is here purely to observe.'*

Henry was meek as a lamb and stripped off, peeking at me all the time. He wasn't wearing panties and had the stiffest cock I'd ever seen! I'd never seen a circumcised cock before; his helmet was huge and crimson, all shiny and menacing as though his peehole was an eye, winking at me. Mum pretended to be really angry at no panties, or maybe not pretending, and got him over her knee for his bare-bum spanking.

He took a spanking for a good fifteen minutes, and he was clenching beautifully; I was longing to wank off, as my thighs were running with come, right into my stocking tops. I wished I had panties on, to sop up my juice. All the time, Mum was telling him he was more insolent than ever and he would get a thorough birching this time, to teach him manners in front of his cousin. She was his 'auntie', you see, so that made me his 'cousin.' It's all about role-playing.

She took the slipper and he had fifteen minutes of that – wip! wip! wip! – very hard, and his bum was a mass of scarlet. I stood up and folded my arms as I watched, pressing my thighs together to try and stop my come flowing; but of course the pressure on my clitty only got me more excited. I could feel my stockings getting quite wet, down my thigh, and wished I'd worn a skirt that covered more of me than my micro-mini! After spanking and the slipper, he was still hard as rock and took his time preening in the mirror and rubbing his sore red bottom.

But Mum got sterner. He knelt over the stool and my help was enlisted, to strap him down. I got the dog leash round his neck and Mum had some cuffs made of PVC, with velcro fastenings, I think they were Japanese. They were very light but extremely strong and I fastened his wrists and ankles very tightly to the legs of the stool, so that his bare bum stuck up well in the air. I had one cuff left and I whipped it round the shaft of his cock and pulled tight, just leaving his bulb and balls free, but well swollen. He squeaked! Mum just grinned. But his cock didn't go down – the helmet bulged and it was yummy to watch; I was really sopping with come.

Then, Mum began his caning. She used the short one for a set of twenty, without a pause, and then let him gasp and splutter, before starting with the long cane at longer range.

He took the long cane in sets of ten, with a minute's breather between each set. He got to look in the mirror and his bum was lovely and puffy, all blue and purple with the welts. After about 60 with the long cane, his cock started to wilt and the cuff slipped off, and Mum said that was satisfactory and he was ready to be birched.

He started to whimper and plead, like the other man and Mum said that she would be merciful. Her daughter, the novice, would birch him! I almost fainted.

I took the birch from her and swished it a bit, getting the feel of it. I saw that his penis was stiff again. God, I was dripping wet! I pressed my thighs together, but that made me want to come even more, so I stood with legs apart and started to birch him. Mum must have seen how moist my stocking tops were, but I didn't care. I swung the flail and cracked right across his bare bum, and he jerked like a startled horse. It was fabulous.

The birch made such a lovely crackle as I whipped his bare bum. He clenched and writhed and the marks sort of seeped over the existing cane-welts, filling them out to a pretty pattern. I gave him a tenner, then paused for breath. Then another tenner, and another. He was groaning and sobbing quite severely now, but I didn't want it to stop and he didn't either, for his tool was still rigid. It was one of the biggest I'd seen, erect. All the time, Mum was talking me up – how kind and thoughtful I was, and what a wonderful nurse I should make, and all that stuff.

He took a whole 100 with the birch! His welts were on the point of bursting and Mum called a halt. I wanted to come, wanted to pee; I felt like bursting myself. That penis was still huge! Actually, it frightened me a bit.

'I suppose you wish extra treatment, for that?' said Mum, tapping his penis with her cane tip.

He stammered that he did and she said extra service cost more, and he blurted 'Please!'

Mum said I could leave the room, if I wished. Did I heck! I said, po-faced, that a nurse's attendance was surely required. Mum told me to put a towel on the sofa, in case his welts burst and he lay down, with his cock standing up like a tree trunk. Mum lifted her skirt. She wasn't wearing panties, either. Then she straddled him, with her back to him, and quite efficiently sank his tool into her quim, holding her skirt up so that he could see her bare bottom. I was amazed she could slide that huge knob inside her so smoothly! She started to writhe on his penis. I could see the sweat on his brow so I bent over and mopped it with the hem of my skirt, and he could see all the way up to my soaking minge.

It was weird, seeing Mum fucked by a man. Although she was fucking him, really. I think they call it the primal scene. I had come out of that hole and another man's spunk would go into the place I'd left. But, so what? It was rather beautiful, in a way; in fact, a bit of a turn-on. Girls are always close to their mums, fucking. Life goes on. We are all flesh, and I was her flesh. Animals mate in the open, why not human animals?

Her bottom was as smooth as a young girl's! He clutched her hips, moving her up and down on his penis. She bounced quite high, sliding almost to his bulb, then plunging down again, so I saw how wet his shaft was, with Mum's own juices. It really turned me on and I wished it were me, especially with Henry's eyes darting from her bottom to my hairy wet quim.

I couldn't resist. As I heard him start to moan and I knew he was going to spurt, I touched my button and brought myself off at once. His groans and gasps masked my own, I think.

Anyway, when it was over, Mum was as bright and brisk as if nothing had happened – except that Henry walked down the street, not chirpy, but all dreamy and content.

Two days later, she got a phone call from Dr Stone's clinic at Harley Street, offering me an assistant nurse's job for the summer, or for as long as I wanted. I wasn't stupid. I figured Henry Stone had spunked in 'Auntie', and wanted to spunk in 'cousin' as well. I wasn't averse to the idea, and Mum agreed.

'Get the money,' she said, with a twinkle in her eye.

Trust Mum . . . but there was more to it than that.

# 3

# Beyond Caning

This was it. Belle took a deep breath as she placed her legs apart, facing the dominatrix and her witness, Belle's friend Geisha. Was she truly her friend? Or Cunliffe's accomplice? It was too late for second thoughts. Belle had committed herself, accepting a bare-bottom caning, with her word as a lady.

She thought back to the dunes, those innocent times, nude on the Atlantic beach. It was normal to see men and women naked. But it had puzzled her to see their buttocks striped with faint pink weals, as though they had been thrashed. Grown men and women? Now, Belle understood. They *had* been thrashed, and willingly, as Belle herself was willing to be caned.

Was she about to join an arcane world of slavery and submission? The next time she bared her body to sand and ocean – if, after this, there could possibly be a next, innocent, time – she would find her own buttocks the object of secret smiles . . .

Dr Cunliffe's fancied empire of slaves had been no fancy. It was Dr Cunliffe's own reality, and Belle was about to submit to its embrace. Belle would be a slave, a submissive; part of a network of human beings who found their humanity through pain and humiliation. Belle would share in that and, at last, she would *belong*.

She touched her toes. Her buttocks were upthrust, bare for the cane, and her cleft spread wide. Belle sighed, heavily, for her cunt was juicing. She *wanted* a naked caning – had *always* wanted it, deep inside herself. Her bare-bottom spanking, by the Japanese girl, had truly turned her on and she was proud – thankful, at last! – to be initiate.

Suppose Dr Cunliffe, and Geisha too, were vicious sadists – Belle's pain would give them pleasure and heal them. She wanted that pain, not just for her own stimulus but to give of herself, with her naked bottom the symbol of her gift, for *their* pleasure and thus her own.

She had read, of course, that a masochistic impulse lies dormant in every human: the need to submit to an adored superior and to express that submission by taking pain. Now, touching her toes, with her bare bottom exposed and ready for the cane, she felt a glimmer of understanding. Physically whipped, Belle would be spiritually helpless. To be in another's power meant to be under her protection. A naked beating seemed such a small way of thanking Dr Cunliffe for wanting her . . .

'Having second thoughts, Belle?' said Dr Cunliffe, distantly. 'The door is there.'

'Quite the opposite, Doctor,' said Belle. 'I want to . . . *appreciate.*'

'It is 21, Belle,' said Dr Cunliffe. 'Without a pause, and at intervals of only four seconds. Are you sure you can take it?'

'Yes!' Belle insisted.

'Once you appreciate, your future beatings will be harder, and longer,' said the Doctor.

Belle trembled at the tingle in her clitoris, untouched. Her pussy flowed with come that seeped onto her thigh. Her *future* beatings . . .

'Oh, I want them so much,' she heard her own voice whimper.

Her whole body tingled, now. All the colours and scents of the spartan room glowed with a new intensity, as her shivering bare buttocks awaited the cane. Her waiting, she knew, was part of the delicious cruelty of her flogging. Still, it did not come.

'*Please* . . .' she whispered.

Suddenly, wood whistled.

42

Wip!

'Oh! Oooh!'

The first slash of the cane took Belle unawares, rocking her on her toes. Liquid fire seemed to pour across her naked fesses and tears sprang to her eyes. She panted harshly; her gorge rose and she swallowed repeatedly to contain her anguish.

'Ahh . . . *uhhh* . . .'

'Tight, eh?' said Dr Cunliffe. 'Worse than you thought.'

'Oh!' Belle gasped, and swallowed again, without words.

The smart of the canestroke dulled to a throbbing, hot ache on her bare flesh. Gasping, Belle found her voice.

'It feels like I've been branded,' she sobbed.

'And that was only one!' mused Dr Cunliffe. 'You have twenty more strokes to take, Belle, and we have exceeded your four-second interval.'

Wip! Wip!

She laid two strokes in immediate succession; and accurately, right on the first welt.

'Ah! *Ahhh!* Oh, God!' Belle shrieked.

The smarting of her bare bottom was unbelievable. Her eyes blurred with tears and she fought, swallowing, to contain the lump that swelled in her throat. Her legs trembled beneath her. She felt a cool hand on her flaming bare arse. It was Geisha's, stroking tenderly.

'It is not the same as spanking,' Geisha said. 'The cane is more beautiful.'

Suddenly, her fingers delved in the crack of Belle's pussy. They came out sopping wet. Geisha put her fingers to Belle's lips and she tasted her own come. Geisha moistened her fingers again, at Belle's wet gash, and tasted them, then put her fingers in Dr Cunliffe's mouth and the dominatrix licked Belle's come from Geisha's skin.

'Eight seconds,' said Dr Cunliffe.

Wip! Wip!

Belle screamed.

'Oh, *God!* God! *Ahhh!*' she sobbed.

Her body shuddered so much that she could scarcely remain standing as her bottom clenched madly, trying to dissipate the agony. The fourth and fifth strokes had taken

43

her hard, one on each haunch, whose thin skin smarted worse than the fleshy central arse.

'An appreciate should take her punishment in silence,' said Dr Cunliffe.

Four seconds lapsed – Belle found herself counting, anything to distract her from the pain, then –

Wip!

The sixth stroke lashed her right beneath the spinal nubbin, on the thin skin of the top fesses.

'One . . . two . . . three . . .'

Wip!

The same welt, on top buttock, flamed in agony, and the force of the seventh stroke was so hard that Belle was knocked forward, shrieking in pain. She fell onto the pouffe, dislodging her bag, which spilled open.

'Very well,' panted Dr Cunliffe. 'You may take the remaining fourteen strokes at crouch.'

Belle raised her buttocks, for the eighth stroke.

'Yes,' she gasped, smiling, '*Yes* . . .'

The smarting, suddenly, had distanced itself from her and joyously, she felt she had reached her plateau of pain. Her eyes were unblurred by tears and her gorge no longer rose. Belle thrust her buttocks up and apart, as wide as she could, exposing her soaking gash and the wet jungle of her pube-hairs. Her heart pounded in gratitude. She *wanted* her naked bottom to be caned . . .

Geisha plucked the rose from her vagina and placed the stem at Belle's anus. She tickled, found the aperture and rammed the oiled stem all the way to Belle's anal root, pushing until only the flower peeped between her buttocks. Belle moaned in pain as the stem invaded her anal cavity. She felt the petals tickle her arse-cleft and the bottom of her pussy lips. Geisha's thighs locked around Belle's neck and Belle felt her wet gash against her nape as the Japanese girl squatted, pinioning Belle's head with her full weight. Geisha's hot come trickled on Belle's shoulders.

'I shall concentrate my caning on your haunches, Belle,' said Dr Cunliffe. 'Your welts are darkening prettily, and the haunches bear marks longer than any other portion of the arse. So you shall wear a constant reminder of your submission, until it is time for your next thrashing.'

At the cold friendliness of these words, Belle felt her gash juicing uncontrollably and a tingle of joy throb in her stiffened clitty. Her bottom would bear thrash-marks, always! *Must* bear them . . .

'Oh, yes! *Yes!*' she gasped. 'Cane my bum! Cane me, cane me . . . Oh!'

She writhed as she spoke, and the rose-stem tickled the whole channel of her anus.

Wip!

The ninth stroke lashed her left haunch.

'Ahh . . .'

Then, at the tenth, the cane's tip took her on the right. The strokes now alternated between the haunches. Belle's bottom squirmed in willing agony; at each stroke, a rose-petal fluttered to the floor.

Wip!

'God . . . yes . . . yes . . . Oh! Oh!'

Wip!

'*Ahhh* . . .'

She could not even shake her head, as Geisha's thighs pinioned her so powerfully. She felt the movement of Geisha's finger at her crotch. Geisha was masturbating, shifting her cunt up so that her come dripped into Belle's hair. So subtle was Dr Cunliffe's caning technique that the full shaft of the cane lashed and embraced Belle's central fesses, before the tip dealt a damaging weal to the haunches. Belle's belly began to spasm. Her anus clutched the rose-stem inside her, rolling her elastic walls on the fibrous rod. She gasped, with tickled pleasure.

Wip!

'Oh! *Nnnh* . . .! Ah! *Ah!*'

The cane slashed again and again, whipping her bare squirming fesses and welting her haunches with an excruciating smart. Belle's breath came in choked gasps and tears ran again from her eyes, not jolted in anguish, but flowing like a melody.

At the fifteenth stroke, she knew that she would orgasm before her caning was finished. There were six strokes to go. *Six of the best*. Her mouth twisted in a smile, and salt tears trickled between her lips. The pain in her flogged bare arse had become a powerful throbbing, like an engine's, heated beyond endurance. Each smarting throb felt like a stroke from a lover's penis.

The first stroke – it seemed an age away! – had seemed to brand her, but now she knew her scalded haunches were truly branded. She needed no telling that her weals would wear long.

'Uhh . . .' Belle said, slack-jawed, as the sixteenth whipped her.

'Uhh . . . uhh . . .' she gasped, at the searing smart of the seventeenth.

Geisha writhed on her neck, her gash squirming almost as fiercely as the whipped globes of Belle's arse. Belle felt the brick of her clitty, as Geisha rubbed it in her come-soaked hair. Geisha's breathing was deep. She, too, was approaching a climax as she masturbated. At the twentieth stroke, Belle exploded in come. Hearing her shrieks, Geisha reached down and slid the rose-stem from her anus, very slowly, so that Belle almost fainted at the intensity of her orgasm. At the same time, Geisha raised her cunt from Belle's head and Belle felt the rose-stem, still warm from her anus, pluck at the Japanese girl's clitty until she, too, grunted in climax, her come fluid lathering Belle's back.

'Oh . . . yes . . .' Belle gasped.

Then – Wip!

'Ahhh!' she screamed.

In the afterglow of orgasm, she had forgotten the twenty-first stroke.

Her bare bum jerked; her whole body leaped sideways, dislodging Geisha, the impact of whose body sent Belle's purse slithering on the floor to Dr Cunliffe's talon toenails. From it spilled the brochure, advertising the south sea research centre. Dr Cunliffe picked it up; her nose and mouth wrinkled in distaste.

Belle rose to her knees, rubbing the coruscated ridges of her flogged bare behind. Her skin felt hard as gnarled wood, yet deliciously hot. The smarting of the welts still pulsed gloriously through her buttocks. She felt her haunches and smiled. They were deeply grooved with hot weals that smarted in agony to the lightest touch. Belle longed to see herself in the mirror.

'What were you doing with this?' Dr Cunliffe snarled.

Her nostrils flared, and her eyes widened; her sleek body fleece stood up, bristling.

'I . . . I brought it for Geisha to translate the Japanese,' Belle said, uncertainly. 'It's –'

'*I know what it is*,' hissed Dr Cunliffe.

She spoke rapidly, to Geisha, in Japanese.

Geisha stood, hesitating for a moment, her nude body trembling. She looked into Belle's eyes, swallowed, then looked back at Dr Cunliffe. Dr Cunliffe's bright eyes stared Geisha down, and Geisha lowered her head. When she looked up, her eyes were blank, like dark glass. She darted to the door and locked it from the inside, handing the key to Dr Cunliffe, who smiled at the kneeling Belle.

'Furvert's Island,' she said. 'The island of the criminal charlatan Dr Darwinia Paine.'

'*Furvert's* Island?' said Belle, frowning. 'That's not the name I saw.'

Geisha moved behind Belle, and Belle's lip trembled.

'Have . . . have I made some mistake?' she quavered; then grunted, her naked breasts quivering suddenly as Geisha's forearm clamped her belly in a lock.

'I hope not,' said Dr Cunliffe. 'And I hope the lesson to come will prevent you from ever doing so. After your caning, Belle, you have learned to *appreciate*.'

She picked the rose stem from the floor and lashed Belle three times across her bare nipples.

'Now, sooner than is customary, and for your own good, you must learn to be *subjugate*.'

# Memoir 3

*Power, that was what it was about. Money is one form of power, and there was plenty of that to smell at the Stone clinic. Dr Stone also had the power of the healer. How those rich bitches gooed over him! He was just as dishy as his son, Henry, only in a silver-flecked, soap opera kind of way. He started off as a gynaecologist, and he knew everything about the pussy that there was to know. Women love that! It makes them feel so helpless, that a male has such knowledge of them. Then, he went for the big money as a plastic surgeon who didn't have to mess around with sick people.*

*I got to love the RBs, as I thought of them. Some of them were scarcely over 30, most in their 40s, and a few older ones. They all looked in terrific shape, but somehow their shape was never quite right. They would come back to Dr Stone for repeat nose jobs, arse jobs or boob jobs, three or four times! And they never blamed him – always themselves, as if they had been unworthy of him or something. Having seen the son's tool, I suspected the dad was fucking most of them; and he was, actually. Later, he admitted it, after I let him fuck me.*

*That was after I had thrashed him, in front of his wife. She watched us fuck, too. It seemed only fair to let her, after she had seen her son, Henry, fucking me. Anyway, I'll get to that.*

*I got to like the RBs, actually. They were so innocent, in a way; so malleable, so frightened of getting old and ugly. Like children. I really got a kick out of helping them feel better about themselves, and all their money.*

*That is when I learned about rich people. You can get money off them easily, as long as it is a lot of money. They turn up their noses at pennies. A big wad of notes, or a cheque with a lot of zeros, or a even credit card slip for them to sign without looking, that's different. That's OK. They say, never give a sucker an even break, you can't cheat an honest man, and so on, and it's all true. Nothing to do with dishonesty; you just make it easy for people to be generous, because they want to be. You plant the seed. Everybody wants to be generous to a glamorous young girl. The glamour might spread to them.*

*Men like a slut, because they always think they are different, they are the one who can tame her. When they can't, they feel guilty for not loving her enough. That summer in Harley Street, and at the health farm in Bucks, I learned to love being a slut.*

*My tasks were mainly decorative. I had to dress as a nurse, of course, but I never had to do anything difficult, just look skimpy and sexy. It dawned on me that I was an ad for Dr Stone: big boobs and arse, narrow waist, long legs, big hair, perfect nose and all. I was the end product. I was perfection.*

*With the RBs, I played dumb. I didn't tell them I had more brains in my left tit than most of them had in their heads, or that I was going to college, hoping to study genetics.*

*I was just a simple nurse, but I acted with a kind of earthy authority, like I understood 'real life' and that. So they confided in me, gave me gifts; and when one saw me wearing a gold neck chain, she had to give me a bigger one, and so on. I played them off against each other. I wanted money. I wanted a lot of it. I had plans. Like mother, like daughter . . .*

*I had some cards printed with my mobile phone number, and the legend 'Teenage Tigress of Discipline, Visiting Service For Naughty Boys'. I put the cards in the phone boxes all round the West End and Mayfair. I was a teenage dominatrix! All perfectly true, too. Truth rules OK.*

*First, I charged 50 per cent more than Mum, but soon I just doubled it. I had a pigskin briefcase and dressed as a visiting nurse, or else a businesswoman. I went to all the big* hotels and the houses in Belgravia and so on. Never too far away. I couldn't be bothered with cheap creeps in Tufnell Park or somewhere.

I had a whole set of whips, cuffs, restraints and bondage gear, that I got in Soho. Mum would not have approved, but this was my style, for me. I also got a lot of kinky costumes, in PVC, rubber and leather. Rubber was most popular, which was handy because rubber is lighter than leather and folds better.

Some of the women – dykes, mostly – who ran these shops, would ask me to parties, and to join what they called 'the scene'; but I was a lone tigress. I made pots of money. I had sex if the guy wanted, and tipped extra, but usually they didn't. They wanted to be my slave and worship me, and I let them. I'd whip them, piss on them, shit on them, everything. What was nice was, my price included everything. Everything I wanted to do, that is. So when I was whopping and humiliating them, they knew it was because I really wanted to. I really was a cruel tigress. Sometimes I'd order them to wank themselves to come, as I watched. Occasionally there was a guy I fancied, and I'd make him fuck me in the arse. I wasn't acting. That's why I got tipped so well, even without fucking.

That went on nicely for a few weeks. Dr Stone was sweet, and he confided in me. He knew heaps about genetics, but he had to compromise and make a living. He told me about reading cells and unlocking them, and closing the cells which trigger ageing, and so on. All to do with DNA. He said people could live for 1,000 years if they could find the DNA code. You could transplant not just organs from other species, but senses, too. Like, you could graft a cat's eyesight, or a dog's sense of smell, into a human. He said that the Japs used to do experiments in the last century, in World War Two. I said it sounded disgusting. Problem was, improvement in one sense led to compensatory reduction in another. If you gave a man a cat's eyesight, he'd be deaf, and so on.

'That's why Jewish men are short, fat and ugly,' I said. 'They compensate with extra virility. But you are quite a dish, Dr Stone. How disappointing!'

50

*I said that all serious but then laughed, and he grinned, shyly! He was always touching me, petting me, almost. Usually on the bottom. Some girls hate that, but I don't. I'm very touchy-feely. So he wanted to fuck me? I'd have been offended otherwise.*

*He was telling me about the human buttocks, how erotically sensitive they are and how, with genetic enhancement, a lady's arse could be like her nipples, or even her clitty. For a guy, the arse would be like his bell-end. There was some stuff about baboons, showing off their red arses as a mating signal. That's when I pounced. Like father, like son.*

*As usual, his hand patted my rump, just on the cleft. I jumped like a scalded cat and slapped his face. His look of bewilderment! I put my really, really angry look on and stared at him, breathing through my nose. The poor dear didn't know what to say.*

*'You cheeky pervert,' I hissed. 'It is your arse that needs to be reddened. Get your pants down this instant and bend over my knee!'*

*I knew I'd hit the spot, because at that, he got a beautiful bulge. It was a monster, too.*

*I spanked him properly, till his buttocks were crimson. About 150 spanks, I think. His knob was rigid and I made him wank off in front of me, over my shoes, then lick his come off them. I wouldn't touch him down there, not yet. I called him all sorts of names and said I would use a cane on his bare bottom, if he was impudent again.*

*Of course, he was impudent. How I made him worship me! Every three or four days, I decided his impudence merited caning. Always in his surgery, with him bent over his desk, and never less than two dozen strokes. After a while, I would rub his penis till the cream came. It never took long. I had to restrain myself, for I'd be soaking in my panties. I wanted his cock inside my pussy. But I remained a teenage tigress, till he was tamed and would do anything for me.*

*I still had a crush on Henry, damn him. I decided on a stunning new trick in the feminine arsenal – I would tell him the truth! No man ever expects that from a female and it throws them sideways. Honesty is the best policy.*

*The family home was up near the health farm, where I used to shuttle back and forth with the RBs. Henry was always sniffing around me (what man wouldn't?) but he was uncharacteristically shy, because I'd witnessed him being flogged and he was afraid I'd tell on him. So I had power.*

*Mrs Stone was a golfing type, about forty. I told Henry the truth. I said I'd had a crush on him for ages and wanted to thrash him like Mum had, only harder. And he was to fuck me, afterwards, in the cunt or anus, whenever I wanted. Otherwise I would tell on him. He was to meet me in a patch of bramble on the golf course, where I knew his mum was playing that day.*

*I made sure she saw me thrash her son, bare bum, while I pretended not to see. I was dressed in my nurse's uniform, with split-crotch rubber knickers. I gave Henry four dozen stingers with a cane, then knelt down and made him take me in the arse, doggy fashion.*

*Later, I went all tearful to Mrs Stone, and said Henry had made me do it, or he'd have me sacked. She was a pretty sexy lady and she petted me and told me not to cry, and so on. I said it was normal for a boy to be lustful, and actually I liked Henry and I'd been arse-fucked before, and liked that too, but when it came to his own father . . .!*

*That got her interested. I didn't tell her I'd already tamed Dr Stone. I said he wanted to paw and cuddle me and what should I do, I was so afraid of losing my job . . .*

*Planting the idea, you see.*

*'Well,' she said, with a gleam in her eye, 'what's good for the son is good for the father.'*

*I lured him to a summerhouse in the garden, on the pretext that I agreed to fuck him. Of course, when we were naked, Mrs Stone arrived, by coincidence with a switch of birch rods. She got seriously angry, wouldn't listen to excuses and proposed to thrash Dr Stone – just as she thrashed her own son every two weeks, she said, on the bare bum.*

*'Better still,' she spat, 'your whore can thrash you while I watch.'*

*She was a fine actress, though the part about thrashing Henry was true. She assured me of that, once I had laid five* or six welts on her husband's bare bum. She whipped her grown son, bare arse, regularly, every fortnight! So I didn't mind telling her I had seen Henry thrashed and fucked, by my own mum. She told me to make Dr Stone squirm!

I birched Dr Stone raw, until there wasn't a twig left: 80 whops at least. His tool was like an oak tree and his bare arse quite purple with welts. I was juicing heavily, so I was pleased when Mrs Stone, as I'd hoped, raised no objection to my mounting him and taking him in my cunt. She was masturbating as she watched, with her skirt up and panties down. When he had come in my cunt, I had to lick her off. I don't mean she told me to; I mean, I knew she wanted to tell me to. Her pussy was really wet and tasted nice, like the sea. She shaved it bare. It was the first time I had full lesbian sex. We are all flesh. Knowing what flesh wants – that's power. Now, I had all the family in mine.

The RBs used to moan all the time; about their men, of course. That was the downside of the boobs 'n' shopping excursions. While they were packed off to the health farm, they imagined hubby laying some pipe, somewhere, to teenage sluts . . . like me.

One lady, Lee, a stunning, big-titted blonde from Hawaii and the last person in the world to need plastic surgery, got close to me. Her man was a stud, and then some. I told her he needed a good thrashing on the bare bottom, like all men. She laughed, of course, but kept asking me questions, and was this normal practice in England, and I confessed that I'd caned plenty of 'boyfriends' and was very experienced. Furthermore, men liked being thrashed bare-arse, by ladies, and tamed that way.

So, it was arranged I'd come to their suite in the Dorchester one evening, for drinks. She would suddenly 'remember' another engagement in Berkeley Square, and leave me with hubby for 'just an hour or two'. I planted the idea, as though it was her own.

It all happened as planned, same as with Dr Stone. I could see why Gary was popular with ladies; he was one of those boyish hunks whose dick just can't seem to stay still. And what a sweet big dick! I did my angry routine, then spanked

him and caned him as well; three dozen stingers, bare arse –
I made him strip completely.

'Now, do you still want to fuck me?' I said, looking at his
rigid knob and wealed arse.

'More than ever!' he blurted.

I had only rubber knickers and bra on, so I dropped them
and let him mount me. That's when Lee came in, after
watching from the vestibule of their suite all this time – and
with a video going. She watched Gary fuck me and he almost
blew me away in two or three strokes, he was so good; and
Lee lifted her skirt and got her panties down and masturbated as she watched. He came like Niagara and Lee came
too. Then she said he was superhuman, and had plenty more,
if she could just thrash it out of him . . .

I stayed till dawn. It was quite a party. I even licked off
Lee, while Gary was buggering me. His arse was covered in
weals, from me and his wife; I took one whopping too, from
him. Only a dozen with the cane. I was pleased I could take
it bare arse, like Mum.

Word got round the RBs and pretty soon, I was a fixture
with most of their husbands. Actually I was glad to keep it
in the family, as it were, for I was starting to get too
aggressive with my phone customers. I mean, I really did
want to hurt them, as they were so despicable, yet it hurt me
to despise them. How weird that seems, today! Finally, I
took the battery out of my mobile.

Lee gave me a gigantic gold bracelet after our party, and
I hinted that as a poor girl, that would be expected for future
'extra nursing'. It suited everyone. The RBs liked their men
tamed, and the men loved being tamed. I began to see the
possibilities of a world-wide network . . . of slaves, at my
beck and call. Men and women who long to be teased,
beaten, shamed, even at long distance; who fall hopelessly in
love with me (most slaves do) and are forced to wank off,
sobbing, over a video of me being gang-fucked . . . then, when
I deign to visit them – at their expense – being treated like
shit. Being treated with shit! Whipped beyond endurance,
humiliated and hurt in ways undreamed of. That's the secret.
Mum always used to know a person's limit, or threshold, and

*take them to the brink. I do too, but I flay the bare body, screaming and terrified, beyond it.*

*They reward me with gold, and they beg for more. It works.*

*Gary and Lee remained my favourites. They were very useful to me, later, when I'd finished my doctoral thesis on Social Darwinism.*

# 4

# Bare Submission

The room was in shadow, and Belle Puget's caned body was naked. On each side of the room, she viewed her nude self in two full-length mirrors, propped against the wall. She saw Geisha – her friend, Oh, please let Geisha be a friend! – and her eyes pleaded to her. Yet, Geisha watched, her face blank and sullen, in cruel betrayal. Belle had been led to a trap.

Her body ached, almost beyond endurance, but it was not from the smarting of her welts. *That* was a warm, dull ache, almost a friendly throbbing, which kept her aware of her body. The tools of discipline, which now restrained her, reduced her to a yoked animal.

Dr Cunliffe intended to crush her utterly. It was a nightmare made flesh, yet, somehow, it was Belle's dream of joy. To submit, to be free, to feel her spirit soar, as her bare buttocks glowed under the whip. She would be enslaved, *willingly*, by this perfect female, not impersonally crushed, like a worm, as was so obviously intended. She *wanted* to submit – to be whipped naked and humilated, in fullest shame – but of her own accord! She tried to explain, through her sobs, as her body screamed to her alone, in mute agony.

'Slavery cannot be negotiated, Belle,' Dr Cunliffe purred. 'Only accepted. As *you* accept.'

Belle was mute. She *did* accept.

*How can I want such things . . .?*

Belle hung from the ceiling, by pincers, which clamped her nipples like vices. Her breasts were stretched to voluminous size, like balloons of skin, taking almost all her body's weight. The lower portion of her body was supported by identical pincers, attached to her cunt lips, which were stretched wide revealing her naked, plugged gash and her clitoris open to view. The pincers had a screw attachment, by which they could be tightened further. As yet, they were only tightened halfway.

Her body was at an angle, facing the floor, at 45°, so that the cords, fastened to her cunt lips and nipples, snaked around her shoulders and hips, biting her further. Her tresses were pulled painfully to their roots, bound in a knot by another cord from the ceiling that stretched her head back, so that her throat was bared and her hair thus supported her head. A monstrous plug of gnarled, wrinkled plastic, filled her anus, and a similar plug filled her cunt. A smaller, toothed clamp was fastened to her clitoris and hung down, pulling the nubbin, as it bit. Her belly was buckled in a hideously tight and painful rubber cincher, spiked on the inside. Yet, the buckle was, as yet, fastened only a few notches.

Her legs were spread wide, anchored by taut ankle-chains to the floor, and the cleft parted to show her filled anus, the tiny arse-pucker distended to a rose. Absurdly, she longed to pee, yet the quim-plug prevented her from even that relief. Behind her, in the shadows, Dr Cunliffe flexed a crop. Not the cane – the friendly cane – but a black riding-crop, that seemed long and heavy enough to tan a bear. Geisha, impassive and blank-eyed, had shown her the instrument before handing it to the Doctor. Belle had nodded, numbed by the intensity of her desire for hurt. Its thong of braided leather, woven over a steel rod, had a snake's tongue at its tip. She was ungagged, yet scarcely dared to speak. But she must.

'Why . . .?' she gasped, from her stretched larynx. 'Why, Doctor?'

'Because you *want* to be cleansed, Belle,' said Dr Cunliffe. 'You want to feel my lash on your bare, smarting buttocks – again, and again, and again, like all my slaves. For your own good! In the future, you will thank me, should you remember your cleansing, after hypnosis.'

'You wish to make me your slave?' said Belle, bitterly. 'Why, I longed for nothing else. But a *willing* slave!'

'You are willing, Belle, but it is no longer possible to enrol you, without hypnosis. I want you so much! I had you picked . . . you are physical perfection, Belle, and that is your greatest danger. You have already been placed under attraction. You have seen the prospectus, and that knowledge must be blanked, because you are too beautiful a creature to waste. And no slave can be completely willing, Belle. My cruelty is the very appeal of my slaves' submission.'

'The prospectus for Dr Paine's research centre, on Sakosha Island!' Belle cried.

'Its name is not Sakosha Island,' said the Doctor. 'It is Furvert's Island. I know a lot about you, Belle Puget. More than you do. My hard drive, locked away, contains many secrets. We shall see how you fare under extreme duress: *peine forte et dure*, or "strong and hard punishment". I intend to crush you to joy, my beautiful Belle.'

'Oh, God . . .! Please . . .'

'My crushing will cleanse you, place you under my *imperium*, and steer you away from your morbid and dangerous interest in genetic research. You must take this with the utmost seriousness, Belle. Furvert's Island is an island of evil.'

'I haven't even read all the prospectus!' Belle sobbed. 'I was going to ask Geisha . . .'

'And corrupt *her*, too?' snapped Dr Cunliffe.

'I glanced at the English part. That is all.'

'And learned?'

'Dr Paine wishes to help mankind! By genetic research, she wishes to arrest the ageing process and improve the senses, using animal gene-splicing. Her aim is human happiness.'

The crop whistled in the air, like a flute.

Wip!

'*Aahhh!*'

Belle screamed, as the nude dominatrix's crop lashed her bare buttocks. Her body shuddered helplessly in her bonds, tearing at her nipples and cunt, and the squirming of her bare arse drove the spiny dildo hard against her anal elastic and cunt walls.

'Oh, God . . .' she sobbed.

The crop was worse than any cane. Her bottom seemed to melt in molten agony. The crop descended again, three times, on her naked fesses. Belle writhed and sobbed, fighting back hysteria. Now, four strokes to her bare breasts, followed by four across the back.

'Oh, please!' she howled. '*Please . . .*'

'Of course,' said Dr Cunliffe, pleasantly. 'You wish your cleansing to cease, Belle. Hmm! I suppose . . .'

Her words dangled in the air. There was a minute, during which the only sounds were Belle's harsh sobbing.

'Well?' said the dominatrix.

'Oh . . . God help me, I do want to be cleansed – to be a slave, forever. I know how Geisha was instructed to lure me, and I'm happy. It is for my own good, to feel that I belong to you, and show it by taking your beating. I want my body to squirm for you.'

'Then say "please" again, Belle.'

'Please, Dr Cunliffe!'

'Please what, Belle?'

'Please whip me to submission,' Belle whimpered. 'Please make me yours. Please make me belong. Please accept my humiliation as my gift. Thrash my bare buttocks raw . . . *please!*'

Dr Cunliffe nodded to Geisha, who screwed the cunt and nipple clamps fully tight, and Belle grunted, as the metal bit deeper into her teats and gash flaps.

'But . . . but how can Dr Paine's dream of human happiness be evil?' she sobbed. 'You . . . you are the slavemistress, Dr Cunliffe. Can there be so many willing slaves like me? Longing, not for contentment, but to submit to a pure and cruel dominatrix . . .?'

'Far more than you know, Belle,' said Dr Cunliffe.

Silently, she dealt a further twelve strokes to Belle's fesses. Belle writhed and shuddered, helpless in her bonds. Her 21 strokes of the cane seemed a distant, pleasant memory.

'Oh! Oh! Oh! *Ahhh* . . .' she cried, a long and unbroken howl of submission.

'The room is sound-proofed, of course,' said Dr Cunliffe, mildly.

She dealt another twelve strokes, at slower intervals, six to the buttocks, and three each on back and teat-flesh, and talked to Belle between each stroke, as to a child.

'I, too, was interested in genetic research,' she said. 'And I know of Furvert's Island. I have . . . been there.'

Her voice faltered.

'And escaped, before I was made inhuman.'

Belle moaned, in uncomprehending pain.

'I thought Dr Paine a do-gooder, a dreamer, a saint,' said Dr Cunliffe, 'and her naivety is the worst evil. By seeking to enhance humans with the flesh of brute beasts, she makes them into beasts. Beasts are happy, for they are ignorant. It is human to know, hence to suffer. My slaves, all over the world, are truly human. As I hope you can be.'

'How can suffering be human? *Why do I want to be whipped, Dr Cunliffe?*'

'How can it be anything else? Beauty like yours *begs* to be whipped. And *how* did that filthy document reach this college? I thought my virus, over the Internet, would prevent *any* dissemination of Dr Paine's filth.'

Another twelve strokes of the crop. Dr Cunliffe whipped her thighs, on her belly, her teats, arse and quim. All of Belle's arse-skin was slowly reddening, to a deeper and ever more voluptuous shade of crimson. Belle writhed, panted for breath and shuddered.

'Furvert's Island was named Sakosha, by the Japanese. They conducted genetic experiments there, on slaves, during the Second World War. After the Japanese surrender, the research was abandoned, though not the island. Sakosha was a speck, in the middle of the south seas, unknown even to the American conquerors. The research recommenced, much later, in this century, with Dr Paine's vast funding. She, too, has slaves – rich fools.'

The crop sliced the air again, landing on Belle's pinched gash-lips and clitoris. Belle jerked her whipped loins and groaned, sobbing incoherently. Three more strokes to the gash, and then Belle felt Geisha's fingers inside her cunt.

'She is juicing heavily,' Geisha said. 'She is a true slave and shall come to orgasm, if the crop continues to lash her arse.'

Belle's anal and vaginal plugs were removed and a flower vase placed under her gash.

'Please,' begged Belle, 'I am willingly your slave. My appreciation – my caning – hadn't you guessed it was what I have always longed for?'

'I did not guess, I *knew*,' hissed Dr Cunliffe. 'You wish your cleansing to stop?'

'N – no . . . I am your slave,' Belle gasped.

Her head was fastened in a metal brank, with a tongue depressor preventing speech.

'You will be left alone under Geisha's supervision, for an hour,' said Dr Cunliffe. 'Geisha shall not speak. Then, I shall flog you again. After more floggings, with pauses between, you will be hypnotised and released. I have informed Dr Sawyer that you have had a nervous break-down and will be transported to a health farm, in Buckinghamshire, to recuperate. After that, you will pass the summer vacation in the nude, at my villa in southwest France. The ocean shall cleanse you, to recommence your proper studies in October. Geisha and I shall be your best friends. You will be determined to succeed in mainstream microbiology. You shall not remember your cleansing, except that any mention of genetic engineering will cause you nausea, without knowing why. In the event that you hear the name Sakosha, or Furvert's Island, again, you will feel repugnance. And, unaware, you shall be my slave. I want you, Belle – *for your own good.*'

Dr Cunliffe left her alone with Geisha.

'Mmm . . .' moaned Belle, wishing her friend – even if her enemy – would break her silence.

Suddenly, she peed; a golden, hissing stream, that splattered the vase beneath her. Her bowels gave way and she filled the vase. Geisha lifted the vase and poured its contents over Belle's head and body. Her hair was matted with her ordures and golden piss streamed on her stretched bare breasts, trickling down her back and belly and returning to her arse-cleft.

Belle wept, uncontrollably. Geisha patted her wet hair and this small caress flooded Belle with joy.

'I am sorry,' said Geisha, 'but it *is* for your own good.'

She sounded doubtful, but would say no more. Belle saw that her sullen eyes were moist with tears. There was fear in Geisha, too; fear of her slavemistress, Dr Cunliffe.

The hour passed and her second flogging took place: 50 hard strokes with the crop, that reddened her buttocks and whipped her mercilessly on gash and perineum. Belle was still gagged by her brank, but at the second flogging with the crop, she did not wish to cry out. Dr Cunliffe was right. The pain on her naked arse was what she desired. Under the crop, her cunt juiced with come and her clitoris throbbed, but her powerlessness to masturbate herself to relief made her subjugation the more thrilling. Then she heard a door close, as Dr Cunliffe departed. Geisha frowned, and loosened Belle's brank, holding her finger to her lips.

'Oh . . . Oh . . . How did she know I wanted it so much?' Belle whispered. '*Why me?*'

'Dr Cunliffe knows of your ancestor,' Geisha replied. 'She knows your curiosity would drive you and wants you for her slave alone. You are too beautiful for your own good, Belle.'

'All I know,' said Belle, 'is, my great-grandfather's family name was Furvert, before he took his wartime name Puget. It is a coincidence.'

'No coincidence. Jean Furvert, the 17th century free-booter, sailed out of Bordeaux and landed on Sakosha. It was then called, by others, Furvert's Island. You would have discovered that in due course, if left undisciplined. Cats are curious. Puget was another Pacific explorer – Puget Sound, in America? Your great-grandpa was a joker. But Captain Furvert himself called the island *l'Ile du Ciel*, Heaven's Island. It doesn't matter, you will remember nothing when Mother has hypnotised you.'

Belle was dumbfounded.

'Dr Cunliffe ... your mother?' she gasped.

That would explain her extraordinary hold over the Japanese girl, and Geisha's simmering resentment of her dominance.

'But she can't have had you when she was ... ten years old!'

'She is not my biological mother,' said Geisha, her voice cold again, like a machine recording. 'My parents both worked in genetic engineering, at a secret island research facility. They were visiting mainland Japan when they died, suddenly.'

'But when? How?' Belle blurted.

'They were in Hiroshima on August 9th, 1945,' said Geisha.

Dr Cunliffe's steps were heard again and Belle's brank was replaced, as were her anal and vaginal dildos. Dr Cunliffe stripped nude, and took the crop from Geisha. Belle took her last bare-bum beating in silence and, though her crimson bottom writhed at each stroke of the crop, her eyes were dry of tears. Her gasps were like a puppy's, panting eagerly.

When Belle's cleansing was finally at an end and the naked globes of her bottom flamed like red suns, Dr Cunliffe fastened golden spirals to piercings in her nipples, and began a sinuous dance, making the spirals whirl. At last, Geisha put her fingers in Belle's soaking cunt and pressed her stiff clitty, making Belle Puget climax immediately.

'You are going into a deep, deep sleep,' the slavemistress said, beginning Belle's hypnosis.

That summer by the Atlantic was the best Belle Puget had ever enjoyed! She was with her best, best friend, Geisha, and nice Dr Cunliffe. They spent almost all day gloriously nude. She had been unwell, but had recuperated quickly at a lovely health farm in Bucks. The men doctors were so nice and lascivious too, which was the best cure of all.

In France, she got a nice new boyfriend, and they soon made love, in an old German bunker. He was a German lad named Heinz, and he admired the welts on Belle's body. She explained that she and her friends liked spanking and caning games. Heinz liked them, too. He said his great-grandfather had been stationed on this very beach and had photos of him and his friends, with some French girls, all nude, and spanked. Germans, he said, were sensual beasts.

Heinz looked glorious, nude. His body was completely hairless, like Geisha's, with not even down on his pubis, and this gave his huge manhood an appealing innocence. He said he did not shave his body, since, apart from the thick flax of his head, his skin was naturally smooth. His penis was especially exciting. The glans of the massive cock was split by two clefts instead of the single urethral gap, with an extra cleft on the front of the helmet, like a cloverleaf, or two-clefted arse. He explained that it made his glans extra-sensitive to pleasure and that the most sensitive, ticklish part of the glans, just below the urethral cleft, was duplicated for him. The first time Heinz fucked Belle's cunt, his cock felt like a ribbed tickler and she orgasmed almost at once. Heinz admired Dr Cunliffe's nudity and her furry brown body. Geisha and Dr Cunliffe liked to watch Belle and Heinz make love. They were all flesh, Dr Cunliffe said. Animals mated in public, so why not human animals? When she watched Belle and Heinz fucking, she would lick herself under the armpits and also bend down, put her face between her thighs and lick her pussy and bumhole. Belle couldn't do that, though she tried. Nor could Geisha. So they licked each other's pussies and bumholes, while Heinz and Dr Cunliffe observed.

Belle and Dr Cunliffe loved to watch Heinz fucking Geisha, too. They would mutually masturbate, watching the lovely slippery bodies writhing. Dr Cunliffe juiced most copiously and her expert fingers brought Belle quickly to come, with more and more juice at each wanking off. Belle felt healthier and healthier. Geisha liked being fucked in her bumhole, which made her squeak with pleasure. Heinz's tool was truly massive – Belle had known boys with big penises, but never one this size – and it never seemed to grow tired. Belle marvelled at the amount of creamy sperm his balls produced, regularly, inexhaustibly, and in long, powerful spurts. The girls called him their spunking machine. Dr Cunliffe demurred from fucking, preferring to watch, and even to time Heinz's sperming. They all took part in spanking and caning games, however.

It was splendid fun, to watch Geisha take twelve of the best, on the bare, from Dr Cunliffe, and Belle loved to offer her own naked bottom, for a playful caning, though it was not always playful. Dr Cunliffe selected branches of driftwood from the beach and caned so hard that they snapped. Her canings made Belle's bottom sore. Sometimes, on a nude ramble through the lovely scented pine forest, she would break off a young branch and cane Belle, Geisha and Heinz in a row. The pine branch did not snap. It was thin and springy, and smarted dreadfully. But the scent of the trees and ocean healed her.

Yet Belle looked forward to her bare-bottom canings. She craved the smart of her bare buttocks. The pain seemed to cleanse her and make her whole. Belle was proud that she could take a whole dozen. She wondered, though, how her arse could stand it, even when it blushed so deep and red. As though she had been caned before.

Heinz, being German, had to outdo them. He insisted on twice the girls' canings, and more. The girls laughed at his gasps and grimaces. Geisha, like Dr Cunliffe, really knew how to cane.

In secret, Heinz admitted to Belle that he felt guilty. After the Second World War, his great-grandfather learned that his French girlfriend Josette had been whipped naked in the village square, for befriending the enemy. In fact, his forebear had enjoyed many French mistresses, as he was part of some secret medical research facility isolated in the pine forests: benign research, Heinz insisted, to improve the sexual enhancement of the human female and thus the breeding capacity of the male. With German thoroughness, females were fucked to repeated orgasm and measurements taken of their pulse, eye-blinking, skin temperature and flow of come oil. Males were simply mutated females, and the greater the female's pleasure – observed most of all, by her flow of come – the stronger were the male sperm. Heinz said that sometimes, bare-bottom spanking produced heavier come than fucking alone. Josette was scapegoat for the pleasures of many. She had been shorn bald and whipped with 100 strokes on her back and arse. She had been tattooed in crimson letters on each buttock: 'P' for *pute* – 'whore'. Belle loved Heinz even more, for his guilt. There was so much pain in this world, and she longed to heal it! At night, Heinz would lie face down on the sand, with the Atlantic waves drenching his naked body and Belle would whip him in silence, to heal him.

They did not make love, on those occasions. But Belle could not help masturbating as she whipped the handsome boy's wet bare arse. The waves were tears, healing the welts from her whip of pine branches. She masturbated her clit to come, loving her power to heal the male.

They were all flesh: glorious, nude young flesh and they would live, spank and fuck, forever. Belle said she intended to win a Nobel Prize in her star subject, microbiology. Mainstream microbiology.

'How about genetic engineering?' said Dr Cunliffe. 'Injecting humans with animal cells, to improve the breed?'

'None of that weird stuff!' Belle cried, gulping air to quell her sudden nausea.

But Belle had strange dreams: of old sailing ships under a tropic sun, of shipwrecks and feline naked monsters, with penises that were whips; of demons.

When she awoke, sobbing, in Dr Cunliffe's villa, Geisha comforted her and Dr Cunliffe lulled her to sleep as, bare-breasted, she twirled her golden nipple-spirals. Geisha looked troubled, then, as though she had dreamed Belle's dream too.

Two nights before their scheduled return to England for the new term at college, Geisha and Belle were left alone. Dr Cunliffe had gone for a midnight bathe with Heinz and Belle said those two seemed to be closer than she would like. Geisha taunted her wth jealousy, which Belle falsely denied. Dr Cunliffe had for once left her laptop computer unlocked and Geisha suggested they had some fun. She proved to be a keyboard witch and they got into files which surpassed Belle's experience, and even her imagination.

'Dr Cunliffe is no benign dominatrix,' she said. 'These images are horrid.'

There were scenes of torture and abasement, sexual practices with deformed women and men with giant organs.

'Like your Japanese comic books,' Belle said. 'How did you know the password?'

'Just a lucky guess,' said Geisha. 'Dr Cunliffe is an Internet dominatrix. She sells images and instructions to her slaves throughout the world.'

The password was *claw*. Now, Geisha's fingers danced again on the keyboard and another site opened. This was Sakosha Island, Dr Paine's website and was full of images of healing, smiling nurses and happiness, in a tropical paradise.

'Dr Cunliffe's world is hell,' Belle said, with a shudder. 'And Dr Paine's seems heaven.'

'They are rivals, in a way I cannot tell you,' Geisha blurted. 'That is, I am . . . programmed, not to speak the words. There is a blank, in my mind. I can only give you these clues, just as I slipped Dr Paine's brochure into your folder. You are submissive, Belle, and are fated to fall under the domain of one pole or another: Dr Cunliffe's hell, or Dr Paine's heaven.'

'Fated?' Belle laughed. 'But why don't you go to Dr Paine, for this . . . this blank in your mind?'

'I'm busy at Paradise Lost,' said Geisha, curtly. 'Perhaps, one day, I'll pay you a visit there.'

That night, after she and Geisha had spanked each other's bare bums and mutually masturbated, she had a dream. Furvert's Island. Paradise, or inferno? Was it a place where things happened to people, to make them into monsters. Or, to cleanse them, by making them pure and whole – uniting animal skill and human wisdom, in supreme harmony? *We are all flesh.* Which was it? Belle had to find out. She *must*. It was in her genes – she must go, and *heal. As she had been healed by the slavemistress, Dr Cunliffe.*

Belle saw herself whipped naked, in her dream, and orgasming as her bottom flowered. She yearned for her bottom to smart once more in slavery. There was something so heavenly about a crimson bottom! Belle knew she wanted hers to be whipped, forever and ever, by her true mistress. Would it prove to be Dr Darwinia Paine? *She must find her true mistress.*

Geisha, and Heinz, and Dr Cunliffe, were in her dream. Dr Cunliffe's bare bottom was caned, and bore the letter 'P' on each raw fesse, while Heinz, a demon, whipped her with the monstrous flail of his spiked penis. Geisha and a row of lookalike Geishas, masturbated. They all had tails at their spinal nubbins, standing erect over open bumholes, fronded like sea anemones. Geisha's cunt was a pink slit, flapping like a fish's mouth.

Then, Dr Paine swam into view. She was an angel, and shooed the others away, welcoming Belle to her embrace. She looked the mirror image of Belle, blonde, big-breasted and with ripe arse-melons, and nude – so she *knew* Belle. She ruled the island Belle's ancestor discovered. Coming drowsily from her dream, Belle flashed that Dr Darwinia Paine had the knowledge she sought – genetic technology, to give humans the beauty of beasts. She was grateful to Dr Cunliffe for awakening her submissive nature, but she especially must understand. Beauty had its destiny. *Optimum attraction of the male of the species*: Belle Puget must accomplish the perfection of her beauty. The summer's play had served to entertain her, for sex and spanking games were healthy. Now, she must go to Furvert's Island, where the summer did not cease, and brown feline bodies were always naked and touching perfection.

For the remainder of the holiday, her relations with Dr Cunliffe were cordial, but once back at college, she avoided her. She contacted Dr Paine, and they corresponded. Yes, Belle sounded ideal as a research student on Sakosha, as Dr Paine called Furvert's Island. Belle sent the requested details – including, to her surprise and secret satisfaction, nude photos of herself. Dates were fixed: she would shortly enrol at the Paine Foundation as research assistant. Dr Paine's own image radiated kindness. She introduced Belle to a special website, showing the effects of her research and treatment. Nude brown women danced in tropic surf, their sexual beauty enhanced by Dr Paine's therapy, with large firm breasts and buttocks, slim bellies and swollen cunt-mounds . . . Belle felt a little bit jealous! There was even – *even!* – a playful sequence of Dr Paine, giving a nude, wriggling Japanese girl a bare-bottom spanking.

*Oh, let it be more than spanking.*

Belle's pussy moistened strongly and she wanked off at once. Done and dusted: she would go immediately. The name of Dr Paine's website was *mutant*.

# 5

# Fresh Flesh

'Hot enough to fry a scorpion, eh?' said Dr Darwinia Paine, as she helped Belle down from the bumboat. 'Welcome to Sakosha, Miss Puget. I am so glad you made it. We are in sore need of fresh flesh.'

Beyond, in the bay, the weekly island-hopping steamer began its turn, to depart. The bumboat hurried to catch it, the outboard motor buzzing like a fly. Furvert's Island loomed green above them. A paved roadway wound into valleys covered in moist heat haze and of startling lushness. The jungle came right to the water's edge, as though hungry to invade the ocean.

Belle was drenched in sweat, already. Her light skirt clung to her buttocks, showing her white knickers clearly, and her bra was visible, as twin mounds under her sodden cotton shirt. Belle was aware of Dr Paine's appraising and unashamed glance at her body, right from her moment of greeting and silky, firm handshake.

Dr Paine's own body, at ten years older than Belle, had the ripeness of a teenage girl's. Her blue nurse's cape, made of thin latex, billowed in the sultry breeze above a tight nurse's uniform revealing long legs, tanned golden yet unbeaded by sweat even in their covering of wide fishnet stockings above high-heeled white shoes. The blouse clung to her breasts, that jutted bra-less, the large nipples quite prominent. Where Belle had primly pinned her hair, Dr Paine's tresses hung free and lush in the breeze, which scarcely eddied them. Her pencil-thin waist, below the big teats, was cinched in a tight studded belt made of glossy animal fur.

Belle suddenly felt a bit foolish, with her white knickers and bra already, now, stained to sluttishness. There had been only the most primitive toilet facilities on the steamer, and certainly not the luxury of toilet paper. Sure that her arse-crease ponged a bit, she wanted to take a shower, or a swim in the turquoise ocean. Belle wondered if Dr Paine was stuffy about swimming costumes, as she had brought none. Bra and knickers would do at a pinch.

They climbed into Dr Paine's land cruiser. Dr Paine explained that the clinic and the sandy beaches were on the other side of the island, but the only harbour was here, on the jungle side.

'It is standard Pacific island paradise, on our side,' she said, 'so you can swim and sunbathe; in the nude, of course. That is one of the attractions for our wealthy customers: while beautifying their bodies, they can enjoy a five-star holiday at the same time, with cuisine to match. Luckily, they don't demand exotic leisure facilities – in any case, their genetic enhancement makes strain ill-advised – just to laze in the sun, which permits us to get on with our research work.'

Flicking the powered steering wheel with a single finger, Dr Paine manoeuvred the land cruiser up and down winding hillsides, with tendrils and creepers whipping the window as though to reach the women. Belle felt engulfed by jungle and said so, but Dr Paine laughed and said the island contained a complete miniature ecology.

'We even grow our own crops, and fruit,' she said. 'Those who cannot pay for their treatment must work for it.'

She asked if Belle understood the relationship between her profession of 'beauty enhancer' and the connected genetic research work, and Belle said she thought so.

'You prefer not to solicit funds from the big chemical companies, and thus remain independent,' she said.

'That is correct. Some of my research is rather delicate, and outside the mainstream. If it fell into untutored hands . . .'

71

Suddenly, the land cruiser emerged from the jungle and Belle saw undulating hills before them, strewn with bougainvillea, palm trees and jacaranda, with patches of cultivation.

'My paying clients are very wealthy women,' she said, 'and I pamper them as they expect. Their treatments are inordinately expensive, but effective, as you will see. One of the concerns of wealthy women married to rich husbands, is to remain wealthy women married to rich husbands. So, the genetic enhancement of their figures is designed not just to improve their bodies, but to instil in them a new and ageless vitality.'

'Sex appeal,' said Belle. 'For rich bitches.'

'Sex appeal, yes,' said Dr Paine, beaming at the girl with dazzling white teeth. 'But please do not use . . . that last term, in or out of my hearing. It causes me displeasure, for reasons you might find petty. I prefer to think of my guests as *females blessed*. My island belongs, freehold, and in its entirety, to the Paine Foundation, which purchased it from the descendants of one Captain Furvert, who discovered it centuries ago. It was formerly known as Furvert's Island, but lay neglected. The Japanese named it Sakosha and then of course, the Americans arrived after the Second World War in the last century; but its constitutional status remained in limbo until the Paine Foundation took the initiative. Japan, France and the United States have a nominal claim to it, but all have enough Pacific territories to worry about and the small harbour makes my island strategically useless. So the place rests as it is. Not least, because the husbands of many of my clients are men of influence in those nations and are content to leave a well-meaning English eccentric to potter about in her straw hat . . .'

Dr Paine flashed her dazzling smile, again.

'In a sense, I am the island's sovereign and have made the rules. For example, men are not permitted to reside on the island in the interests of order and discipline, so we take a relaxed attitude towards nudity outdoors, or during therapy; although our guests appreciate strict dress at mealtimes and formal occasions. I understand you are a nudist, Belle?'

Belle said she loved to be naked.

'Good! Although most of the time, you will dress as a nurse, or wear a white coat, or other clothing of authority,' Dr Paine continued. 'Speaking of discipline, Belle, can you also confirm that you favour the idea of corporal punishment?'

'Why, yes,' Belle blurted. 'I believe I made that clear in our email correspondence.'

'Sometimes, corporal discipline is necessary, for my workers,' said Dr Paine slowly. 'They are orientals, and what may seem old-fashioned, or cruel, to Europeans, is normal and even desirable to them, and, sometimes, for my patients as well. You may not be aware how closely corporal chastisement, that is, controlled whipping and caning, is linked to my research, as well as my body enhancement program – the link between the pain and pleasure centres of the brain, and certain nerve endings of the female body; notably the buttocks, breasts and pudenda.'

'I am no stranger to caning on the bare bottom, Dr Paine,' Belle murmured. 'I went to a rather old-fashioned school . . .'

She shifted in her sticky dress and knickers, reassuring herself that she had not, strictly, lied.

'So, you have been caned, as punishment, on the bare buttocks?' said Dr Paine.

'I can take quite a lot,' said Belle, easy with the absolute truth.

'Heaven, I'm not suggesting *you* should be caned, Belle,' said Dr Paine, laughing. 'I am simply ascertaining your readiness to *administer* the cane, to the bare bottoms of compliant subjects, and under strictly controlled lab conditions, as part of your nurse's duties.'

'I have no problem with that, Doctor,' said Belle.

'Good. You see, the practice of gluteal caning has a distorted image,' Dr Paine said sombrely, 'because flagellant therapy is associated with hostility, cruelty and the

73

desire to dominate, out of pure malice. There are certain evil women who call themselves *dominatrixes*, and use their female wiles to enslave others. The healing impulse, present in all humans, can be distorted, Belle, into its nightmare mirror image. We must not forget that the saintly Dr Albert Schweitzer, who tended the natives of Cameroun, shared the same initials as Adolf Schickelgrueber, who later took his *mother's* name of Hitler . . . *Our* therapeutic caning is a process of joyful self-awareness, not of subjugation.'

'I shall fulfil all my duties to my best ability, Dr Paine,' said Belle. 'But I should hate to administer any caning that I was unprepared to take, myself.'

The sweat in Belle's panties now mingled with a seepage of juice from her pussy lips.

'Belle!' cried Dr Paine. 'You're my assistant, and shan't be caned, of course! Unless, that is, you are *naughty*, and break my rules – or *wish* to help our research . . .'

They were silent, as their vehicle traversed a wide valley, with distant plantations of fruits and legumes, patched between clumps of trees hanging with Spanish moss. Belle saw females, a few to each field, who did not seem to be working as field hands, but rather playing. They darted hither and thither, hatless and nude under the scorching sun. Dr Paine explained that they were catching those pestilent insects as yet resistant to her genetically-modified food crops. In the heat haze, Belle fancied that the girls were trapping the pests with their tongues. In the most distant field, shrouded in blue mist, sowing was taking place. A nude girl, in harness, pulled a plough and was dealt occasional, lazy whiplashes to the bare buttocks by another naked female, who squatted briefly behind the plough, to eject seeds from her vagina and anus. The skins of all these nude workers gleamed with pearl-white scales, under the sun.

They came to a high fence of sharpened wooden staves, about twice the height of a man, linked together by coils of barbed wire and topped with a frosting of broken glass. The area it enclosed looked as big as several city blocks.

Dr Paine pressed a key on her dashboard, and a section of the palisade swung open, to close again, rapidly, after their ingress. Belle saw pairs of muscular guards, all female, patrolling the perimeter. All had cropped heads and seemed nude, until she saw they wore flesh-coloured skin-suits, zipped at crotch and neck. They drove for two hundred metres down a sandy track, shaded by coconut palms and emerged at the research complex. The Paine Foundation was the same as any luxury beach resort: a large complex of wooden bungalows, shaded by palms and with palm leaves for a roof. White sand swept down to a turquoise sea and a sprinkling of behatted ladies basked or swam, all nude, all golden brown and superb of figure: the breasts and buttocks exaggerated, bellies taut and waists thin beyond the dreams of any cosmetic surgeon.

The land cruiser pulled to a halt outside one of the larger buildings, signalled by a flag bearing a green snake twined around a rod; the ancient Aesculapian healer's symbol, except that this rod had a crook handle and splayed tip, like a disciplinary cane. They were greeted by an elfin Japanese girl in a white nurse's blouse, tight around her breast-buds and tucked into the waistband of billowing harem pantaloons of crimson cotton that clung closely to the taut peach of her bum; beneath the pants, she was barefoot. Her strong porcelain face with rosebud lips, was framed by cropped black hair. Belle stifled a gasp of shock: the girl was Geisha. But Geisha was a world away, at college in England! Her twin, then – but Geisha had not mentioned any immediate family, save to say, mysteriously, that Dr Jolita Cunliffe was her 'mother' – that her biological parents had perished in the atomic holocaust of Hiroshima long ago in 1945.

The Japanese girl stretched out her arms, and, with her head bowed, caught Dr Paine's rubber cape as she shed it, but she was careful not to touch it with her fingers. She followed Belle and the doctor into the building.

'This is Sushi, my helpmate, and soon to be yours, Belle,' said Dr Paine.

'How do you do, Sushi,' said Belle.

Sushi bowed to her, but did not return her greeting.

'Sushi is mute,' said Dr Paine. 'Tragically, she was born without a tongue and can eat only liquid or emulsified food, though her vocal chords are intact. But she understands everything.'

Sushi bowed again, without smiling.

'I call her Sushi because she has such a sweet little slice,' whispered Dr Paine and giggled girlishly at her own joke, which Belle thought in curious taste. 'However, today she is wearing caning pants, for she was naughty yesterday – weren't you, Sushi?'

Sushi nodded agreement and smiled for the first time, showing teeth as white as Dr Paine's.

'In the less humane society of the orient, the disabled, such as Sushi, would be left to starve,' said the Doctor. 'We at Paine pride ourselves on care for the unfortunate, as well as the rich. Those unfortunate enough to have been naughty must be caned on their bare bottoms, and there are no divisions of rank in bare-bottom caning.'

Sushi nodded again enthusiastically, and held up two fingers; a gesture which Belle thought rude, but which obviously had a different meaning in the orient. Dr Paine looked at her diver's watch and nodded.

'Yes, we have plenty of time before luncheon,' she said. 'Belle, I invite you to witness your first scientifically monitored caning at the Paine Foundation – you might as well plunge in at the deep end. First, Sushi will show you to your quarters and assist you while you shower.'

Belle nodded agreement, scarcely able to breathe or contain the seepage of come in her panties in her excitement at witnessing chastisement. Sushi knelt and Dr Paine placed Belle's suitcase on the girl's head. Sushi straightened and, carrying the case with perfect poise, led Belle through a maze of corridors to her room, which occupied a corner of the building and gave directly out onto the beach. Belle gasped in joy: it was perfect! A simple apartment with a whirring fan, refrigerator, table and chairs and armoire. Belle helped herself to a glass of ice water from the fridge and gave one to Sushi.

'How happy I am!' she cried. 'Turquoise sea, white sand and useful nursing work – it is every girl's dream!'

Then she frowned, mindful that she was to watch the girl caned on her bare bum and that her cunt was juicing heavily at the prospect. She decided not to be embarrassed by her caning tendencies, obviously normal in the Paine Foundation. Perhaps that *was* every girl's dream! Sushi watched, as Belle squatted on the toilet and peed noisily, then, silently, moved to wipe Belle's anus with tissue when she had copiously evacuated. Then, she sponged Belle under the cold shower. Her fingers lingered on the jungle of Belle's pube-hairs and her lips curled shyly in a smile. When Belle reached for a towel, Sushi made a moue and motioned the tall blonde girl to kneel under the fan. Then, crawling under and over Belle's wet body, Sushi mopped every droplet of water from her skin with her hair, her body capable of effortless gyration.

Trembling, and her cunt gushing with new come, Belle changed into a plain white frock, before her throbbing clitty could make her betray herself with a rash gesture. She persuaded herself that her drying was merely Sushi's oriental form of submission, despite the swishing touch of the girl's clothing, that had seemed to glow with intimacy meant for Belle alone. She also reminded herself that they were awaited for Sushi's caning. Belle was dripping with sweat again, though Sushi, like Dr Paine, seemed immune to heat and without perspiration.

Belle debated whether to wear undies or not. She knew her cunt would continue to juice as she watched a girl's bare bum flogged – especially this sweet reminder of her beloved Geisha – and wondered if she could excuse herself, shut the door on the Japanese and privately wank off, before the beating. But, she knew also that one wank would make her want another and sensed that Sushi did not understand a European's bathroom privacy.

Eventually, she settled for no knickers, which evidently meant no bra, either. Her big teats flopped under the thin cotton, her nipples plainly erect and she knew that her crotch would be stained with come but hopefully, it would soon be indistinguishable from sweat. Wearing only rope sandals, and her light dress swaying above her knees, as her naked breasts bounced beneath a deep cleavage, she followed Sushi to the caning room. A sign on the door said, in English and Japanese: CANING IN PROGRESS – PLEASE ENTER QUIETLY.

Dr Paine awaited them in an airy, spacious chamber, whose brightness did not conceal its function as a whipping room. It was furnished with a wooden table, at waist height and slightly aslant, with metal cuffs at each corner and a rise in the middle, to present the buttocks. Above and below the rise, thick rubber straps, with buckles, hung down from the table's sides. Set an arm's length from one corner was a whipping post, made of a sawn palm trunk, with a collar at its head, handcuffs midway on its trunk and ankle-cuffs at the base. There was a rack of canes and whips of various lengths and thongage. There was no fan, although the heat was oppressive.

Beneath the whipping post, and under the caning table, ran gutters which emptied into a hole in the centre of the floor. The floor was slightly concave, so that any liquid spilled would flow towards this central drain hole. Two video cameras, mounted on tripods, completed the apparatus of punishment, and one of them, pointed at Belle, was already blinking. Dr Paine held a palmed remote control, by which she could control the focus of each video. Belle smiled for the camera, which promptly moved to Sushi, who bowed, but did not smile. Then, the camera swivelled to a panoramic view of the caning table, the twin camera being closer, and focused on the place where the caned buttocks would rest.

Dr Paine wore nothing but a black rubber bikini, whose gossamer fabric clung to her breasts and buttock like a second skin. The panties were a mere thong, leaving her massive, firm buttocks almost entirely nude, and the bra was an uplift, whose scalloped cups pointed her teats like golden marrows.

'I generally put myself at my ease, for caning,' said Dr Paine. 'You may feel free to do so as well, Belle.'

Belle blushed and stammered that she had no under-things.

'I think I am aware of that,' smiled the doctor and selected a long, thin cane from her rack.

'This is a rattan,' she said, showing it to Belle. 'Feel how supple and strong she is, despite her thinness. I cut her myself. Were you ever caned with a rattan, Belle?'

'N . . . not to my knowledge, Doctor,' said Belle.

'It is awfully painful. But then, Sushi is awfully naughty. You may assume position for your caning, Sushi,' Dr Paine announced, 'and Belle will make the strapping arrangements.'

Sushi positioned herself face down on the caning table, with her bum slightly raised by the wooden dimple. She stretched her arms and legs, making an X shape, and laid her wrists and ankles in the cuffs, ready for fastening. Belle now saw that her caning pants, though fastened tightly at the waist, had a row of buttons extending down a seam which clung neatly to the cleft of her buttocks. Dr Paine watched in silence.

Belle locked the Japanese girl in her wrist and ankle cuffs. Sushi's body was splayed rigid and she made no sound other than a quiet gasp, as Belle tightened the waist strap on the small of her back above her caning pants. Belle strapped the lower thong over Sushi's trousered thighs, so that the twin straps now pinioned her belly to the table, and pressed her pubis to the dimple. With trembling fingers, Belle began to unbutton the back seam of the caning pants. Her cunt gushed with come, as each opened button revealed more of the Japanese girl's pure white arse flesh. When all the buttons were undone, both buttock-flaps fell aside, leaving bare flesh between Sushi's belt and about four inches at the tops of her thighs. Her anus bud was clearly visible between her stretched buttocks, and the pink pucker was ringed with a down of stiff, shiny hairs. Belle saw the lips of Sushi's cunt gleaming deep red and shiny wet with come. The finny hairs opened and closed on her anus bud, as though gasping. Above her cleft, her spinal nubbin was elongated, like a little tail and shiny with the same crystal down.

Dr Paine stepped to Sushi's head and lifted her cane, then repeated the girl's gesture of two fingers. Sushi nodded agreement and Dr Paine returned to assume her caning position, with her feet stretched wide to brace herself and standing at just over the cane's length from Sushi's completely naked buttocks.

'Two it is, then, Sushi,' she said, pleasantly. 'Five second pauses between strokes, and no break, I'm afraid, or we should be late for luncheon.'

Belle was confused, then understood that the two fingers indicated Sushi was to take two dozen strokes. She shivered: two dozen, on the bare, with that fearsome rattan!

'One,' said Dr Paine.

Her body coiled backwards, like a snake's then lunged, so that, although her caning stance was further than the cane's length, her body swung forward over Sushi's fesses and delivered the canestroke right across the centre of the bare bum.

Vip!

Her torso followed the cane on its downward path, before looping back, as she righted herself. Belle's hand flew to her lips: she had never witnessed a canestroke delivered with such momentum and yet, all the time, Dr Paine's feet remained firmly on the floor, as though gripped by suction pads. A vivid pink stripe appeared almost at once on Sushi's bottom, which quivered only slightly, with no sound from the girl's lips.

'Two,' said Dr Paine, after five seconds had elapsed.

Vip!

Again, she lunged back, whirled, then lunged forwards, feet firmly anchored and thighs quivering hard with muscle. The cane took Sushi on the buttock tops, below her spinal nubbin and now her fesses clenched very slightly, as a sister weal appeared on her naked skin. The video cameras glided in and out, now focusing on the weals, now on the entirety of the bare bottom or from below, on the swollen cunt lips.

'Three . . .'

Vip!
'Four . . .'
Vip!
'Five . . .'
Vip!
'Six . . .'
Vip!

The cane took Sushi in every portion of her exposed fesses. Belle lost count of the strokes, as she was mesmerised by the delicate quivering of the girl's buttocks under her caning and the purity of pink on her porcelain skin, as the cheeks clenched in silence under Dr Paine's rod. Belle's cunt was gushing and her knickers drenched in come. Her clit and nipples were rock hard and she felt an intense desire to masturbate, even if the reward would be a caning for her own bottom. Well, two dozen – she could manage *that*. She slipped her hand under her dress and clamped her throbbing clitty, her fingers sopped instantly by oily come, and could not suppress a groan of pleasure as a jolt of pleasure electrified her spinal cord. The beating continued, Dr Paine's body animal-like in the lithe intensity of her thrashing as though flogging a captured prey. Her teeth gleamed like knives and her tongue protruded, licking her lips as each vip! of the cane on naked flesh echoed through the room.

Belle was soaked in sweat, her dress almost transparent. She fingered her clit, wanting her wank to last and timing her masturbation to the canestrokes, with one surge of pleasure for each cut to the reddening bare bum, whose flogged tight jellies quivered before her eyes. Dr Paine had begun to slice the Japanese girl right on her finny bumhole, lashing the inside of her wet cunt with the cane tip, which caused Sushi to jump against the rubber fastenings at her back and thighs. But still, she did not even whimper.

'Fifty-seven . . .' said Dr Paine.
Vip!
*Fifty-seven!*
'By the way, Belle, your dress is going to get stained with your come and masturbating is much more agreeable in the

nude, so I suggest you shed it. There will be other ladies here soon – they can hear the cane above the sound of the sea – and they'll want to wank off before luncheon, too. In fact, Sushi has well over a hundred strokes to go, so you can have more than one wank, if you like. A lovely way to acquaint yourself with our guests.'

Numbly, Belle did as invited, or ordered. She shed her dress and, as the bare-bum caning continued, with strokes delivered at precise intervals of five seconds, her hand pushed into the wet cavern of her cunt and with her thumb flicking at her clitty, she began to masturbate hard. Sushi's twitching white buttocks lay in a puddle of come that seeped visibly from her red cunt lips, their lush hue equalled by the dark red quilt of weals that suffused her buttocks. The pool of Sushi's come flowed towards the table's edge and began to drip into the runnel carved in the floor. Belle longed to lick and swallow every drop of that come, while Sushi sat heavy on her face, squashing her lips with her cunt and spanking her bare tits; and at this thought, Belle gasped repeatedly as her fingers wanked her clit to a shuddering climax. Sushi had earned, and accepted, a caning of *200 strokes, on the bare!* The door opened and a lady slid quietly into the flogging chamber.

She was nude, her magnificent teats thrusting firm and ripe, topped by big brown nipple-pots, the breasts with no need of support. The firm pears of her derriere scarcely quivered as she tiptoed, with thighs rippling below the smooth, shaven bulge of her pubic hill, her gash a glistening crevasse with the well-extruded clitty peeping like a thick pink worm. Like Dr Jolita Cunliffe, she had a pelt of glossy brown fur which covered all of her below the collarbone, except the nipples and quim lips. Even her buttocks gleamed with shiny fur.

'A deuce, eh?' she whispered. 'I'm Bluebird. That's my nickname, my *nom de cravache* . . . I guess you are the new nurse, Miss Puget. You're lovely! I know we'll be friends.'

She giggled, and Dr Paine said mildly that Bluebird was a naughty girl, and would be caned herself, if she disturbed the punishmnent.

'Well, Doctor, thanks to you, I love that more than anything, even cock,' said Bluebird, her accent definitely American. '*Not* caning me would be punishment.'

'It's a thought,' said Dr Paine, and chuckled, as she caned Sushi hard in the cleft, right on the wet flesh of her gash. 'Imagine, Belle – where caning is pleasure, what can we use for punishment? Other than caning beyond the limit of pleasure. A hundred and thirteen . . .'

Vip!

'*Uhhh* . . .' mewled Sushi and a flow of golden pee suddenly pissed from her cunt, onto the table and down into the runnel.

Sushi strained against her bonds and, still pissing copiously, began to whimper at the next few strokes to her cleft, as though she wished to remain the centre of attention. Her come and pee, mixed now, flowed quite rapidly in the channel. Belle stared at Bluebird's bare bum. It was golden tan, the perfect glow of a true nudist and without a cane weal.

Suddenly, Bluebird's fingers were cool and firm, pressing Belle's wet gash. She did not stop there, but began to masturbate Belle's clitty, which soon tingled anew. Belle's head whirled in pleasure and confusion. To be wanked off, cool as you please, by a gorgeous female to whom she had not even introduced herself . . .! Her fingers rapidly found Bluebird's clitty, as stiff as her own, and the come already flowing copiously from her swollen cunt onto her hard muscular thighs. Belle could not help herself and joined her new friend in a slow wank, as they watched Sushi's crimson bare bum twitching and shivering under the strokes of the rattan. Bluebird's belly began to heave, and her breath grew fierce.

'God, you wank superbly,' she whispered to Belle, as she squeezed and pinched her bulbous nipples. 'Such tits, and such buns! You're gorgeous! I can't wait to see your ass caned!'

This stunned Belle but then, as the full import sank in, her cunt gushed with more come. Even as Dr Paine's assistant, she was free to live nude and submit to bare-bum caning . . . suddenly excited, she felt the urge to pee.

'Well,' panted Belle, 'I'm not sure I could take two hundred . . . two dozen, perhaps.'

Bluebird laughed and her balled fist rammed into Belle's soaking cunt, right to the neck of her womb. She continued to wank off the English girl with her thumb flicking the stiff clit.

'A deuce is just tickling! When you've been gene-spliced, sweet baby, you'll be able to take much more. And if she won't cane me, please say *you* will! Oh, please, please, pretty please! Serious cane fun, and we'll wank off as much as you like, Miss Puget! Say yes!'

*Serious* bare-bum caning . . .! Belle thought back to Geisha and her desired spanking of over 1,000. Bluebird's thighs clasped Belle's hands like rocks, as her cunt spewed come and she began to pant in the onrush of orgasm. Sushi's bare bum was now a twitching landscape of ridges and furrows, as crimson as the caning pants which enclosed her buttocks. Belle thought of Geisha caning her bare arse, hard, with a rattan – then, Geisha merged with Sushi and both had canes, flogging Belle's bare nates to the bone. Belle let a hot stream of piss flow at last from her cunt to mingle with the oily come on her thighs, and whinnied in orgasm once more.

'Yes,' she gasped, 'Oh! Ah! *Ahhh . . . Yes . . .*'

# Memoir 4

*My exam results weren't as good as I'd hoped, so I couldn't pick and choose my university, or even my courses. Genetics was the hot thing at that time, and I had to settle for anthropology, which kind of dovetails into it, and that is what got me to my thesis on Social Darwinism. Geneticists sometimes can't see the wood for the trees, but in anthropology you can expand your horizons, and I read a lot of genetics on the side. Eugenics, that kind of thing, offbeat stuff that the uni course wouldn't cover. I worked like a bugger at college of course, so in due course I got a First and sailed on towards my doctorate. Meanwhile, I had plenty of money. Money is the key. With money, you can get proper equipment, and with proper equipment you can rule the world. The Germans would have won the Second World War, if they'd had enough petrol, although maybe they did win it, in the long run, them and the Japs. Anyway I was always off to London, in my own BMW, and didn't have to sit around with grotty students drinking grotty instant coffee, instead of working. I kept my job at Dr Stone's: most weekends, and in the super long holidays, when I wasn't busy travelling. Being a student was great, especially since I was a slut at the same time. I got my phone thing working again, in London, with absolutely extortionate fees; only this time, I wasn't a teenage tigress, I was Miss Claw. That sounded grander, and more dangerous. After a while, I refused to discuss my fee saying that if they had to ask, they couldn't afford me. And then I just left my 'tip' up to the man I had just beaten and* shat on and everything. If it was insufficient, I said he'd never again lick my dirty arse clean, while he wanked off. It is a great sense of power, making a man wank off while you watch, but not letting him touch you – except to lick your shitty bumhole, of course. Also, I had the Stone family, mother, dad and sonny, eating out of the palm of my hand. My own Mum encouraged me, without asking too much, when I hinted that I was taking a leaf out of her book; or a twig from her birch . . .

I didn't make friends at college, on purpose. I let them think I was a rich bitch. I didn't want anyone to know my secrets. Mum, you see, had a certain reticence, a sense of shame, even. I mean, when she flogged a man, she knew she was punishing him for being naughty. If she fucked him, too, it compounded his naughtiness. I was shameless. I wasn't naughty, I was amoral. I was Miss Claw. If I put a guy in bondage, he really was helpless and really didn't know what to expect. I might whip or birch him a few hundred or more, and then leave him tied up, in the dark, with my shitty panties stuffed in his gob and not saying when, or if, I was coming back. Sometimes I'd truss him, then shit and pee on his face, then tell him I was going to birch his bum raw but not flog him at all, even though his cock was stiff and begging for it. Then, after a couple of hours, I'd say he was too disgusting to whip and order him out, wearing a cock restraint which he was forbidden to remove until his next visit, when I might consider lashing him . . .

That's all men really understand: the whip, the lash, the cane. On their bare bums, making them squirm till they beg for mercy . . . or beg for more. That's all anybody understands. Men and women are no different; all the same flesh. Flesh only understands power and control. All humans are in bondage from minute one – meat in bondage of skin. The appeal of submission to flogging is that people want to celebrate their skin, their bondage. To feel their skin alive, whipped.

Studying anthropology, and the Stone family too, fused more and more into the same thing. Anthropology teaches you that everyone does everything to everyone, all the time.

*Categories and value judgements are worthless. For example,
I stopped thinking of myself as lesbian, or bisexual, or any
other stupid restriction. What I did with Mrs Stone was just
what I did. And usually in front of one or other of her
menfolk. Or else, one of us would be the voyeuse. Kinky?
Another stupid category. I was a nurse at heart! My function
was to heal, with pleasure, which – I was gradually learning
– is at its purest in submission, especially to whipping on the
bare. This is where the nurse, or slut, comes in. Everybody
tries to compromise with life. They want to balance regularity with excitement. So, happily married guys expect to have
a reliable little wife to go to bed with but they also like to
play with uninvolved sluts, or aunties, or nurses. Of course it
works both ways and couples like Lee and Gary find they can
remain couples while playing their games together, either
with submissive sluts or with a clinical and dominant nurse,
like me. Any scenario is OK, as long as somebody exerts
naked power. That is why my Internet slaves worship me. I
know all about them, their tastes, histories, everything. I
have an encyclopaedic memory, even without my hard drive.
I'm their goddess that they can never turn off.*

*The Stones were my first field project, if you like; my first
exercise in prolonged domination. All that golf kept Mrs
Stone in superb shape and our lesbian sex was a joy, as it
got more and more exotic. But we kept our activities strictly
separate from my clinic work and also from my 'private
practice' with the RBs and their submissive men. Detachment
is important for proper joy in power, even detachment from
your own person. That is why I began to volunteer my own
bare bottom for canings and birchings; longer and longer
ones. Always by Mrs Stone, never by either male. It hurt
dreadfully, but I was learning not to mind the pain as though
my thrashed bum was another person's. When you become
indifferent to your own pain, you are free to enjoy everyone
else's.*

*Mrs Stone and I enjoyed ourselves with her two males, but
never with both together and always with her properly
dressed in front of her son, though she got naked with me and
her husband, if she wanted. Especially if he was rubbing his*

birched bum and wanking off on my orders, while I tongued or dildoed his wife's cunt, or else tongued her clit while dildoing her anus with a big rubber tool sunk right to her root, making her squeal and gush with come oil from her slit, wetting her thighs and stockings.

When I took a thrashing myself, I was not nude at that stage. I had my nurse's uniform and pulled down my knickers to show my bare bum on Mrs Stone's instructions. I was to be punished for some misdemeanour and either Dr Stone or Henry was permitted to watch. A couple of dozen was normal, then it went up to three or four, even with the birch, and the idea was that the male voyeur would get an erection, and as punishment for his own misdemeanour would have to strip completely and take two strokes for every one I had taken, twice as hard. Mrs Stone pretended to be outraged and we would share the flogging equally. Naturally, with my own bum smarting – Mrs Stone whipped hard – I was genuinely eager to wreak vengeance on a naked male arse.

A typical scenario, at first, would be that I, in my nurse's uniform, would witness Mrs Stone's regular bare-bum thrashing of Henry. The bugger stiffened even before he was stroked! Mrs Stone pretended not to notice. He would take two dozen stingers with her cane, and then I would feel his wealed bum and note his erection and state solemnly that his flogging had been insufficient. Then I would give him another two dozen with the birch. He was practically coming by that time – Mrs Stone would be modestly dressed but with no knickers, and would be discreetly wanking off – and when I got his cock into my wet gash, it would only take a few squeezes to milk his spunk while she ogled my bare bum threshing on his balls. Or I would wear Mrs Stone's knickers and skirts, and make-up like hers and everything, and make Henry or Dr Stone fuck me in the cunt while she watched. If it was her husband, she would wank herself off while I licked come from her gash. Dr Stone would bugger Mrs Stone while I birched his bare arse, or else I would be buggered by his massive cock while she flogged him, always masturbating. Mrs Stone confided that before my arrival, she masturbated to orgasm at least once a day, whether Dr

88

Stone fucked her or not and usually two or three times on the days she caned Henry. She confided that she was addicted to wanking and I said there were worse addictions and made her wank just for me, which she liked immensely. I began to understand why Henry visited my own mum – it was youthful rebellion, showing that he was free to submit to whoever he chose! Frequent bare-bum thrashing had addicted him to submission. The two males never witnessed each other, but I dare say we broke all sorts of taboos, though an anthropologist learns that everything is taboo somewhere and sacred somewhere else. And the whole point of a taboo is that it wouldn't exist, unless someone enjoyed it.

My computer was always state of the art, which helped my studies and also helped me keep in touch with the RBs and their husbands over the net, like Lee and Gary in Hawaii. As Miss Claw, I conned my way into a Visa account in the name 'Independent Nursing Consultants' so that visiting business types could put their floggings and bondage on their expense accounts, saying they had gout or something. It was also useful worldwide, because I made videos of everything, including 'introductory' videos of me wanking, fucking – usually a black stud – shitting, or pissing and sold them over the net to RBs and their hubbies and friends they introduced. Usually, they would send me amateur videos back, begging for my approval. I built up a network of slaves, paying big money to receive my orders. Like, they were to wear cock rings, ball clamps and suchlike, or drink their wives' piss, or take so many strokes of the cane daily and send me the videoed proof. I ordered some of them to have their cocks pierced, or their pouches and arse puckers, and have rings put in; then show me, say, their 'albert' [that's a cock-ring right through the glans] pulled by a taut wire while their women flogged them.

Lee and Gary were actually my friends. Gary's arse was as hard as his tool and he loved being caned for video by Lee, nude; I would wank off just watching her titties bounce and her gash shiny with come as she herself masturbated, with her cane striping Gary's bum and his cock stiff. Sometimes, Lee would take a bare-arse whipping from Gary, just to

89

*prove she had balls. They were seriously rich, of course, and lived in a huge house, very isolated, on the northern side of Hawaii island in the middle of a sort of volcanic moonscape. There were no other houses for miles and you could only get there by helicopter, or something. They started to include their housemaids in their videos.*

*They wore frilly French maids' uniforms, all with dolls' faces, like Japs, only sultry. Lee said they came from some weird little island in Micronesia. At first, I saw them clothed and helping with canes and bondage, their faces deliciously impassive yet somehow glowing with lust, while Lee and Gary whipped each other or fucked. I got cross that I wasn't sharing in the things that went unvideoed, for I was sure those maids weren't there just to serve breakfast. Then, I started to get videos of the maids, nude or in nude bondage, taking the cane or the rattan or birch, both on naked bums and breasts. And being fucked by Gary of course, in cunt and anus. How their little taut buttocks wriggled as his monster tooled their bumholes, sinking in right to the balls and with their arms clutching his arse, to pull him in to their roots.*

*Usually, a buggered maid would tongue Lee's wet clit and drink her come, as Gary bum-fucked her while the other two licked and chewed her nips. There were all sorts of lustful combinations that had me wanking off like some prisoner. Anyway, the maids' bums squirmed so deliciously and their titties were so luscious and trembling, that I wanked myself off to come after come, just watching those bare tight arses flogged to purple. Like little sleek mice I thought, and squeaking with delight as they were whipped! Now, at that stage, I still had a few shreds of stupid morality and I worried that these sluts were sex slaves, like you heard about in the Orient. Lee assured me they were free, but the girls actually begged to be flogged, once they had learned of her and Gary's new passion for the cane. The proof was in close-up shots of their come flowing, as the cane thrashed their arses and their heaves of unsimulated orgasm.*

*Afterwards they would hold up score cards, with the number of strokes they had taken and the number of comes, like a kind of tournament. The winner was allowed to wank* herself off, in close-up and very expertly, with big gushes of come oiling her thighs for my benefit. They all had large whorled clitties, I noticed; like helmets. And with these wonderful, inscrutable smiles. Lee said that caning actually made them come without their clitties being touched, as though their arses themselves were clitties! That sounded weird to me. I've known plenty of male submissives who will ejaculate while I cane them and female ones who masturbate under cane, but nothing like this. Yet the evidence was there. These girls had bottoms so sensitive, they orgasmed repeatedly and automatically, when caned bare.

Furthermore, Lee could whip their bums raw, I mean, right to the bone, and they would come and come, gushing juice and crying 'Harder!', with their bums absolutely shredded, and crimson with weals – yet, the next day, their buttocks were as smooth and creamy as ever. I wanted to find out where they came from, because I figured it must be one strange island indeed, the people hopelessly inbred and ripe for anthropological pickings. But Lee said that the girls didn't even know exactly where it was! Or couldn't – wouldn't? – tell, with their limited English. Of course, there was no way to thrash it from them, as they longed to be thrashed! She begged me to come over and help out, in a working holiday, or her caning arm would get as big as Gary's cock. Hawaii began to seem a very tempting place. Not least, because I wondered where all their money came from.

# 6

# Pleasure Girls

'Actually, I've ... I've never been caned, myself,' said Linda Folsom. The pretty brunette lowered her face, whose blush was mirrored by her bowl of crayfish soup.

Belle paused in her enthusiastic description of Sushi's caning that morning, although she had omitted the excessive detail of her wanking off with Bluebird.

'Oh!' she said. 'Well, you must be very well-behaved, Linda. I'm afraid *I've* never been well-behaved. Always getting into trouble at school.'

Belle giggled at the mischief of her white lie. Soon, she decided, she would tell her new friend and supervisor that she liked baring her bottom for the cane ... but not just yet.

'It's not that,' said Linda, smiling through her blush. 'Not that at all. Some day, I'll be caned, I know. But' – deftly changing the subject – 'Dr Paine says British schools have been forbidden to cane for a long time.'

'State schools, perhaps,' Belle sniffed, 'but at my school, we got caned for the slightest thing. Knickers down and a dozen fast stingers on the bare bum.'

Her quim began to moisten slightly, in the juiciness of her own fantasy.

'Yes, the prefects would take us in the gym, before all our class, and we had to bend over a vaulting horse in gym slips, raised of course, and panties at our ankles. We would be caned by two prefects, each taking a long run-up, so that after one stroke was delivered, there was never a pause of more than two seconds before the next. Oh, the awful thudding of those runners on the gym floor! Then the whistle of the cane – they lifted very high – and then the awful crack across your bare bum, which you had to hold with your own hands to stretch the skin tight and stop you clenching the cheeks.'

'Oh, don't,' Linda murmured, grinning in delight. 'You're getting me all excited.'

'Don't you witness canings here?' said Belle.

'Sometimes. But I can't bear it . . . I mean, I juice so much, I have to masturbate.'

'I don't think Dr Paine objects,' said Belle gravely. 'She believes it to be healthy.'

'But I masturbate to excess,' said Linda. 'I really do – I'm a wankaholic. And when I see something that turns me on, like a caning – well, *only* caning, really – then I can't stop masturbating. I do myself till my fingers are numb, and I'm useless for work. Dr Paine encourages girls to masturbate, actually, and insists we keep our come for the lab, in little rubber jars. I suppose that's why she puts up with my clumsiness, because I provide her with so much wank juice. I wear special sponge panties, you see. The runnels in the caning room lead to a central collection tank underneath the floor and Dr Paine likes a good audience for her canings, with all the ladies wanking and juicing well. "Liquid health" she calls it . . . But we're supposed to be talking about work and your duties, aren't we?'

She giggled. Linda Folsom was slim, with firm, jutting young breasts and coltish legs, but surprisingly pale in comparison with Belle's golden tan. She wore a white lab coat, buttoned right to her chin, but which clung to her ample breast swellings; her ripe buttocks and stockinged thighs were pressed tightly against the clammy cotton of her coat which was unbuttoned almost to the crotch. Under the tight coat, it seemed that Linda wore only rather bulky panties, with stockings but no bra.

She sipped her soup and munched a piece of bread, as Belle did the same. Most of the food was raw fish or fruit, exquisitely diced. A huge tank of seawater, the size of a small swimming-pool, thrashed with live lobsters, which were extracted by pincers and painlessly killed by a needle through the neck, before being boiled in a cauldron. Belle, too, was dressed in a white lab coat over blouse, skirt, knickers and bra. It was the done thing to dress at mealtimes and indoors and the rich guests, nude on the beach only minutes before, enjoyed the occasion of dressing up. Bluebird held court at a nearby table in the palm-roofed refectory, wearing pearls, gold and a pink silk sarong that tightly sheathed her teats and bum, with rope sandals.

The table of a dozen or so nurses were all Japanese, like Sushi, and all prettily starched, with net stockings, except for some who wore baggy caning pants. Their voices twittered like birdsong. The nurses whose turn it was to serve as maids – among them Sushi, who served Belle and Linda – were attired as French maids, in perfect frilly costumes whose thin latex micro-skirts allowed their black knickers and garter straps, also rubber, to be seen on the flowered tops of their seamed lycra stockings, while black uplift bras were clearly visible under gossamer blouses.

Linda was Senior Research Assistant and Belle her junior, as plain Research Assistant. To Belle's surprise, they were the only two of this rank, the other duties being carried out by Sushi and her sister nurses. Linda had warmly welcomed her, not least, as she frankly admitted, because she would be glad of a helpmate, but mostly because the two girls took that instant liking to each other of compatriots who bond quickly in strange climes. Linda was truly shy and Belle felt her own residue of shyness harden to boldness, in an instinct to protect her. The brunette said the other principals were Dr Paine herself, Miss Budgen, the terrain mistress and –'

'And what does *la* Budgen supervise, on the *terrain?*' Belle interrupted, remembering the nude field girls she had seen working, hatless in the sun.

'Oh, well,' blurted Linda, 'first things first, Belle. I mean, there are no secrets here – except, of course, that only Dr Paine is allowed into her computer room, which is locked at all times, and we must only work in the labs under her personal or video supervision; but that's not really secret, is it? You'll spend some time free for your own research, approved by Dr Paine, but mostly we will be supervising the preparation of genetic sera to Dr Paine's own specifications. Then in turn, we must supervise the nurses as they administer the sera to our subjects – that is, guests. The sera are administered through the mucous membranes of the vagina or anus and by solid suppository or liquid injection, which isn't actually more painful than a strong enema. Then, there is Dr Cazenove, the dermatologist. We call her the skin mistress. You'll get to know everything, in the proper time, you see . . .'

Linda smiled shyly and blushed again, and Belle rescued her new friend from her evident embarrassment, saying that she was more interested in Linda herself at the moment: in particular, her sex life, if addiction to masturbation could be called so. Belle gloomily reminded herself that there were no males resident on Furvert's Island.

'I can't imagine you've never been caned, Linda,' she said, 'especially when it seems to excite you so much. Or are you a dominant, only interested in caning others?'

It was equally hard to imagine a girl less dominant than the beautiful but timid Linda Folsom, and Linda duly assured her that she longed to be caned naked and had been promised a pure bare-bum thrashing by Dr Paine, when it was her time.

'Oh, God . . .' she moaned, and her hand darted between the folds of her lab coat.

Belle did not see her press her clitoris under the garment, but her wank was vigorous and brought her to such a rapid come that Linda's single whimper, and her gasping, were over before Belle realised that her luncheon companion had just masturbated to orgasm before her eyes – and that Sushi, her blank porcelain face giving no indication that she had just received a bare-bottom caning, watched slyly.

'Sorry,' said Linda, her face scarlet, 'I just *had* to . . .'

Her fingers glistened and she wiped them on a paper napkin. Belle caught a glimpse of pink panties stained dark and oozing with come.

'Well,' said Belle, 'It would be foolish to think myself alone in my excitement. Dr Paine's research into the gluteal nerve-endings ... I mean, you cannot separate purely academic interest from personal interest, can you?'

'In bare-bum caning?' said Linda. 'Hardly a subject for a doctorate ...'

Now it was Belle's turn to blush.

'OK,' she said. 'I admit that I'm submissive, like you – that bare-bum caning turns me on, to receive, or even to watch. But I can imagine myself dominant as well, and actually giving a thrashing ... as long as the bare bottom squirms.'

She felt her pussy moisten, thinking of Sushi's naked buttocks reddened by the cane.

'Oh, you'll have the opportunity,' said Linda. 'I helped Dr Paine check your psych-profile and we agreed you have the perfect makings of a switch. Someone who can be dominant or submissive. I'm submissive, pure and simple.'

'Then how is it you have never been caned?' Belle cried, looking at Linda's haunches. 'You've a bum crying out for stripes, Linda – Oh! Sorry, I didn't mean ...'

'I rather hoped you did, Belle,' said Linda. 'After checking you with Dr Paine and now meeting you at last, in the lovely strong flesh, I hoped *you'd* be the one to ...'

She shook her head.

'But it's out of the question, until Dr Paine decides. There are a lot of things I'm not sure of ... even that Dr Paine isn't sure of.'

Linda herself, in her devotion to Dr Paine, did not mind being kept in the dark about aspects of her own work. The doctor seemed to have a hold over the girl, or a gift promised: perhaps the longed-for caning.

'Linda, are you lesbian?' Belle asked.

Linda threw back her chestnut mane and laughed.

'We are an island of females, Belle,' she said, whispering in sudden earnest. 'What does that tell you? Don't pretend you haven't played girly games like the rest of us.'

'No,' said Belle, 'I can't deny it. Spanking and caning, and ... well, wanking off, tonguing ... *you* know. But that's not the same as ...'

'As what?' said Linda. 'I thought I knew what words like "lesbian" meant. Then I realised we are all just flesh. I knew, once, that all human beings have 23 pairs of chromosomes, but since I came to Sakosha I know even that isn't certain. Dr Paine still has much to decipher, from research by the Japanese, in the Second World War. We mustn't embarrass her by asking questions she cannot yet answer, although I *know* she will have all the answers, one day.'

Linda spoke with the ferocity of a religious zealot.

'How can questions embarrass a scientist?' said Belle.

'The Japanese research was originally sexual in nature. You may have heard of the thousands of women sex slaves, or pleasure girls, used by the Japanese army. There were some humanitarian Japanese scientists, who understood the unavoidable brutish appetites of males and especially Japanese ones, who like to cause their females pain during sex. They wanted to know if females could be genetically enhanced so that pleasure girls *would* actually feel sex pleasure, even being whipped and hurt. The scientists wanted to aid women and the military; to boost a soldier's morale once he knew his pleasure girl had genuinely orgasmed for him, even under the vilest whipping. But once you start tinkering with genes . . . well!'

Linda sighed and shrugged.

'After the war, the Sakosha experiments were hushed up, until Dr Paine rediscovered them, and realised how they could be developed for human goodness!'

She had her zealot's voice again.

'Oh . . . I'm sorry, Belle,' she whispered. 'It's just that I want so much to be caned and whipped and made to submit, but to a *man*, with a big penis, and have him fuck me in my cunt and my bumhole, and wank me off as he fucked me, and . . . and not to be a virgin any more.'

Their conversation was interrupted by a clatter, as one of the frilly maids dropped a dish of lobster. Dr Paine said mildly that the girl should report to the caning room immediately after luncheon and there was a buzz of excitement from the guests. The girl took the news of her punishment with a blank face, and bowed to the doctor.

'How I wish that could be me . . .' sighed Linda. 'But no matter how clumsy I am, the doctor says I must wait till my skin is ripe.'

'We can watch that girl caned,' said Belle, 'and . . . and wank each other, if our come juice makes Dr Paine happy.'

Linda said the afternoon would be taken by her showing Belle the labs and work areas and explaining things generally.

'But don't worry,' she said, 'there is no shortage of canings for you to watch, Belle. Except the one *I* want . . .'

Linda's lab – now to be shared with Belle – was spotlessly clean. A video camera winked in the middle of the ceiling, swivelling as it followed the girls. The first thing Linda did upon entering the fan-cooled room was to wriggle out of her panties, unstopper a rubber jar and squeeze the copious come fluid from her lunchtime wank into the jar, which she then labelled and placed in a refrigerator full of identical jars. Then, she put her panties into a laundry chute and selected a fresh pair from a drawer.

Belle was beginning to feel tired after her day of travel and excitement and Linda agreed that a nap would be in order, after a quick tour of the other labs. They visited a succession of equally spotless rooms, in one of which Belle was introduced to Dr Cazenove, who looked up from her microscope and gave Belle a perfunctory handshake, but pressing hard; and a more than perfunctory looking-over. Dr Cazenove, Belle guessed, was about Dr Paine's age and as youthful, with a pale skin under jet-black hair. Like Dr Paine, Linda and, Belle realised, Belle herself, her large breasts and especially, her wide, pear-shaped arse were her most prominent features. Her lab coat was carelessly buttoned and Belle was sure she was nude underneath it, and in fact had only donned it on hearing the girls knock. Some of the labs had nurses decanting fluids into syringes or rubber bottles and Linda gave a summary of the work that went on: tests, injections, suppositories and the like, her recital growing in enthusiasm.

Dr Paine, in one lab, was supervising a rectal injection of a nude female, strapped to an operating table by a heavy rubber thong across her breasts and with her legs apart and feet clamped in stirrups. The prongs of a steel speculum spread the lips of her anal cavity apart, so that her hole gaped to at least seven or eight times its normal width. She groaned, as one of the Japanese nurses inserted a syringe of clear fluid to the root of her anus and pressed the plunger, slowly evacuating all the liquid into the intestine. Belle saw that the woman had the same finny hairs around her bunhole as Sushi and a little nubbin of a tail at the kundalini of her spine. Also, her clitoris, though not in an erect or stimulated state, was large and extruded like a thumb.

'Yes, Belle,' Dr Paine said, distractedly, watching this operation. 'Linda is taking care of you . . . very good.'

When the woman's anus had ceased writhing, she turned to appraise Belle's body, as though seeing her for the first time

'Soon,' she said, 'you will be supervising anal injection or even experiencing mild genetic enhancement yourself, should you prove worthy. There is no danger of an imperfect experiment these days, since a . . . a certain unstable person was expelled from Sakosha. Carry on, girls.'

'What did she mean, Linda?' said Belle, as soon as they left Dr Paine's lab.

'Oh,' said Linda, flustered, 'I'm not sure. Dr Paine is so dedicated, sometimes she sees those who are less dedicated as enemies. But you said you'd like a nap, Belle. My room's much closer than yours, so why not lie down on my bed.'

She made it sound more like an order than a question – Linda seemed to slip easily from her submissive personality to her scientist's detachment, so Belle was happy to follow her the short distance to her room, without thinking the invitation anything but innocent. The heat made her too drowsy to think of anything but rest, and perhaps a shower, to clean herself of the sweat that glued her clothing to her body. Linda's window looked out on dense jungle, with the sea crashing a long way off, but was otherwise like

Belle's own. Belle sighed and accepted Linda's command to stretch out on the bed. The fan did little to cool her and Belle fumbled with her buttons and sussies, before starting, and asking Linda if she minded her stripping for comfort. Linda smiled. Under her gaze, Belle wriggled out of her damp things and lay nude, with arms and legs splayed on the bed and her pussy open.

Linda made no move to unbutton her own lab coat, though her face, too, was beaded with sweat and there were damp patches at her armpits. When Belle playfully urged her to strip, Linda blushed and said she was comfortable but would take a shower when Belle was asleep. Belle closed her eyes and fell into a dreamy doze, listening to the distant sea, and now a furtive rustling. It was Linda's clothing; the coat being parted at the legs, but not removed. She heard Linda's breath grow heavy and realised that her friend was masturbating at the sight of her nude body. Her first instinct was to wake up and throw a teasing pillow at her new friend, but then she reconsidered and feigned sleep.

She too began to breathe heavily, as though asleep, and all the time listened to the soft plopping noises of Linda's fingers rubbing her wet cunt. The thought of someone, especially a luscious female like Linda, masturbating just at the sight of her naked body, made Belle's own cunt start to seep. She grunted sleepily and flopped over on her tummy, knowing that Linda would be excited by the sight of her bare bum. Linda's breath became a harsh panting and as Belle opened her thighs, sudden gasps alerted her that her hostess had orgasmed at the spectacle of her spread quim and buttocks, Belle's cunt well moistened with her own come.

Finally, there was the sound of the bathroom door, a shower starting, and Linda's clothing discarded before she stepped under the spray. Belle sat up, grinning. She tiptoed to the bathroom door and pushed it open. There was no shower curtain, and Linda's body was revealed wet and shining, in voluptuous and perfectly-proportioned nudity: the breasts and arse swelling like dunes, the belly flat and

100

muscled and the thighs quivering, as the girl washed her come-ooze from her gash. Her clitty was still swollen from her wank and, in fact, looked oversized, like that of the guest who had received the anal injection. Belle shivered and closed the bathroom door, then regained her bed, and resumed her drowse.

Linda emerged from the bathroom, her towel fastened beneath her chin, and opened her armoire to select a wine-dark polo-neck shirt into which she slipped, with high white cotton panties and a white skirt, leaving her long legs bare. From the corner of her eye, Belle watched, as Linda took out a book and began to study at her desk. It was impossible for Belle to sleep, now that she had seen Linda nude. Should she speak? She had seen, albeit by peeking – but surely Linda knew Belle must see, some time. And it was ridiculous to think that the others did not know. Belle understood how lonely Linda must be in her virgin state and a wave of affection washed over her. She yawned, deliberately making lots of noise, then sat up and stretched.

'Feel better?' said Linda.

Belle leaped from the bed and suddenly embraced Linda and kissed her hair. Linda started in surprise, but did not resist the caress.

'Linda,' whispered Belle, 'I think you are the loveliest girl I have ever seen.'

'Oh, Belle,' sighed Linda, 'you should look at yourself in the mirror, first. Anyway, you wouldn't say that, if you saw all of me.'

Belle stepped back, and stood with legs apart, and hands on her hips.

'Then let me see all of you, and we can look together in the mirror,' she said.

'No! I can't!' Linda cried.

'So you want to be a virgin all your life?' Belle taunted, then suddenly embraced Linda again.

'Oh, I'm sorry, Linda!' she pleaded. 'That was cruel, and I don't want to be cruel! I deserve to be whipped for my remark, and for . . . for what I did. I wasn't really asleep. I peeked at you, in the shower.'

'Then you *have* seen all of me,' said Linda bitterly.

'And I want to see all of you again,' said Belle, 'lots and lots. Linda, I want you to strip, and *show* yourself to me.'

Still, Linda hesitated.

'Linda Folsom, I order you to strip naked!' Belle barked, marvelling at the authority in her voice and the wetness in her gash. 'You have already earned a spanking on your bare bottom, and any further insolence will merit a caning!'

Linda's eyes were glazed with desire and she let her skirt ride up, to show her cotton knickers already soaked at the cunt.

'Off!' cried Belle.

She felt the giddy pleasure of acting, in giving the orders she herself wanted to hear from another, stronger dominatrix. She knew the role. Numbly, Linda let her skirt fall to the floor, then slipped out of her wet panties. Turning her back to Belle, she lifted her polo and pulled it up to free the ripe melons of her breasts, which swayed as the garment caught her hair then dropped to the floor like a discarded skin. Belle gazed at the magnificence of Linda's arse-pears. She reached out a hand and stroked Linda's left bare buttock with shivering fingertips.

'Turn round,' she said. 'I've seen your arse and thought of how I'm going to cane you, Linda, and now I want to see your tits and pussy.'

Slowly, Linda turned, her eyes averted and glistening with tears. Belle took a breast in each hand and cupped them, as though weighing fruit, then let her thumbs slide to the engorged saucers of the nipples and press the erect pimpled areolae.

'I want to cane you, Linda,' Belle said. 'I want to spank and cane your naked breasts and bum and pussy. I wasn't telling the whole truth – I have caned before and I'm very good at it. I won't hurt you.'

'But I want to be hurt by you, Belle,' sobbed Linda, 'only Dr Paine says my skin is not ripe yet! The serum hasn't taken . . .'

'Hang the serum,' said Belle. 'Can't you see how wet my cunt is at the thought of bare-caning you?'

She stuck her fingers rudely into Linda's gash and the girl shuddered. Her cunt was soaked in oily come and her clitoris throbbed, fully erect.

'Now you know why I am a virgin and a submissive as yet uncaned,' she said faintly. 'It is called a hemangioma – I suppose you know that.'

'A birthmark,' said Belle. 'Yes, I knew, and suspected why you covered up.'

Linda's body was cruelly disfigured with a lurid red lake of puffy and gnarled skin, exending across both her teats, her belly and the tops of her buttocks, ending only at her shoulders and the tops of her thighs but leaving the swelling of her cunt-hillock white under its jungle of lustrous black pube-hairs. The skin surrounding her nipples was redder than the nipples themselves and the crusty, scaly solidity of the birthmark made it look the result of some hideous skin disease. Belle began to masturbate Linda's clitoris.

'You are a silly goose,' she said, 'and it's plain you don't know much about blokes. Why, all they want is pussy: this beautiful gash makes up for a thousand hemangiomas. And as for spanking and caning you, there is plenty of terrain for me to work on.'

'What if Dr Paine sees the marks?' cried Linda.

'I won't leave marks, Linda, I'll spank you, then paddle you. You'll be well marked, but the imprint will be gone by tomorrow. I mean to spank you right now, girl. My cunt's wet too.'

'Oh, I think I'm going to come!' Linda cried.

Belle resisted her urge to masturbate along with Linda, although her own clitty was throbbing and desperately in need of a wank. Instead, she pressed Linda's stiff nubbin between finger and thumb and tweaked hard, while cupping her other palm to catch the flow of Linda's come, with which she bathed the girl's stiff nipples. Linda sighed, squealed and gasped, as her belly and cunt heaved with her orgasm and Belle's palm overflowed with her love-juice. Belle explained to Linda how she would thrash her, all on places untouched by hemangioma: the inside of her thighs;

her nipples; her lower fesses; her arse-cleft; and her cunt-lips themselves.

'I assure you it will hurt a lot, Linda,' she whispered, 'maybe more than a full-buttock caning.'

'Oh, please hurt me as much as you can,' Linda pleaded, 'and wank me while you beat me.'

'Yes,' Belle said. 'Now, I want you to position yourself so I can reach all those places . . .'

Linda glowed with happiness as she was forced to twist her body, while grasping the bed knobs and with her feet on the floor, to allow Belle a full target of clear skin. Her thighs were spread wide and Belle fingered her gash-lips and bumhole open.

'Oh, God! This is fabulous!' cried Linda. 'I feel so – so –'

'So submissive?' said Belle. 'I'll warm you up with a good hard spanking, then proceed to paddle you with this bed-slat, which looks very painful indeed. By the time I've finished, girl, your skin will all be the same shade of red.'

She removed a slat from the bed and showed it to her new submissive.

'I wonder if you aren't truly a dominant, after all, Belle,' said Linda, shivering at the board that was to smack her bare skin.

'No, it is just that I know what submission is about. But who cares? We are all flesh.'

Thwack!

The first slap of Linda Folsom's first spanking, cracked on her bare cunt lips.

'Oh! God! Yes!' Linda cried.

Thwack!

'There are a couple of conditions, though,' said Belle.

Thwack! Still on the bare gash.

'Anything . . .' panted Linda, squirming.

Thwack! A spank right on the clitty, fingertips slapping the inner thigh.

'*Ahh* . . .!'

'First, I want to know everything you know about this place, *and* Dr Paine, right away. I'm not a ninny. None of this "in good time" stuff.'

Thwack!

Now, Belle twisted and began to spank Linda hard on the lower portion of her quivering buttocks. Linda gurgled in her throat.

Thwack! Thwack! Thwack! Thwack!

The spanks rained thick and fast and merciless.

'Oh! Oh! Oh! I never dreamed it would hurt so much! Yes . . . I suppose . . . Oh, don't stop!'

Thwack! Thwack! Thwack! Thwack!

'You suppose *what*, slave?' spat Belle.

'That I can tell you everything, right away!'

Linda's white lower buttocks began to glow a livid pink under her spanking. Belle alternated spanks to the buttocks with very hard blows to the erect nipples.

Thwack! Vip! Thwack! Vip! Vip! Vip!

Linda's body jerked and writhed, as her buttocks clenched and her heavy bare teats wobbled like jellies under their nipple-spanking.

'Supposing isn't good enough, slave!'

Thwack! Thwack! Vip! Vip!

'I mean, yes, yes, Mistress, your slave will tell you everything. Oh! I think I'm going to come! It hurts so! My bum's smarting! God, it's better than I ever . . .'

Vip! Vip! Vip! Vip!

'Oh! Ahhh! *Oooo* . . .!'

Belle wasn't sure she wanted to own a slave, rather than be one, at this juncture. But Linda was superb, her beauty accentuated rather than marred by her blemish – especially as her arse squirmed so deliciously, making the horned red skin dance. Besides, she would be a useful ally – or tool. Maybe Belle's psych profile as 'switch' was correct. Belle's own cunt was juicing profusely, as she imagined the blotched buttocks squirming under her spanks to be her own. She did not want the glorious deformity of her slave's hemangioma to be obliterated . . .

Thwack! Thwack! Thwack! Thack! Vip! Vip! Vip! Vip!

By pinching her fingertips together, she managed to land some hard spanks, clawing right in the taut arse-cleft and on the anus bud itself, which made Linda sob.

'The other condition . . .' she panted.

Thwack! Vip! Vip! Vip!

'Yes, Mistress? Oh, I'm coming! Oh, Belle, wank me, please!'

Belle grasped the stiff wet clit and began to squeeze it fiercely, as Linda's nude, reddening body writhed under her spanking. Her hand was drenched in the girl's come.

'When I'm done with you, I must be punished with a naked thrashing for peeking at you. You can beat my bare arse black and blue with the slat still warm from your own bum.'

'Oh! Mistress! I couldn't! Not hurt *you!* I love to watch girls' bums beaten, but yours is so perfect, so pure, so round . . . I couldn't be so cruel!'

Thwack! Vip! Thwack! Vip! Thwack! Vip!

Belle attacked every beating zone, while tugging and scratching at Linda's erect clit.

'Couldn't you? I *command* you to thrash my bare bum, slave!'

Vip! Vip! Vip! Vip!

Belle pinched and pummelled Linda's clitoris quite savagely and the girl's back arched, as she squealed in her come.

'Oh! Oh! Oh! Yes, Mistress, yes . . . I'll spank your bare, thrash you, cane you . . . *anything!*'

# 7

# First Thrashing

Belle Puget beat Linda Folsom to over 200 strokes, carefully using the flat of her paddle, except for strokes to the cleft of the arse. She whipped every portion of her body that was clear of the hemangioma birthmark, concentrating on the fesses, the cunt and the nipples. Linda's cunt spewed come and she climaxed a further three times, as Belle wanked her distended clitty. At Linda's suggestion, her whipped cunt was positioned over her chamber pot, which collected come juice an inch deep. At the end of the beating, Linda's body was, as promised, a uniform red. She inspected herself, face flushed in delight, in the mirror.

'You are expert, Belle – my Mistress!'

'Long practice at taking it,' Belle gasped, then said it was time for her own spanking.

Her come flowed so heavily, she could hardly think, but she restrained herself from the single flick to her nubbin that she knew would bring her off, preferring instead to savour her longing.

'Have you addressed Dr Paine as Mistress?' asked Belle, suddenly.

'No. She says it wouldn't be right, until she has caned me.'

'Then, I don't think you should ever call her Mistress,' whispered Belle, as she positioned herself for a bare-bum thrashing; this one, she explained to Linda, to be full buttock.

'I'm awfully scared,' said Linda. 'It seems wrong to cane such a beautiful bum.'

'You are not caning me, Linda,' snapped Belle, 'you are giving me a simple paddling, which is not the same thing, even when taken to several hundred strokes. The sound, the impact and the type of pain are all different according to the implement, and you must learn the difference. Now, you'll be thrashing me with the flat of the board. I want you to hold it right at the end, for maximum impact, and I'm going to stretch my bum tight with my fingers, so my bumhole will be widened and a good target; but you'll have to aim carefully and catch my pucker with the very tip of the board, getting the flat across the adjoining buttock at the same time – that hurts most, and I shall complain if I think you are soft on me.'

'Heavens!' cried Linda, ' are all submissives so demanding?'

'Yes,' said Belle. 'Now, get on with it, Linda. Beat my arse beyond crimson.'

'And how many will that be?' Linda quavered.

'You'll know,' said Belle. 'It'll be when my bum's well blotched and I beg you to stop.'

'I see,' said Linda. 'I stop when you beg me to.'

'No!' said Belle. 'That's exactly when you *don't* stop . . .'

By the 143rd stroke of the bedboard, Belle's cunt was well dripping with come and her thrashed buttocks were seared hot. After a few hesitant strokes to begin, Linda's lithe muscles had proved admirable for administering firm corporal punishment to Belle's bare fesses – Belle continually reminding her that peeping at a girl in her bathroom was a frightful offence, worthy of deep wealing. Furthermore, she showed no signs of tiring. If anything, her enthusiasm seemed to grow as Belle's buttocks purpled, her fesses clenched and squirmed more desperately and her squeals of pain grew shriller.

Slap! Slap! Slap! Slap!

'Ouch! Oh! *Oooh* . . .!'

The squirming of Belle's clenched arse was unfeigned.

'That must be nearly 200,' Linda panted. 'May I please pause for a wank, Belle – I mean, Mistress?'

'Certainly not,' groaned Belle. You may wank again, as you thrash me. And it's only 147 – you've a long way to go.'

'But, Mistress, your bum's all purple and blotchy.'

'As I said, you've a long way to go. And you haven't explained half of what happens here on Furv – I mean, Sakosha.'

Slap! Slap! Slap!

Linda's three strokes of the paddle, taking Belle to 150, hid the slip of the tongue.

'That's because I don't know half of it,' said Linda. 'I stick to my own field, of dominant and regressive genes. Your interest in recombinant DNA touches it barely, but it's more in line with Dr Paine's own research, which is partly why she favoured you. But what a juicy peach! That was really your ticket here, I'm sure.'

Slap! Slap! Slap! Slap! Slap! Slap!

'Oh! Oh! Mmm ...' Belle whimpered, her hot bare buttocks writhing.

'Dr Paine is interested in slowing the ageing process,' said Linda. 'Each time our cells duplicate, free radicals – excess oxygen – shorten the telomeres, or the tips of the chromosomes. It's as though they are being burned up by the oxygen from the red blood cells. So, each cell duplication is imperfect, like making a photocopy of a photocopy, and that is why we age. If the ingestion of free radical oxygen can be controlled, then our cells could duplicate themselves perfectly, or even improve – regress back to their original purity. The skin is the test of ageing, Dr Paine says. Everything lies in the skin.'

'Don't forget –' Belle began.

Slap! Slap! Slap! Slap!

'There,' gasped Linda, 'I haven't forgotten.'

'Oh! Oh! You beast! So that is where caning comes in,' Belle panted. 'The power of the skin to regenerate. If the skin can regenerate, it follows that everything else can.'

Slap! Slap! Slap! Slap!

'Oh, God, you whip well, Linda,' Belle gasped, her buttocks squirming in unfeigned distress. 'You may take that wank, if you like, now.'

'Thank you, Mistress,' said Linda, slyly, 'but I'm already wanking.'

Slap! Slap! Slap! Slap!

'Oh! *Ahhh* . . .!' Belle groaned. 'God, I think I'm going to come myself – I must have puddled your floorboards terribly.'

'You have,' said Linda, 'and I intend to make you pay for it. Your puddle will be a lake, before I've done with your bum.'

'Minx!'

'Vixen!'

Slap! Slap! Slap!

'Uhhh . . .'

Belle jumped, as the paddle's tip stung her naked anus pucker.

Slap! Slap! Slap!

'Oh! Ooh . . .'

Belle removed one hand from the floor and, supporting herself on a single arm, began to wank vigorously using her left hand's fingertips to rub her swollen, throbbing clitty.

'How gorgeous – to live forever, and wank and fuck forever!' she moaned.

'I don't yet know the second part,' sighed Linda. 'But eternal wanking would please me. Dr Paine's serum is based on a simple virus, in solution, female come juice being the ideal solvent. The virus first has the disease nucleus removed and replaced by a mutated gene. Since a virus is designed to attack cells, it is the perfect vehicle for invading the cells with an enhancing gene. If Dr Paine can find the perfect gene mutation, it will protect the cells against toxins, ultraviolet, heat decay . . . everything that causes us to age.'

Slap! Slap! Slap!

'Oh! Oh! Oh! Mmm . . . So, you could stay out in the sun all day and never wrinkle, and take the cane and never scar . . .?' Belle gasped.

'Yes, I suppose so.'

Slap! Slap! Slap! Slap!

'Oh! I'm going to come! Oh, beat me, Linda. Make me smart! Oh! Oh! Oh! I'm coming . . .'

Belle's come oil splashed into her puddle, as her belly quaked in deep orgasm – but Linda's thrashing did not cease. Now, she began to beat Belle's bare breasts, flattening the teats with each stroke and pressing the nipples agonisingly against Belle's ribcage.

'*Ah! Ah! Ah!*' cried Belle, her bottom clenching as her melons wobbled. 'My titties . . . not fair!'

Slap! Slap! Slap! Slap! Slap! Slap! Three each, to titties and arse-crevice.

'Oh, God!' Belle shrieked, 'It smarts like hell! Please stop!'

'No,' said Linda, thrashing Belle again, with three to the breasts and three to the very tops of the buttocks, beneath her spinal nubbin.

'*Ahhhh . . .*' Belle wailed, and felt Linda's fingers probe her cunt-slit. The thumb briefly flicked Belle's expanded clitty and she shivered.

'I had to be sure, Mistress,' said Linda, licking Belle's come from her fingertips. 'Tit-spanking makes you juice.'

'You beast . . .'

Slap! Slap! Slap! Slap! All four strokes across the nipples.

The beating now alternated between the breasts and buttocks and soon Belle's tit-melons were as raw and crimson as the globes of her bare wealed arse. She panted in joyous submission, feeling her cunt liquid with her new and copious flow of come.

'Cloning . . .' she managed to gasp, as the paddle slid from her whipped titties and her bum clenched for another slash.

'I don't know about that,' said Linda.

'But Dr Paine does. That's why I'm here.'

Slap! Slap! Slap! Slap! Slap! Slap!

'Oh! Oh! Ouch! Ooo . . .!' All right, it's *partly* why I'm here,' Belle blurted.

'Human cloning is forbidden by law, in most western countries,' said Linda.

'But not cloning of beasts,' Belle gasped. 'We clone animals, from an omnipotent embryo cell, growing, but before it has redivided four times.'

Slap! Slap! Slap!

'Ahhh . . . those were hard!'

Linda's strokes now took Belle right on her spread wet cunt-flaps and Belle whimpered, as lashes now cracked against her cunt, buttocks and titties in rapid, random succession.

'When one cell has divided to sixteen,' Belle blurted, 'the cells differentiate and although each one still contains the whole DNA alphabet, certain letters are blanked and each cell now governs precise characteristics – it is a hair cell or a skin cell and can only replicate more of the same. But an embryonic omnipotent cell can replicate a whole creature, so if –'

Slap! Slap! Slap! Slap! Four stingers, two on each tender haunch.

'Ah! *Ooh*! Suppose the Japs were working on a way to reverse the process and *undifferentiate* cells? So that you could clone a whole person from a hair, or a drop of come?'

Slap! Slap! Slap! Slap! Slap! Slap! Two each to tits, cunt and anus bud.

'Oooh! You bitch! Don't stop! I want to wank again!'

'It's a far cry from research on pleasure girls, Belle.'

'Is it? To change pain response to pleasure responses, you have to get right into the nerve endings, in the original DNA alphabet . . . who knows what else the Japs discovered? They expected to *win* the war, remember? To create an eternal Japanese empire, longer than the Nazi thousand-year Reich! It wouldn't stop there – you could clone organs to your own specifications, like . . . like a big penis, clit, or titties. You could insert animal or fish letters into human DNA alphabet. Maybe Dr Paine is keeping you in the dark, Linda. What has *she* discovered?'

Slap!

Belle shrieked, as the thin edge of the board took her right on her wet clitty and suddenly her cunt flowed with hot piss, that streamed down her thighs and calves and joined her puddle of come, the acrid, steaming ooze invading her nostrils. Linda took no notice.

'If Dr Paine has a fault, it is caution,' said Linda. 'Not just her computer room but a whole wing of the building, her own research lab, is kept locked.'

Slap! On the gash-flaps again . . .

'*Uh!* Th-that sounds like paranoia,' said Belle. 'Oh, Linda! Those cunt-strokes really hurt . . .'

'No! The research woman, who was expelled, vowed vengeance. We know her only as the clawed woman and her interest was purely evil. She was interested in recombinant DNA, but to create monsters. Dr Paine's computer must even have special protection against her viruses.'

'What protection is there against Dr Paine's viruses?' said Belle, then yelped as a particularly hard stroke took her in the anus cleft. 'Ouch! Linda, how much of Dr Paine's research is her own, and how much was there already, from the Japs?'

'*I don't know, Belle,*' said Linda, throwing down the caning board. 'But I think *you* know a good deal more than I want to. *I* know Dr Paine has promised to cure me of my hemangioma – in good time. Meanwhile, I hear no evil, see no evil and try to do no evil.'

Belle rose, rubbing her inflamed bare bottom and scooped Linda in her arms, then carried her to the bed, soaking the cloth in her flowing come juice. She straddled Linda with her own wet cunt on Linda's mouth and plunged her tongue into the girl's slit, while rubbing her stiff clitty with the tip of her nose and waiting for Linda's immediate orgasm to subside, before continuing with a gentler, yet more insistent frottage.

'I couldn't beat your lovely bum any more, Mistress,' Linda whimpered.

'What if Dr Paine has no intention of curing you?' Belle whispered.

'Oh! Don't say that! But don't stop tonguing me!'

Belle now thrust a fingernail into Linda's bum-pucker and, finding it yielding, put her whole finger down the elastic passage, right to the anal root. Linda moaned, writhing under spear.

'And what if your hemangioma isn't *meant* to be cured?' Belle said. 'What if the hemangioma is simply an arrested process, which will make you into the most radiant beauty on this planet?'

Second, third and fourth fingers joined her first, probing Linda's anus.

'Me . . . a beautiful woman!' wailed Linda. 'Don't tease, Mistress!'

Belle began to bugger Linda vigorously with her bunched fingers, while chewing hard on the girl's hard clitty, her lips washed by the girl's river of come.

'Yes . . . all red and glowing, like a goddess. But we'll only know if you'll tell me *everything* . . . *slave!*' she hissed.

'I will! Oh, I'm coming again!'

Belle balled her fingers and began to fist-fuck the squirming girl's anal hole. Linda's mouth and tongue were frantic, frotting her own cunt lips and clitty.

'*You* are as beautiful as a human can be, Belle,' gasped Linda. 'Oh! Yes! *Yesss* . . .!'

Come flowed copiously from both cunts, as the girls exploded in mutal orgasm.

'But perhaps we're not talking about *human* beauty,' Belle said.

# Memoir 5

*My trip to Hawaii was fun; I hate anything that isn't fun.*
*First, I had to go to Los Angeles, then get a connecting*
*flight. The flight to LA was eleven hours or something,*
*overnight; so I packed a super new vibrator in my handbag,*
*fancying I'd treat myself to a soothing wank or two before*
*getting some shuteye. It was more like a Black and Decker*
*drill than anything else; battery-operated, with all sorts of*
*little buzzy, whirry attachments and two giant bendy prongs*
*to go in your cunt, or your bum, or two cunts, or – well, you*
*get the idea. It was German, of course. Also, I had a sweet*
*little gadget, also German – a collapsible cane. The Germans*
*think of everything. It was steel, about as long as a pencil;*
*but at the push of a button you could pop it out to either half*
*a metre or a metre in length.*

*Most people have heard of the so-called Mile High Club,*
*and my flight to LA was when I became a member; several*
*times over, in fact. The fun started at the security X-ray.*
*Of course, I had to open my bag and show my things to the*
*dyke bitch in uniform, and she tried hard not to blush when*
*I explained what they were and where the various prongs and*
*bits went, all in a loud voice and very serious. I had to show*
*how the cane worked and that it wasn't a weapon or*
*anything. I was right at the front of the queue and the cabin*
*staff and flight crew had gone through first, and a particu-*
*larly dishy blond guy looked at me with a lop-sided grin that*
*I found appealing until I remembered that all male flight*
*attendants are supposed to be gay – and all female ones*

*nymphos.* He was the one who showed me to my First Class seat and I gave him a few touches and let him see a good portion of my tits. I was wearing a little cocktail dress, very rich bitch, with a cashmere wraparound; and when he offered to put the cashmere up for me, I wiggled my tits so they almost flopped out of my little black number and made sure that my hem rode up as I sat down, so he could see I had sheer stockings and sussies but no panties. I crossed my legs and gave him a good flash of pube hair. To my surprise, he had a bulge, right where it should be!

Well, this being First Class, they served champagne and everything before we started moving. There was a dishy female attendant, with big tits and dyed blonde hair, and I figured her for a proper slut, like me. The blond guy had a name tag that said Derek, and hers said Cindi, and I told him that he didn't look like a Derek, more the action man type. Cindi wanted to know if she was the Cindi type, and I told her I hoped so. There were quite a few attendants in First Class, and not too many passengers, so I was well fussed over. Another one caught my eye – an oriental, called Susan. She was slim and dishy, too; small hard tits, long legs and a boyish bum. I asked her about her name and it seemed she was Singapore Chinese, who all have English names. There was a ravishing black girl, with pefect tits and bum, a real hour-glass named Claudette and with a thick London accent like Cindi's, but a bit sullen; and I thought, there is one slut who needs a bare-bum spanking to put a smile on her face. But I was more interested in Derek's cock for the moment; it seemed to have possibilities.

I had plenty of champagne, and had to go to pee a lot. I made out I was a bit oopsy and unlocked the door before I had finished peeing, so that it swung open and whoever was there had a good flash of my bum and cunt. By the time we were halfway over the Atlantic, it was all first names, even with Claudette. There was a meal and a stupid movie with all the naughty bits cut – which I complained about to Derek and Susan – and more drinks all the time. Then they brought round the sleeping gear. I said it was so boring to sleep on my own and stuff like that, and everybody laughed. When

116

Derek was idling by the loo, I told him it was time for my midnight tinkle, and he mustn't get alarmed if I was a long time. He eyed my handbag and said I shouldn't be too long, as he was bursting to go himself. Actually, he had a full erection just talking to me, so I brushed its tip with my purse and said I thought all stewards were gay and here was his chance to prove he wasn't. I just nodded him into the loo, before me.

He got in and I locked the door and pulled my dress over my head, so I was standing bare, apart from sussies, stockings and stilettos. Right away, I unzipped him and got his pants down and began to suck his hard cock, as I fingered my clit, which was already quite tingly. I could feel the come start to ooze from my pussy. He was well-hung – not like Gary, but pleasing. I squeezed his balls and licked his peehole, the tip of my tongue going round and round, which drives men wild, and pulled his prepuce all the way back, to tickle the base of his glans. I didn't want him coming in my mouth and said I hoped he was up to fucking me, and he sort of sighed that he was straight as an arrow; and I said I didn't believe him and he couldn't fuck me till he'd passed my test. First of all, I was going to spank – or more accurately, cane – his bare bum, and I clicked my pencil cane to half a metre. He bent over without protest and I gave him a dozen hard ones, which he took in silence and without too much clenching.

As I caned him, I explained what I did for a living and Miss Claw and everything, and I saw his cock tremble, with my saliva shining all over his big purple bell-end. I clicked the cane again and it extended to a metre, and I gave him another dozen, and now he was squirming quite satisfactorily so I added a third dozen, real stingers and making a whop! whop! so loud that anyone outside would know what was happening. I was wanking myself all the time I was caning his lovely tight arse, which crimsoned beautifully, and I knew the welts on his haunches and top bum would be visible for ages. His buttocks were twitching madly when I got out my vibrator and started it humming, then greased one prong with my own come and pushed it an inch into his arsehole. I said

117

that if he could take an arse-fucking without coming, I'd know he was straight. He dropped his pants completely and spread his bum-cheeks so that I got the dildo right to his root. Then I switched the vibrations to maximum, and began to wank my stiff clitty with the other prong, rubbing my belly against his caned bum.

He insisted he really wasn't gay, but me buggering him and wanking off made him want to come, so, ordering him to hold the dildo inside his anus, I turned him round, lifted my thighs and hopped up to straddle him, shoving his cock into my soaking cunt and getting him all the way in. I could feel the vibrations of the bum-dildo through his skin and had the other prong wedged between us, humming on my clit. I wasn't far off coming myself, especially when he began to fuck me quite hard, and I began to ram his hole with the dildo, buggering him in time with his strokes to my cunt. My slit was really flowing with juice, all down the insides of my pumping thighs, and it splattered all over the floor and toilet seat. It wasn't long before I felt myself coming, and he sensed it too, for at my first squeak there was a shudder of his cock, then a lovely hot jet of cream spurting right up me. I came and came! I reckoned his balls had a good week's spunk in them, I told him; but that wasn't enough for a thirsty pussy like mine. I was going to clean up the loo and wipe my equipment – excluding my wet cunt – and he was to leave the door unlocked, in case I needed rescuing . . .

It wasn't long before another bloke came in, called Glen, or Greg, or something. He wasn't as hunky as Derek, but his cock was bigger and like Derek, he took a caning with only a little whimpering. I didn't have to explain what I was, for Derek had evidently done so and instead, I asked him jokily if all flight attendants were into spanking and he said quite a few, including the ladies; and spanking was good fun because it didn't matter who was gay and who wasn't. My dildo slid into his arsehole with no trouble and his anus sucked it in like a pro. I got him to stick his cock up my own arse, with my feet curled round his neck, my bare bum-cheeks slapping against his belly as I buggered his mineshaft with my dildo. He was darn good at arse-fucking, hammering right at my root, and I came again in no time . . . of course I was wanking off more or less continuously, now. I felt a good spurt of cream up my bumhole root and when he had finished his come, I sat on the toilet and peed, still wanking, as I hissed and told him I didn't believe what he had said about the ladies.

Talk about a grapevine! I'd hardly sat down to have a shit, when Cindi and Claudette came in, together; Cindi giggling and Claudette sort of sneering at me. I always figure Londoners are in a sort of cabal together. Anyway I finished my business and was going to wipe my arse, when Claudette said suddenly that I could save myself the trouble. The black girl, cool as you please, took my dildo and pencil cane, flicked the cane open and started the vibrator humming, then told me to present my arse for cleaning. Suddenly, she was all boss woman and I obeyed, out of curiosity, but also with a little tingle of fear; and delight, too. I was going to learn what it was like to be a submissive, for a while!

Cindi knelt and I presented my spread arse-cheeks and she began to lick my bumhole clean. Her tongue was lovely and raspy, like sandpaper, and tickled my hole so much that my come would not stop gushing. I saw Claudette had Cindi's skirt lifted and the point of her shoe pushing aside the almost invisible thong of Cindi's g-string and the toe going right into her anus, thrusting and kicking hard. Then, I jumped as I felt the cane cut my bare arse, at its half-metre length. Well, at the Stones', I had toughened my hide under Mrs Stone's cane, and her birch, too; but I hadn't been caned in a long time and it really hurt.

The strokes whipped me harder and harder and I felt my bum clench on Cindi's protruded tongue; it was all I could do not to shriek. Claudette said a dozen was enough, but she meant with the short cane, for now she lengthened it to the full and I took another whacking bare arse – a dozen again. I was wanking furiously, because I had got used to the smarting and remembered all my loving sessions with Mrs Stone and I knew I was juicing to a splendid come. But I wanted some clit action, so I straddled the toilet with my thighs clamping the seat, staring at my poo which I hadn't

119

*flushed, and got Cindi's tongue on my wet cunt-lips. My bum-squirm under Claudette's canestrokes pushed her tongue right inside me and had her lapping at my stiff nubbin. I saw everything in the mirror: Claudette had her blouse and bra off and skirt up, showing a huge shiny black mound that was shaven bare, with the pink pussy gleaming wet and the nubbin as stiff as mine; and she had no knickers at all or rather, a pair of stained white briefs evidently long unwashed, clasped in her palm.*

*She unfolded them and pissed very noisily on them, then wiped my cunt until my come was mingled with her own pee. Then, she knotted the panties in a hood over Cindi's head, but so that her tongue stuck out of a leghole and she could continue to gamahuche me. Claudette strapped on my double dildo and got one prong in her own cunt and the other in Cindi's anus, kneeling, so that she could fuck Cindi in the arse while she masturbated her own clitty and rubbed her big black titties with the end of my cane, between lashes to my bare bum, which was well smarting by now. I almost came, just looking at those bare boobs as big and stiff as castles and shiny smooth, with huge bulbous nips. Her arse moved in a rhythm quite separate from the rest of her body as she buggered Cindi, masturbated her own tits and cunt and caned me all at the same time; she had superb control.*

*I think I had taken 50 with the cane when I came and Claudette sneered, 'Some manners, at last'. Cindi started to whimper and she came too, and I saw she had been wanking off all the time she was being bum-fucked. Claudette came, or I think she did, with a long sigh, then removed the dildo from her cunt and Cindi's arse and, without bothering to wipe it, fitted on an attachment called a reamer. This was a thick knobbed ring that went at the bulb of the dildo and whirled round and round, like a drill, to caress the neck of the womb. But Claudette turned me arse about and rammed it into my bumhole! My head sank as I felt the reamer whir right at my root and by accident, I flushed the toilet; which was just as well, because when the bowl cleared, my hair sank right into it as my arse wriggled in a frenzy to escape that deadly reamer, buzzing right inside my shaft. I was filled to bursting and thought Claudette would split me in half.*

Cindi clambered onto the other prong of the dildo and sat astride my arse, bouncing up and down so that she was buggering me and also fucking herself, while Claudette, still masturbating, caned Cindi's bare bum. Claudette aimed superbly, for Cindi's buttocks writhed and squirmed like pistons and every canestroke hit them with unerring precision. Cindi was juicing copiously and her come oozed down the cleft of my buggered arse and all over my stocking-tops, which were already wet with my own come. My arse-fucking, with that reamer, was the most powerful and the most glorious I had ever taken, and I pissed myself without realising it, until I felt the hot pee along with our come oils trickling inside my stockings. Cindi was caned to come, and I wanked myself to orgasm and then Cindi was obliged to ball my stockings in her mouth, still poking through the hood of Claudette's well-stained panties, and suck all the pee and come from them while Claudette continued her caning. The finale was that Claudette towered over both of us girls, kneeling, and made Cindi tongue her arsehole while I licked her huge clitty and she peed a huge flood of golden pee right into my mouth, just as I used to do with my male clients. When she and Cindi had orgasmed again, they left me, saying they had yet another meal to serve, so I figured that was about it. I stuck my wet panties over the smoke alarm and had just lit a Marlboro, when the door swung open again.

This time, Susan, the Chinese girl, slipped noiselessly in and before I could stub out the cigarette, was stretched nude between the opposite shelves of the bathroom, her legs straight with hands on her hips like a ballerina's splits, and her cunt and arse-cleft stretched wide open. She whispered would I please cane her anus bud, cunt lips and her clitoris itself, as well as a normal thrashing on the bare buttocks, and would I be so kind as to apply at least 100 strokes to each area. Susan, unlike the voluptuous black girl, was elfin, yet her cunt gaped even bigger than Claudette's; a truly monstrous gash in her slender white furrow, with a clitoris to match, as though inflated by invisible lips. I was amazed. She was just as dominant as Claudette, but in a way that seemed quietly submissive. She had her clitoris actually pierced, like an 'albert' through a man's glans, with a little pale jewel attached to her clitty-tip like a miniature bell-end. She said it was a tourmaline: a gem that generated an electric field when heated and changed colour with the body's warmth or mood. My cigarette was dangling from my fingers and with a smile, she said 'no smoking' and pissed, directing her jet of pee right to the burning cigarette end and arching it to spray my erect clit. I started to cane her right on the gash and she took it with little yelps, saying 'oh' and 'ah' at each stroke – nothing more, not a squeal, no matter how hard I caned, with the cane-tip catching the nubbin fully. Her tourmaline began to glow pink, like her clit.

My come had stopped dripping, as I was so awed by her endurance, but when she said 'the buttocks, now please,' I started to juice again, for there is nothing as tasty as a quivering bum-flan. At the first stroke, very hard on the bare, she gasped and said, 'Oh! I come, now!' and then gasped twice more. I couldn't believe she had come, just by a stroke to the bum and without even touching her clit. The tourmaline was now crimson. Then I remembered Lee's videos and the strange housemaids I was so looking forward to meeting in Hawaii, and I asked her if oriental girls had a secret western girls didn't. I was caning her cunt again, with alternating strokes to the swollen clitty and she murmured something about her parents being interned at Changi camp in Singapore during the Second World War, by the Japanese, and medical experiments and suchlike. It was hard to hear her above the aircraft noise and I didn't take it all in, nor think there was anything odd about this long gap between generations. Of course, I didn't know everything, then.

Also, I was fascinated by the way her own cunt juiced: the flow came straight down, like piss, and formed an oily pool on the floor that was a perfect circle. She said, 'two more to my bare bum, please, and two to the haunches,' like a riding instructor, and I obeyed. Then she gasped and said she was coming again! I was flabbergasted, and continued to cane the buttocks, striping her a lovely pink, deepening to crimson all over the skin, with plenty of really painful welts to the top bum underneath the nubbin of her spine, which was strangely swollen like a second erect clitty. The tourmaline was pulsing from pink to crimson and it was eerily beautiful. At every second or third stroke to the bare bum, she gasped and came! Her come juice was now a hearty flow, and she invited me very politely to kneel and drink her come and that it might give me a surprise. I thought, you precious little madam, I'll give you a worse thrashing for your cheek, but when I opened my mouth under her cunt, the flow of fishy come into my throat was nectar. I swallowed every drop, and I felt tingly all over, my titties and bum and everywhere, as though my whole body was a clitoris, pulsing like her cunt-jewel.

After a while, when I must have drunk a glassful of hot come, she invited me to recommence her gash-caning, which I did. She said that my poor bottom was frightfully wealed and that Claudette was a harsh mistress, and would I like her to stroke it to make it feel better. This required some manoeuvring in the cramped loo, but I was able to present my buttocks and thrash her arse-cleft, cunt and thighs from below, while her slender fingertips prepared to stroke my arse. I didn't know what she had in mind but continued the caning she had demanded and then suddenly I cried out, as I felt her fingers like petals, brushing the ridges of the deep welts of Claudette's caning. One touch of her fingers to my arse and I shuddered in the most delicious orgasm I could remember!

She asked me to keep caning and I obliged; and after a few strokes more, I felt her fingers on my bum, lower down but still on my weals, and I was almost knocked off my feet by another come. I was glowing and shuddering and tingling and had never felt such pleasure in my life – with my clit untouched! She kept at it. As I caned her arse crevice, she would stroke my bare bum and just her touch on my buttocks made me come. Her bum was furrowed with livid red welts, the white skin now mottled and puffy, and each of my strokes to her weals would make her shiver and gasp in another climax.

123

*There is multiple orgasm and multiple orgasm plus; and this was the second. I don't know how many times I climaxed, or if it was as many comes as her, but when she finally left me, I really appreciated another smoke. I didn't need any champagne to get me to sleep, though. When we disembarked at Los Angeles, Derek solemnly handed me my panties: I had left them draped over the smoke detector and he whispered that naughty girls should be spanked. Very funny, I said, I can think of one naughty girl who's escaped spanking and her black bum should be purple. At that, Claudette appeared and lifted her skirt very shyly, to show me her bottom glowing with welts. Susan curtsied in obeisance as she handed me back my pencil cane. I supposed it was funny after all, until Susan too lifted her skirt to reveal her knickerless bum, prettily framed by white sussies, garter straps and stockings. Her bare buttocks, which I had caned crimson, shone white and unblemished as porcelain.*

# 8

# Aquarium

Many of the Japanese nurses wore fluorescent gems at their
eyebrows and navels, or even pierced in their cunts or anus
buds, Belle observed when invited to witness a bare-bum
caning. She began to ask where these gems came from, but
got only vague replies. On her third day of acquainting
herself with routine lab work, mostly preparing suppositories and syringes for anal injection and labelling
them for each subject, Dr Paine summoned her for a
'private chat'.

The door to Dr Paine's inner sanctum hummed open
electronically and Belle expected to see some chamber of
wonders – or horrors. Instead, she found herself in a
chintzy drawing room, which reminded her of some villa
on the south coast of England, except for the turquoise sea
and dazzling white sand visible through the open window.
A ceiling fan whirred. There were two other doors leading
from the airy salon, both electronically locked. Dr Paine,
dressed in white lab coat with formal shoes and stockings,
sat in a floral-pattern armchair sipping a cup of tea and
motioned Belle to take the opposite one. Belle herself wore
a lab coat but was bare-legged and had nothing underneath except bra and panties. She was not sure if this
constituted an imperfection, but kept her coat demurely
closed and her legs crossed, just in case it did. No sooner
had Belle accepted a cup of tea, served by a Japanese maid
in frilly starched uniform with full hose and undies, than
the smiling Dr Paine took Belle by surprise.

'We are very alike, Belle; physically, I mean. I wonder if the resemblance is more than skin deep. Having witnessed me caning several girls bare-bottom, you probably think me very cruel.'

Belle disagreed politely, though Dr Paine's fierce and evident joy as she whipped bare rumps, made Belle's disagreement insincere.

'Oh, but I am!' cried Dr Paine. 'That is, I try to be.'

She sighed.

'The girls – the subjects, and nurses – like to feel their therapist is truly in charge . . . dominant, I mean. So I do my best to act the part.'

'And very convincingly, Doctor,' said Belle.

'It is an act which can not falter in any detail,' said Dr Paine, 'so that whenever I am displeased with a member of my staff I must deal with it strictly, whether heartfelt or not.'

'Is that why you summoned me, Doctor?' said Belle. 'Have you reason to be displeased with me?'

Dr Paine sighed again.

'Not exactly displeased, Belle. Worried, more. I think that it would be advisable for you to begin receiving bodily enhancement sooner, rather than later.'

'You mean, anal injections, Doctor? I'm not sure . . . it's rather sudden.'

'Not just anal injections, Belle. There is the cane, too. Of course, it is your privilege to demur, but it is not really the done thing. Team spirit counts a lot here at Paine. Initiative is welcome, but all in good time. I am pleased with you in general, Belle. Linda is very taken with you – I hope that the poor girl will one day be cured of her disfigurement, which prevents her submission to the healing cane for which she longs so much. She is a submissive, you see.'

Belle made no comment.

'But Dr Cazenove reported you for excessive curiosity, Belle, about these pretty gemstones with which the girls like to adorn themselves. I believe naked skin alone is supreme beauty – a nudist belief I understand you share, Belle – but I am no dictator. To be frank, I'd like the excuse to cane you, Belle. I look at my own derriere, and think how like yours it is and . . . I'd like to observe your bum – so like my own! – under the cane. I know that a caning would be good for you. I'm afraid I am too much of a scaredy cat to take it myself. But I understand it was the practice at your girls' school to cane bare-bottom.'

Belle nodded.

'As it was at mine. I didn't like it very much, but I knew it was good for me,' said Dr Paine. 'I became aware of the healing virtue of the lash on bare skin. We were caned nude, in the assembly hall and in front of the other girls. Usually, for a caning of two or more dozen, we would be tied to a flogging-frame. How well I remember!'

'With us, it was humiliation that counted,' said Belle. 'We were caned bare-bum all right, but not nude – rather, with knickers at ankles, skirts lifted and stockings at half-mast, for shame. It was sport for the prefects to cane a girl so painfully that she urinated and spoiled her stockings and panties. A nude caning, I agree, Doctor, is far more healing – and so, you have summoned me here, to heal me with a bare caning?'

'I suppose so,' said the doctor. 'But only if you'd like . . . Oh! You must think me a bit of a silly.'

'Not at all,' Belle responded promptly. 'I am quite ready to be caned, Doctor.'

'Would you call yourself submissive, Belle?' said Dr Paine.

'Yes, Doctor,' answered Belle, promptly.

'So I guessed, from our correspondence. Yet you take delight in watching others caned.'

'My masturbating must prove that, Doctor. I imagine myself caned in their place.'

'And you have no objections to caning errant nurses yourself, on their bare bottoms? Some of them like it, you see – they are not happy without a daily thrashing.'

'Which I should be happy to administer, Doctor,' said Belle, 'on the same principle.'

'Bare caning forms a bond amongst us, Belle. Ladies should look inside themselves, not outward, or beneath the ground. Miss Budgen is mistress of things outside our palisade, like these precious stones and the . . . and other things, and I am happy to let her remain so.'

Dr Paine unbuttoned her lab coat, revealing her massive bare breasts, the nipples standing erect as though stiffened by prongs inside the skin. Pierced through each nipple was a gemstone, glowing soft cream. Her breasts began to sway, as though in an unseen breeze. The lab coat, dangling loose, revealed her sussies and stockings, and black split-crotch panties through which the lips of her vulva gleamed wet, like swollen red worms.

'Shall I hypnotise you?' she said. 'For a proper *healing*, in the hundreds of strokes – as opposed to the school beating in the mere dozens, which do not quite bring a girl to her plateau of sublimity. The tourmalines at my nipples – please don't think me a hypocrite, Belle – they are for therapeutic, not cosmetic purpose; that is, purely for hypnosis.'

Belle said that she would rather not be hypnotised and that she would prefer to take an old-fashion school beating, if Dr Paine didn't mind.

'Why, of course! You are a new girl still,' she said warmly, without refastening her lab coat. 'I think I have my old school cane somewhere . . .'

She got up, making sure her breasts still swayed within Belle's gaze, and rummaged in a drawer until she found a three-foot wooden rod with a crook handle and blew the dust from it.

'A fond memento,' she said. 'This *is* a good game. I dreamed of being a schoolmistress, perhaps a headmistress, myself. But the cane is outlawed nowadays, and I don't know if I would have the stomach anyway, to give a really stern beating. My role as healer enables me to cane and to know that I am providing health and pleasure. Well, how many do you deserve, Miss Puget? Let this be our special game. How about three dozen stingers?'

She whopped the armchair and the cane made a frightening whistle.

'Or let's say four.'

'Whatever you think best, Doctor,' said Belle, feeling moisture seeping from her gash at the prospect of a proper, no-nonsense, bare-bum caning.

'And your first anal injection afterwards, when your bum's warmed and you feel like bonding,' said Dr Paine suddenly. 'It's a mild one and a lovely surprise for you, Belle.'

Belle eyed the cane and her heart jumped as the oil flowed from her cunt.

'Anything you say, Doctor,' she heard herself reply, faintly.

'We must do things properly – this cane is so dry,' said Dr Paine. 'The eucalyptus trees are to blame, as they suck moisture from the air and the earth.'

She put her fingers deep in her own wet cunt and used her come to oil the cane.

'You may bend over the arm of my chair, Belle,' she said. 'First, remove your coat – Oh! You are wearing only undies! So sluttish and, I think, worthy of an extra dozen. Don't you agree?'

'It was so hot, Doctor,' said Belle.

'Your bum will be hot, too, when my cane has whipped her to crimson,' said Dr Paine. 'We'll have the knickers down, too, stretched between your thighs, in case you pee yourself.'

Belle complied, trembling and cunt-wet, in submissive relief. At last, a bare-bum thrashing! And from a dominatrix who pretended, with charming hypocrisy, that she wasn't. With luck, the sweet pain of Dr Cunliffe's lash would fade to a dream. Belle spread her arse-cheeks and thighs as wide as her knickers would allow and bent over the chair, scented from Dr Paine's bum and damp from her fluids. Dr Paine had been juicing through her split-crotch panties all the time she was discussing Belle's caning! This caused Belle's own cunt to wet profusely at the thrill of her power over her caner. Dr Paine had deliberately invited Belle to bend over *her* chair ... Belle pressed her face into the come-damp cushion and gripped the sides of the chair with arms splayed. She swallowed, nervously, relishing the moments of suspense before the always-dreadful smart of a naked beating's first cut.

'Four dozen then,' said Dr Paine.

'I believe you said five, Doctor,' Belle murmured.

'Why, so I did. Let us begin, then – we've plenty of time and if you want to call a halt, or think I'm caning too hard . . .'

'Please get on with it, Doctor,' said Belle, instantly regretting her waspish tone – the arrogance of a submissive!

'Very well, Miss,' said Dr Paine coldly, and the cane whistled in the air.

Vip!

Belle jumped as the cane struck her skin. God! It stung like hell! The first cut took her right at top buttock, below her spinal nubbin where the skin was thinnest. Belle gasped and felt her arse-cheeks helplessly clench.

Vip!

The second stroke followed almost at once, this one to the left haunch, followed – Vip! – with a fierce stinger to the right haunch. Then – Vip! Vip! Vip! – three squarely on the central fesses and then – Vip! Vip! Vip! Three hard ones to the underbuttock, stroking the tops of her thighs. Belle danced on tiptoe, her bum squirming in real agony. There was no let-up.

Vip! Vip! Vip!

Three in a row, right to the first weal, at top bum. Belle gasped, fighting back her tears and the lump that rose in her gorge. Her breath was raucous.

'Tight, eh?' said Dr Paine.

'God, yes, Doctor! It smarts awfully . . . I'd forgotten . . .' Belle panted.

Vip! Vip! Vip! Vip! – two each to each haunch.

'*Ah . . . Ahh . . .*' Belle sobbed, in a choked wail.

A flatboard paddling was fun, compared to the sting of a thin cane on the bare.

'I'll take that as a compliment,' said Dr Paine.

Vip! Vip! Vip! Vip! Vip! Vip!

'*Ahhhhh!*' Belle screamed.

130

*Six* stingers, in an unbroken flurry and *all in the same weal*, on her left haunch! Belle sobbed, her fesses churning, as she knew what was to come.

Vip! Vip! Vip! Vip! Vip! Vip!

The scalding weals on her left haunch were matched by equal strokes to her right.

'Ah ... Ah ... *Ohh* ...!' Belle sobbed, knowing haunch-weals to be the darkest and most lasting.

Yet, as her buttocks squirmed, she felt her erect nubbin tingle, in the delicious agony of her submission. Her cunt was flowing, under cane, and she felt her belly glow and tremble, aware that she was reaching her girl's plateau – of sublimity, Dr Paine had called it – where the cane's smart became a pleasure craved. Dr Paine let her rest, panting, for a moment while the warmth and glow of her beaten buttocks seeped through every pore of her tingling skin.

'Please, I . . .' Belle sobbed.

'Yes, Belle? You were going to say?'

'Please, Doctor, continue my beating,' Belle whispered. 'I want it so much . . .'

'Good, Belle. Now, I think you understand the . . . cravings of our Japanese girls, and of our lovely guests, too. You realise it is time you took anal injection – gene enhancement, for your own greater submissive pleasure. *This* is only a school caning . . .'

Vip! Vip!

'*Ahhh! Ahhh!*'

The two whistling swishes to the underfesses took Belle unawares. Dr Paine's fingers suddenly clutched Belle's wet cunt lips, pressing them together to squeeze drops of come.

'A mere 30, and already you are sopping – your clit's hard, too. Think of the orgasms you may enjoy, like mute Sushi and the others, when your buttocks are sensitised by anal injection.'

'Yes, Doctor,' Belle groaned, her body flooding with the pleasure of her weals as her cunt flowed with grateful come. 'Oh, *yes* . . .'

Dr Paine touched her nubbin with the cane's tip, hot from her flogging, and Belle suddenly and piercingly climaxed. Her beating was halfway complete.

'*Ahh . . . ahh . . . mmm . . .*' Belle sighed, as her pleasure drenched her.

Dr Paine's fingers were at her own extruded clitty, like a tight pink sea anemone that seemed to sprout from the aperture of her panties.

'If you are going to come under cane, Belle, it is only fair that I wank off as I complete your thrashing,' Dr Paine said, frotting her erect clit, 'before your first anal injection . . .'

The bare-bottom caning continued, with Belle's naked fesses well squirming and clenching in staccato rhythm to her caner's approval.

'You will bear lovely weals, Belle,' said the doctor, 'but imagine – with gluteal enhancement, you can take the cane every single day and awake unwealed for a new day's pleasure.'

Belle knew she wanted it! She had come here to submit . . . how foolish she had been, to doubt her own deep submissive needs. Wanking over Sushi's bare bum squirming on the flogging frame was one thing, but Belle wanted it to be *her* bum's caning that made other girls wank. The clenching and wriggling of her beaten buttocks now seemed a graceful ballet, celebrating her submissive's power; her glowing smarts on her bare skin, the furnace of that power.

Belle Puget went to the full 60 strokes of the cane, without crying out again, but at the 49th stroke she allowed her piss to spurt, wetting her stretched knickers. This made Dr Paine's frotting harder and she paused, moving into Belle's view, so that Belle could observe the doctor's masturbation. Dr Paine dipped her fingers into Belle's smelly panties and pressed her fingers across her nose and lips.

'Mmm . . .' she gasped. 'Please wank off with me, Belle.'

Belle's hand stretched to her engorged nubbin and she plunged her fingers in the bath of cunt oil that was her slit. When her thumb brushed her throbbing clitty, she came immediately and her gasps of coming brought the doctor off, her fingers wanking fast at her nubbin as she breathed the aroma of Belle's pee and come. Neither woman touched the other. The doctor's come-howls were like a hyena's yelp, but after her orgasm had passed she was brisk again.

'Only another eleven to go, Belle. I'll make them as hard as I can and then we'll proceed next door, for your treatment,' she said, caning Belle twice across the tops of her naked fesses.

Vip! Vip!

Belle scarcely felt the strokes, her skin seemed a protective hide of pain, each further lash adding to her store of pleasure.

'Mutual wanking is one of the greatest pleasures, Belle, haven't you found?' said Dr Paine.

Vip! Vip!

'*Urrggh . . .!*'

Belle did not respond, except with a gurgle in her throat, as two hard strokes took her vertically in the arse-cleft and lashed her full on the anus and cunt. Dr Paine chuckled that she must expect real stingers for the last seven.

'And that means cleft-strokes, Belle.'

Vip!

'*Oh! God!* Oh, it hurts . . .'

Belle's come dripped as the cane's tip caught her on the very clitoris, maddening her with the pain and pleasure of humiliance, even as her tears flowed.

'I mean, two girls, innocently wanking, stroking their own breasts and clits but not touching each other's bodies, except perhaps an embrace at the moment of climax. The same, I confess, with boyfriends. Such a delight to wank slowly and watch the naked penis rise, the glans shiny and trembling, as the cream surges in the balls, yet knowing it may not touch the female's sacred person. Then the first drop of come at the cock's tip, the bucking of the shaft, the spurt of glorious cream, as the male gasps in frustrated ecstacy. How he longs to touch the sweet softness of female skin, and give his spunk to her warm wet depths! A girl may bring herself to come, controlling her body, as a brute male can never control his; after coming, perhaps a single touch, or a chaste caress to his balls, as a token of the female power.'

Vip! Vip!

Strokes repeated on the drumskin of Belle's cleft, shuddering pain through her clitty and gash.

'Never forget, Belle, that males are merely mutant females. Popular wisdom calls our clits the remnants of penises, but the truth is converse. A penis is merely an enhanced clitoris, for brute breeding. A male can never be anything but a brute, while a female can be everything.'

Vip! Vip! Vip! Vip!

'*Ahhh! Uhhh . . .*' Belle sobbed, tears and cunt streaming, as the final four strokes took her firmly on the anus bud, which flamed like a red-hot coal between her wealed arse-melons.

Their frantic clenching made her anus open and close like a fish's mouth and Belle felt Dr Paine's finger slide into her bumhole, to about half its length, and hold there, waggling and reaming the lips of the anus, to keep it distended. As Belle's squirming calmed, she found her anus stayed slack, so that Dr Paine was easily able to penetrate the bumshaft with a second finger. Both fingers now slid easily to Belle's anal root.

'Good!' she said. 'We may proceed directly to your anal injection.'

Dr Paine moved to the locked door, pressing a coded sequence, and it slid open. Belle rose unsteadily, rubbing her flamed buttocks and grateful for the cool of the sopping wet knickers as she pulled them over her welts. Her bottom felt like red-hot corrugated iron. Clutching her bottom, she followed Dr Paine into a cool chamber, all in beige, with soft lights and the hiss of bubbling water. Belle had to rub her eyes a long time to dissipate the blur of her tears, then saw an operating table and tubes, jars and other surgery apparatus. Around the walls of the room stood water tanks, each hissing with oxygen bubbles. Below the ceiling, the wall was fringed with a gallery of framed photographs. Belle focused on the nearest water tank, then at the photo gallery and gasped in shock.

'Welcome to the aquarium, Belle,' said Dr Paine, as the door slid shut behind them.

'Miss Budgen and I do not always see eye to eye,' said Dr Paine, 'which is understandable. She is a mistress of terrain, while I am mistress of water; hence, her superior, as water is the female element. If you care to twist your head, you may admire my record of success. The photos illustrate Miss Budgen's clumsy attempts, now discontinued, to emulate my own genetic work, and my successful repairs to bodies botched under the claw woman's malign influence.'

The photos showed naked female bodies, before and after. Belle blanched; the 'before' shots showed women without noses, or with three breasts; legs webbed together like mermaids; navels extruded like floppy penises; buttocks spread to show twin anal holes, or double vaginas; scaly holes where nose, mouth and ears should be; long oxtails at the spine, webbed toes and fingers; or arses of a single buttock. Some girls were androgynes, with abnormally large penises and testicles on otherwise perfect female bodies. In the 'after' shots, the girls were as normal as Geisha, or Sushi. Belle said she had not had the pleasure of Miss Budgen's acquaintance.

'And you have no need of it, Belle, for your own good,' replied the doctor, pleasantly. 'I overlook her shortcomings and ambition, because she is useful. It will not shock you to learn that she, too, fell under the empire of the dreadful clawed woman and that I had to administer a public naked whipping of 500 lashes – to her bottom and shoulders, *without* genetic enhancement. That made her see reason.'

Belle was completely nude and strapped face down on the operating table. Her ankles and wrists were locked in rubber gloves at each corner and her belly was thrust up by a strong rubber balloon. Her thighs and buttcks were fully splayed and a steel speculum was inserted into her arsehole, holding the anal lips wide apart. Inside the prongs of the speculum, a monstrous tube filled her anus and pressed painfully at her root, its ends sucking and cupping the innermost orifice. The other end of the tube was plugged into a valve beneath the tank, whose contents had made Belle gasp. Dr Paine positioned herself by the stopcock, ready to open the valve and flood Belle's bumhole. Between Belle's teeth was a rubber bar.

A nude girl floated inside the tank, completely submerged and supported only by a breathing tube rammed in her mouth. Her wrists were bound and her legs bent backwards, the ankles fastened in the same clasp thus exposing her cunt and thrusting her pert conic teats forward. The girl was Sushi. Her eyes were shut and her face contorted with pain, for the tank seethed with live black lobsters who tussled for her body; several of them had their claws clamped to her nipples, bum and cunt-lips. One lobster had her big extruded clitty held fast between its crusted pincers. Cunt oil flowed from Sushi's cooze, floating like a cloud in the milky water. At short intervals, the steady flow of come was joined by a spurt of yellow pee. This liquid was to be Belle's first anal injection.

'Sushi has been naughty again,' said Dr Paine, 'and merited a non-flagellant chastisement. Her own enhanced juices will nourish your body, Belle. Only half the tank is water . . .'

She turned the stopcock and Belle gasped, as a flood of warm fluid penetrated her anus. Her belly felt full to bursting and to stifle her squeal she bit hard on her rubber bar, but could not stop her body writhing in agony as the liquid penetrated her remorselessly. She looked round; Dr Paine was blatantly frotting herself, at Belle's discomfort and, trapped in the lobster tank, Sushi had open eyes and her lips smiled at Belle around her breathing tube. Her eyes were fixed on Belle's squirming buttocks and the flow of come from her cunt increased to a torrent.

The other tanks, five in number, swam into Belle's view. None was occupied save the furthest, in the corner of the lab. It contained a nude Japanese girl, not festooned with lobsters but caressed by a horde of water snakes, which made Belle's gorge rise. They slithered and slimed over the nude girl's body, diving in and out of her cunt and her

136

anus, which was stretched open like Belle's with a speculum, but even wider, so that the snakes could penetrate her anus as easily as they penetrated her vagina. The girl's mouth and eyes were shut, but her face was strangely calm and her only movement was a quivering of her oddly distended earlobes. Her anal ring bubbled, fringed with downy fronds, which waved in the waters like the tentacles of an open anemone, as the snakes brushed past on their way into her anal shaft. Every few moments, her body shuddered as though whipped and her lips creased in silent pleasure.

'Electric eels,' said Dr Paine. 'Are my punishments chastisements or pleasure? How do you whip those who crave the lash . . .? Perhaps you are the one to help me find out, Belle.'

The grip of Belle's teeth on her rubber bar loosened as she grew used to the stretching of her loins and belly by Sushi's coursing fluids. Gradually, the smart of her bum-welts faded, to be replaced by a strange tingling pleasure, as though her clit were being caressed; yet her clit was untouched, Dr Paine's fingers being busy masturbating her own. Belle began to gasp as she felt her own cunt gushing come. Sushi's enhanced fluid seemed to seep from Belle's anus and belly, into every crevice of her wealed arse, caressing and tickling the bruised flesh, making each welt a sliver of clitoral nerve. Her bottom glowed, throbbed and tingled, as though her buttocks were an extension of her now-stiffened nubbin. Belle began to pant with joy, as she understood the true beauty of gene enhancement. *This* was what Sushi felt when she was caned . . .

Dr Paine was panting as she masturbated and her gasps of pleasure made Belle's gash flow with more copious come, knowing it was the sight of her squirming buttock-flesh which moved the woman to wank off. The liquid seemed to fill Belle entirely; she shut her eyes, and imagined her whole nude form a giant anus, or vagina, with Sushi's come and pee pulsing within her as a vast cock and the whole skin of her buttocks, its clitoris. Dr Paine began to pant as her orgasm approached and, as she came, her fingertips touched Belle's wealed arse, just once.

Belle screamed. She came, in an orgasm harder and stronger than any before, just at that one touch to her bum-skin. Her eyelids fluttered; she saw Sushi staring and smiling at her over her rubber tube, with come pouring from her nibbled cunt; the other Japanese girl, awakened by Belle's pleasure, smiled too, as the electric eels flitted in and out of her cunt and anus, making her buttocks clench as her breasts quivered and her stiff nipples twanged. Jets of bubbles spurted from her bumhole and globules of come from her cunt, to her shudders of delight. Belle became aware of something odd about the second Japanese girl. Like Sushi, she was totally immersed in water, but she had no breathing tube.

# 9

# Cane Virgins

'We're quite safe in daytime,' said Linda. 'The ferals only come out at night.'

They sat in Linda's jeep, which she piloted easily along a rutted mud road, swathed by jungle. Both women were nude, though Belle wore a sun hat.

'Did I miss something?' she said. 'Why shouldn't we be safe? And what are ferals?'

Linda's fingers flew to her mouth.

'Oh! And I promised to tell you everything I know, Mistress!' she said, guiltily. 'You get to take things for granted, and forget they are unfamiliar to others.'

It was a month since Belle's arrival at the Paine Foundation and, as the jeep careered through the jungle, she cast her mind back. During that time, she had become accustomed to an undemanding daily routine: lab work, supervision of treatment, some time to lay the ground for her own research and nude sea bathing with the guests. Even the cool Dr Cazenove treated her politely, when Belle witnessed Linda taking her daily anal gene injection for her hemangioma – which did not seem to be working, Belle thought secretly – as the fiery blotched skin seemed to spread over further portions of Linda's buttocks and teats. If Dr Cazenove had 'reported' Belle to Dr Paine, for over-curiosity, Belle reasoned that it had been with good intent. Dr Paine herself, though always in a hurry, or locked away in her secret lab, always had time for a smile: especially when she administered Belle's own anal injection, twice a week, in the aquarium. Although Dr Paine always masturbated as Belle squirmed under enema and made Belle orgasm with a gentle clit-rub and a light spanking of her newly-sensitive buttocks, she did not cane her again and Belle had not been treated again to the eerie spectacle of nursemaids in underwater chastisement. Nor did she ask questions, but manifested a drowsy acceptance of 'all in good time'. She realised that her nagging questions would be answered not by Drs Paine or Cazenove, nor even Bluebird – but by Linda.

She witnessed numerous canings, mostly judicial, of Japanese nurses who had committed some imperfection, and occasionally of guests, including Bluebird. Bluebird regularly took 500 stripes of the rattan on her bare bottom, administered by Drs Paine and Cazenove together. Belle had not been caned again herself and demurred from asking Linda, though her arse thirsted for whipping. She still had trouble reconciling her own submissive impulse with her newly assumed dominant one towards Linda and it was clear that Linda would prefer not to thrash her mistress, even though the paddling had left meagre welts and her bum had quickly cleared of them. Yet, with the glowing enhancement of her buttocks under Dr Paine's anal treatment, Belle's arse began to long for the cane: not the school caning she had enjoyed, but a serious flogging, like the Japanese girls or Bluebird. She sensed that Dr Paine was teasing her, making her hungry and thus obedient.

After Bluebird had been caned, she would join Belle for a naked swim, an hour or so later, with her furry bottom shining sleek and unscarred. Belle had marvelled at her stamina in taking the fearful thrashings, whose weals she had actually witnessed and wanked over, and which would have left any normal woman's arse wealed for weeks, but Bluebird gushed enthusiastically about her hormone and gene treatments and how the skin repaired itself so quickly. She boasted that she orgasmed five times during a beating of 45 or 50 minutes. No praise was enough for the good Dr Paine and her genetic therapy and the evidence of her pure buttocks obliged Belle to agree.

On her second day at Paine, before her own school caning, anal injection and witnessing of Sushi in the lobster tank, Sushi had been her 'toilette nursemaid'; hygienic assistance being a privilege, or necessity, of research staff. Both girls had showered nude and Sushi had licked Belle's anus clean after she had evacuated, this being a nursemaid's duty. The Japanese girl's bottom was snow-white, though the caning Belle had witnessed the day before had marked her buttocks deeply with crimson and purple welts. Sushi had wanked Belle off, as an accepted part of her hygienic assistance, but had demurred when Belle offered to return the favour. Instead, Sushi scratched the globes of her own arse, just as Belle climaxed, her come gushing into the Japanese girl's mouth. Sushi had gasped just as orgasmically as Belle, though both her hands were massaging Belle's stiff nipples and her own clit, though erect, was unstimulated. Later, and alone, Belle tried to masturbate by rubbing her bare arse and not touching her clit, but, though her bum tingled, the pleasure was not sufficient to bring her off. She needed a clit-wank, and, more important, she needed *the cane*. She began to beat her own arse, with a flatboard, as she wanked and found that after an exhausting self-flagellation, with a vigorous masturbation of her nubbin, she *could* climax. But, for true pleasure, she needed the cane, in submission to another dominant female. *Or even a male,* she thought, guiltily. Linda insisted that her personal gene treatment worked, though her unblemished nates were not really evidence of its efficacity, since Belle had been careful to thrash her without leaving lasting marks.

'I know what I'm getting,' Belle said. 'Pure femme-juices, come and pee ... But aren't you curious to know exactly what Dr Paine or Dr Cazenove are shoving up your bum every day? Mine hurts just a bit, but yours looks extraordinarily painful, with that pointed nozzle and the largest anal speculum.'

'It is,' said Linda, 'and I love it. I like to squirm under anal injection, even if she won't cane me. As for the gene serum, only Dr Paine knows its composition. You can understand why Dr Paine is frightened of spies, Mistress. If her secrets were known – especially by that awful clawed woman – it would change the world.'

'Then why doesn't she tell them to the right people?' said Belle.

'It is a matter of great precision,' said Linda, uncertainly. 'The slightest imbalance could lead to *over-medication*. So Dr Paine must be cautious. Perfection takes time.'

Belle did not say 'all in good time' on the occasions Bluebird invited to her luxurious cabana for spanking games, for Belle was as yet unsure of the thin dividing line between supervisory staff and plain nurses. Bluebird seemed to take no account of it as she offered Belle tea, let her loose robe fall open and asked Belle if she admired her sleek pelt and bristling, furry mound. Belle said, truthfully, that she did and was invited to exhibit her own hairy pube-jungle. Their tea left to cool, both females wanked each other until both were swimming with juice and Bluebird asked Belle if she would like to suck some elixir, meaning her come juice. That way, some of Bluebird's 'magic' might find its way into Belle's own system. Belle remembered her joyful wanking of Bluebird while watching Sushi caned and knelt submissively, to press her face into Bluebird's cunt, while the American woman kneaded Belle's quivering teats between her fingers. Bluebird, who like all the guests, was known only by nickname, asked if Belle was comfortable, and Belle did not take her lips from the woman's sopping quim to say that a submissive was not supposed to be comfortable. Bluebird seemed an odd nickname for a woman whose downy skin smelled so deliciously vaginal. Even her teats smelled of cunt juice.

Bluebird's spanking games were only for Belle's bottom, though Belle enjoyed being bent over the woman's thighs for a beating of 100 or so spanks, which made her clench quite hard towards the end, and she saw with pleasure that her bare bum was prettily reddened by the spanking. Her belly full of Bluebird's come juice, of which she had drunk copiously, Belle found her spanking unusally exciting, each slap making her gluteal nerve-ends tingle with pleasure. It was scarcely more than playful, however, and insufficient for gluteal orgasm without clitoral stimulation. Hard whipping was reserved for Bluebird's own naked buttocks, to which Belle was asked to apply a thorough scourging of 200 strokes with a three-thonger. Belle accepted her spankings gracefully and did not ask for more: she sensed Bluebird, as a paying guest, considered spanking a tip and expected staff to be content with that.

She whipped the American woman, with Bluebird strapped by ankles and wrists to her bedposts and her waist cinched in a pincer corset that Belle surmised was very painful. Her large teats were squashed under her ribs like pancakes. Bluebird was talkative, and noisy, expressing her appreciation of each whiplash by loud cries and enthusiastic clenching of the fesses, and announcing with gleeful gasps whenever her flogging was bringing her close to her frequent comes. She said her husband and she played such games all the time and, although males were not allowed at the Paine Foundation, she had found that by making him drink pints of her come juice, she could increase his own bottom's orgasmic potential. Belle found herself charmed by Bluebird's American friendliness, yet slightly disappointed at the absence of the mysteries of humiliation, dominance and submission which she had learned in Europe, after her introduction to a slave's role by Dr Jolita Cunliffe. For Bluebird, the lash was a merry game.

Not that her whippings were gentle: Belle raised dark crimson and even grey or black welts, all over the honey-coloured bare bum, which Bluebird assured her would be gone by suppertime. She said it was nice to watch the little Japanese mice whipped, as she called the nursemaids, but they did not orgasm so frequently: the constancy of their treatment, Bluebird suspected, had addicted them to the lash and they needed it just as a morphine addict needed a fix. Without regular whipping, the Japanese girls just 'didn't feel right'. Like every other enhancement, Dr Paine's gene cocktails were enjoyed best in moderation. Bluebird seemed to enjoy her assumed submissive's role as another American-style fitness programme.

Belle was quite pleased when Bluebird made her strap on a dildo and fuck her vigorously in her cunt, while Bluebird masturbated herself to another orgasm and then consented to fuck Belle with the dildo still wet from her own come. Bluebird liked to be whipped and fucked in the cunt, her anus crammed with shiny pale tourmalines, which plopped out like bullets at her moment of orgasm and which Belle replaced before her whipping continued, noting that the stones had brightened to fiery pink. Belle insisted on taking it in the anus, with the tickling gemstones filling her cunt; and when Bluebird kept enquiring if it hurt too much, would snap with a submissive's demanding arrogance, that it did not hurt enough. Eventually, Belle was satisfied, by taking Bluebird's full weight, her hard teats slapping her back and squashing her flat, as her anus was vigorously buggered and the dildo thrust really hard, hurting her anal root. Masturbating herself on clit and titties, she wanked herself to a satisfying climax at the pronging of her bumhole, imagining Bluebird as some horrid monster of Geisha's Japanese comic books. The gemstones filling her cunt seemed to tingle electrically at the neck of her womb, like battery terminals pressed to her clit.

Belle recognised that she had come here with subtler intent: to find proper submission, as the whipped slave of the dominant Dr Paine: a submission which would be anything but routine and chillingly unpredictable, like the attentions of the true dominatrix Dr Cunliffe. She was unsure whether Dr Paine *was* a true mistress. Rather, she seemed a genuine healer. Her resemblance to Belle herself became more and more striking, as, in Belle's recollection, did her own resemblance to Dr Cunliffe. Dr Paine had admitted that her delight in caning Belle was in imagining she caned her own bottom; and perhaps that had also been Dr Cunliffe's pleasure, seeing Belle as a mirror of her own beauty. Dr Paine's aqua-punishments and her canings of the nurses were therapeutic rather than cruel or lustful, even though she wanked off when caning. Did Belle wish to bare her bottom to a lady who would not appreciate her submission? Or – awful thought – was Dr Paine *herself* secretly submissive? Belle faithfully acted the part of Linda's mistress, aware that the sub/dom bargain must be equal on both sides. But if she was to enslave herself to another woman, her bare-bum caning must *hurt*. So far, the true submission she craved eluded her. Bluebird's friendly spanks and dildo-fucking or her own self-whipping, however savagely she thrashed her own bare buttocks, were not enough.

Only a month and Belle was already part of the quiet routine of the Paine Foundation. The very normality of Dr Paine's world seemed puzzling. Voices were not raised in argument, or delight; the women rose at dawn and retired at sundown, except for a rotating roster of nurses on security duty, in addition to the ever-present paramilitary guard corps. Linda confided that these women received a special anal formula whose molecules were unstable. Treatments and canings and sea-bathing took place in a dreamy, contented stillness. Everything, including frequent caning or masturbating to orgasm, proceeded in good time. Belle understood, from the constant tingling of her own enhanced – and, she was sure, *enlarged* – buttocks, that the females of Furvert's Island were in permanent gluteal arousal. Even sitting down pantied, on a rattan chair, or with bare bottom on the hot sand, gave a warm thrill.

Japanese nurses changed, as a few left, to be replaced by others; 'cane virgins,' as Linda put it. That, too, was normal: Dr Paine placed her trainees in prestigious jobs throughout the world. Furvert's Island – Belle had to remind herself of the true name – was paradise. Dr Paine kindly hypnotised cane virgins for their first beatings, before their arse-skin was sensitised. The mute Sushi, Belle's occasional handmaiden, would never leave for a prestigious job. Certain other of the nurses suffered from deformities like her and would remain in Dr Paine's employ forever. The nurses shared handmaidens' duties, and Belle got to know two of the others, each bearing a resemblance to Geisha but not as startling as Sushi's. Both were cane virgins on arrival, but after a week or so of daily discipline and frequent anal injection, were able to take the cane on their bare bottoms as coolly as Sushi, or Geisha, far away in Europe.

There was Jo, svelte and Eurasian, with lustrous dark hair, short, like Geisha's; like Geisha, she had no body hair at all. Jo's buttocks were disproportionately large, emphasised by her almost flat, muscular chest, with little pin-pricks of pink nipple. The arse-cleft was a canyon between the two perfectly smooth mountains of her buttocks, and her labia were stretched like rubber pillows. Her single leg was adorned with powerful slabs of muscle, for her left leg was absent – she coyly refused to give details of its amputation, or otherwise – and she normally wore a rubber prosthesis in its place. The prosthesis was very obvious, since her good leg was shiny with small scales, like a fish's. She, too, had finny hairs at her anus bud, which were the only hairs on her whole body, and she had two lobes on each ear. As she was happy to demonstrate, she could move by hopping on one leg only with deft use of her long, prehensile fingers. She was coy, too, about saying where she had been before coming to the Paine Foundation – or else forbidden to speak. When she did speak, her voice sounded slurpy, because she had two tongues: the normal one long and spiny and beneath it, a small, thick one.

Its purpose became obvious when she hygienically assisted Belle for the first time and, while sponging her in the shower, asked if Belle wished to be wanked off. When Belle agreed – her clit already tingling at the sight of the nude Eurasian balancing herself on the single leg, her stump shiny with green scales – Jo lowered herself to her one knee in a fluid motion of surprising grace and proceeded to tongue-fuck Belle. Her long tongue hardened like a penis, as if cartilage had suddenly grown and probed the pouch of Belle's cunt far more expertly than any cock; while the short second tongue was perfectly shaped as an anus plug, or clit-tickler, depending on the angle of the girl's head. Belle writhed in ecstacy as Jo gamahuched her, alternating the second tongue between vigorous anal penetration and clit-frotting.

As a result, Belle's slit gushed, matting her pube jungle in oily come and she climaxed twice in as many minutes, while the girl's soft fingertips, with no nails or cutaneous matter at all, caressed Belle's bum and nipples. Jo's only demanded tip was a vigorous hand-spanking on her wet bottom, upside down, while she clung to Belle's neck with her single leg and masturbated her powerful clit by rubbing it against Belle's nipples. Belle was obliged to lift her arms high to spank the girl in this position, using both palms, with simultaneous slaps to each bare buttock and Jo came three or four times at each spanking of 90 or 100, even without her clit-rubbing. When she buckled on her rubber artificial leg and covered it with a yellow lycra stocking, she showed Belle, solemnly, that she was able to do knee bends and squats quite effortlessly.

Like Dr Jolita Cunliffe and Bluebird, Japanese Kiki was covered in sleek fur and could bend her spine to lick her own clit. She was obliged to wear specially thick rubber condoms at all times, on her fingers and toes, since the edges of her nails were razor-sharp and thus dangerous, no matter how much she filed them. If she did not cut them twice a day, they grew rapidly into long diamond-pointed claws a hand's length, and with razor edges. She, too, liked to be spanked, but with Belle using the Japanese girl's own unsheathed hand as a tool of chastisement, the claws raising sharp welts on her tight white bottom.

Spanking was accompanied by her enthusiastic licking of Belle's clit, with a rasping tongue, and her zeal in servitude almost exceeded Linda's when Belle consented to bugger her elastic anus with a dildo of her own fabrication, made of clam-shells, glued and bound together by strings of barnacles. Kiki explained that she had been buggered so hard and so frequently as a geisha girl in Tokyo, that her anus could only respond to the harshest penetration for her to achieve orgasm. Her attraction as a geisha had been her claws, which she used to scratch the balls, penises and arses of her customers, while spanking them on the buttocks with her untrimmed nails. Pain alone would make them erect and, in the fashion of the Japanese male, eager to take revenge on the person of the tormentress by anally penetrating her as painfully as possible. Kiki had been released from her duties as prostitute – so she claimed – because, by age 21, a 'poke-geisha' had normally grown to enjoy anal penetration so much and her arse had grown so elastic, that the customers no longer derived satisfaction from hurting her. In fact, a seasoned poke-geisha actually craved buggery. Kiki's anus bud was a prune, her shaft a rubbery cavern. She was nineteen years old.

Witnessing the regularity and ease of corporal punishment, and masturbatory practice made Belle readier to administer the discipline demanded by her slave, as the price of her confidance. Belle obliged her slave Linda with three long spankings of 1,000 on the bare during her first week, followed by wanking and anal penetration of the submissive with a dildo. Also, Linda was being trained to swallow her mistress's come and her flood of piss, as she tongued her clit. However, Belle's true motive was to gain knowledge, and she concluded that Linda was completely honest in describing herself as clumsy. She *was* physically clumsy, vague and absent-minded: a dreamer with low self-esteem, quite the opposite of Belle who, having been subjugated, increasingly found in herself the arrogance of the true submissive. She was irritated that knowledge still must be prised from her slave, not because Linda dissembled, but because she forgot things, or thought they didn't matter. She was suspicious, not of the girl's motives, but of her ignorance. She claimed she had never heard of Furvert's Island, although she lived on it. Linda had wished Belle to pierce her clitoris and affix a tourmaline but Belle had refused, mindful of Dr Paine's possible anger.

'But it's so lovely!' Linda cried. 'I've been saving it . . . for when I was deflowered. But now you are my mistress, Belle . . . lots of girls have them, there are so many under the ground!'

The girl blushed adorably, and Belle had to gently interrogate her, to find out that the stone came from a mine on Furvert's Island itself. Belle was shown it and recognised it as one of the gems that had filled Bluebird's anus during whipping and then her own cunt, under bum-fucking; and that Dr Paine had worn at her nipples, as tools of hypnosis. Linda admitted reluctantly that she knew where it came from.

'The gem mine, Mistress,' Linda said, 'is not our – my – business. It is in Miss Budgen's domain. Girls work there, sometimes.'

'As punishment, or full time?'

'I . . . hadn't really thought.'

'You mean you didn't want to think. And where do these stones go?'

Linda wiped a tear from her eye.

'How should I know that? Oh . . . you're cross with me, and I'll be spanked.'

'Yes, I'm cross with you, slave, and that is why you shan't be spanked. Instead, you will take me to pay a call at the mine. I have yet to meet Miss Budgen, so there is my excuse.'

Petrol had to be signed for at the supply shed, and Belle put 'recreation' as her reason for the trip. For their excursion, Belle permitted Linda to wear a slave bracelet at her ankle made merely of seashells, and only outside the Paine compound. One of Belle's first demands had been for an explanation of the palisade surrounding the complex. It was reasonable enough: there were wild beasts on the island, and felines were attracted by the fishy smell from the canteen: hence the paramilitaries, adept at martial arts. Now, on their way to the mine, Linda spoke casually of ferals, which hinted at *cognisant* wild beasts. Belle sighed. Another explanation to extract.

'Are these ferals related to the Paine Foundation?' she said.

'I suppose they might be,' said Linda. 'You are so curious, Mistress!'

Belle told her to stop the jeep, while they were still in the jungle. The heat was oppressive and the noises of the jungle fauna seemed to swathe them like a blanket. The range of hillocks a mile away, in the savannah, was the location of the mine.

'We are scientists,' she said, 'and must be curious.'

Linda stared at her, with a glassiness in her eyes. Suddenly, Belle asked her if she had ever been hypnotised. Her answer came too fast.

'No! Never! I've never been hypnotised in my life!'

But her eyes now flickered in panic.

Of course! Linda's confused reticence was genuine. She was not concealing what she knew but, deep down, knew more than she realised. Belle fingered her nipples, pinching and clawing them to bricklike stiffness. She had no need of tourmalines, as her nipples were larger and harder than any other girl's. She began to sway her back, swinging her pendulous bare breasts back and forth.

'I want you to look at my nipples, slave. Both at once. Look only at my nipples, Linda . . .'

# 10

# The Mineshaft

'No, I've never been hypnotised, Mistress,' said Linda, rubbing her eyes. 'Why do you ask?'

'Just curious,' said Belle. 'I know Dr Paine is an expert at the art. Maybe you have been hypnotised without knowing it.'

'Then maybe you have, too, Mistress,' said Linda.

It was over half an hour since Linda had slipped into her truth-telling trance, lulled by the swaying of Belle's bare breasts and the hard pink jewels of her nipples. Now, they approached the squat single hut that signalled the entrance to the jewel mines. There was no protective palisade to hinder their approach. Linda's knowledge of the Paine Foundation was genuinely incomplete – and Belle understood why. She wrinkled her nose at the fishy stench which assailed her, even over the scent of the eucalyptus grove through which they approached the mine.

They emerged from the grove and into the clearing, where the mine building stood. Though there was no protective fence against ferals, the hut itself was of hardwood, with a single entrance of two enormous steel flaps which seemed bolted rigidly shut, from the inside. There was a large window in the steel door, armoured with crossed steel wires but no entry handle. Linda braked the jeep to a halt and both girls gazed at the source of the fishy stink.

Outside the steel door, a nude girl was belted and strapped, by her wrists and ankles, between two whipping-posts. Her head hung limp as if in faint, and no hair protruded from the black rubber hood that shielded her from the sun. Rivulets of sweat cascaded down her breasts and back. Her whole bare body was a mass of whip-marks, mostly fresh, including weals on her thighs, teats, buttocks and gash so harsh, that it seemed she must shed her skin at any moment. Yet her cunt oozed slimy come, pink and viscous, like cod's roe and dripping in a large puddle on the baked earth. The weals on her thrashed buttocks also dripped, but with clear fluid, powerfully scented with the unmistakable tang of cunt oil. Even hanging, and striped with weals, her bare breasts jutted very long, with conical nipples that ended in sharp points and stuck out from the slender ribcage as though hardened with rubber filling. Her body was furred, including the gash: the pubic forest did not stop at her hillock, but grew from her clitoris and the cunt lips themselves. Her buttocks, too, were furry and the bum-bud, clearly visible in her taut cleft, had a thick jungle of fronds that sprouted from within the anal shaft. Her toes were webbed, like a duck's. A rubber tube was fixed in her cunt-hole and led to the steel door, which it penetrated. Sporadically, spurts of golden fluid hissed from the tube in the strapped girl's cunt and mingled with her pink exuded come, to lighten the puddle between her legs. This fluid was woman's piss. The two girls, still nude, got out of the jeep.

'A feral,' said Belle, 'and obviously tamed, or captured.'

'But why?' said Linda, genuinely puzzled and with fear in her voice.

'As bait,' said Belle. 'Look . . .'

Beyond the steel door, inside the building and visible in the window as in a mirror, another nude female was hung between two flogging posts. Her face was unmasked and her mouth was opened in a scream, as she writhed under a whipping on the buttocks delivered by a figure in shadow, also female. The tube's other nozzle was inserted into her gash, so that as the pain of her whipping made her juice and piss herself, the pee was siphoned along with her gushing clear come, into the cunt of the girl outside. Belle

152

found herself having to explain to Linda things she herself had got from Linda's suppressed memory. She reached for her bush jacket and skirt.

'Ferals,' she said, 'are descendants of the Japanese experiments, left to run wild after the end of World War Two. They are genetic experiments gone wrong and they augment their numbers with escapers from the Paine Foundation who are ... Dr Paine's mistakes. They are addicted to the scent and taste of genetically enhanced cunt juice. The whipped girl here is intended to entice them through the steel doors to the other girl undergoing whipping, and pissing and juicing more copiously. I'll bet the doors open easily, but won't open again, from the inside.'

'I can't believe it ...' Linda murmured, yet obviously stirred by her own deep memory.

'But it makes sense,' Belle said, 'since no other explanation presents itself. The mines need more fresh bodies than Dr Paine provides. It must be horrid work.'

'How do the ferals breed?' Linda asked. 'Hybrids are sterile, normally.'

'I don't know that part ...' Belle answered quickly.

Suddenly, a trapdoor slid open from its concealment beneath a clump of trailing tree roots, and revealed a brightly lit steel staircase. A woman hoisted herself nimbly from the subterranean passage and smiled at the girls. She was tall, a ravishing cropped blonde, with taut arse and tits sandwiching a flat muscled belly over a mountainous furry cunt-swelling and nutcracker thighs. She carried a whip and was nude, her downy golden body covered with hideous whip scars.

'No need to dress,' she said, 'it's quite hot down the mineshaft. I'm Miss Budgen, the overseer, and pleased to welcome you, though you might have called first. This way, ladies.'

She cracked her whip gently on her thigh. Belle gaped, mesmerised by the evidence of the overseer's hideous flagellation, until she saw the zip fasteners at the crotch and neck. Miss Budgen was not nude, but wore a second skin. She cracked her whip again, loudly this time and inches from Belle's bare breasts.

'I said, *this way*, ladies, if you please,' she repeated.

Suddenly, a trio of furry nude girls emerged from the bolthole and surrounded them, jaws slavering with white razor teeth. Their breasts were hard, perfect cones with razor-sharp nipples. Spinal nubbins lengthened into bony whiplash tails over a foot long, with clubbed tips that flicked the air in menace. Their thighs were parted, in wrestler's stance, showing their hairy pink gashes open like mouths, with clits dangling, not standing and inside the pink slits, gleams of ivory. Trembling, the two nude girls descended into the mineshaft, followed by their new hosts and the trapdoor slid shut with a clang, above them.

'I'm scared, Mistress,' sobbed Linda.

'It . . . it'll be all right,' Belle whispered, wishing she were unbound and able to soothe the girl.

How could she explain to her submissive that this was *real* submission, and that her cunt was flowing with come at the prospect of imminent whipping, by a genuinely cruel dominatrix – one who would fashion her own, terrible garment from the shed skins of her victims? The two girls were spreadeagled beside each other, their nude bodies splayed face down on simple metal bedframes. The stifling caning chamber, underground, held over a dozen of these flogging frames, grouped in a circle with heads at the centre; all but two were occupied by Miss Budgen's slave-girls, as she unabashedly called them. Their Japanese dolls' faces glowed with excitement. The other two contained girls face upwards. Their faces were nervous and fearful, their hard conic breasts trembling and goose-pimpled even in the heat. Dim phosphorescent light glowed from the rock itself; there was a dank odour, of girl-sweat, metal and clay mingled with urine, for the feral slave-girls pissed casually, whenever a tiny dribble pressed.

The bed-frames were empty with no supporting struts or wire mesh, thus obliging each girl to strain, supporting herself. Beneath each bed was a pegboard of holes in the

154

rock. In the hole appropriate to each body, a sharpened wooden stake was embedded, just below the stretched cunt lips with its shaft sunk halfway into her vagina. The shaft was of quite large penile girth, not in itself uncomfortable, but if a girl allowed her body to sag even an inch the sharp tip would pierce the neck of her womb. The two feral girls who awaited their whipping face up had similar stakes, but embedded in anus rather than cunt and, it seemed, already had the points tickling the anal root, for the girls sobbed and shivered in an incessant squirm. They were ill at ease, whereas the other girls, face down like Belle and Linda, had lustful, longing faces and awaited whipping with genuine impatience. It seemed, in the eerie glow, that most of the slave girls were Japanese, *or had once been* . . . Miss Budgen re-entered the whipping chamber, followed by her retinue of females. Belle whispered Dr Cunliffe's words to Linda:

'It is not the pain of penetration or the lash which matter, but the joy of submission, of which they are symbols and reminders.'

Miss Budgen cracked her stockwhip, a heavy leather thong studded with milky gemstones, coloured tan in emulation of their leather nests. Linda shivered, whimpering.

'You wanted to be submissive, Linda,' Belle said. 'Be brave and watch me. Afterwards, you may not want me for Mistress, for you'll see how a true submissive screams.'

'I shall always want you, Mistress,' Linda replied. 'But . . . *why?* Why this?'

'Power is its own reward, Linda, and our offence is to be victims,' Belle said.

Both girls fell silent, gasping in the strain of holding their bodies stiff, above the threatening vaginal prong. Belle's cunt quivered: the stave was unoiled and she began to rub the walls of her vagina against the rough, pungent eucalyptus wood, to make her slit juicy and ease its intrusion. She allowed her body to sag, lowering her belly until the spearpoint inched closer and closer up her cunt, towards her womb's mouth, then stifled a gasp as the point penetrated her uterine hole. Tears sprang to her eyes, but her cunt spurted suddenly with heavy come at this shameful pain. She felt the eucalyptus stave moisten with her flowing cunt oil. Her buttocks clenched, clasping the penile spear inside her flowing slit.

Miss Budgen approached Belle, accompanied by a Japanese girl whose skin was porcelain and not furred, but bare, like Geisha and Sushi, with the same big arse and cropped hair: a third mirror of those beauties. Her cunt-mound and the lips below, were monstrously distended and a rippling pouch of muscle. The tailed girls fanned out around the circle of beds; one guard, or chastiser, to each prisoner. Each guard raised a single leg and curled it around her nape, then bent down with her head between her thighs and licked her clitoris, until come flowed on her furry sleek legs. While they licked their clits, the girls' tails rose from their spinal nubbins and stood erect, like penises. The Japanese girl took position beside Linda, knelt and lifted Linda's haunches to free her cunt of its piercing spear, wet with Linda's own cunt juice.

Linda's body sagged free, but only until a fresh stave was brought, shaped in a Y like a large catapult, with hinges halfway along the two branches. This was pegged in the rock and Linda's lower spine clasped by its curve. The ends of the branches now folded on their hinges, pressing deeply into Linda's back and top buttocks and snapped shut, thus imprisoning her waist in a wooden cincher. The height of the stave lifted Linda's buttocks well higher than Belle's and with her ankles thonged firmly to the bed corners, forced the arse-globes well apart to display the cleft, gash and anus bud, the skin drum-taut.

'Your skin-blossom is not yet ripe,' said Miss Budgen, 'so you shall be cunt-whipped.'

Linda whimpered again, softly and her eyes filled with tears.

'Let me take her punishment, Miss!' Belle gasped.

'Why, so you shall,' said the dominatrix, 'but not in her stead. My slave Kaa will attend to the blossomed girl, with cunt-asp. My whip shall be for your buttocks, hole and slit, Miss Puget.'

The Japanese girl parted her thighs and reached a finger into her cunt, then rapidly withdrew it. Between the huge wet cunt lips, an eye appeared; then, a flickering tongue and finally, the whole head of a snake. As it uncoiled itself, the snake slithered from Kaa's slimy cunt pouch and lifted its body in the air, tongue darting and eyes wide. Kaa hissed, spitting on the snake.

The beast began to coil its body down between her parted thighs and slithered across her perineum and arse-cleft, until its flickering tongue lapped her wide anal hole. The tongue darted inside her bumhole which clamped shut, imprisoning the snake, whose tail was now embedded in Kaa's cunt, with the head quivering at her anus. Kaa hissed again and loosened her anal aperture to allow the snake's head to enter. The snake penetrated her anus to about two inches beyond its neck, then three, four ... finally, Kaa tightened her buttocks, when a good nine or ten inches of the reptile's body were embedded in her anal shaft with the rest of it, shiny with Kaa's come, stretched taut in her arse-cleft. Her fingers grasped the cunt lips again and held them wide. The nether portion of the snake, oiled from her gash, emerged with a plop. She caught it in her hand and squeezed it. The snake's tip was bony, like a second skull but with no eyes: only a second mouth and flickering tongue. Now, Kaa let the snake drop, with the head held fast in her anus; it gave her a scaly green tail, whipping the air between her legs. She stood, staring impassively at Linda's spread bum and the blotch of her hemangioma.

'Are you a cane virgin, Miss Puget?' asked Miss Budgen.

'No, Miss,' said Belle.

'You have been whipped?'

'I ... yes, Miss, I have been whipped,' Belle murmured.

'Bare bum, I take it.'

'And bare back, Miss.'

Miss Budgen cracked her whip in the air, making a fierce clap. Belle shivered and her cunt twitched; she winced, as the stave-point brushed her womb's neck. Yet, the stave was wet with come that spurted faster, as Miss Budgen touched the thong gently to Belle's bottom, then removed it and cracked it inches from her skin, sending a rush of hot air into her anal crevice.

'Linda is a tadpole,' said Miss Budgen. 'Who has caned you, Miss Puget, and how often?'

'Why, Dr Paine, Miss,' Belle said, as the leather stroked her taut cleft and poked into her anal pucker. 'I am undergoing gluteal enhancement.'

Belle's anus squeezed on the whip's tip, holding it between her shivering buttocks until Miss Budgen sharply withdrew it. She gave Belle a very light spank on each fesse.

'Naughty girl,' she said. 'Were there others, before? For whipping, I mean.'

'Yes, Miss,' Belle replied.

'One in particular? A mistress?'

'I choose not to say, Miss,' Belle stammered, her heart pounding. 'Please consider me virgin.'

The whip cracked again, closer to her body.

'Secretive, as well as naughty,' mused Miss Budgen. 'Though I can guess . . . there was a mischief-maker here, whom I had to thrash to 500 on the bare back and arse, before sending her away to her world, squealing in shame. The slaves had formed unhealthy attachments to her – she is somewhere in the world, a dominant pervert. But each flogging from me dims the awe of my ferals for her memory. Be warned that a whip virgin receives strokes limited only by my judgement – a free-thrashing. The strokes will be regular, hard and very painful. I do not insist on silence, for I know how much this whip hurts. Dr Paine will know too, when I choose to release you, unable to walk or sit comfortably, because your bottom will be so very sore.'

'I . . . I accept a free-thrashing, Miss,' Belle blurted, her cunt a sea of flowing come.

'You have no choice,' spat Miss Budgen, lifting her whip. '*Submissive bitch* . . .'

As she did so, Kaa leapt onto Linda's bed and stood on the girl's strapped ankles, straddling her with her hands pressed on her own buttocks. She began a sinuous writhing of her hips, growing faster and faster, until the snake extruded from her anus whirled the air like a lariat. Miss Budgen's whip flashed and a thunderous crack echoed in the foetid cavern, as the studded leather seared Belle's bare buttocks, wrapping its tongue around her thighs and cunt. Belle screamed, but not loud enough to drown the crack of the snake's lashing Linda's anal hole and cunt-lips. The snake's second tongue landed on Linda's clit and flickered on the stiffened nubbin. Linda too, screamed as the scaly skin of the snake left a bruise right up her perineum and cleft, beyond her bumhole.

As the two girls took their second strokes, the furred females began to emulate Kaa, each attending to one of the strapped ferals. Twisting their loins and with backs to their victims, each lashed the bare buttocks with the cartilage of her erect tail. The slap of tails on bare skin was as loud and precise as that of a cane and the flogged girls sighed in a chorus of relief. Only the two girls who were face up screamed, along with Belle and Linda, as they were tail-whipped. Their whippings were directly on the bare breasts and nipples and left brutal weals, even from the first, deadly accurate strokes. After only the second stroke, one of the girls pissed herself, the yellow jet spurting from her stretched cunt like a geyser. Belle sobbed helplessly, unable to prevent herself from writhing and clenching her welted nates, as a third whiplash cut her bum raw and impaled her on the cunt-stave. Now, the second tit-whipped girl pissed, her jet steaming onto the rock floor to join the existing golden puddle. The cracks of tails on the naked titty-flesh made even the hard Japanese tits wobble, with the nipples erect amid the streaks of punishment on the breasts.

Crack! Crack! Crack! Crack!

'*Oh! Ahhhh . . .!* Oh, God . . .' Belle sobbed, as her bare arse was whipped. '*Oh! Oh! Oh, God . . .*'

Crack! Crack! Crack! Crack!

'You probably wonder why two slaves have been chosen for teat-whipping,' said Miss Budgen as she flogged Belle's squirming bare arse, her strokes covering the whole expanse of buttock, from spinal nubbin to cleft and thighs: over 40 strokes, now, and each more vicious.

'*Ahhh! Ahhh! Uhhh* . . .!' Belle screamed, her bare bum a cauldron of pain.

Linda's scream had become an incessant whimper as she was whipped on the cunt and anus and her whole arse-cleft was crimson. She too, let go a hissing flood of pee, which sprayed the Japanese girl's feet. But the golden stream glistened with pearls of come as well, and Kaa paused for an instant, to kick up first one foot, then the other and take her toes right in her mouth, where she licked and swallowed the splash of Linda's come and piss.

'Wash *me*,' Belle whimpered.

Linda had a second jet already dribbling and she directed the fine spray of pee on Belle's wealed buttocks, where it trickled down her inner thighs and into her come-soaked gash. The girls who took whipping on their bare extruded their tongues, which were long and hard, like pink lizards. As the whips fell on their furry sleek arses, their tongues stiffened and their tips joined in the centre of the circle. As they were bum-whipped, the furry girls stroked each other with their tongues and, through her blur of tears, Belle saw that all drooled, not with spit but with thick oily fluid that smelled of cunt juice. The girls moaned and squirmed, faces flushed, in apparent ecstasy at their bare-arse whippings. Belle's cunt juiced too, as she watched Linda's perineal cleft quiver and redden under lashes with the snake and the cruel precision with which the reptile's tongue flickered, stinging Linda at each stroke on her stiffened clitty.

Belle too, put out her tongue, longing to join the other girls in their tongue-wank, even though she knew it was in vain: she had only a normal girl's tongue, not the monstrous enhancements of the furry girls. The crack of lashes was broken by the squeals of each girl in turn, as her whipping brought her to orgasm. Belle's own whipping was so fierce that the tourmaline gems were dislodged from their nests on the whipthong and dropped like stools into her lake of come on the floor, except for one: an agonising stroke caught her right on her distended anus bud and she felt a tourmaline dislodge and stick at her bumhole. Clenching her bum and sphincter muscle, she sucked the gem deep inside her anus and held it there. At each further whipstroke, the electrified gem delivered an orgasmic shock at her anal root.

'Enhanced ferals are quickly addicted to the whip,' said Miss Budgen, continuing to lash Belle's bare buttocks. 'They must be whipped to orgasm frequently, or they cannot shed – just as a cow must be milked, if her udders are not to burst. But, if whipping is pleasure, how are these sluts to be punished?'

Crack! Crack! Crack! Crack!

'*Oh! Oh! Ahhhh . . .!*' Belle shrieked, as the whip wrapped itself twice around each haunch.

Her scream opened her mouth agape and her tongue protruded fully, like a hanged woman's. She felt its tip touch one, then another, of the hard wet tongues of the flogged ferals. The tongues seemed prehensile, sticking to her own and drawing it from her throat. She felt the whip again, cracking on full centre fesse, its smart now suffusing her body with submissive glow and she knew she had reached her plateau of serenity. She could no longer scream as her tongue was drawn to its full length by other tongues, stickily caressing hers. The stave's dagger in her cunt prodded sharp against her womb-neck at each jolt of the whip on her buttocks. Miss Budgen's fingers quickly pinched Belle's throbbing clitty, dipping in her cunt-bath of come.

'The trick,' said Miss Budgen, 'is to leave them an Achilles' heel, or rather, breast – a place that is not orgasm-sensitised and where whipping is truly painful. These two girls are here for punishment, not come-milking, and the whip on naked nipples causes them exquisite pain.'

Now, Belle's tongue felt torn from its roots, but of its own volition – a swollen and throbbing organ of pleasure, like her erect clitty. She joined the circle of tongues: hers, too, was a pink lizard, hard and sucking as she tasted the oily drool from the girls' lips. All tongues suddenly poked each other and Belle felt an electric shudder of pleasure, as though she had touched her own nubbin. Her tongue was a second clitty . . . her cunt flowed with come and she could not help peeing, the stream hissing acrid down her inner thighs to pool the floor, with her lake of cunt-juice. The whip descended on her bare, as Belle tongue-wanked with the moaning, pleasured girls, who writhed in a bath of orgasm from the flogging of their naked bottoms.

Crack! Crack! Crack! Crack!

'*Mmmm! Ahhhh . . .!*'

Beside her, Linda's bum-cleft was bright crimson as the snake whipped her cunt and hole. Kaa had removed one hand from her whirling bum and had it on her grossly extruded nubbin, wanking off, as she flogged Linda with practised flicks. The snake's tongue flashed on Linda's stiff clitty and Linda moaned in her come. Kaa's thighs dripped with her own cunt-oil and as her victim came, she continued to flick and pinch her own clitoris and rubbed her swollen pubic mound with the heel of her hand, pressing on the snake, visibly writhing and gnawing inside her cunt. She squeaked softly, as her come flowed in torrents and her belly heaved in her own climax. One sound was louder than all.

'*Ah! Ah! Ah! Uhhh . . .!*' Belle screamed, pissing herself in come-drenched orgasm.

# Memoir 6

Chinese girls have smaller feet, but Japanese girls are more elfin and have bigger, firmer bums. That's what Lee told me anyway. Susan's bum was firm, and in fact I was thinking about her all the way from the airport and getting wet remembering all the super comes I'd enjoyed from her stroking my bum-weals. I hoped Lee had a proper welcome party ready, for I was sitting next to Gary and just wanted to get that huge cock out of his pants and suck him off, but I couldn't really, as he was flying the helicopter. As soon as we landed at their house, Lee came to greet us, nude and with five of her frilly maids all wearing the most delicious costumes, with stockings and stilettos and everything. The house stood on a plateau of grey lava, a moonscape, with nothing for miles around, just like in the photos; but all around were gardens, three swimming pools and a lawn, irrigated from artesian wells – a real ideal home. I thought Lee had changed; for the better, if that were possible. Her tits and bum were bigger and firmer, her belly flatter and as we embraced, I felt a sort of silky fur all over her body. Her shaven cunt had the same silky fur, though it wasn't like normal pube-hair and I could see her clit, peeping quite big, though not yet erect, through the folds of her labia, which seemed bigger as well. I said as much and she clapped her hands in delight and said I should wait till her clit got stiff; and I said I hoped I wouldn't have to wait long, because mine was throbbing already at the gorgeous sight of her. I said I wanted to pee – naturally! – and Lee said Koo or Kee or

163

*somebody would attend me. One of the gorgeous little tartlets accompanied me to the bathroom and the girl knelt suddenly beside the bowl and placed the back of her head on the toilet seat. She didn't speak, but indicated I was to squat on her face! I was bursting for pee, so I did, and Lee came in halfway through my stream and began to finger her clit as my piss poured down the girl's throat. Afterwards, the girl licked my pussy dry, though it juiced again at once when Lee said I was to take part in the 'daily reckoning' as soon as we'd eaten. She said it would be a cute surprise. I went straight in for a nude swim and was joined by Lee and Gary; his cock always was a monster, but now it was like a shark in the water with balls the size of grapefruit. I thought, maybe it was the refraction of the water. What a silly! The five girls lined up to watch us, solemnly, as though longing to join us, till Lee invited two of them to do that. She winked at me. One of the Japs stripped in an instant and folded her clothes neatly, then jumped in. Her nude body was lovely, completely hairless, even at her cunt – I mean, it looked as if she didn't need to shave; she just didn't have any hair at all. But the other one burst into tears! Lee laughed and said she had earned extra punishment at the reckoning and that made her smile. Aha, I thought, a sub. Then Lee said she must strip, to earn punishment, even if she didn't go in the water. The girl stripped naked and she had hair like Lee, only far thicker and more like a sleek pelt of fur. Also, she had a cute little nubbin dangling from her spine like a toy tail. Well, we splashed around and played silly games, like racing for Gary's cock and so on – he was erect, by now – and I wondered where the swimmer girl was. She was right at the bottom of the pool at the deep end, with her legs wrapped round the back of her neck, ogling my cunt and bum quite unashamedly and wanking herself off! There were little air bubbles spurting from her arsehole. I started to wank myself, grinning at her because her slit was so big and red and her clit, even from here, was stiff like a little ruby palace under the sea . . . The furry girl was masturbating too, pinching her stiff clit as she stared at the wanking girl underwater and her come dripped into the pool, plop! plop!*

*plop! Like that. Then, she dipped her head, bending her spine right over and looped one leg around the back of her neck, while she began to lick and chew her own clitty! I was mesmerised. But I didn't get to come, because Lee said it was time for drinks and food, which were served on the patio by the frilly maids, minus the girl underwater. We were still nude and Gary was powerfully erect and we just let the sunset dry our skin, except that Lee wasn't wet at all. The girl must have been down there fifteen minutes, so I was worried and asked how long she could hold her breath, but Gary laughed and said that she wasn't holding her breath, she breathed through her asshole for all he knew and anyway, whatever goddam species they were, the maids were all airheads. He had a coarse sense of humour, sometimes. She emerged, dripping and scampered past us with a shy little smile and her tits bobbing and her cunt still swollen from her wank. There was a big cloud of oily come swirling in the pool and Lee said she liked the girls to masturbate there, as it 'boosted the water'. But they could only wank alone – if they were wanking together, they got too playful and 'went to the bathroom'.*

*I was itching to start some serious fun and regretting that I hadn't brought myself off during our swim, so I was glad when the reckoning started. Gary busied himself with video and disciplinary equipment and Lee showed me a schedule of misdemeanours and an accompanying tariff of chastisement. The punishments were ferocious! Lee said it was the only way to control them and at first I misunderstood, but realised later that they actually craved whipping as part of their genetic programme; so there had to be some order to it, otherwise Lee and Gary would be worked off their feet, or caning arms!*

*Lee was a great fan of old-fashioned whopping England, as she put it, and all the lovely formalities of corporal punishment. So she had this list in calligraphy, that she had drawn herself, with little drawings in the margin to illustrate the nature of the offence and what its punishment looked like. It was supposed to be medieval or something and gave me quite a laugh. 'For unseemlie behavior, 300 strokes of ye rod*

*on ye bared buttockes; for insolence, 200 lashes of ye scourge
on coynte bared, and 200 each on buttockes and bubbies
bared'* ... *that kind of thing. The drawings were very
detailed, showing oriental girls weeping and in bondage, with
their cunts and bums and titties striped, either by a
dominatrix, Lee, or a master, Gary, whose huge erection
they were obliged to worship as they were flogged. In real
life, as I was just about to learn, they needed little
encouragement.*

*Gary laid out the instruments of punishment and donned
black rubber trousers belted with a string and a hood, like a
hangman's, with his torso bare. Lee remained nude, but had
little gems at piercings in her nipples, quim-lips and anus
bud; even her clitty was pierced. The gems were milky and
were called tourmalines. Lee said that when heated, they
gave off a mild electric current – hence the gem pierced in
her clit and nipples – and changed colour with body heat. Lee
said they reflected the wearer's mood. Right now they were
pink. At last, I discovered where Gary's wealth came from.
He was a dealer in precious stones, and that was how he had
hooked up to these submissive oriental maids – because they
were used as couriers, from the gem mines of their home
island. They would transport the stones in their cunts and
arseholes! Not just the orifices, but they had such muscle
control that they could get ... right in there, as it were. That
was if they were travelling legally ... but Hawaii had so
much deserted coastline and was the USA proper, so there
were no further customs hassles. I didn't pry, as I understood
Gary's own indifference to where these gems and girls
actually came from. You don't look a gift horse in the mouth.*

*The chastisement tools were hand-crafted and almost
works of art. My own spring-cane looked humdrum in
comparison. I wondered what Mum would say! There was a
long, pearl-handled cane and Gary said the 'fish gals' made
useful pearl-divers to supplement his income, as they could
stay underwater almost indefinitely. The furry ones he called
'pussy gals'. There was a leather scourge, like a cat, only
with 18 tails, the thongs inlaid with split pearl; a bullwhip,
six feet long; various shorter 'clitty-canes', and so on. The*

equipment was very thoughtful. For bondage, there were hoods, cinchers, spiked collars, leg-irons, handcuffs and cunt-clamps; also surgical speculums, to hold the cunt and anus open for penetration. That was for free bondage. At the side of the room was a small stage, like a gallows platform, with a pole at each end. This overlooked Lee's throne, like an electric chair with a very high back and wide arms, with buckles on each and a single rail poking out from the top of the chair-back, so that it would be above the head of the sitter. The whole throne tilted backwards at an adjustable angle. There were also nipple-clamps on the top of the chair-back. Lee said that riding a rail was an old custom in the Wild West. A whore was whipped, sitting pantieless on a sharpened rail, with her legs and arms trussed so that the sharp bar pressed against her cunt, which took her whole weight.

The girls lined up for reckoning, each wearing only light caning pyjamas: pantaloons held up at the back by a drawstring, with a large aperture that left the buttocks exposed at all times. The girls were bare-breasted and barefoot. They seemed to enjoy the ritual as Lee read out the first punishment: it was to the girl who had wanked herself in the swimming pool and she was to take 100 strokes each with cane, scourge and bullwhip, on her bare buttocks. Lithely, she clambered onto the throne and placed her feet in the grooves by the ankle-cuffs, which Lee fastened. Her legs were fully stretched and her cunt pulled down over the protruding rail, which ended an inch from her cleft. The rail stuck her buttocks well up in the air and Lee ceremonially tugged at her drawstring, so that her caning pyjamas fell to her ankles. The other girls hissed, which I learned was their way of applauding. I looked at that juicy bum, all white and ripe for strokes and felt my cunt juicing. I didn't think it was against etiquette to begin masturbating, so I did, with slow wanks of my clitty, getting myself going for the furious wank I knew I'd have when I saw that bum reddening. Lee was tickling her own clit and Gary's bulge almost split his rubber pants. I said I hoped Miss Claw might get a turn at flogging the girl and was rewarded with a yes. The girl's nipples were

*clamped ferociously tight on the back of the chair and her*
*arms bent backwards almost to her nape, where they were*
*cuffed to a spiked collar which loosely fitted her, only with*
*the spikes on the inside so that any movement would hurt.*
*The nipple-clamps were spiked too, but were not clamped*
*loosely: the spikes dug right into the buds, which were*
*already erect and poking brick-hard out of their tiny spiked*
*cincher. Thus, the only support for her body was the rail*
*itself, which sliced deep in her cunt and obliged her to stick*
*her bum high. With the nipple clamps pinioning her, she*
*could not rest her belly on the chair-back.*

*Lee seated herself on the throne with her legs spread, so*
*that I saw she was already juicing with plentiful come and*
*her clitty was stiffened. Gary ascended the stage, standing*
*over the throne and began caning the girl's bare buttocks*
*with very hard swishes, at one-second intervals. The girl*
*twitched and her tits strained against the nipple-clamps – her*
*cunt began to drip come almost at once. Lee's mouth was*
*open and the girl's come fell right into her throat. She*
*swallowed it with lttle grunts of pleasure and some of it*
*slopped over her bare titties and stiff nips. I began to wank*
*harder, seeing Lee's own fingers at work and I knelt in front*
*of her and pushed her fingers out of the way with my lips,*
*then began to tongue her clitty. I paused often, to swallow*
*her own come, which was nectar. Above us, I heard the girl*
*squeal in orgasm and was reminded of Susan. She could*
*come, just at bare-bum caning. Lee's tourmalines were*
*glowing bright crimson as I tongued and her come almost*
*drowned me as I brought her off.*

*The girl took 100 with the cane and then Lee offered me*
*her place, while she scourged the girl's bum. Gary was to*
*have a rest; his pants came off and he sat in the throne before*
*me, so that on sitting, myself, I impaled my bumhole on his*
*monstrous cock. I had taken the precaution of lubricating my*
*cleft with my own come, so he sank in smoothly, right to my*
*root and I clutched his cock with the walls of my arsehole,*
*bouncing gently up and down on his shaft, while Lee began*
*the scourging of the girl's buttocks. The Jap maid's come*
*washed my mouth and throat as I was buggered by Gary.*

*Her come was sweeter even than Lee's and I drank eagerly. Lee was masturbating her clit as she whipped the girl and Gary needed no encouragement to diddle my own nubbin as I squeezed his bell-end inside my anus. I saw the point of the hood – he was an anonymous male animal, buggering me. God, there is something devilishly thrilling about taking a man's cock up the bum! Like a sinful place . . . He murmured something about coming in my cunt, but I squeezed his bell harder with my bum-root and began to milk him seriously, all the while swallowing great gulps of the Jap girl's come, which made my whole body tingle like my clitty. Gary was masturbating me hard and I could feel his cock tremble as he was about to spurt, so I squeezed harder and felt his spunk shoot right into my anal root. That is such a marvellous feeling, to have a bloke squirt his whole load of spunk right inside your bumhole and as his come jetted, I came too; a glorious orgasm that seemed to wash my whole body in pleasure and left me gasping.*

*After her 100 with the scourge, the girl's arse was black and purple and the bullwhip was still to come. The honour was given to me; Lee resumed her throne, with Gary upended on her lap, and his cock fucking her cunt upside down, while she drank girl-come. The bullwhip was very heavy and made a fearful crack as I flogged the Jap's arse and, watching Gary, who was stiff again, upended and pumping into his wife, I had the bright idea of whopping his bum too. I was Miss Claw, all right! This meant extra work, but it was worth it for the pleasure of seeing two arses squirm and redden at once. Lee said I should go easy on Gary, as he was only a poor male and couldn't take more than a few hundred, unlike us girls. When he was about to come again, the furry girl who had masturbated at the swimming pool darted forward and knelt, pleading; Gary withdrew his cock and plunged it into her throat and she drank all his come. I wanked myself to two more comes, by the time I had delivered the 100 to the girl on the throne-rail and then had a mad impulse to submit my own bum to whipping.*

*I had no time to change my mind, for I was seized and stretched between the two posts on the gallows platform,* strapped by ankles and wrists and splayed in an X. Lee placed a chamber pot under my cunt, to catch my come. It was awfully pretty – eighteenth-century Venetian, I think. The cane cracked on my bare arse and I thought, God, what have I let myself in for? But at the second stroke, my bum came alive, like a clitty or a man's bell-end [I suppose] and at the third cut I convulsed in orgasm again! Lee was caning my bum from behind and Gary took a shorter cane, standing in front of me for titty and cunt work. He alternated strokes to my nipples and right between my gash-lips, catching my clitty iself, usually. I didn't care – it was glorious; my whole whipped body was a clitoris, pulsing with pleasure. From time to time, Lee would drink from the potful of my come and after 150 or so strokes to bum, tits and cunt and several of my comes, she pressed it to my lips and I must have drunk a wineglass of my own cunt juice.

For the next girl, I reverted to Miss Claw. It was the 'pussy gal' who had drunk Gary's come and she was stretched between the posts, with me caning her bum and Gary gash-fucking from the front, while Lee buggered Gary with a strap-on. We swapped roles and chastisees all evening, and all the time, I felt the wonderful glow of the come I had swallowed and the tingling whole-body clitoral excitement I had first experienced with Susan on the plane. All the girls were flogged raw, with vicious black and purple welts all over their naked behinds, and pulled up their caning pyjamas to troop off to bed, flushed and squeaking at all the comes they had enjoyed. The next day, they were back in their frilly maids' uniforms – which left nothing to the imagination, bumwise! – and their arses shone fresh and white as new! My own was lovely and hard, like corrugated iron, while Lee's was not pure but her weals had faded very fast. Poor Gary was nursing a lovely sore crop of welts, though, where I had thrashed him. Mum would have been proud.

Anyway, I stayed a week with my friends, a lovely lotus-eating time of swimming, wanking, fucking and of course naked whipping. Lee was fond of teaching the girls 'come conrol' – lining them in a row, on tiptoe and fingertips, with their maids' skirts raised and knickers down to reveal their bums and caning them each with a dozen quickfire strokes, repeated and repeated. The girl with the driest knickers won a prize, which was an exra-hard caning for herself – when she could let her juice flow freely – and for her best friend. My suggestion of adding bladder control was most welcome, so the girls had to restrain themselves from wetting their knickers with pee. I can assure you it is very difficult for an excited woman to hold in her come, or for a whipped one to stop herself pissing. I learned more than Lee and Gary intended, but not everything. Lee herself seemed nervous when I broached the subject of the girls' always-fresh arses. She said that was their one totally private affair – that they had been 'come-enhanced' back home, far longer than Lee had and obviously I was just a beginner. My arse would stay hard, so that I could enjoy limitless canings – which I did, as well as dishing them out – but I would know, somehow, when it was time for 'fresh skin'. Lee had gleaned as much from the maids, who didn't speak much English, or pretended so. She herself would be mysteriously informed when she was ready, as though these sluts were somehow in charge! Gary, a mere male, was just a spunk-provider, like all mere males. The 'pussy gals' had to drink his come regularly, so he was kept virile, forcibly. All the maids could lick themselves clean; I mean bend their spines and lick their own cunts and bumholes, or indeed each others', a talent I envied . . .

I made it my business to befriend the girl who seemed brightest and most promising – the fishy girl I had seen immersed in the swimming pool, wanking off underwater. Her name was Kaa; we conversed mostly in sign language, and I learned the secret of where she came from. I was a bit naughty and said, if she told me, I would help her get back there as it seemed she missed her twin sisters – she was one of triplets. Not that Lee and Gary detained her – it was just that she craved being whipped and fucked and wanked off so much, she was frightened to return and find constant lashing unavailable. I promised to be there, waiting for her and that she would be lashed and wanked off as much as she could stand. Well, I'd known whip and come addicts before.

*It was a place called Furvert's Island, discovered by some ancient French tar and there were two of them apparently, but one was good and one bad – heaven and hell, she said, with good monsters and bad monsters, which I thought a bit odd; I mean, surely a monster was a monster either way? She came from the heaven one. I figured I would find some dynamite stuff there, for my doctorate in Social Darwinism, and videos and stuff for my Internet slave-ring and . . . who knows? I imagined selling bottles of live oriental girl-come, over the net! But I didn't tell Lee and Gary. I found out where this frog island was, in Micronesia and how to get there and after fond farewells – meaning whopping and anal or cunt penetration for all three of us – I set off, pretty bruised and sore in both my holes, but excited. I hoped there weren't any frogs there, or I would wave my magic wand [my cane] and turn them into proper frogs! Ha Ha, just my little joke.*

# 11

# Whipped Raw

Belle orgasmed three more times before her whipping was over, and Linda twice. In the closing dozen of her beating – Miss Budgen said she had taken 144 lashes and 156 would suffice, for the moment – Belle watched Linda's final come, though not under whip. Linda's cleft was a solid mass of blotchy puffed skin, where the asp had whipped her most tender parts and the serpent itself glistened with Linda's come oil. Kaa, who had masturbated constantly as she delivered the flogging, now stroked the shaft of her reptilian whip and hissed and spat. The snake's body at once went rigid, like an obscenely distended penis and Kaa climbed onto Linda's buttocks, clamping the girl's thighs with her own, to steady herself.

With a savage thrust of her hips, she thrust the stiff snake into Linda's anal shaft, paused when the anus was filled halfway and allowed Linda's squeals of pain to subside. Then, she delivered another thrust, which plunged almost the whole shaft of the snake-whip into Linda's arsehole and began to bugger her with a fierce jerking of her loins. Belle, squirming as her own bare was flogged, watched in horrified fascination as Kaa pressed her distended nubbin to the tiny tail-sprout at the base of Linda's spine and began to rub her clitty against this abnormal organ. Kaa's cunt flowed with come, all down Linda's cleft and buttocks, as her hips slammed again and again in more and more powerful thrusts, forcing the rigid snake to the full depth of the anus as she buggered the girl to squirms of agonised pleasure. Kaa's fingers snaked over Linda's belly and to her clit, which she took between finger and thumb and pinched hard, not ceasing her buggering of the squealing girl's bumhole. After only a few seconds of this frottage, Linda's squeals grew to a moan of climax and her own come oil joined her bugger's, streaming on the backs of her thighs. In the eerie half-light, her hemangioma seemed to have grown larger and spread down her thighs, covering her whole pubic hillock as well as her shoulders.

But Belle's final dozen took her down from her plateau and reduced her to a sobbing, squealing schoolgirl. Miss Budgen doubled her whip in two and whipped Belle with two tongues at close quarters, the beating now resembling a school caning. She raised her whipping arm high and the strokes of the shortened instrument concentrated on precise weals.

Vip! Vip! Vip!

'*Ahh! Ahhhh!*'

Belle screamed as she took three lashes right in the cleft, the handle of the whip – now one of its two tongues – smacking her squarely between the cunt lips and on her clitoris. There were three strokes to each haunch, three to top buttocks, three to the underfesses and, with Belle now sobbing and shuddering in near-hysteria, a final, merciless three cuts to her arse-cleft.

'*Ahhh! Oh! Oh!* Oh, God! Heavens, Miss, you are cruel . . .'

Miss Budgen laughed.

'I despise sluts like you,' she sneered and Belle's cunt gushed in an ecstacy of shame.

Kaa passed around the furry girls sponging their wet cunts, wringing the sponge into a pail after each cleansing. When she had finished, the pail brimmed with come and she presented it to Miss Budgen. Kaa's pubic mound now bulged and writhed as before, since her snake had returned to her pouch. All the ferals were released and purred with satisfaction as they felt the ridges on their whipped arses: sleek fur now gleamed with black and purple welts. The two mischievous ferals, who had taken whipping on the breasts, were released also but made to lick the entire floor clean of girl's pee and swallow every drop.

Linda's come was collected in a separate vial, which was only half full; Miss Budgen filled it from the pail, swirled the mixture and poured it into a large anal syringe. Belle shuddered as the giant syringe, full with oily liquid, came near her open bumhole. Kaa oiled the syringe with come from her own cunt, then inserted it at Belle's anus bud, making sure the anal bum-lips had clutched the glass tube before sliding it deep into Belle's bumshaft. Belle felt a tickling at her bumhole, which involuntarily clenched, but was powerless to prevent the invasion of the enema tube. The massive cylinder poked halfway up her channel, with Belle's buttocks writhing and sobs choking her throat. Suddenly, her anus yielded, the syringe plunged right to the hilt and Belle groaned as pleasure washed her anal chamber. She sighed deeply as the tube pulsed at her root, filling her abdomen with the hot come. The tube stretched her anus so wide that the pain seeped back, until Miss Budgen decided the fluid was now dispersed inside Belle and ordered the tube removed and both girls released. Only a few drops of oil were left in the syringe; Belle rubbed her raw, whipped buttocks and grimaced, though her belly was warm and bursting with injected fluid. She wiped the tears from her eyes, and embraced Linda, thanking her for the come that had washed her anus.

'Now what?' she murmured, her head lowered to Miss Budgen.

'You came to visit, so I suppose you must see,' said the dominatrix. 'You may be here for a long time, unless I decide to release you. Kaa came, as you did, and has not asked for release.'

Belle knelt and kissed Miss Budgen's webbed toes. After some seconds of licking, Miss Budgen kicked Belle's face and she slipped on the shiny film of come and sprawled on the rock floor. Then she kicked her wealed cunt and Belle cried out. She rose, unsteadily.

'Have I offended, Mistress?' she whispered. 'Must I be whipped again?'

175

Miss Budgen spat.

'*That* goes without saying. The question is, to enslave you now, or later? Follow me, sluts.'

The mine was on two levels: hard rock and aquifer. Miss Budgen and Kaa led, down twisting passages hewn from rock, sometimes barely large enough to pass without stooping. Always they descended and the temperature rose, until even Kaa's smooth body was beaded with sweat, while Belle and Linda were dripping heavily. The tunnel widened and suddenly they found themselves on a narrow gallery, overlooking a vast excavation domed with fluorescent rock. At the pit and walls of the cavern, furry nude girls were mining, supervised by overseers wearing the same striped skin-suits as Miss Budgen and carrying whips. If a girl seemed to idle, she was whipped across her bare breasts and the air was full of squeals. They scratched the earth with long unsheathed claws. Furry girls passed the other way, into the tunnel, with bulging cheeks and cunt-mounds. Miss Budgen said that the girls carried the gemstones in mouths, bumholes and pouches, for safety, lest a precious tourmaline be dropped. At the receiving station, their crevices were thoroughly searched and evacuated. Girls were also supervised at communal stooling, so that any girl foolish enough to swallow a gem, in the hope of retrieving it from her excrement, would be severely punished. A few miners wore white bras and these were girls guilty of attempted theft, whose bare breasts had been whipped with 500 lashes.

'Here are rubies, opals and emeralds,' said Miss Budgen. 'The French came here 400 years ago, led by a buccaneer called Furvert and found tin, on the upper levels. This chamber is our own excavation. Furvert did not know that where you find tin, you find gemstones. And of course, the lower level is flooded, so when the tin was exhausted, they left. The best gems, the tourmalines, are found in the earth strata submerged. Occasionally, on either level, a girl unearths a human rib and keeps it as her prize, to masturbate with.'

Miss Budgen made a moue of distaste.

'I do not visit their quarters, neither of the earth slaves nor the water slaves. I do not wish to observe their barbarities. My spies say there is some kind of cult . . .'

She grimaced again and patted her coiled whip. They descended to the floor of the pit, the size of a hockey pitch and Belle noticed that all the nude girls, even those whose hair was so fine as to be almost invisible, had unblemished bottoms. She recognised one or two of her tonguing partners, now sweating as they scrabbled for gems. Their bums too, though striped not an hour before, gleamed pure and unbruised as though they had never been whipped. They passed into another tunnel, sloping sharply downwards and the stink of earth now mingled with the scent of sea. Now, they were passed by hairless Japanese girls like Kaa, their nude bodies gleaming with water and the fronds of their anal anemones flapping at their bumholes. This anal excesescence was the only evidence of hair on their bodies, apart from the black, cropped scalp and several girls were completely bald, their scalps shining like their pubic mounds. Like the furry slaves, they had bulging cheeks and cunt-pouches.

'The Japanese discovered much,' said Miss Budgen, 'of which the so-called Dr Paine is ignorant. Beauty treatment for rich fools! Hah!'

She spat again, her oily, viscous saliva like female come.

'The only true beauty is slavery. The ferals who escape from Dr Paine's torture chambers find themselves already addicted to anal come injection and bare-buttock lashes. There is no palisade around my mineshaft, for any feral who wishes to leave, despite her enhancement and subjugation, is free to return to the wild. Each slave is enslaved by her own desires.'

Belle said she did not understand – the good Dr Paine a torturer? And, if that were the case, why did every feral not plead for enslavement in the mines? Why remain free at all, when there was whipping and come injection to be had?

'They can whip each other,' said Miss Budgen, 'and wank off to come. But embarrassment deters them. Ferals

177

are human girls and even the most debased human females have vanity. You have seen the good doctor's photo gallery – the "before" and "after" shots?'

Belle admitted she had, and Linda agreed.

'They are wrongly labelled,' said Miss Budgen drily. 'They are not before and after, they are after and before. The photos illustrate Paine's clumsy genetic experiments, horribly botched.'

Belle and Linda stared, horrified, at each other and at Linda's vivid red hemangioma.

'Escaped genetic experiments meet the remnants of the Japanese experiments in the last century and find themselves sisters under the skin. You know that Furvert's Island was abandoned by the Japanese scientists in 1945? Well, the experimental pleasure girls were left to run wild, in various stages of deformity or enhancement. Every scientific process has its side effects and every medicine can be overprescribed. The Japanese bred pleasure girls for their soldiers, after the Nazi Germans taught them their discovery of *in vitro* fertilisation. Their aim was a hairless girl with prehensile cunt and anus, buttocks and teats that craved long whipping. But they found that a longevity gene intruded. A genetically enhanced pleasure girl could remain a teenager until an advanced age.'

They entered another gallery, only a few metres above the underwater minefield, where pale bodies swam in shoals searching for tourmalines. They did not come up for air. Little bubbles spurted from their anus holes.

'Another curiosity of the Japanese,' said Miss Budgen, 'is their passion for seafood and all things fishy. A female with piscine attributes – so reasoned the scientists in the 1940s – must surely provide a Japanese soldier with his greatest sex pleasure. Not all of their research has been thoroughly decoded, for it was cleverly encrypted and, as well as this island, there was another Furvert's Island. The buccaneer Furvert logged two discoveries, the other island was valueless.'

The chamber narrowed to another cave, or tunnel, through which they could glimpse the ocean and a green speck in the distance, clouded in heat haze with a reddish tinge.

'That is the second Furvert's Island,' said Miss Budgen. 'However, it is unvisited, for we have deciphered that the Japanese conducted nerve gas experiments there. They called it the island of the chestnut blossom, which is the scent of male sperm. I believe they used a mixture of male sperm and enhanced female come juice, suspended in the inert gas argon. A superior hybrid, orgasm-enhanced by the very air she breathes! Yet there were no survivors of these experiments, since the enhancement was so intense that it destroyed those enhanced; and the island is taboo, for argon gas does not burn or dissipate. One stupid and disloyal scientist did go there, I believe, and never returned; or else Dr Paine, in her paranoia, abandoned her there – the female now scorned as Miss Claw. So, our ferals here either remain in the jungle, or come to the mine. I believe they are long past the desire for revenge on poor, deluded Dr Paine, but she has her uses and her fear of ferals is really fear of herself. There is another reason why ferals choose to remain in the wild. Genetic hybrids, like mules, are sterile. But, somehow, *ferals are able to breed.*'

'I am so confused,' said Linda. 'I have never heard Sakosha called Furvert's Island, nor was I aware of a second one . . .'

'Really,' said Miss Budgen. 'And you, Miss Puget?'

'Why, no, Mistress,' said Belle, lowering her head to lie, but then raising it, to stare straight into Miss Budgen's piercing blue eyes. 'I knew nothing.'

Slowly, Miss Budgen unzipped her skin suit and let it fall to the floor. Her nude body, smooth and hairless and with the massive firm teats, cunt-mound and buttocks quivering like huge white flans, stunned Belle to silence.

'You know you will be severely flogged if I find you are lying?' she said.

'Yes, Mistress,' said Belle.

'I must supervise the divers,' she said. 'You will obey Kaa at all times.'

Miss Budgen slipped into the water and disappeared amid the shoal of swimming girls. Belle and Linda watched uncertainly; after ten minutes, Miss Budgen had not surfaced once. There was a touch of fingertips to Belle's clit. Kaa twisted her mouth in a faint smile and nodded, then led the two girls back up the tunnel. She walked with a graceful sway of her bottom, which betrayed a jaunty air of office, and Belle wondered whether Kaa or Miss Budgen was enslaved.

In the smoky, still air of the slaves' den, the girl's wig of long, auburn curls made her sweat. The smoke came from candles in a circle, around a whipping post in the form of a carved and polished stone phallus, standing waist high. The girl was white and diminutive, her heavy wig seeming to capsize her elfin Japanese body. Like Kaa, or Geisha, she was hairless but very full at the buttocks and cunt-mound. She knelt in front of the phallus, hands cupping her buttocks apart in a submissive position, with her head bowed, allowing the auburn wig to cascade over her upper arms and jutting bare breasts. The slaves squatted in a circle, furry and smooth intermingled; paying little heed to Linda and Belle, the visitors who joined them. Their bodies were whipped, just like the other slaves', except that Linda and Belle still bore the marks of whipping, which caused a few hisses of surprise as every other bare bum was pure as white silk. The place stank of sweat, urine and fish; the floor was littered with leaves and live creepers, and hollows in the rock indicated bedding-places. The slave-girls hissed and chattered in Japanese, but fell silent as Kaa lifted the kneeling girl by both nipples.

She was draped over the helmet of the phallus, so that the gash of the stone peehole was directly beneath her cunt lips. The glans of the massive cock was split by two clefts instead of the single urethral gap, with an extra cleft on the front of the helmet, like a cloverleaf, or two-clefted arse. Her wrists and ankles dangled by the massive ball-sac, until they were encircled with separate rubber thongs, buckled tightly to imprison her on the penile shaft, with her limbs stretched and quivering. The mounds of her bared buttocks resembled the glans of a giant phallus, with her cleft the slit of the peehole. Kaa lifted a thin, short cane with a sharp quartzite gem embedded at the tip. She stepped well back, with her arm extended and the cane hovering over the naked buttocks. There was a crack, as the first lash of a bare-bum caning stroked the girl's skin. A second stroke and a third, followed almost at once, and then there was a steady Vip! Vip! Vip!, as the girl took her caning on bare.

Kaa's caning arm scarcely moved as the chastisement was effected by wrist alone, changing slant and direction as she whipped the girl's arse, but striking only with the cane's tip. She worked on each fesse for two or three minutes, shifted to the other, then shifted again after welts had formed. The girl's crack clenched slightly as the pink darkened on her wealed arse, but she did not whimper or cry and there were only a few wriggles of her bum, when the cane landed twice on the same welt. Come oil flowed from her gash and fell inside the peehole of the great stone phallus, although some of it slipped over the glans, moistening it to a shine; the phallus seemed to glow as the girl's whipped nates trembled over it, anointing the rock with her come.

After over 100 strokes of the cane, Kaa stepped back to reveal, and admire, her art. Each bare buttock bore the letter 'P' etched in deep, but minute, crimson welts. The slave girls' hissing grew to a tumult. Kaa released the girl from her wrist-thong, leaving her secured by the ankles. The girl rose of her own accord, until her spine was vertical. Kaa picked two long creepers from the floor and hurled them up, looping them in the groove of a knobbed protrusion in the stone wall. One end of each creeper was tied around an ankle and the girl stretched her arms in a vee shape, bowing her head to bare her shoulders. Her wig-hair fell over her breasts and Kaa pulled on the tendrils until they were tight, then knotted the other ends around the girl's wrists, stretching her body in a position for flogging on the naked back.·

A second pair of lianas were looped around the knob but, before fastening them, Kaa affixed metal clamps to one end of each. She delved into the wig-hair that covered the girl's breasts and withdrew each nipple in turn, to clamp it into the pincer. When both nipples were clamped, she pulled hard on the tendrils until they twanged like violin strings, and quickly knotted them around the girl's ankles. The thongs made her back arch, with her head still bowed, but her breasts stretched like tongues nuzzling her chin and the nipples distended to almost the same length as the white teat-skin. The stretching of her body lifted her hairless cunt a few inches from the peehole of the stone phallus, still tightly gripped by her tethered ankles.

Kaa picked up a bundle of creepers from the rock floor and wrenched them from their roots to fashion a long quirt of a dozen or more thongs. These creepers were thin and hard, like ivy stems, and whirred as she swished the air beside the girl's marked bottom. Now the feral slave-girls' hissing bcame an audible, though distorted word: *poot* . . . *poot* . . . *poot* . . . chanted hypnotically, over and over and rising in crescendo, as Kaa raised and aimed the whip, lashing the girl's bare back. The whip crackled and left vivid weals, almost at once. Kaa delivered a second and third stroke, as the chanting – *pooot* . . .! – continued, and it was clear to Belle that this was a sacrificial scourging. Every one of the slave-girls began to finger her clit, slowly and solemnly, as though masturbation was part of the sacred whipping. Belle's own cunt was juicing with heavy come and her nubbin was stiff as brick, as she watched the girl shudder under the whipping of her naked back and shoulders. Her finger, too, crept to her swollen clitty and she began to masturbate.

'Linda!' she gasped. '*Pute* . . . Don't you remember? Heinz's story of the flogged French girl who collaborated with the Germans, her bum marked with a P . . .?'

Linda was masturbating faster than Belle and frowned, not understanding. Belle remembered Linda hadn't been there, on the nude beach. But Heinz had been Belle's lover, as his forebear in the German army had taken poor Josette . . . and so many other women. Were they sex slaves, or sex goddesses? Belle's cunt tingled, as she imagined being fucked by virile male after virile male, strapped to a whipping post, perhaps, with her come collected by scientists and her bum raw from caning to the hundreds of strokes.

Belle felt a finger stroking her perineum. It was Linda's. The finger passed from anus bud to wet cunt and back. Linda's fingertip, oiled with Belle's come, slid into the anal cavity. Belle shifted, parting her buttocks, and Linda's whole finger slid easily into the elastic bumshaft, its nail sawing at her anal root. She began to finger-fuck Belle's anus and her first finger was joined by another and then, packing her bumshaft to the brim, a third. Belle imagined Heinz again, with his fellows, all with massive cocks surrounded by forests of flaxen pube-curls and now, the first – not Heinz, who must fret as he awaited his turn! – had his glans at her bum-bud, was poking into her, and the full penile shaft stroked mightily until her entire anus was filled with hot muscle. Her come flowed and her clitty throbbed madly, as another cock took her from the front, the penis plunging brutally into her swimming cunt, both men fucking her hard in arse and gash until the whipping-post was slippery with her come and pee . . .

'Ah! Ah! *Ahh!*' Belle yelped in tiny squeaks, as she masturbated to a full, pulsing orgasm.

The slave-girls began to caress each other on the buttocks and at once, their hissing turned to gasps as they too wanked off to copious come, the tendrils and leaves seeming to writhe in delight as they hungrily soaked up the dripping cunt-juice. Linda slowly withdrew her fingers from Belle's anus and began to wank her stiff clitty with them, bringing herself rapidly to her own whimpering climax. The flogged girl, shuddering under Kaa's relentless whip, now had a back entirely covered in welts with not an inch of white skin to be seen and Kaa descended, to whip her thighs and calves. These, too, were soon dark with weals and Kaa whipped the soles of her feet, which wriggled far more than her buttocks. The arse marked with dual 'P' now seemed lily-pure compared to the rest of her raw skin. Kaa passed to the girl's front and recommenced the whipping on her teats, cunt and belly. The crooning slave-girls masturbated continuously and Belle envied them their orgasmic power, though she too felt another come well, inside her gushing cunt. The whip striped the girl's distended breast-skin and clanked as it struck the nipple-clamps, between which were squeezed the buds of the nipples. These too were thrashed raw and then Kaa worked on the naked cunt-mound and the tops of the thighs. Come-oil dripped faster and faster from the flogged girl's cunt into the peehole of the stone phallus. Kaa, too, had thighs glistening with her flow of come.

When the girl's entire body was dark purple with weals and it seemed she had no more skin left to whip, Kaa returned to the buttocks. The circle of slave-girls inched hungrily forward. Kaa bent and opened a tap at the cleft of the stone ball-sac and at once, a fine spray of come began to spurt in a fountain from the peehole, to drip down the shaft of the penis and on to the stone balls. The slave-girls knelt and began to lick the come from balls and cock, hissing with pleasure and now masturbating each other's distended clits, the sleek fur or bare porcelain of quivering thighs glistening with cunt juices. Suddenly, there was a flash of dark skin: from the peehole of the phallus, an electric eel emerged, tail first, and shot straight into the flogged girl's cunt, inserting its body until only its head remained in the peehole. The eel's body began to writhe and twitch inside the girl's cunt and her come became a torrent. Kaa applied the whip to her bare, now frantically squirming buttocks, until they melded in the purple of the rest of her skin. The girl began to drool and her torso arched, shuddered and writhed, with gurgling squeals growing louder and louder in the back of her throat.

*Poot* . . .! *Poot* . . .! hissed the masturbating slave-girls. Belle and Linda were both masturbating, too, as though their wanks of minutes before were long past. Belle looked at the giant phallus and knew it reminded her . . . of a boyfriend's cock? No . . . the monstrous, distorted penis of one of the demons in Geisha's Japanese comic strip! Her come flowed over her wrist as she thumbed her clit and balled three fingers, punching her uterus deep in the sopping walls of her cunt and imagining herself back in the scented French pine forest, by the surf and dunes, buggered and cunt-fucked and whipped raw by endless legions of virile young blond men ...

Suddenly, the flogged girl screamed and her whole body shuddered, the buttocks squirming as though jolted by electricity. Her nipples wrenched loose from their clamps, but her spine arched upright so that she did not even require the support of her wrist-ropes.

'Ah! Ah! Ah! Ah! ...'

They were unmistakably the sounds of orgasm, an orgasm so incredibly long and powerful that Belle and Linda both whimpered, as they wanked their raw nubbins rapidly to a new come. As the girl writhed in climax, the eel's body disappeared entirely inside her cunt, whose lips closed on it like a vice. The girl's flogged skin began to peel from her body, first at her neck, then splitting asunder, neatly, down her spine and arse-cleft, then falling from her legs and feet and arms, until her whole purpled skin lay neatly in one piece, on the ball-sac of the stone phallus. Her bare body shone white as porcelain. The slave-girls began to lick the new skin until it was glistening with come from the fountain. A shadow fell over Belle and Linda, and both girls paused from their renewed wanking, to look up at Miss Budgen, zippered again in her own second skin.

'So, you have witnessed your first shedding,' she said. 'I wonder if the sperm god of their imagination will ever come, in answer to their sympathetic magic? He is supposed to live in the forest, where he breeds with ferals. Of course, if they had him, they would not have sought the mineshaft. Now, I wonder if I should enslave you, or let you beg for enslavement later.'

'Please, Miss – with your permission, Belle – I beg for it now,' Linda blurted.

'Belle is in no position to permit anything,' snapped Miss Budgen, 'as you are in my domain. Will Dr Paine miss you? I dare say she will, and her intrusion would be a further nuisance.'

Her fingers stroked the blotch of Linda's hemangioma, then suddenly delved at Belle's soaking cunt and pinched her perineum, anus ring and lower buttocks. Belle's anus thirsted for more of the come injection. She lifted her leg and saw the unmistakable blush of a hemangioma beginning to spread in her arse-cleft.

'Linda may stay,' said Miss Budgen. She is ripe. You, Belle, may go, after I have branded you my slave. Then, I know you'll be back.'

She nodded; Kaa leapt on Belle, pinioning her, and Linda helped her hold Belle's legs apart.

'Don't worry,' said Miss Budgen, unzipping her skin suit and showing her massive teats shiny with sweat, the nipples like stiff red chimneys. 'I'm going to hypnotise you, so you won't feel a thing . . .'

She began to sway her breasts, and Belle was mesmerised by the whirling of her nipples. Slowly, she slipped into a trance. She awoke in the shadow of a eucalyptus tree, outside the mineshaft and by the whipped girl's inert, though juicing, body. Starting with fear, she inspected her body for brand marks. There were none; nor was there the expected pain, save for a tingling at her clit and the neck of her womb and a strange stimulation at the root of her anus, which filled her with longing pleasure. She gasped, finding that her clitoris had been pierced and a tourmaline inserted, which would press forever on her nubbin, emitting its faint surge of electricity as it fluoresced to her body heat. She explored both her holes and found that she was similarly pierced; a smooth gemstone placed at the very neck of her womb and at her anal root. Miss Budgen's 'branding' was thus to keep her slave's loins in constant sexual tension and bring her back to the mineshaft, to beg for whipping and orgasmic relief . . .

As Belle staggered, still nude, into the sunlight towards the jeep, she remembered the likeness of the stone phallus, with the twin-clefted fesses at its helmet. It was the penis which had pleasured her, ages ago, on the nudist beach in France. It was that of the German, Heinz.

# 12

# The Juicing Room

'You have been a naughty schoolgirl, haven't you?' said Dr
Paine, sympathetically. 'So, I'm afraid you'll have to be
punished – severely, this time.'

'I meant no harm, Doctor,' pleaded Belle, her voice
muffled by her own piss-soaked panties.

'Heaven knows what you might see, or imagine, next,'
said Dr Paine. 'I did advise you – "all in good time" –
didn't I? But girls are headstrong, and won't listen, so I
suppose your bare buttocks must be caned, right to the
bone.'

She spoke as casually as if inviting Belle to a cup of tea.

'I don't think you'll be needing your caning pants for a
while, so, if you don't object, I'll remove them,' she added.

'I do not object, Doctor,' Belle whispered.

Belle was already nude from the waist up, and now she
felt the cotton slide down her legs to her splayed calves,
leaving her bottom bare.

'That's the spirit,' said Dr Paine. 'And you shan't mind
if I masturbate, as I watch Sushi cane you. She is so much
stronger than I, and will hurt you more.'

'No, Doctor,' said Belle, 'I shan't mind.'

Dr Paine and Sushi, who revealed unexpected muscle,
had strapped her to a flogging frame like an iron bedstead,
with a single curved strut at its centre which raised Belle's
loins and bum for chastisement, with the narrow metal
biting her belly. Belle still had to strain, to support her
back and legs. Her wrists and ankles were cuffed at each

corner and her panties formed a sloppy gag. After stripping her, Dr Paine had ordered her to piss in her panties before their removal and her ritual, unnecessary donning of caning pants. Beneath the frame was a runnel and the six adjacent, but empty, frames had similar gutters, all draining into an unseen tank. This was the juicing room, where miscreant nurses' come was collected for later injection to the guests. Already, Belle's come was dripping into the runnel. Sushi was handed a rattan cane and ordered to position herself several paces behind Belle's raised bottom, as she was to deliver the caning at a run. The mute Japanese girl obeyed; she wore a frilly maid's uniform, with very high skirt and panties and thong knickers for freedom of movement. She was permitted to remove her shoes, one of which Dr Paine balanced on Belle's head.

'Your caning will hurt you very much, Belle,' she said, 'but no matter how much it hurts, you must not let the shoe be dislodged, as I would be very cross. Poise, Belle, is all.'

Belle asked what punishment could be worse than that she had already earned.

'Oh dear,' sighed Dr Paine, 'I do hope I am not obliged to show you . . . yet.'

At a signal from the doctor, Belle's caning started. Belle heard Sushi's stockinged feet padding, then racing, on the floor, towards her defenceless bare behind, then the whistle of the rod and the vip! as the cane bit her buttocks and the searing flash of pain across her taut bum-skin, making her gorge rise and her fesses clench hard. Belle moaned.

'I shall not count strokes, Belle, for your caning shall continue until you wish it to stop,' said Dr Paine. 'And, when you have signalled you can take no more, the caning shall still continue.'

Vip!

Belle gasped and her fesses began to squirm. The second stroke was on the tender top of the buttock, beneath the noticeable growth of her spinal nubbin into a minute tail.

Vip! Vip! Vip!

The third, fourth and fifth also lashed her top bum. Belle opened her mouth to scream, but the breath was knocked from her by two hard cuts to the underfesse and a vertical cleft stroke, slamming on her exposed cunt and anus.

Vip! Vip! Vip!

'*Ughh* . . . Oh! *Ohhh!*'

'Only eight strokes, Belle,' said Dr Paine, 'and your bottom is squirming like a cane virgin's. I must say you are marking prettily.'

'They are very tight, Doctor,' Belle sobbed.

'One of Sushi's talents, on the rare occasions when she is permitted the pleasure of caning, as well being caned. I know of your improper visit to Miss Budgen's domain. Where is Linda?'

Vip! Vip! Vip!

'Oh! Oh! *Ahh* . . . L–Linda elected to stay, Doctor.'

'Linda, a traitor?'

Vip! Vip! Vip! Vip!

Belle took four in rapid succession, to the soft flesh of each haunch, the cane slicing almost up to her belly. For these rapid strokes, Sushi made her run for the first impact, then delivered further strokes in alternate forehand and backhand, twirling her body in a blur.

'*Ahhhh* . . .! Ahhhh! Ah! *Oh, God* . . . I don't know, Doctor.'

'You'll have to do better, Belle. Take your time. We have all day for you to squirm.'

Vip! Vip! Vip! Vip!

'*Urrghhh! Oooh! Ah! Ah!*'

'What happened at the mineshaft, and what did you observe?'

Vip! Vip! Vip! Vip! Vip!

'*Ah! Ah! Ah! Oh, God, please* . . .'

'Vip! Vip! Vip! Vip! Vip!'

Belle sweated, with the effort of keeping the stiletto shoe balanced on her head. Her squirming buttocks seemed seared by molten lava and she could not remember a worse caning, nor one which caused her bare skin to smart so. Each cut made her whole body jerk against her restraints, yet still she kept her head raised and the shoe balanced; and as Sushi retreated for her next strokes, Belle heard the drip of her own come, faster and faster, in the juicing runnel.

'Your wet cunt betrays your pleasure, Belle,' said Dr Paine, moving in front of Belle's head and parting her gown, to reveal her own naked breasts and gash, with her fingers slowly and luxuriously masturbating her nipples and hard extruded clitty.

Why was the doctor so insistent? As though the mineshaft were some enemy fortress and not part of the Paine Foundation at all.

Vip! Vip! Vip! Vip!

'Oh! *Ooh* . . .'

*Bare buttocks caned right to the bone . . .*

Sushi recommenced single strokes, from runup.

Vip!

'*Ahhh!* Ohhh . . .' Belle sobbed, her voice choked and broken.

'You met Miss Budgen,' said Dr Paine. 'There are some foolish girls here who believe that the despicable Miss Claw is still on Sakosha . . . that she never left the island at all.'

Vip!

'Oh! Oh!'

'There are some who say that Miss Budgen is Miss Claw.'

Vip!

'No . . . No . . .'

Vip!

'Speak, Belle. Submit,' purred Dr Paine. 'Your voice will make me climax, just as your squirming bum makes her juice with lovely wet come. Strokes to the cleft, now, please, Sushi.'

Vip!

'*AHHHH* . . .'

Belle screamed through her piss-soaked panties gag, as a stroke took her right on anus, in gash, and the cane's tip on the clitoral nubbin. Her cunt was flowing with hot come as the agony pulsed through her body.

190

Vip!

'*AHHHH* . . .!'

Another cunt-stroke raked her slit and Belle felt her belly give way and a flow of hot piss join her flood of come. Her head jerked and the shoe fell off, damming the runnel.

Vip!

'*AH! AH! God! Ohhh* . . .'

After several more agonising slices right in her gash and perineum, Belle blurted out the whole truth. Dr Paine masturbated as she spoke and climaxed when she described the whipping of the girl at the stone phallus. Her own copious come joined Belle's in the flowing runnel.

'Sympathetic magic, Belle – just as we take the whip ourselves, in the hope of avoiding the whips of demons. But don't you realise, foolish girl – Budgen's injection has undone my work on your anus. Your buttocks have been desensitised, and that is why this caning hurts so much.'

'But . . . Dr Paine . . .' Belle sobbed, 'I *want* to be hurt . . . to *feel* the pain of naked whipping.'

As Belle heard her own submissive words, she cried out in joy as her cunt spasmed in a long, throbbing orgasm. Dr Paine waited until Belle's cunt lips had ceased to flutter.

'You offer me no alternative,' said Dr Paine, icily. 'It seems that to avoid being Budgen's specimen, you must become my own. Kaa, Geisha and now Linda, have escaped me, but you shan't, Miss Puget.'

At her mention of Kaa and Geisha, Sushi's eyes flashed in sudden icy hatred.

'The shedding of buttock-skin through caning, and the resulting tolerance of caning and multiple orgasm under the lash, are valuable enhancements,' Dr Paine said. 'But that is only step one of my guests' enhancement. You are familiar, Belle, with the techniques of cloning – the Japanese search for the omnipotent, undifferentiated cell. Well, *I deciphered their research*. My cocktails of come juice can speak to the omnipotent cell, anally introduced, and cause glandular variations in growing organisms at will. The brain cells too can be accessed, for memory implant or modification. There is no limit to a woman's strengthening, like my perimeter guards, or the sun-proof scales of the lizard-women who work the fields. Even such frivolities as changing the shape of her nipples, or clitoris, or the colour of her hair, at will! If you were X-rayed, Belle, you would find that your removed appendix is already regrowing. In time, it would have been an internal clitoris, mobilised by a mere contraction of the belly, to allow a female unlimited orgasmic pleasure. Our brute sperm-carrying ancestors worshipped *females* as their goddesses. Our power of self-pleasure awed them . . . and that is what my successful guests take with them, back to their males: skins and internal organs which are clitorally sensitive, female pleasure thus enslaving the male. Healing is power, Belle, and not just with renewed breasts, cunts and bums, but with *new ones*, from my fungible organ banks.'

'Kaa, Geisha, and Sushi . . .?' Belle gasped.

'Clones, of course. From genetic material preserved after the Japanese scientists departed. Some early experiments were not entirely successful . . . and of course, fungible organ banks can be punishments, as well. Miscreant nurses do not always enjoy the hideous deformations of the sex organs which a hostile injection can induce, and which I fear you are now about to experience, Belle. But think of the pleasure you will provide as a lookalike for Bluebird and others to come, enhanced by your constantly renewed tits, fesses and *multiple clitties . . .*'

She pressed a buzzer, and heavy boots were heard shortly afterwards approaching from the lab. Suddenly, Sushi lifted the rattan and slashed Dr Paine's bare breasts. Dr Paine screamed and slipped in the puddle of come and piss which had spread from the runnel, dammed by Sushi's shoe. The steps were almost at the door by the time Sushi, her bare foot squashing Dr Paine's face in the come puddle, had released Belle from her bondage. Together, the two women fled through the far door and found themselves in the aquarium. Sushi beckoned Belle to follow her and Belle did so, trying to knot her caning pants around her waist but abandoning the attempt at modesty. Instead, she used the caning pants as a bag, on impulse, scooping up the three entire shelves of juice jars. The two women ran into a corridor, and hauled themselves through a window just in front of the rubber-clad, crop-headed guards. They were on the beach. They ran past the astonished nudists, Bluebird amongst them, and plunged into the sea, swimming away in the rapidly deepening water with firm strokes, Belle holding her bag of specimen jars in her teeth. Behind them, she heard Dr Paine screaming at her guard-girls and promising to find them and capture the fugitives, wherever they hid.

'You'll never come back alive from *there*!' she taunted. 'Nobody survives heaven!'

Heading towards the second Furvert's Island, now radiant in the glow of sunset, the two girls swam on.

The second island of Furvert was approached by a shallow strand, so that after swimming for four kilometres, the girls found themselves with an extra kilometre to wade. They took turns carrying the bag of specimen jars, Sushi being, if anything, more protective of it than Belle, who had snatched it partly to spite Dr Paine and partly for possible leverage over her. The whole island was ringed by pure white beach and Belle flashed back to her nudist days on the dunes in France. *I've come home*, she thought.

'Anyone here will certainly see us,' said Belle, as the water lapped at her nipples and tongueless Sushi nodded agreement.

This second island was flat, but covered in dense jungle, almost to the shoreline, with a strange hazy mist that seemed to creep around the bases of the trees, ferns and gaudy flowers, like the smoke of dry ice on a stage. As they neared, with the water tickling their pubic mounds, the powerful scent of the jungle overcame the sea air: in addition to the shady blossom of flowers and the stench of decaying vegetation, there was an unmistakable aroma of chestnut blossom, mingled with that of female come. Both girls blushed and giggled, and Belle explained what a chestnut blossom was and how its scent was like the scent of sperm.

They waded up the shallow white beach and the gaseous mist seemed to creep down the sand to greet them. Belle looked down and saw her feet a blur. When they stepped onto grass, then ferns and finally onto a matted carpet of tendrils, the mist covered her to her ankles. Suddenly they were in shadow, the sun filtering through the clustered treetops only in thin, dazzling rays, so that they seemed to be in a cave of bright stalactites. The mist seemed to claw, like a sentient force writhing at Belle's calves, as though creeping up to embrace her; and Sushi's body was also enveloped. Belle felt giddy and tingling and Sushi opened her mouth wide; she clutched the cotton sack, pressing it against her loins. Belle felt her cunt begin to gush with unexpected come juice and electricity flooded her spine, stiffening her nipples to rocks.

The weals on her whipped bottom began to pulse with energy, like gashes of raw clitoral flesh on her bum-skin. The tourmalines pierced at her clit, anal root and womb, sent jolts of electric pleasure through her; and the clit-gem glowed fiery crimson. Her belly shook and she heard herself cry, over the whistles and croaks of insects, as her body was washed in sudden, shattering orgasm. Sushi's shrill yelps of pleasure indicated the same experience. Belle panted, as much in surprise as in pleasure. Her foot caught a tendril, stretched between two trees, and her panting turned to shrill cries of dismay as there was a swish and a net sprang from the ground, trapping the two girls. They were bundled high in the air to dangle helplessly, as naked girls, some furry and some smooth, crept from hiding and scrutinised their captives. Their skins glowed, changing tint from pink to gold to crimson as they hissed in excitement, and their tails stood trembling like erect penises above bulbous, sleek bare buttocks.

The ferals were not uniform of appearance. Hair colours varied from snow-blonde to jet and the bodies from slim to muscular. Many were deformed, with webbed fingers or buttocks, arses with no cleft, but a plain swollen sheet of bum-skin, and some even dangled miniature penises with tiny ball-sacs beneath their tails, or from the finny lips of

194

their bumholes. Some had a single leg, which ended in a stump above the knee. But all were distinguished by enhanced, even deformed extrusions of clitoris and startling enlargements of cunt, buttocks and breasts, as though these sexual lures had been outrageously grafted onto the shapes of smaller women. They assumed, in Belle's eyes, a sexual potency and magic, like totems worn as parts of the feral bodies. One bare girl, very elfin but with huge breasts and derriere, a vastly extruded clitoris and cropped black head-hair, seemed to be the leader. They took Belle and Sushi, still wrapped, to their village.

It was a cluster of open huts, roofed in palm leaves and grouped around a central clearing. Although the clearing was girt with palms, jacaranda and other plants jostling for light, with fronds dangling and ground creepers that seemed in constant invasion of the human space, the air was heavy with the scent of eucalyptus. Two giant, moisture-sucking eucalyptus trees dominated the clearing and kept the jungle and the strange ground-mist at bay. The gas hovered into the clearing for about a metre, then stopped, shivering as though afraid. The trees stood an armspan apart, with branches intertwined as though in love, or combat. Their foliage shaded a large stone, milky-green and carved in the shape of a phallus. The glans of the penis bore words, evidently carved when the stone had been in its original boulder shape, with the phallus hewn around them to give them prominence. The inscription was in old French. The girls were loosed from their net and imprisoning tendrils, still rooted to their trees, were knotted around their necks. Belle was able to decipher the polished words:

*'Lieu maudit beni*
*Con est noyade*
*Garde semence a jamais*
*Ciel enfer de jouissance*
*Femme fourrure fouet – JF'*

Sushi looked at Belle for explanation and Belle translated into English, which she hoped the girl understood.

'It says, "Accursed blessed place, Cunt is drowning, Keeps sperm forever, Heaven hell of pleasure, Woman fur whip"' Belle said, 'and the signature "JF" must mean Jean Furvert, who discovered these islands. *Jouissance*, in French, means either enjoyment, or sexual orgasm . . .'

The girls were given food and drink, which they took, squatting in the clearing with their new companions. Bound by their neck-fronds, they had no means of escape since the forest itself was their captor. And the girls seemed in awe of Belle, rather than contempt. The specimen jars were removed from Belle's caning pants and placed around the sacred rock, like icons. She and Sushi were in the centre of the circle of squatting girls, who watched them eat, with Sushi swallowing cold broth: the ferals understood she had no tongue.

The ferals crouched in their circle like dogs, each girl's face sniffing at her neighbour's cunt. Belle had a coconut shell full of squashed vegetables, which tasted vaguely medicinal, but which she devoured while the girls themselves feasted. Each girl's cunt-pouch contained a cargo of baby eels, which emerged from her hole wriggling and sauced in gash oil, to be sucked up by the girl behind her. A dark, mushy substance was sucked likewise from the girls' anuses and Belle was revolted when portions of both these foodstuffs were placed in her coconut shell. The anal substance was a puree of mushroom and she swallowed it, with the live eels. When she drank water from another shell and set both shells aside, the ferals hissed loudly, acclaiming her:

'*Meekro . . . meekro cambak . . . weekam meetret . . .!*'

Their hair changed from rusty brown to shimmering gold, then to black and pink, the tribe of ferals a rainbow of joy. Belle suddenly understood their mangled words:

'*Miss Claw – Miss Claw come back – Welcome, Mistress!*'

A new orgasmic pleasure began to seep through her body, afire with the tourmalines piercing her organs of womanhood. She bowed, and opened her arms, accepting her tribe's welcome. She did not resist as furry arms clasped her waist and raised her until her cunt lips touched the top of the gleaming tourmaline, which at her cunt's touch, began to pulse and glow a brighter green. Her arms and legs were splayed and her ankles and wrists bound with fronds to the twin eucalyptus trunks, suspending her nude body with her back and buttocks to the throng of ferals, who retreated to the edge of the clearing until their ankles were immersed in the swirling, sperm-coloured gas. Each girl had her palm covering her gash and was masturbating. Belle's clitoris was stiff and throbbing, pressed against the warm, pulsing stone, which made shivers of pleasure course through her as though electrified by the phallus. Already, Belle's cunt was dripping come onto the glans of the gem penis, as she awaited her whipping.

She watched as Sushi was bent over and her anus presented; the ferals' leader paused in her masturbation, ceremonially picked one of the specimen jars, and emptied its contents into a whorled conch shell which she oiled with her own come. Sushi parted the cheeks of her bum and the already wide aperture of her anus enlarged itself to a mouth. Her face glowed, radiant with joy, as the conch shell was upended and thrust all the way into her bumshaft until the shell disappeared and the anal lips closed again around it in a jagged pucker.

Belle stifled a gasp as the first stroke of her whipping took her unawares, hard across the bare back. The whip felt like leather, but she could not see which feral was whipping her. The leader was still crouching over Sushi's body, now masturbating both her own and the Japanese girl's clitty, with either hand. The second lash knocked the wind from Belle and stung her shoulders, to be followed almost at once by a third, midway down her back. The whip was heavy and made a resounding crack in the clearing. Tears sprang to her eyes at the smarting agony of her bare back, but her flow of come increased, dripping from her swollen gash onto the phallus.

It was pulsing and glowing with eerie light beneath her, seeming to respond to each stroke of her flogging and

197

Sushi now knelt with the ferals' leader, each with tongue buried in the other's cunt, gamahuching and masturbating each others' clitties with flicking fingers, their bellies cupping the stone balls of the carving's base. Belle counted 50 searing whipstrokes on her naked back, each buffetting her hard, so that she writhed on her ropes between the treetrunks, which swayed at her shudders. Then, she ceased counting, her back a mass of welts and Belle knew that the whip would descend soon to her already wealed buttocks. She cried out, as the whip took her right at top buttock again and again, before proceeding to harsh stripes on the haunches. Only when Belle was sobbing uncontrollably from the smarting to those areas, did the whip apply itself to her full central buttock-skin and then the underfesses, each stroke relentless, mechanical and expert. Her whipper knew how to impose the maximum pain from the main thong of the whip, then add extra agony with a cunning flick of the tip.

'*Ahhhh!*'

It was at the first lash between her thighs, taking her full on the wet cunt lips and exposed hard clitty, that Belle finally screamed. She did not stop screaming, even when her attention was distracted by a rustling in the branches of the eucalyptus trees, just above her juddering head; but her mouth hung open to scream and her howl of agony was mingled with astonishment. Through eyes blurred by tears, she saw a monstrous serpent slither towards her. It was the engorged penis of a male and above it, the heavily-muscled torso of the nude man directed his swollen glans towards Belle's mouth. The glans came nearer and nearer, hypnotising Belle with its awful hugeness. The bulb and shaft of this cock seemed too big for her, for any woman, to take, whether in cunt or mouth. The cock trembled as Belle's squirming buttocks made the trees writhe, where the male effortlessly perched, his body lowered in an arc, to invade the woman. The peehole creased in a sneer as it came nearer and nearer Belle and she felt the hot meat of the glans caress her lips and her tongue.

'*No ... no ... Ahhhh!*' she moaned, as the whip continued to lashed her bare buttocks.

Every second stroke now took her in the anal cleft, with the tip of the lash searing her clitoris and she could feel her flogged arse-bud swelling. Her come juice flowed, a torrent; the welting of her cleft made her peach throb with pleasure, like twin clitties, awakened by the whip.

'*AHH! ... Mmm!*'

The whip landed with full thong on her erect nubbin and Belle's body quivered like a leaf as the glans of the naked penis entered her mouth, parting her jaws fully. Still, the monstrous cock thrust into her open mouth, filling it until the peehole was at her throat. Belle fastened her lips and, with swift, bobbing movements of her head, began to suck the glans in time with the cock's thrusts. Her lips could scarcely engorge the whole glans and encompassed only a short section of the massive, knobbed shaft that soon became wet with her saliva. She felt her bladder loosen and her strong hiss of pee engulf the masturbating girls below her, but all she knew was the power of the hot cock in her mouth. The stone phallus beneath her now pulsed with bright, glowing light as her come flowed into its peehole and spurted over the glans onto the balls, where Sushi and the feral leader continued to masturbate to orgasm after orgasm, while licking Belle's vaginal juices from the stone balls.

Above Belle's sucking mouth, the belly and pubic mound of the male gleamed in the reflected glow of the tourmaline. His skin was pure and hairless, the pubic mound a bare dimple. While the first thrusts had been fierce and slamming the back of Belle's throat, the cock now withdrew a little, so that her tongue was able to lick the glans and peehole. Belle heard a deep male voice moan as the cock trembled and she knew he was about to spurt. She licked the furrows of the glans and started, recognising the cloverleaf mutation of the cock-bulb.

The whip continued to lash Belle in the cleft of her buttocks and on the fesses, but now each stroke was a shudder of orgasmic delight, bringing her closer and closer to come. Then, a jet of spunk washed the back of her throat, the male's come spurting so powerfully that she gagged. Belle's fesses ached with pleasure and she felt her belly slide into a quaking, shuddering come. More piss flowed from her cunt, mingling with a new and heavier gush of cunt-juice, as jet after jet of sperm filled her mouth and she swallowed thirstily, yet still could not contain the load, which dripped down her chin and onto her erect nipples, topping them like cream on cupcakes. The male jerked his loins, thrusting against Belle's tongue and palate as his come flowed. His spunk seemed endless, each spurt as hot and creamy as the last and Belle howled, in an orgasm stronger than the pain of whipping. A woman spoke behind her.

'Thank you, Heinz,' she said.

The whipping stopped and Belle twisted her head to look, aghast. The woman wore a Second World War gas mask, apparently of Japanese manufacture, and her nude body was sleek and furry, like the feral girls'. Her tail was erect. Her hair hung long over her massive bare teats and was no longer jet black, but blonde. Her feet were wreathed in tendrils of the misty gas, which she seemed to have drawn with her into the clearing. The masturbating ferals continued to sob, howl and stroke each others' clitties and buttocks, in continual orgasm.

'Dr Cunliffe!' Belle cried.

'I am glad you came home, Belle,' said Dr Jolita Cunliffe. 'I tried to persuade you against going to the hell island, but it is seemly that you have escaped. You have brought Sushi for me, too! No doubt you will wish to resume your rightful domain, in due course. You are, after all, Miss Claw, since the girls have acclaimed you. They have long awaited Miss Claw's return, just as Miss Budgen's slaves pray for the sperm god . . .'

'I thought *you* . . .' Belle blurted. 'Or Miss Budgen . . .'

'Miss Budgen is not a demon, like Dr Paine,' she said, 'merely a sadistic lesbian who pursues sensual pleasure. She and Paine coexist in uneasy cooperation, like God and Satan. Miss Budgen accepts ferals who have escaped from

Dr Paine's clutches, but still crave whipping and anal injection. In return, Miss Budgen supplies Paine with freshly shed skins and lizard girls to work the fields. She sends slaves into the world as gem-sellers, but Dr Paine sends hers as recruiters. This second island is inhabited by mutated ferals who date from Japanese times and who bred with those who had *always been here, before Furvert*. Furvert himself managed to escape the clutches of ecstasy, seeing his men fucked and wanked literally to madness, but with their sperm preserved within the tourmaline rock itself. The ferals were already here, living on come and captured sperm, long before the Japs arrived. Our island here is embedded on solid tourmaline, the orgasmic gemstone. I knew you were special, Belle, from the first time I saw you at my lecture and instructed my daughter Geisha to seduce you. It remains to rescue my third triplet, Kaa, from her bondage in the mines.'

Dr Cunliffe twirled and showed Belle her bottom. Each of her buttocks was tattooed, with a crimson 'P'.

'I have decided to revert to one of my old skins,' she said, coquettishly. 'Don't you like this one? I was Josette Couzier, then – branded as *pute*, or whore, by those who disapproved of my dalliance with Heinz in the Second World War ... not just Heinz, but *all* of the soldiers fucked me, and the genetic scientists too, and drank my come. I was such a naughty mademoiselle ...'

Heinz sprang to the ground, his penis dripping with Belle's cunt-oil and still massively erect. At this, the masturbating ferals jostled forward to kneel and lick his balls and cock.

'The longevity come gene has long been known,' said Dr Cunliffe. 'The charlatan Paine must pay, at last, for her conceit. She is a true, cruel, dominatrix, interested in power merely for the sake of power. I am a dominatrix, I admit, but devoted to physical pleasure. Dr Paine would have used you as a lookalike, Belle: sent you, or your genetic replica, into the world to enslave rich men and attract their funds to her. My task has been to rescue those sexually enslaved with my own, more powerful, dominion. It is male nature to crave enslavement by female, and the thrall of a malicious dominatrix can only be replaced by that of a benign one. Submissive males, which is most of them, are addicted to a woman's whip, whatever its source.'

She smiled, coy as a teenager. Her cunt was shiny with come and her clitoris erect.

'I admit that I take pleasure in whipping, so I am indeed a whore and look forward to my own punishment – my first proper whipping in ages, Belle, from you. Mmm ... Watch me, Belle. Watch me wank myself, at your beauty. Do you agree that Dr Paine must be punished?'

Dr Cunliffe began to masturbate, staring at Belle.

'Y–Yes,' said Belle. 'I suppose so . . .'

Though she had glimpsed Dr Paine's satanic nature, she did not know *whom* to believe! She looked at her flogged bottom and saw, even beneath her welts, that her hemangioma had spread from her perineum to her lower buttocks. It looked like a crimson butterfly. Dr Cunliffe's fingers were a blur as she rapidly wanked her stiff clitty.

'Uhh . . . *Ooh!* And do you agree to whip *me*? Josette Couzier, the whore? *Mmm . . .*'

Belle thought of Dr Cunliffe's nude body, so like Belle's, beneath her pelt, whipped raw.

'Please, Belle,' panted Dr Cunliffe, 'I'm going to come ... Oh! Oh! Ahh! I'm coming! *Ahhh . . .!* Please say you'll whip my bare skin, Belle. I'm coming! Oh, yes! *Ahhh! Yes . . .!*'

'*Yes*,' said Belle.

# Memoir 7

*It was just as well that my practice with the Stones and my discoveries with Lee and Gary had made me able to assume a 100 per cent lesbian role; for my director of studies, Miss Budgen was 100 per cent lesbian; all the more of a cow because I envied her her gorgeous body. Well, I had enough pleasure from it to compensate. She was a bull dyke who looked like a femme and I had to dress frilly to please her. I didn't mind . . . She caned me on the bare arse very hard, before we got to some serious gamahuching and strap-on buggery, and I didn't let her into the secret of my experiences on Hawaii and how I could take caning or anal penetration so hard and so long, which of course made me irrestistible. Actually, the dildo was the only activity where she enjoyed being sub and liked me to bugger her in the anus, as soon as I was sore and squirming from my own anal fucking. Well, I loved that too, so we got on OK, even though we loathed one another, as women friends do.*

*She wanted to know where Furvert's Island was, and accused me of making it all up, and stuff. She seemed to think there was something sinister in my enthusiasm, sexual, even – as though she was jealous of a whole island! Mind you, I suppose she had every right to be. There was a more recent Japanese name, Sakosha, but I didn't tell that to Miss Budgen, lest she find it on the map. So nosy! I had a half a mind to flatten her and cane the living daylights out of her naked arse, sometimes; but I had to be careful. She had influence, and there was my precious thesis to care for. I would tease her by slyly inviting her to go to a nude beach with me, for I knew she didn't like dropping her tight rubber knickers, corset and bra, even rubber stockings, that she called her second skin. Except to go to bed with me, of course. I certainly didn't tell her about Miss Claw, or how I seemed to have so much money. If she gave me a particularly vicious bare-bum caning, which got to be most of the time, I would take it out on Dr or Mrs Stone, or especially Henry, even though he loved me to welt his arse raw with his big erection to taunt me, especially if his mum was watching. It got so that I didn't care if she watched, as her son tooled my bumhole after his beating, or I dildoed his and she wanked off. After my visit to Furvert's Island I had given up bothering about what was normal. He'd been naked inside her once, hadn't he? Yes, Furvert's Island . . .*

*It was hell getting there, but so richly worth it! I had to get on some shitty plane, then a shittier plane, then get a boat crew who would take me there; and all the time they were jabbering about demons and stuff, and only one of them would take me ashore in a bumboat, and that was only because I'd let him ram me in the arsehole. It took six days to get there and I was sunbathing nude most of the time, so I had every one of the four crew, including the skipper. The sea was gorgeous, pure turquoise, with flying fish and dolphins and so on, and a huge sun in a perfect sky. It made me horny as hell and I used to lie with my legs apart and wank off, quite blatantly, with my come streaming over my thighs; and they couldn't ignore the invitation. I could sense that they would have had me anyway, which I wouldn't have minded, but I wanted to be in control of the situation. So I made them gang-fuck me, one after the other, two or three times every day; and made them strip completely, which they were shy about. So, right from the first fuck, I insisted they remain nude all the time, like me, and I enjoyed a genuine nudist cruise.*

*I chose the one with the biggest cock to bugger me and gave him the reaming of his life, so I knew I wouldn't have to swim ashore. Actually I guessed correctly that without a female on board, which was most of the time, they used to do it to each other, or rather to the one who liked it. He was smaller than the rest, with a lovely hairless body and a huge dick, and he was the only one with a foreskin – from a different tribe, or something – which I used to pull back and bite, to make him squeal. When we got to know each other, I asked for a demonstration – and I got it. All of them took turns at buggering the slim one and he really squealed, though he said he loved it. I was sucking his cock with his balls on my tits, while they did him, or else tit-wanking him, and he was ramrod stiff. Afterwards, I showed them felching, which I used to do with the Stones – that is, when Dr Stone had cunt-fucked or buggered me, I'd make Mrs Stone suck his spunk from my pussy or bumhole and swallow it all. I did that, felched the young seaman, after they had all buggered him. I sucked all their spunk from his bum, which was brim full by that time, and as I swallowed, I wanked him off to a really hard spurt.*

*That's where I realised that human bodies aren't that different; I mean the bits are interchangeable. It's like when you are whipping a sub in bondage, sometimes only the screams tell you it is a male or female sub, and sometimes not even then. Under the hot sun, we are all melting flesh. A clitty is supposed to be a remnant of penis, but I thought, what if a cock is really an enhanced clitty? The tropics make you see connections, not barriers, between flesh. Once you have accepted yourself as a sexual animal, nothing is taboo. I even introduced a little spanking into our fun and games, followed by caning, just to keep in practice for my meeting with these weird little Jap girls who supplied Gary with gemstones. The rule was, if a poking didn't make me come, I'd spank the matelot bare-bum. Well, I always came, when I felt the spunk hit my uterus, but I'm good at pretending, so I got to spank them all, in turn.*

*Then we graduated to the cane – on the bare, of course, and the joy was, a good caning of four or five dozen would make the stud hard again and I got a fresh poke, or else I would suck his stiff cock to spunk, when it was still oily from fucking my cunt. I love the taste of my own come. It was wonderful, to be nude and alone on the Pacific, gang-fucked* by naked young studs, sucking their cocks and caning their bare bums at my pleasure, and nobody on Earth knowing where I was! I milked them dry, and so trusted them to pick me up in two weeks for a second helping, when they were fruity again. It's all about power. Men will do anything for a tight cunt or ringpiece. Hunt, steal, kill, sacrifice themselves. Anything. Slaves, all of them.

Of course, I wasn't alone on Furvert's Island, though at first I felt like the last woman on Earth, or the first. I had a tent and stuff, but I knew there had to be some buildings left over from the Japs, so I set out to find them. In the distance, I could see a second island and was afraid that might actually be the main one. But I came across the Jap settlement quite soon, as I figured if I was dumped at a convenient beach, so must they have been. I was really blown away when I found somebody else had got there first! Couple of do-gooder bitches who I disliked at first sight; one, Dr Cazenove, was English, and her nurse was Anglo-French, speaking both lingos. They were pleasant enough, had some sort of healing mission to help the leftovers from the Jap experiments who were runnng wild in the jungle. They didn't know anything about gemstones, though. Cazenove was the one in charge, and I had her sussed straight way. I know a sub, and a lesbo type . . . the other was drop-dead gorgeous, looked a bit like me; so of course I hated her guts. I wondered if they had a thing going, but apparently not.

They welcomed me well enough, the fools, and I gave them some story about photography and coral reefs and that. Cazenove was a scientific geek, the other was a nudist it turned out, like me, so we became as close as ladies who detest each other can be. The ferals, as they called the deformed girls, were amazing, and I took masses of photos: girls with distended tits and cunts, scarlet hemangiomas on their arses, ones with a single leg or even no legs: she had the biggest cunt and most extruded clitty I had ever seen and she could actually move by flapping her cunt lips on the dirt, like some amphibian. They got various injections but it didn't seem to help them much. I almost forgot my mission, romping in the sea all day, but one day I persuaded Cazenove to drive me round the island in her jeep. She explained that the ferals suffered from retardism, after the Jap experiments: that is, a regressive gene would appear, at the same time as human gene enhancement. So, if you got a tighter pussy, you grew gills, or a tail, or claws, something way down the food chain. Cazenove said she was on the point of isolating the regressive gene so that the body enhancement could coexist with the regressive animal feature, using the benefits of both. In other words you could have fish gills and human tits and lungs . . . you could have your tail and wag it, so to speak.

This didn't sound too much like healing, more like the Jap research – the nudist bitch was a plain nurse, but I figured Cazenove was up to more. Frontal assault, I thought. We stopped in the jungle and I hypnotised the slut, by wiggling my bare titties, and she told me about her experiments on herself – masochistic, sort of. She would inject herself with various chemicals, then wank off and collect her come, which she would feed or convey to the tribe of ferals in the jungle. In return, she would drink their come, or inject herself anally with it, for she was interested in how they seemed so young, after all this time. Did they breed, or had the Japs discovered the longevity gene? Their language was a sort of hissing, like snakes. They, and she, were guinea pigs and she noted that come was addictive and which strains were most addictive. She said they had 'itchy arses'! I asked Cazenove if she ever suffered from itchy arse and under hypnosis she said, yes. Then I asked if she suffered from itchy pussy, since she wanked a lot and she said yes, too. She admitted she spanked her own bum, with tree branches and it made her come.

Well, I knew what she wanted, and she got it; bare-bum spanking, then whipping; several hundred strokes with a bunch of knotted tendrils, her tits pressed to the hot bonnet of the jeep. Her come flowed over the radiator and hissed to steam. I knew why she wouldn't strip, like the nudist nurse: there was a red hemangioma that covered the cleft of her arse and thigh-backs; also, the nubbin of her spine grew into a little furry tail, her arsehole was covered in finny gills, and when I plunged my fist in her pussy to wank her off, she came at once and the stumps of milk teeth fastened round my wrist. I grabbed her tail and wanked it like a man's penis and she came again! She said it was like a clitoris. She was a shy femme lesbo, not like Budgen the bull dyke. She would wank off watching the nudist nurse but didn't wish to spoil their friendship by coming on to her. I tongued her giant clitty to another orgasm and drank mouthful after mouthful of her love juice, feeling like an electric discharge had gone off in my cunt. I orgasmed without wanking, just by drinking her come!

We didn't find the gem lode on that first trip, but I had a good idea where it might be, where a hill looked disturbed, then camouflaged. For the moment I wanted Cazenove in my dominion. She didn't protest when I said that the feral girls knew more than they let on and that the truth could be got from them by caning them raw. I saw the nurse bitch didn't like this, but Cazenove gave the orders. Once 'submission' therapy started, the ferals flocked to get bare-bum caning! They orgasmed, those furry little beauties, almost at every canestroke. The nurse bitch was blue with envy, and stopped stripping, so I was the only nudist. The ferals worshipped me for whipping them and drinking their come! I was kind of side-lining both Cazenove and the nurse. I befriended one elfin Jap girl by sign language, and she took me to where the gems were. Tourmalines, deep in a crude hole in the ground [like a giant bumshaft, I thought, as we went down] and there were all these ferals, hard-scrabbling with their claws. I introduced them to spanking at first and they hissed with delight, and then of course to the cane.

One of them had orgasm after orgasm and actually shed her bum-skin when I'd welted her with several hundred, to reveal a new white skin beneath! It just sort of peeled off, like giftwrap. Now I knew the secret of Lee's slave-maids in Hawaii. I kept wanking her and the others, until I had several jars of come, which I kept secretly and drank every day until I saw the changes in myself. I pierced my nipples and clitty and inserted tourmalines, which gave off a slight electric charge to the body's heat and I orgasmed at once, and repeatedly, till I was exhausted and had just the strength to remove the gems from my piercings. My Jap girlfriend

208

also took me to their breeding ground. We had to swim to the second island, which was covered in thick mist. Cazenove had said this was Jap poison gas and nobody could go there, but the ferals obviously did, and hell, I was becoming one of them. Nobody else knew how, or even if, they bred.

As soon as we landed on the island and my feet were tickled by that layer of mist, I exploded in an orgasm, like a thousand volts coursed through my clit; in fact, my whole body seemed a clit! At once I understood that the second island was the key to the whole thing. She led me to the centre of the island through groves of eucalyptus trees, with my clitty throbbing all the time in that swamp gas, and I came three more times! Maybe four. The breeding ground wasn't a ground at all; it was a lake. There was a village there, of decaying old Jap nissen huts; and another tribe of ferals, these ones all smooth and hairless – fishy ones, like my girl, whom they welcomed. They took me to the lake and under the surface there were a whole lot of nude, hairless Jap girls, asleep. I tasted the water and it wasn't water at all, but salty and fragrant, like come. It was a lake of amniotic fluid, a lake of pure come-juice.

I said my name was Miss Claw and they jabbered 'Mee Kro! Mee Kro!' and took me to their treasure hut. They had two treasures: one was a vial of vacuum packed cream, which by lewd gestures they indicated as male sperm with some Jap writing on the vial – from World War Two I guessed. The other was buried in the dry ground – eucalyptus trees suck up moisture. It was a handwritten diary, bound in skin and in French, and it was the log of Captain Furvert. I could only scan a few pages before they reburied it and I looked at the end. He was saying that he was a prisoner of she-demons and must escape this place or die of pleasure. There were two tribes of ferals: piscine and feline, both from the same seed which in the seventeenth century seemed a demonic mystery. They thought that men were simply mutant women, but with the ability to spunk. He was kept for his sperm . . . they wanked him several times a day, for the breeding lake needed male seed. He also took sacred whippings, tied between two eucalyptus trees; for they thought a whipped body would make the eucalyptus weep spunk into the come-pond. They prayed for some mythical sperm king to return and, when they had no male captive, they whipped each other to make him come to them, pretending the welts on their flogged bottoms were cunts. Of course, I had to whip every white little bottom in the place and was happy to do so, though my arm was sore. I kept coming and coming, as I watched their crimson skins peel off their buttocks like clingfilm. I realised the Japs hadn't invented this genetic stuff, but rediscovered it. I thought of eternal life, organ farms, sexual enhancement to irresistably enslave men, shedding skin to remain youthful – the whole nine yards . . . and all the money to be made from the RBs who would pay for my secret treatments. When I left, they were all sobbing and begging "Mee Kro" to stay, and I promised to return. Except that all that coming exhausted me and I had to be careful, because heaven can be addictive and even in the Garden of Eden, too many apples make you sick. I wasn't sure what they would put in me if I fell asleep . . .

# 13

# Voyeur Slit

'I knew you'd come back,' was Miss Budgen's terse greeting, either to Belle or Dr Cunliffe, or both. 'Miss Puget's escape with Sushi, from the slut Paine, has stirred up a nest of vipers, I hear. Her guards no longer worship Paine and their gene-splice makes them unstable.'

'Josette Couzier has a score to settle,' murmured Dr Cunliffe. 'With Belle's permission.'

They stood in the flogging room, which was the nearest thing the mineshaft had to a lounge. Kaa hugged Dr Cunliffe and Miss Budgen said she had a pleasant duty for them; another trespasser to deal with. Kaa, nude, left Dr Cunliffe's embrace. She returned leading a Japanese youth, also nude, on a dog leash.

'Intruders, usually Japanese, are usually given a bare-bum caning and then examined, to see if they are suitable for sperming purposes. Those too young are sent away, of course, minus their cash and wristwatches,' said Miss Budgen. 'We must replenish our stock, as feral girls go into the world to seduce males, and we have plenty of voyeurs to catch. The Japs think an island of orgasmic females must be paradise. We see their boats, capture them and flog them on the back, with the cat – not their bums, yet – and keep them in a cave, hollowed from the tourmaline, until they are full of spunk and ripe for bum-caning. Now, you'll excuse me. I must scourge an escaped feral, a slave-girl named Bluebird who claims her real name is Lee, a guest, and that a lookalike has been sent home in her place! Sent *home* . . .!'

Miss Budgen laughed and departed, her skin suit rustling.

'Make him masturbate,' Belle ordered, opening her thighs to the naked Japanese youth. 'Then cane him till he is erect and wank him off again. I want him drained and tame.'

The intruder's whole body had newly been shaven and weals of whipping shone blue on his bare back. He cowered, grimacing in fear but hungrily eyeing the two females, armed with canes. His penis stood rock-hard.

'Shall I wank him off, Belle?' said Dr Cunliffe. 'Or should Sushi do him, while I cane her? It would be faster.'

Dr Cunliffe wore only caning pants and her bare breasts quivered as she spoke, with the nipples visibly stiffening. Belle herself was nude, as was Sushi.

'No,' said Belle,' I want to see him do it. I'm curious.'

'You're not the submissive girl I remember,' said Dr Cunliffe.

'I'm in a different place, now,' Belle replied. 'I was totally submissive, before I came here. Now, having had a slave of my own, Linda . . . and Sushi and everything, I'm not sure.'

'Your thoughts will clear, back at college,' said Dr Cunliffe.

'Back *there* . . .?' said Belle, after a pause.

Belle spread her cunt lips and fingered her erect clitty. Her cunt was already shiny with come and the youth reached out to touch her but jumped, as Dr Cunliffe's cane lashed his buttocks.

'No touchy lady,' said Belle.

She accompanied her words with a lewd gesture that conveyed her order. Hesitantly, the Japanese youth stroked his glans, then grasped the shaft of his cock and began to rub.

'I bet you speak English,' Belle said, nodding to Dr Cunliffe who encouraged the boy with a sharp cut to his top buttocks, which made him yelp.

The youth nodded miserably.

'I am a student,' he said.

'Then, tell me what you think about when you do this,' said Belle, frotting her own clit and making his eyes goggle. 'I know that smutty boys wank themselves all the time, but ladies also like to masturbate. I suppose you read filthy Japanese comic books.'

'Yes, Miss. At twenty years, I have no girlfriend. Must look . . .'

'The really dirty ones, with demons and naked women flogged and tortured.'

'Yes, Miss. I . . . I masturbate over them. All Japanese men do.'

'So, what is your fantasy?'

'Golden lady, like you, Miss,' stammered the boy, rubbing his penis very fast.

'With an ugly hemangioma?' said Belle, rubbing the dark puce skin that now adorned her buttocks, perineum and cunt-hillock and crept up her belly, approaching her nipples. 'And what would I be doing, in your fantasy?'

She began wanking harder.

'What you are doing now, Miss. Masturbating with me,' the boy blurted. 'Or whipping me for my filthiness. And . . . your skin is beautiful, not ugly.'

'Fantasy,' Belle drawled. 'Have you never fucked a woman?'

'No, Miss. It is very expensive. But I've watched.'

'A voyeur! Describe what you saw,' Belle snapped. 'If it is satisfactory, you will receive one bare-bum caning. If not, two. Satisfactory means making me excited enough to orgasm. I want your whole story, every filthy detail; and you may continue to wank as you tell it, but you may not spurt. Is that clear? Otherwise you shall be triply flogged.'

'Y–yes, Miss,' he stammered.

In truth, Belle was having difficulty holding her orgasm back, as her clit and nipples tingled at the slender white body and the penis rising like a birch tree. Her cunt was sopping wet. The boy admitted that he used to buy used schoolgirls' panties from vending machines in the geisha district of Tokyo and masturbate with them. From that, it was a short step to purloining the stained panties of

213

Mikyo, one of his two twin elder sisters, the other called Tana. He would take either of the twins' panties from the family laundry, returning them after ejaculating in them, but preferred Mikyo's: Tana was an intellectual and professed no interest in boys, but Mikyo had a steady boyfriend, so her panties were generally stained with come fluid after petting sessions. Also, in her excitement, she would have to go to piss several times and be in too much of a hurry to wash her pussy, so her panties also bore generous pee stains. She was very careless with her panties and underthings generally, leaving them unwrapped and dangling over the side of the laundry bin, instead of wrapped in paper, like Tana's. It was almost as if Mikyo was daring him to take them. Sometimes, he got underthings of both Mikyo's and Tana's and would put Mikyo's over his head, while he spermed in Tana's, breathing in Mikyo's fruity odours as he ejaculated into Tana's satin panties or bra.

'Oh, Miss,' he whimpered, 'the scent of a lady's stained panties . . . it is heaven!'

In due course he began to spy on Mikyo, when she thought she was alone in the family home with her boyfriend. He observed her entire sexual education, from shyness to boldness to defloration, which he witnessed in her bedroom through the lattice door and thus, his own sexual education was accomplished as a voyeur. This, he insisted, was normal for Japanese males, but with a readily available stimulation of pornographic films and sadistic comic books, he had the advantage of a live sister to spy on. Belle wanked harder as she listened.

One night, Mikyo accompanied her boyfriend to the bedroom she shared with Tana, when she thought the entire family had gone to the cinema, and the student voyeur was at some college seminar. The couple lay down on the bed and made heavy petting, the boyfriend easily getting his hands under Mikyo's bra and then her panties, though she put up a struggle when he tried to remove the garments. The student was agog, recognising the panties – white satin, with a frilly bow at the front of the waistband

– into which he had spurted his own sperm so many times. Mikyo was whimpering, over and over, like a prayer, that she was virgin and he must not penetrate her with his cock.

It was the custom for Japanese families to share the bathtub, so he had often seen his twin sisters nude, but never before as sexual animals. Now he saw that under her boyfriend's frotting fingers, Mikyo's white panties were stained dark with her come oil. He also saw that she had shaved her pubis bare of its bushy forest, for the occasion, so that her resistance must be feigned or an accepted part of the ritual of defloration. The boyfriend had his pants off but kept his shirt hanging unbuttoned, revealing his massive erection. The student was not offended by this sight but rather stimulated further, for the man's penis was much bigger than his own and this gave him a curious thrill, as though his sister's body, which he had come to consider the sexual property of his own penis, must necessarily be ceded to the more virile organ.

The boyfriend teased Mikyo's cunt with his glans, tickling her distended clitty until she was dripping come all over her thighs and onto the bedcloth, and now her whimpers of resistance had turned to high-pitched pleas that if he must penetrate her cunt he should not hurt her. He had her breasts out of her bra, also white satin, which dangled sloppily beneath the big stiff nipples and he was squeezing them together quite hard. She moaned as he did this, and then he began to slap her erect nipples with his palms, pausing to pinch each nipple between his finger and thumb. Her moans were now definitely of pain. Yet she did not try to escape his embrace; rather, to get his penis inside her cunt, which she opened fully so that the inside pink flesh was visible, wet and squashy. The voyeur's own penis was rock-hard and trembled at his slightest touch, yet he timed his self-stimulation carefully, as he did not wish to ejaculate before his sister or her young man. His glasses were misty and his eyes blurred with sweat, fixed on her pulsing wet cunt, which seemed in his fever to be like a sea-snail with the swollen clitoris its head, rearing above the pink shell and jerking at each slap to her bare breasts.

Mikyo's half-naked body gleamed white and shiny with sweat.

The boyfriend suddenly ripped Mikyo's panties, tearing them in two, and turned her over across his thighs, as he squatted on the futon. He placed her bare bottom cheeks up and began a hard hand-spanking, holding her down by her neck and squashing her face in her pillow, so that her squeals of distress were muffled. Her legs and bottom wriggled like eels under the force of the man's strong spanking and very soon, her white fesses turned pink, then darkened to crimson, with deep blotches left by his fingers. Her cries of pain grew louder and louder but as her spanking progressed, the flow of her cunt's juices increased. She inched her hips so that the lips of her cunt touched her boyfriend's tight ball-sac. Contemptuously, he lifted her whole loins, by the hips, and poised her cunt above his glans. Then, with a swift thrust, he slammed her cunt onto him and plunged his cock inside her, to the hilt, so that only his ball-sac showed, pressing her hips hard against him before resuming the spanking. Now, her bottom bounced up and down at each spank, revealing the man's cock-shaft, slimy with her come.

The student wondered why there was no evidence of breaking his sister's virgin hymen and the male, too, demanded an answer, increasing the force of his spanks as he fucked her. She squealed in pain and insisted that she had broken her own hymen with her vibrating dildo, with which she masturbated almost every night. The male called her a lying slut and said her cunt was wide enough for a ship and had taken many cocks before his own. Proper Japanese girls did not masturbate, or use vibrators. She whimpered again, that it was not so, and he was her only love, but he was not satisfied. She gave a great wail of distress when he lifted her from the shaft of his cock and knelt on her thighs, while he unfastened his studded belt from his trousers. He recommenced beating her naked buttocks, strapping her now, with the belt-thong doubled and the heavy studs laying welts on skin already spanked crimson. His cock rubbed against her jerking hips as he whipped her bum. The sister screamed but was powerless, or unwilling, to escape. The male had her neck down and as he thrashed her bare bum with the leather, her fingers fastened on her cunt, three of them sliding inside, with her thumb frotting her clitty. Whipped on her naked bottom, his sister was masturbating. Her fingernails were long and pointed which excited the voyeur, as he imagined them clawing the walls of her cunt.

Her wails turned to choking and increasingly hysterical sobs, as the skin of her shuddering bare buttocks was severely welted by the leather. The man snarled and cast aside his whip, then straddled the threshing bum, and spread the cheeks. The sister's hand was still masturbating her cunt and the male revealed her anus bud, then wiped his fingers in her gash and greased his cock with her come. He poked the tip of his glans inside her bumhole. The girl's shrieks and sobs grew louder and with a fierce grin, he plunged his penis right to the balls, inside her anus, and began to fuck vigorously. All the time, he squashed the sister's face to her pillow but her screams, as he buggered her, might well have been unmuffled. Her fingers flickered on her clitty and come poured from her cunt. The student's own movements grew more vigorous, as he sensed the boyfriend was about to spurt and that his sister was going to masturbate herself to simultaneous orgasm. The male howled and released Mikyo's head, which twisted, gasping on the pillow as she screamed 'Fuck me! Do me hard!' and masturbated furiously. The boyfriend began to spank her twitching bum again with slaps to each buttock from both hands; then, suddenly, he grabbed her by the hips and pressed her bum into his belly, as he cried out that he was spurting at her anal root. Mikyo squealed 'Come in my hole! Fuck my poohole! Fuck hard! Hurt me! Hurt me!' Her squeals became a rasping sob, 'Oh! I come! I come! Fuck me . . .' and the words were dissolved in cries of ecstacy. The student was on the brink of spurting in his own self-stimulation, when he felt a hand grasp the back of his neck and a female voice call him a filthy pervert and a voyeur. It was Mikyo's twin sister, Tana.

217

With his erect penis still naked, the student was dragged into the twins' bedroom by Tana, livid with rage and angrier still when she saw her buggered sister, the cause of his excitement. Mikyo cried that it was not her fault, that her resistance was swept away by passion and brute male force. Tana's glasses misted as she stared at the male's flopping, come-slimed cock and then at the voyeur's erect organ. Obviously, the brute male force was *there* – it was somehow, obscurely, the fault of the voyeuristic student that Mikyo had been whipped and buggered. The boyfriend and the two twin sisters agreed that they must punish the miscreant, as a deterrent and example, to himself at least. They agreed, too, that the punishment should fit the crime. Protest was in vain. The voyeur was stripped naked and obliged to lie face down on the futon, while Tana sat with his head clamped between her powerful thighs and the full weight of her buttocks and loins pressing on his neck, through her panties. To his delight, her skimpy satin panties were oily wet! His penis remained fully erect.

He screamed, as the first lash of the belt struck his bare buttocks; then again, and again. He had never been whipped before and could not understand how Mikyo had seemed to take pleasure in it. The pain was unbearable. He squirmed and squealed and felt tears blur his eyes, dripping onto his glasses as his gorge rose at each smarting welt. Finally, he heard a rustle above him as Tana shed her blouse and then her bra. She wadded her bra in his mouth, filling it to muffle his cries. All he could do was squirm in her thighs' vice and moan, as his buttocks seared under lash after agonising lash. His mouth and nose filled with the aroma of Tana's breasts and his balls ached with pleasure. He had no idea who was whipping him. He hoped it was Mikyo! At this, his stiff cock throbbed. The welts on his whipped arse seemed alive, like red-hot leeches on his skin.

Suddenly, he felt the cheeks of his arse being parted and something hard and warm nuzzle the pucker of his bumhole. He started in terror. Convinced that Mikyo was

218

whipping him, he knew that the boyfriend must be preparing to penetrate his anus with his cock. He let out a moan of shame which turned to a squeal of agony, as the oiled shaft thrust all the way into his anus until his walls were helpless to resist. He wept at the indignity of being buggered. The whipping did not abate, but now the lashes were applied to his haunches and thighs, while a heavy belly slapped his buttocks as the tool pierced his anus. He felt a trickle of hot liquid on his face and neck: Tana was masturbating as she watched him suffer! He managed to twist his head, to peer over the tops of Tana's thighs; for she had shed her skirt, too, and was now masturbating completely nude, save for white nylon stockings and a lace suspender belt. She wiped her fingers on her stocking-tops, making them gleam with her copious come.

The boyfriend was whipping him and Mikyo's lips were fastened on his engorged member, sucking and licking his glans like a huge lollipop. Her body was aslant, her breasts clamped in his fingers, which pinched and clawed her stiff bruised nipples. Mikyo gave little whimpers of pain, or satisfaction. She herself was buggering the voyeur, with the dildo she used to masturbate fastened by a rubber cord at her waist. As her boyfriend pinched her nipples harder and began to thrust his own buttocks between her lips, fucking her in the throat, her buggery of the voyeur grew harder and faster, striking his anal root at each thrust. He squealed and buried his face in his pillow, now soaked with his own tears and Tana's come. Tana, squashing him like an insect with her buttocks, was now masturbating very fast at the spectacle of his buggery. Her laughter at his squeals was music.

For one blissful moment his whipping stopped, but only so that Mikyo's boyfriend could hand the lash to Tana. Mikyo released his cock and he moved behind her, inserting his penis once more into her own anus as she rammed the voyeur – and now Tana recommenced his flogging, with lashes to the bare buttocks at close range. The pulsing of the dildo at his root was heavier, now that the weight of the male's body slammed against Mikyo's own buttocks; suddenly the electric motor was turned on, and the dildo vibrated at maximum speed inside his filled bumhole. The pain of whipping on bare skin and the dildo throbbing in his squirming arse was so intense that he thought he should faint, yet still his cock stood as he began to relish a new and delightful thrill, that of total shame at female hands. Part of his shame was the nearing of his spurt, on his sister's futon. As the voyeur spoke, he continued to wank himself off, on Belle's instructions, while she slowly toyed with her erect clitty, spreading her gash as wide as possible with her fingers.

'Humiliation,' she said. 'You enjoyed your shame . . .'

'Yes, Miss!'

'I propose to shame you – by bare-bottom caning, I mean – until you don't enjoy it.'

'Scarcely possible. Have learned, can never be shamed enough, by lady . . .'

'And I know that,' said Belle.

She looked at Dr Cunliffe, whose nipples were fully erect. She, too, was playing with herself, the visible bare buttocks goose-fleshed under her caning pants and the gusset stained by her wet cunt, which she fingered through the cotton. The youth switched suddenly, to describe his initiation into the world of closed geisha houses. He was still virgin and still voyeuristic, but now unashamed of his voyeurism, which he insisted was an honourable Japanese tradition.

'A friend of mine from my schooldays has enviable job as slop-boy in a geisha house,' he said. 'He is paid not in cash, but in geisha girls' stained panties, which he sells. Sometimes, a geisha wears paper panties, so that salaryman can pierce through her garment with his penis, simulating power. It is a special geisha house, owned by the wife of a powerful yakuza gangster. My friend sold me a copy of the key to the secret corridor upstairs, where the geisha girls entertain rich salarymen. I slip in through the sky window and can look through slits in all the door panels. Each room has its own voyeur slit, unknown to the guests, and for women friends of the owner. There is a throne at each slit, with a hole, to drain the watcher's come juice into an urn as she masturbates. The voyeurs are all female in this geisha house, and all wear masks with big robes, naked underneath. It is easy for me to disguise myself in Tana's or Mikyo's robe. There are nine rooms and always a good show. The watchers exchange seats, or move, and so it is easy to slip from one slit to the next. It is the slop-boy's task to empty the urns when they are brimming with come, into a larger, wheeled vessel, which he must push on hands and knees, naked, without looking up. If a lady voyeur chooses to cane his bare bottom, he must endure it for as long as she pleases. Many ladies like to cane him as they orgasm.' The nine rooms were of various 'strengths', and he described his most recent visit:

Room 1: a nude girl stood bent over a toilet, with her head padlocked in the bowl, and in a spiked collar. A second nude girl squatted on the seat, with her cunt touching the girl's hair, and pissed down her face. As she pissed, she masturbated. When her piss had finished, her place was taken by a second girl, then a third – all the time it took a group of men to fuck the toilet girl in her anus. Each male lashed the girl's bare buttocks with twenty strokes of a bamboo cane, before he buggered her. The group of piss-girls masturbated before, during and after their evacuations, and those who had just evacuated knelt to lick the clits of the girls about to piss, while they squatted in turn beneath the buggered girl, licking her clit and swallowing her pee and come.

Room 2: a naked male, bound and hooded, was scourged on the bare buttocks and back by a nude girl, with only one leg, the other replaced by a rubber prosthesis. After his scourging, she unstrapped her artificial leg and balanced on one foot. He was permitted to kneel and lick the one-legged girl's clitoris and naked stump, while she toed his cock to spurt.

Room 3: the 'honeymoon suite', where a newly-wed couple, naked but for their traditional wedding-wigs, hung from the ceiling by their chained ankles, facing each other, their wrists clamped in sockets on the floor. Their legs were stretched fully, and molten wax was poured into the anus of both bridegroom and bride. While this solidified, a girl, naked but for a dragon mask, caned the male on his buttocks; another caned the bride's bare arse; while a third whipped the female on her titties, belly and cunt, using a short flail of three thongs. A male in a yakuza's robe watched, with arms folded. The bride's nipples were bruised raw by whipping but stood erect and her cunt juiced heavily. Her come flowed over her belly and breasts and into her mouth, which swallowed it. The suspended couple were ordered to extrude their anal wax, which they did, pushing, until two dildos were in the hands of their tormentors. The male was now buggered with the dildo in the form of his wife's anus, and the woman with her husband's. Her screams were louder, due to the larger size of the shaft that penetrated her and each was buggered for several minutes, until the pucker's lips touched the hilt and the wax dildos disappeared inside the anal shafts. The male thrust open his yakuza's robe to reveal his monstrous, erect penis, which he thrust into the screaming mouth of the bride and began a vigorous mouth-fucking, while her husband was obliged to watch.

A nude girl lay beneath the bride and collected her come in her mouth, but without swallowing. The bride witnessed her husband's cock sucked by the dragon woman who had caned her cunt and breasts. When he spurted, she kept his cream in her mouth; then, the two women with mouthfuls of fluid pressed their lips to the anus of each of the bridal pair. The husband's bumhole was filled with his wife's come and the bride's with her husband's sperm. Both were released from their bonds and obliged, one after the other, to suck and swallow the contents of the other's anus, while the nude women pissed on them. The yakuza played bridal music on a flute, while his cock was sucked by the bride, whose husband was obliged to cane her bare bottom. When she was crimson with stripes, the yakuza, still playing, mounted and buggered her, while her sobbing husband was whipped and caned by all three dragon girls.

Room 4: a male in bondage had his cock and balls smeared with honey and a trio of nude, furry girls, wearing parrot's beaks, pecked at the caraway seeds with which his genitals were covered. A fourth nude girl stood on a chair above and caned him, drinking glass after glass of emetic lemonade, so that every minute she pissed copiously on his face, or wealed bum.

Room 5: an audience of yakuza and their mistresses sat before an enormous fish-tank. Inside, a nude girl, her head and body completely shaven, was suspended in water by a thin chain pierced through her clitoris. Her gash was open and her legs fully outstretched, with each ankle clamped to each wrist, so that the girl's body was a perfect diamond shape, with her torso a bar at its centre. A lobster had its claws fastened on each of her nipples. The girl wore nothing but a gas mask; two other girls, in rubber diving suits and helmets with snorkels, flogged her on the cunt with stinging jellyfish, their tentacles about an arm's length. Other jellyfish stung every portion of her bared body and streams of yellow piss issued every few seconds from her cunt, accompanied by air bubbles from her anus. The female members of the audience were nude and sat, masturbating and rocking on the laps of their companions in yakuza robes, which hung open to permit the cock's passage in cunt or anus.

Room 6: an 'arsepoke-geisha', standing and touching her toes, presented her anal hole to a succession of males, who buggered her. She wore rubber socks and rubber gloves. The movements of her buttocks indicated her specialised skill of anally milking the men who poked her bumhole. Most of the males spurted after less than five seconds, so powerful was the clutch of her anal elastic. Nevertheless, she screamed and trembled, in real or simulated agony. A second group of men arse-fucked her, but now she lay on her back in missionary position, her rubber gauntlets removed to reveal sharp tiger's claws. These men buggered her, enjoying the pain and hatred in her face and her vengeful clawing of their backs, buttocks and even ball-sacs, as she screamed and sobbed at her anal penetration.

Room 7: another arse-geisha, this one horizontal, with her legs strapped to an upended horsehoe-shaped harness which stretched her thighs to present both cunt and bumhole. One male fucked her cunt from beneath, a second took her in the anus, while a third mouth-fucked her.

Room 8: a male, suspended in full rubber bondage and gas mask was whipped by one nude girl in a dragon mask, while a second girl tit-wanked his erect cock.

Room 9: two nude girls were suspended by their wrists from ceiling chains. Their bodies were clamped together by thin copper wires through piercings in their nipples, cunt lips and extruded clitties. Their mouths and teats pressed in kisses: any separation of their skins must cause hideous pain. Their bodies swayed and shuddered as their naked buttocks were flogged with a leather scourge of nine thongs, wielded by two girls, also nude, but unmasked, with sleek furry pelts and erect tail nubbins, who masturbated as they whipped. Come oil flowed down the bare white thighs of the scourged girls, yet the whippers made the only noises, squeaking in come after come, until the flogged girls, too, joined in cries of orgasm. When they had come, the girls were unbound and one knelt with buttocks and anus presented, while the other straddled them. Her already extruded clit had distended to monstrous size, like a baby penis, and she inserted this organ into her companion's anus, her buttocks quivering as she thrust, buggering her very rapidly to a further orgasm.

'And which room made you wank off the best? The truth!' Belle said, her fingers playing in the torrent of come that flowed from her swollen cunt.

'The ninth room, Miss. The whipped girls were my twin sisters, Tana and Mikyo. Tana buggered her twin with her own clit. Tana is enhanced, you see . . .'

'What *was* the end of your chastisement for peeping at Mikyo?' Belle demanded.

'After this event, I accessed Tana's computer and saw videos the twins had made, with this boyfriend and others. Always, the male was humiliated – a favourite scenario was that the twins subjugated a young man, who was obliged to watch his wife whipped and buggered by their boyfriend, dressed as a yakuza, while the twins did the same to their captive. Sadistically, they made their victims enjoy, or even beg for, humiliation! They knew the male would enjoy being caned by females and seeing his wife thrashed and penetrated by a more powerful male, just as she would love her naked bottom whipped and her anus fucked by the bigger cock. There was an address in England, to which these dreadful things were sent. Tana is a student of genetics, Miss. I saw her correspondence with Dr Paine, and that is what drew me here. Tana experimented on herself. I ... I was buggered by her, Miss, with her unnatural, distended clitoris, as I licked Mikyo's clit, while she herself was whipped and buggered by her boyfriend. When Tana had fucked me anally with her monstrous clit, enough for several comes, she withdrew from my bumhole and whipped my bare buttocks again, so severely that I myself came and spurted all over the futon, still swallowing the heavenly rain of Mikyo's cunt juice. They all laughed and said it had been wonderful sport! I sobbed in shame, that I had been willingly enticed into humiliation of their design, and enjoyed it! That is why I am still virgin, Miss. Myself a voyeur, I cannot orgasm unless whipped and shamed, before voyeurs. Before my caning, please tell me – which one of you ladies is Dr Paine?'

Belle caressed her clitoris with her cane, eyeing the youth's buttocks, unblemished save for the weal of Dr Cunliffe's single stroke. Her come flowed, shining on the skin of her growing hemangioma.

'Why, *I* am,' she said.

'That's right,' said Sushi, licking her lips with her big pink tongue.

# Memoir 8

*My plans had changed. This place was a gold mine, and more. I had my laptop and modem with me, of course, so I kept in touch with my network of e-slaves; only now I was able to sell videos of really super-kinky stuff, mutant girls wanking, coming in waterfalls, gamahuching and whipping each other [or me] and so on. Oh, yes, I started to offer my own body to the whip, stretched naked between two eucalyptus trees and the earth swallowing my floods of come, and pee, too, until the magic day when I shed my bumskin for the first time. The process of shedding itself was orgasmic, in addition to the numerous comes I had enjoyed while being whipped on my sensitised buttocks. And with fresh skin, tender as a clitoris, I could take another whipping at once. After I hit on the right formula, I dosed myself to the maximum with feral come. My tail grew, sensitive like a clit; I found I could breathe underwater – though with some difficulty, and through my anus – and I found I could change my hair colour ever so slightly, and that I could grow or shed body hair at will. And the sales piled up, all electronic – what wonderful things credit cards are. My own platinum card was upgraded to iridium or something; I had the Bank of England to spend. I emailed Lee in Hawaii, at bluebird.com, and told her to order me up the most sophisticated computer gear and lab stuff; enough to equip the whole hospital. I'd come and collect it and accompany the shipment back here. I figured I could do my doctoral thesis by email. Why not? You can do everything else. First, I had to make sure the island was* mine. I had enslaved Cazenove, for sure, but I didn't want the snotty nudist nurse getting uppity. She had high regard for Cazenove, so when I made Cazenove suggest a series of anal injections – pretending to keep it secret from me! – she didn't protest too much. Being a dominatrix is all about relationships, you see. My tame sailor-boy returned, and I told him the skipper was going to take me to Hawaii and back. They all came ashore this time and, after they had all drunk my come and been allowed to fuck several of the feral girls, that was their heart's desire. I didn't allow my spunk-boy to do any fucking, as I wanted all his cream for me, on the long voyage, but I liked wanking off as I watched the others do the girls. They weren't allowed to come in their girl's pussy or bumhole: two girls stood by with cupped hands, to collect their cream when they spurted. They didn't mind, as they got to do it so much.

I paid another visit to the tourmaline lode, to get some gems for Lee, and this time I was able to dig them myself. I was truly Miss Claw. The thing was, I had to do something about the nurse bitch. She started absenting herself without explanation, but she kept taking her anal come injection, and I saw her skin was getting furry, really beautiful and sleek. In truth, I fancied her – she was so like me, physically, and I suspected that underneath her French snottiness she was probably like me in spirit, too, hence an enemy, who must be subjugated. I was worried, when she started to ask for more, and varied, injections – there was a gleam in those newly-feral eyes, just like my own. So, after a brief whipping-visit to my subjects on the second island, I gave her an exra-special anal injection, to put paid to whatever schemes she had. Did she know everything I had learned? Was she in league with one of the feral tribes? You have to be paranoid. Have to. It's common sense. Eventually, I scourged her.

The three of us had an argument – well, between me and the nurse, really. I dominated Cazenove and she was on my side. The Anglo-French bitch accused me of all kinds of wicked schemes, most injuriously, because she was right. She said I was the darkness and she was the light and other mumbo-jumbo. I knew this had to be nipped in the bud, because, strange as it sounds, we were so alike that I suspected the Jap ferals had difficulty telling us apart! I imagined her hatching all sorts of plots, even getting rid of me and acting as my lookalike with the slave-girls ... an example had to be made, I had to show them that Miss Claw was the boss, darkness or not. I began to suspect that the French bitch had been here before any of us and knew stuff that I couldn't get out of Cazenove, even when thrashed raw and hypnotised. She knew all sorts of spooky stuff about secret research in World War Two, but I reckoned she was just swanking, I mean she couldn't have been alive then. But I thought of the early days, when we'd been nude together in the sea and I wanted to do her, do everything to her. I fancied her so much, because she was turning into a replica of me and like all dominas, I fancy only myself.

I slapped her and she reared up; nude, we wrestled like tigers, punching and slapping and gouging until I was sitting on her face, with her titties in a thigh lock. To my surprise, she ceased resisting and put out a big sandpaper tongue and started to lick my clitty. I started gushing with come and orgasmed straight away. The ferals seemed to creep out of nowhere, as though for a ritual, and the slut didn't resist as they strung her between two eucalyptus trees and I flogged her with a scourge of several branches knotted together. It was one of the most severe lashings I had ever administered and the girls took turns to squat under her gaping cunt and drink her come, or her piss, as she frequently peed herself as well as orgasming profusely. I was wanking myself off too, though I scarcely needed to: the sight of that magnificent nude bum, so like my own, twitching and squirming under my scourge, was enough to bring me off.

Then, I roped her by her four limbs, cunt, tits and neck and swam, floating her behind me, to the second island, where I delivered her to the breeding pool, in the care of the tribe. I told them she was to remain in restraint at all times, even when my special come injection took effect, in three months ...

I was gone three months and returned from Hawaii with everything I desired to set up my lab and hospital. I had to

228

let Lee into the secret and told her she would be an extra-special guest. I didn't tell her the Lee who returned to Gary might not be the original one, nor that I had discovered the longevity gene, just before I whipped Couzier. Imagine my horror, when I found Miss Budgen had arrived! Cazenove was terribly embarrassed, but said she was powerless to stop her and so on. I whipped her bare arse till she screamed, I was so cross, and quite forgot the breeding pool until I had figured out what to do about Budgen. She had tracked me, of course, over the net. You can't hide, totally. But it was OK. I knew Budgen. She was at the gem lode and had enslaved a few ferals. She was a sleazy sensual beast, content to have wealth and girls to whip and wank off. We came to an understanding, of mutually guarded suspicion. I was to have my domain and she hers, sort of like God and Lucifer, though I didn't know who was which. I would supply her with fresh come and fresh skins and she would attend to the worldly things, like fieldwork by mutant girls. In addition, I agreed to satisfy her personal longings for me, once a month and, to be honest, I did relish Budgen's caresses and my submissive sessions of being flogged, just like the old days; only now I shed my bumskin for her.

I found Miss Couzier, the nurse, still in severe bondage on my second island and her triplet girls were happily swimming in the gene pool, still attached by their umbilical cords. In a few more months they would be full-grown and already they could swim back to the large island with me, where I had a tank set up for them. I knew they were really mine! The nurse bitch was only the carrier. But she objected and I sensed grumblings, as some of the fishy sluts thought she was their new goddess and suchlike. I sent them to Budgen, as slaves, and set about the expulsion of Couzier, as I could see she was always going to be a nuisance – even being a surrogate mum hadn't subjugated her. First, she was to be scourged more fiercely than ever, between the eucalyptus trees, and I tied her feet in a bag of sperm-gas so that she could not help exhausting herself with come after come, even screaming in agony as my whip lashed her naked furry pelt right to the bone. I wondered what dear Mum would say if she saw me.

It was funny, because down there on the sunny south coast of England, 'Miss Pain' was what she called herself, as a professional dominatrix. All she had to do was leave the last 'e' off her real name.

'That's right, you cunt!' I snarled. 'Remember me! Paine by name and pain by nature! Squirm, you bitch! I'm ruler of this island! I'm ruler of everything! Don't ever return, you stinking whore, or you won't leave again! Doctor Darwinia Paine is going to live a young woman forever, as supreme mistress . . .!'

My tame matelots were happy to take charge of the bitch, still rubbing her welts and sobbing in bondage and to follow their instructions to fuck, cane and bugger her senseless on the long sea voyage to Australia or somewhere. I didn't care. She had fulfilled her purpose and given me three delicious little mutant ferals, blank young bodies, to rear in my own image. They swam home with me and gladly settled in their tank, but spending more and more time on dry land until a few months later, I had three ravishing Jap surrogate daughters who would be luscious teenage girls forever. I wondered who their real father was, or their real mother, at that, amongst all the women's come in the gene pool. I had a story to tell them later, about frozen sperm from Japs killed in the war, but they could be descendants of Furvert himself, for all I knew.

Nothing ever goes perfectly smoothly, even for a young goddess who is going to live forever. When girls are born as teenagers, they are real teenagers, and rebellious, in this case forever . . . Geisha escaped, I didn't know where to, but, to be safe, I put the second island off limits and spread the story about Jap nerve gas. Those feral girls were capable of any madness, like starting up some darned cult about the wretched slut Couzier. Any intruders were to be enslaved, with maximum severity, by my enhanced guards, and the happily cooperative Budgen. Kaa deserted to her and I didn't mind that, for I knew where she was and she whipped me sometimes, while Budgen wanked off or licked my bum and extruded clitty, as part of our deal. I was proud of Kaa's whipping skill, as though she were my flesh. To prevent Sushi *blabbing and ensure her obedience, I made her tongue grow away, but lied to her that I'd find a way to make it grow again. That kept her docile. I made sure that any research assistants had some disability or imperfection, which I promised to cure – in fact, worsen – by anal injection. Meanwhile, the cash pours in, from my RBs and the slaves, sexually enhanced and mutated, that I send out into the world to seduce and fleece rich men. Some RBs I keep in my fungible organ banks, for their come, and undifferentiated cells, and send lookalikes back in their place. The husbands are delighted.*

*Right now I'm awaiting a new assistant, Belle Puget by name, and the first risk I've taken, for she isn't deformed. What beauty! God, I wanked off just looking at her photo! She's the image of me. I wonder what I'll do with her? Mutate her, of course, and tame her with my whip, which I gather she is no stranger to. Her psych profile has her down to a T as a lovely, squirming sub. I wonder if I should share with her? The longevity gene, I mean. Maybe I'll get her to reproduce, in my own breeding pool. Heaven knows, I have enough come available. Three more like Kaa, Geisha and Sushi; only I'll get it absolutely right this time, with a submissive carrier like the gorgeous Miss Puget. Well, I have all the time in the world, for I'm a beautful young woman who is going to live forever.*

# 14

# Skin Slave

'Scared?' said Belle, as her cane swished the air.

'Yes, Miss,' stammered the Japanese boy.

His upraised buttocks shone like snow, in the dim glow of the tourmaline rock. Sushi lay on her back, on the bedframe, with her thighs clamped around the male's neck, pressing his face to her belly. Beneath him lay the nude figure of Dr Cunliffe, her caning pants at her ankles. His cock was erect, inches from her gaping slit.

'You should not be scared of losing your virginity,' said Belle.

'It is your cane that scares me, Miss.'

'Why? You have been thrashed before. Your back is still raw from Miss Budgen's whipping.'

'I have never been thrashed by my beautiful dream, Miss,' he blurted.

Vip!

'*Ahh!*'

The boy howled, as Belle laid the first stroke across bare skin.

Vip! Vip!

'*Oh!* Oh, Miss . . .!'

Vip! Vip! Vip!

'*Ahhh . . .!*'

His body squirmed, as lines of pink appeared on his clenched fesses and his head bobbed up and down, striking Sushi's navel with his glasses. But the hammerlock of her thighs prevented his escape. Beneath him, Dr Cunliffe was masturbating with smooth, easy strokes, flicking her nubbin to ripeness as her quim began to seep copious come. Triple cunt juices dripped into the runnels beneath the whipping-frame.

'That was only six,' said Belle, her fingers toying with her own enlarged clitty and wiping off the oily wetness that now trickled from her gash onto her thighs. 'There is much more.'

Vip! Vip! Vip! Vip! Vip! Vip!

'Oh! Oh! *Oooh! Ahhh!*' he screamed, as a second half-dozen striped his buttocks, in no more than three seconds.

Vip! Vip! Vip! Vip! Vip! Vip!

'*Urrrnngh . . . AH! AH! Oh!*'

The buttocks now jerked in frantic spasms, with the cleft clenching like a fish gasping for air. The skin was darkened to a ripe crimson. Dr Cunliffe shook off her caning pants and in a swift movement, jackknifed her legs to clamp the small of his back and thrust his engorged penis into her soaking wet gash. Under him, she began to buck, slapping the bedframe with her own buttocks, as she fucked him.

Vip! Vip! Vip! Vip! Vip! Vip!

'*Oh! No! No . . . Mmm . . . Mmm . . .*'

His loins twitched in a massive spurt and cream dribbled over Dr Cunliffe's quim lips. Belle paused in her caning and told him he was no longer virgin, so would be treated as an adult. Sushi shifted her hips, so that his face was now clamped against her own cunt and she wriggled and jerked her hips to make him tongue her clitty. Her come seeped over his face as he pleasured her and soon his cock was stiff again. Belle resumed her caning as he plunged his tongue in and out of Sushi's cunt, and nosed her distended clitty.

Vip! Vip! Vip! Vip! Vip! Vip!

'*Ahhh! AHHH!*'

His screams were muffled in Sushi's slit.

'*Mm! Mm! Mm!*'

Sushi moaned in orgasm, as the boy's howls of agony pulsed through her cunt. Dr Cunliffe now moved her legs up to grasp his neck, lifting her own bum so that the anus was now below his glans. She oiled his cock, and her own bumhole, with come and spunk from her fucked cunt.

Vip! Vip! Vip! Vip! Vip! Vip!

By the 36th canestroke, the male's buttocks were puffed and blotchy with rapidly darkening weals and the whole skin of his arse blushed crimson. As Belle lifted her cane for the next half-dozen stingers, Dr Cunliffe slammed her buttocks against the ball-sac of the voyeur, and drove his swollen cock betwen her anus lips.

Vip! Vip! Vip! Vip Vip! Vip!

*'Ahhhh . . . please stop!'*

A second thrust, and Dr Cunliffe had the cock plunged all the way to her root, her buttocks clenching as she gripped the tool with her anal elastic and began to milk it. Now, he groaned in pleasure.

'Oh . . . cane me, Miss! Oh, I am dirty!'

Vip! Vip! Vip! Vip! Vip! Vip!

He began a vigorous bum-fucking in Dr Cunliffe's anus, and his hips slapped like hammers on her upraised thigh-backs.

'Oh! So dirty . . .'

Vip! Vip! Vip! Vip! Vip! Vip!

Sushi quelled his moans by squashing her sopping cunt over his mouth, making his head a dildo for her own wanking off. Belle, too, was masturbating, as she watched the flogged buttocks of the male jerk like pistons in his frantic buggery of the squirming female, who trapped him with her legs. Belle's come flowed down her thighs and the cane handle was slippery with oil from her fingers. Yet her aim remained sure, and now she framed the boy's seared central fesses with artful strokes to the top buttock, haunches and underfesses.

Vip! Vip! Vip! Vip! Vip! Vip! Vip! Vip!

*'AHH.!'* he screamed, but the raw welting of his bare increased his bugger's fury, as though in ramming Dr Cunliffe's anus, he was trying to punish a woman for his thrashing by a woman.

Belle flicked hard at her throbbing stiff clitty and she could no longer hold back from orgasm. She came in a rush, her strokes faltering slightly, as her bum, nipples and clit glowed in the fire of her pleasure. Her skin was pulsing like a jewel, from pink to crimson, with the dark lustre of her hemangioma glowing sullenly like hot coals. Dr Cunliffe's sleek pelt shimmered fiery orange, while she masturbated under the hard buggery in her squelching anus hole.

'Oh, God! That hurts!' squealed Dr Cunliffe. 'You'll split my bum . . .!'

The Japanese rammed harder, until the buggered woman too gave way to orgasm, and amid panting gasps of pleasure, ordered the boy to give her his come.

Vip! Vip! Vip! Vip!

'*Ahhhh . . .!*'

The Japanese twitched and sobbed once more, as his copious spurt filled Dr Cunliffe's bumhole, with dribbles of hot cream splashing her perineum and thighs. Sushi, too, gasped in another come as she clasped his head and rammed her clit with his mouth. At that moment a girl, wearing a plain white kimono, entered the chamber. 'Hello, Belle,' she said. 'Hello, Dr Cunliffe, Sushi . . .'

'Welcome, Geisha,' said Sushi. 'I've found my voice.'

Geisha undid the knot of her waistband and let her kimono fall to the ground. She was nude; tourmalines glowed milky pink at her nipples and cunt lips. A golden chain looped her waist, with tendrils pierced through her cunt lips holding them open to show her extruded clitoris, itself pierced by a gemstone. Her only other adornment was a cane, hanging from her waistband. She looked at Dr Cunliffe and stroked the handle of her cane.

'Between the eucalyptus trees?' said Dr Cunliffe, with a shiver.

'Of course,' said Belle. 'A promise is a promise.'

'I thought you mght have forgotten, Belle,' sighed the doctor. My, how you've changed! Radiant before, and now . . . more than that. I spoke in the heat of orgasm.'

'The desires you cry in orgasm,' said Belle, 'are your true moments. Geisha will cane your buttocks, while Sushi whips your back. I shall drink your come and piss, Dr Cunliffe.'

'And the pervert?' said Dr Cunliffe.

'He shall cane me, then fuck my bumhole while I drink you.'

The sun was waning in the clearing. A short distance away was a sobbing moan. Bluebird's freshly-whipped body hung between the posts, as bait for night ferals. Her teats and buttocks were grotesquely huge, as was her clit, distended further by a rock which dangled between her thighs, attached to a wire pierced through her nubbin. The sky glowed with distant fire, at the Paine Foundation. Nude, Dr Cunliffe was bound between eucalyptus trees. Already her cunt was moist with come, as she awaited her double thrashing.

'You'll forgive me, Doctor, for using your credit card to get here?' said Geisha meekly.

'No,' said Dr Cunliffe. 'You must cane me until I do.'

'Very well.'

Geisha lifted her cane and Sushi, the thonged leather scourge. Two cracks rang out, as the thongs bit Dr Cunliffe's bare shoulders, while the cane sliced her buttocks. After three seconds, and at the same interval thereafter, the flogging tools lashed bare skin again, and again ...

Belle knelt, with her head upturned between Dr Cunliffe's thighs and her swollen gash-lips. Her mouth opened wide as she presented her naked buttocks to the male's cane. The flogged woman's come dripped into her mouth and she swallowed, ordering the voyeur to cane her to orgasm. She shuddered, as the first, muscular canestroke took her on top buttock; another, in mid-fesse; two more, on the haunches, and her own come flowed into the ground as she squirmed in her ecstacy of submission. After 100 strokes, she was nearing climax and on the 103rd, she groaned as her body pulsed with come, the sleek microscopic hairs of her pelt glowing from pink to crimson. Dr Cunliffe's body writhed in her bonds, as her daughters caned and whipped her. A golden stream of pee suddenly hissed from her wet gash lips into Belle's mouth and thirstily, Belle swallowed the mixed pee and come juice.

She felt her wealed buttocks parted and fingers at her cunt, getting oil for the penis. The tip of the Japanese tool thrust into her arse-pucker, then, with a savage poke, filled her anal cavity, the glans slamming against her belly's root. At once, she convulsed in orgasm as the penis touched the clitoral nerve-ends in her deep anus. The Japanese pervert bum-fucked her very hard, but with slow, deliberate strokes and at each touch of his penis to her anal root, her wealed bottom glowed and throbbed with an electric tingle and she squealed in the little orgasms that pulsed through her body like strobe lights, her entire skin now clitoral. Above her, Dr Cunliffe's thrashed body swayed and shuddered, as if blown by gusts. Each lash to her bruised bare skin brought droplets of heavenly rain to Belle's throat.

The Japanese orgasmed in her anus and she gasped in pleasure at his spurts of hot cream. Then, his penis shrank and slipped from her hole, only to be replaced, moments later, by a massive, clover-leafed helmet whose size made her shriek with pain, as it pierced her bumshaft and drove straight to her root, buggering her anew with hard, powerful strokes. After only a few seconds of Heinz's buggery, Belle climaxed again. Fingers stabbed her clitty and the penis slid from her bumshaft, now to plunge into her sopping wet cunt. Belle squeezed; the walls of her cunt clutched Heinz's cock, more massive than she remembered, and he began to fuck her vigorously, the cloverleaf glans thrashing her hard, clit-sensitive womb-neck.

It was completely dark and there was no moon, though the stars cast a faint glow; it was pale compared to the pulsing shimmer of Belle's tourmaline body and the luminescent fur of Dr Cunliffe, moaning as her daughters whipped and caned her naked pelt. The gems adorning Geisha and Sushi glowed too, tracer beams in the dark, as they swayed in the rhythm of their flogging. As Heinz fucked her to the cracking of cane and whip on Cunliffe's body, Belle felt a slithering caress, as a gossamer web embraced her, drenched in a new flood of come from Cunliffe's cunt. Cunliffe cried out in orgasm: she had shed her skin. The skin flowed over Belle like gas, caressing her stiff nipples, her belly, thighs, buttocks and clit, until she felt the first jet of Heinz's cream spurt at her womb. Fucked by the sperm king and enveloped in the mantle of her dominatrix, Belle sobbed helplessly in come after wet, gushing come.

Dr Jolita Cunliffe stood with her three Japanese daughters, as naked as they were and indistinguishable from them. Her new skin glowed pearl-white in the starlight and her hair was short and black. She turned, smiling radiantly, to Belle, and showed the red 'P' blotched on the massive pale moons of her buttocks.

'Your turn,' she murmured, '*Mistress*.'

Strapped and helpless between the eucalyptus trees, Belle watched as Heinz disappeared towards the slave-girls' den. Meanwhile, the Japanese voyeur was crushed to the ground, with Dr Cunliffe's foot on his face and Geisha's on his balls and throbbing penis. He crooned in delight at his humiliance. The first cracks of whip and cane shook Belle and the pain seared, but with joy, like a kiss to her clitoris. She screamed aloud as each lash welted her bare skin; Dr Cunliffe and the Japanese trio flogged Belle raw and she begged for more as her cunt spurted endless come and streams of hot piss. When Belle had reached her 1200th lash, they were joined by Dr Cazenove, Kiki and Jo, all wearing caning pants and gasping, soaked in sweat, with Jo hobbling determinedly on her one good leg and rubber prosthesis.

'Hell has broken loose,' cried Dr Cazenove. 'Where is the Mistress? We seek refuge – the guards are burning everything and Dr Paine is missing.'

'The Mistress is being whipped,' said Dr Cunliffe.

The Japanese boy looked up at Jo and Kiki and cried 'Ahhh ...!' as Kaa began to toe-frot his glans and he sighed blissfully, crushed beneath the women's bare feet.

'The one-legged girl . . . and the poke-geisha! How many times have I shamefully spied on you!'

'Then, you shall serve them as slaves,' said Dr Cazenove. 'As must I, to atone . . .'

The boy ejaculated his spunk over Kaa's toes, with a cry of ecstacy.

'Thank you,' he sobbed.

Heinz returned, bearing Linda Folsom, her nude body curled foetally and carried by his erect cock in her cunt. Her slippery wet slit slid easily from his cock and he deposited her carefully beneath Belle's squirming buttocks; Linda opened her mouth, like a baby bird, to drink Belle's come. Her body was as white and pure as Geisha's, her hemangioma gone, and there were tiny fins at her anus bud. Dr Cazenove gasped.

'How . . .? Unless the anal injections Dr Paine gave were false!'

'They were,' said Dr Cunliffe, still caning Belle's buttocks. 'Another score to settle.'

'Prepare to settle it soon, then, for she's on her way here, with whatever guards remain loyal,' blurted Dr Cunliffe. 'She hopes Miss Budgen will receive her as a friend . . .'

'Miss Budgen will do nothing of the kind,' said the mine supervisor's voice, emerging from the trapdoor entrance. 'As a slave, perhaps, if she has only her person to offer in transaction.'

They were distracted by the moans of Bluebird, strapped between the bait posts.

'*Awwwmm . . .*' she moaned, 'I want cock, I haven't had it for so long, I'm so *horny* . . .'

Heinz approached and inserted his stiff penis between her thighs, found her vaginal opening and plunged his cock inside her, to begin a vigorous poking. Bluebird cried in pleasure as the massive shaft rammed her cunt and streams of come flowed from her gash, down quivering, muscled thighs.

'Oh, yeah! I need it, you know I need it! But you've grown so big! Whip me and I'll come.'

Still fucking her, Heinz seized a branch and began to cane her quivering bare buttocks. She came almost at once, with howls of pleasure, and Heinz transferred his cock, slimy with come, to her anal pucker. He thrust powerfully inside her bumhole and she shrieked again, at a second orgasm, as he buggered her while continuing to whip her massive, squirming arse-globes.

'I've got a clit, right up my hole! Fuck my hole, fuck me, fuck me, *fuck me* . . . Oh, *yes* . . .!'

At the 50th or 60th stroke to Bluebird's glowing buttocks, Heinz cupped his ear and suddenly withdrew. He had not spurted in her and his penis was still erect. He returned to the others and motioned that they should unfasten Belle from her whipping-trees.

'Feral,' he whispered.

'Oh . . .' Belle moaned, 'but I'm about to . . . I *know* I'm just about to . . . Oh, so *glorious* . . . just one more canestroke, *please,* on my bum, just *one* . . .'

Dr Cunliffe shrouded her in her own discarded skin, which rustled and crackled, its weals replicating those on Belle's own flogged body. Not one inch of her skin had escaped welts. She and the skin-suited Miss Budgen seemed skin twins. There was the sound of running and breaking branches, and a figure wearing a white lab coat, torn and stained, burst into the clearing where the group stood in shadow. It was Dr Paine. She stopped, sniffed and saw Bluebird hanging between the whipping-posts. She flung aside her lab coat, revealing her nude body, the teats and bum massively distended like Bluebird's.

'Freshly whipped!' she slavered. 'Come! I must drink come!'

She knelt, and began to suck and chew at Bluebird's cunt, slurping her generous cunt-juices and feverishly masturbating her own grossly distended clitty.

'*Ahhh . . . ahhhh* . . . Budgen, where are you? We'll make a deal – you can fuck me and whip me, just like before. Get rid of that slut Kaa and I'll be your helper. Budgen! *Ahh . . . God . . . come* . . .'

Belle stepped forward, cane in hand, but her face still in shadow.

'There you are! Cane me to a come, Budgen! Then I'll tongue your clit, do you in the bumhole, everything you like! I need it, Budgen, need cane to come . . . *I've overmedicated, and I'm addicted.* Oh, God, I've made myself feral . . .!'

Belle lifted her cane, but remained silent.

'Please! Just touch my bare arse, and I'll come. Ah, God, I need it so much! Wanking myself won't do any more, you *know* that! *Please* make me come ... *cane me on the bare!*'

Belle slashed Dr Paine across the nipples, once, and the doctor screamed and crouched, slobbering, presenting her arse and wanking her gushing cunt-lips.

'On the bare arse, or I can't come! Oh, God, *make me come! I'll be your slave ... Mistress!*'

Belle handed her cane to Heinz and stepped forward.

*Just one more canestroke ...*

Dr Paine clawed, pleading, at her skin suit, which fell away from her body and Belle shuddered as the crack of the cane lashed her bare buttocks just once, harder than ever before. Slowly, her wealed skin began to rustle and come apart, slithering from her, as she shed. She took back her cane from Heinz as her old skin melted to the ground and Belle Puget stood, raven-haired at head and cunt, her whole nude body glowing dark crimson and pulsing like a gemstone. On each of her buttocks, the letter 'P' glowed, blushing pink. Miss Budgen shed her skin suit and joined the other nude women in a curtsy of obeisance to Belle Puget, their Mistress. They raised their wands of chastisement.

The caning of Dr Darwinia Paine was so savage that the doctor was unable to rise before a flurry of new canestrokes subjugated her and she fell, screaming, with her face scrabbling the dirt. She screamed, too, as Belle lifted her by the hair, so that the others could whip her cunt and titties while Heinz buggered her. She begged to be fucked in cunt, as her anal clitoris was numb, worn out from masturbation, but Heinz ignored her gaping wet gash and continued his merciless ramming of her bumshaft. They flogged her back, belly, breasts and thighs; everywhere except her buttocks. Dr Cunliffe whipped the nipples and the teats turned black and purple, while her daughters caned the jerking pink mass of the extruded clitoris. When her body was livid with welts and her sobs uncontrollable, Dr Paine pleaded again for bum-caning.

'Belle, *please!* We've drunk the same come and shall live forever, and I'll be your skin slave *forever!* My clitty's whipped raw! *Please* cane my arse! Make me orgasm!'

Belle ordered Bluebird released from the whipping-posts and her body replaced in fetters by Dr Paine's. When the doctor was bound and trussed, she and her company turned to leave.

'Oh, God! Belle, *please* . . .!'

'All in good time, Dr Paine,' said Belle. 'Bare-bum caning is a privilege a skin slave must *earn,* and we have all the time in the world, here on Furvert's Island.'

# Memoir 9

I have a few moments free of my Mistress's lash, and unshackled, when I may amuse myself by scribbling in my diary. I read the many pages written above and cannot believe that I really wrote such things! I, the humblest and most submissive girl in the world, who long for eternal shame, submission and crushing, my naked buttocks flogged to the bone by my beautiful Mistress! Sometimes she merely watches with a sneer, pissing in my face, or masturbating and rubbing her come juice into my weals, as my bare bottom is caned by her slave Couzier or by the Japanese triplets. But I squirm most, and my skin smarts most, when my Mistress herself flogs me, for she is cruellest to her own skin slave. The Stones have arrived, at the open invitation I sent them long ago. They did not know that the Mistress who welcomed them would be the true one. I believe that she knew them before, which causes her to show no mercy, for I have heard them all scream under whiplash. Henry is ordered to fuck like a brute, for when he returns to England, his penis shall be enhanced and in permanent erection. Miss Puget has no mercy at all. There! I have committed a whipping offence just by writing her secret name. Belle Puget . . . Belle Puget . . . I must masturbate, at her name rolling on my lips. It took Miss Belle Puget, the real Miss Claw, to bring me to true understanding and pleasure. I hope you read this diary, Mistress, and once more cane my bare bottom raw of skin for my impudence, making my come flow in your worship. Women can never know what mysteries they breed! But, like my Mistress, I am a beautiful young woman who is going to live forever.

# NEW BOOKS

## Coming up from Nexus and Black Lace

### *Brought to Heel* by Arabella Knight

July 2000   Price £5.99   ISBN 0 352 33508 4

Lustful desires provoke these girls to their perverted pleasures, but such wickedness is soon exposed by that most stern mistress, the cane, and then the guilty must come under her cruel kiss to suffer sharp sorrow and sweet pain. The pest, the predator, the pilferer – each with appetites for dark delights. Tempted, they feast upon forbidden fruit, but they cannot escape paying painful penalties. All must submit to discipline as they are sternly brought to heel.

### *Purity* by Aishling Morgan

July 2000   Price £5.99   ISBN 0 352 33510 6

Henry Truscott, dissipated hero of *The Rake*, finds himself faced with the prospect of living on his brother's charity. His efforts to create a new fortune lead him along a path of debauchery and perversion, from stripping girls in Mother Agie's brothel to indulging three ladies at once in a Belgravia drawing room. Nor are his associates idle, with his wife being pursued by the sadistic d'Aignan while the flame-haired Judith Cates becomes embroiled in Sir Joseph Snapes' bizarre sexual experiments.

### *Serving Time* by Sarah Veitch

July 2000   Price £5.99   ISBN 0 352 33509 2

The House of Compulsion is the unofficial name of an experimental reformatory. Fern Terris, a twenty-four year old temptress, finds herself facing ten years in prison – unless she agrees to submit to Compulsion's disciplinary regime. Fern agrees to the apparently easy option, but soon discovers that the chastisements at Compulsion involve a wide variety of belts, canes and tawses, her pert bottom – and unexpected sexual pleasure.

### *Surrender* by Laura Bowen
August 2000   Price £5.99   ISBN 0 352 33524 6
When Melanie joins the staff of The Hotel she enters a world of new sexual experiences and frightening demands, in which there are three kinds of duty she must perform. In this place of luxury and beauty there are many pleasures, serving her deepest desires, but there is also perversity and pain. The Hotel is founded on a strict regime, but Melanie cannot help but break the rules. How can she survive the severe torments that follow?

### *An Education in the Private House* by Esme Ombreux
August 2000   Price £5.99   ISBN 0 352 33525 4
Eloise Highfield is left in charge of the upbringing of Celia Bright's orphaned daughter, Anne. Disturbed and excited by the instructions left by Celia for Anne's education, Eloise invites Michael, a painter of erotic subjects, to assist her. As they read Celia's explicit account of servitude to her own master, they embark on ever more extreme experiments. But Anne is keeping her own diary of events . . . Celia, Eloise, Anne – three women discovering the pleasures of submission; three interwoven accounts of a shared journey into blissful depravity. By the author of the *Private House* series.

### *The Training Grounds* by Sarah Veitch
August 2000   Price £5.99   ISBN 0 352 33526 2
Charlotte was looking forward to her holiday in the sun. Two months on a remote tropical island with her rich, handsome boyfriend: who could ask for more? She is more than a little surprised, then, when she arrives to find that the island is in fact a vast correction centre – the Training Grounds – presided over by a swarthy and handsome figure known only as the Master. But greater shocks are in store, not least Charlotte's discovery that she is there not as a guest, but as a slave . . .

BLACK
*lace*

### *Primal Skin* by Leona Benkt Rhys
July 2000   Price £5.99   ISBN 0 352 33500 9
Set in the mysterious northern and central Europe of the last Ice Age, *Primal Skin* is the story of a female Neanderthal shaman who is on a quest to find magical talismans for her primal rituals. Her nomadic journey, accompanied by her friends, is fraught with danger, adventure and sexual experimentation. The mood is eerie and full of symbolism, and the book is evocative of the best-selling novel *Clan of the Cave Bear*.

### *A Sporting Chance* by Susie Raymond
July 2000   Price £5.99   ISBN 0 352 33501 7
Maggie is an avid supporter of her local ice hockey team, The Trojans, and when her manager mentions he has some spare tickets to their next away game, it doesn't take long to twist him around her little finger. Once at the match she wastes no time in getting intimately associated with the Trojans – especially Troy, their powerfully built star player. But their manager is not impressed with Maggie's antics; he's worried she's distracting them from their game. At first she finds his threats amusing, but then she realises she's being stalked.

### *Wicked Words 3* various
August 2000   Price £5.99   ISBN 0 352 33522 X
Wild women. Wicked words. Guaranteed to turn you on! Black Lace short story collections are a showcase of erotic-writing talent. With contributions from the UK and the USA, and settings and stories that are deliciously daring, this is erotica at the cutting edge. Fresh, cheeky, dazzling and upbeat – only the most arousing fiction makes it into a Black Lace compilation.

### *A Scandalous Affair* by Holly Graham
August 2000   Price £5.99   ISBN 0 352 33523 8
Young, well groomed and spoilt, Olivia Standish is the epitome of a trophy wife. Her husband is a successful politician, and Olivia is confident that she can look forward to a life of luxury and prestige. Then she finds a video of her husband cavorting with whores and engaging in some very bizarre behaviour, and suddenly her future looks uncertain. Realising that her marriage is one of convenience and not love, she vows to take her revenge. Her goal is to have her errant husband on his knees and begging for mercy.

## NEXUS BACKLIST

All books are priced £5.99 unless another price is given. If a date is supplied, the book in question will not be available until that month in 2000.

### CONTEMPORARY EROTICA

| | | |
|---|---|---|
| THE BLACK MASQUE | Lisette Ashton | |
| THE BLACK WIDOW | Lisette Ashton | |
| THE BOND | Lindsay Gordon | |
| BRAT | Penny Birch | |
| BROUGHT TO HEEL | Arabella Knight | July |
| DANCE OF SUBMISSION | Lisette Ashton | |
| DISCIPLES OF SHAME | Stephanie Calvin | |
| DISCIPLINE OF THE PRIVATE HOUSE | Esme Ombreux | |
| DISCIPLINED SKIN | Wendy Swanscombe | Nov |
| DISPLAYS OF EXPERIENCE | Lucy Golden | |
| AN EDUCATION IN THE PRIVATE HOUSE | Esme Ombreux | Aug |
| EMMA'S SECRET DOMINATION | Hilary James | |
| GISELLE | Jean Aveline | |
| GROOMING LUCY | Yvonne Marshall | Sept |
| HEART OF DESIRE | Maria del Rey | |
| HOUSE RULES | G.C. Scott | |
| IN FOR A PENNY | Penny Birch | |
| LESSONS OF OBEDIENCE | Lucy Golden | Dec |
| ONE WEEK IN THE PRIVATE HOUSE | Esme Ombreux | |
| THE ORDER | Nadine Somers | |
| THE PALACE OF EROS | Delver Maddingley | |
| PEEPING AT PAMELA | Yolanda Celbridge | Oct |
| PLAYTHING | Penny Birch | |

| | | |
|---|---|---|
| THE PLEASURE CHAMBER | Brigitte Markham | |
| POLICE LADIES | Yolanda Celbridge | |
| THE RELUCTANT VIRGIN | Kendal Grahame | |
| SANDRA'S NEW SCHOOL | Yolanda Celbridge | |
| SKIN SLAVE | Yolanda Celbridge | June |
| THE SLAVE AUCTION | Lisette Ashton | |
| SLAVE EXODUS | Jennifer Jane Pope | Dec |
| SLAVE GENESIS | Jennifer Jane Pope | |
| SLAVE SENTENCE | Lisette Ashton | |
| THE SUBMISSION GALLERY | Lindsay Gordon | |
| SURRENDER | Laura Bowen | Aug |
| TAKING PAINS TO PLEASE | Arabella Knight | |
| TIGHT WHITE COTTON | Penny Birch | Oct |
| THE TORTURE CHAMBER | Lisette Ashton | Sept |
| THE TRAINING OF FALLEN ANGELS | Kendal Grahame | |
| THE YOUNG WIFE | Stephanie Calvin | May |

## ANCIENT & FANTASY SETTINGS

| | | |
|---|---|---|
| THE CASTLE OF MALDONA | Yolanda Celbridge | |
| NYMPHS OF DIONYSUS | Susan Tinoff | £4.99 |
| MAIDEN | Aishling Morgan | |
| TIGER, TIGER | Aishling Morgan | |
| THE WARRIOR QUEEN | Kendal Grahame | |

## EDWARDIAN, VICTORIAN & OLDER EROTICA

| | | |
|---|---|---|
| BEATRICE | Anonymous | |
| CONFESSION OF AN ENGLISH SLAVE | Yolanda Celbridge | |
| DEVON CREAM | Aishling Morgan | |
| THE GOVERNESS AT ST AGATHA'S | Yolanda Celbridge | |
| PURITY | Aishling Morgan | July |
| THE RAKE | Aishling Morgan | |
| THE TRAINING OF AN ENGLISH GENTLEMAN | Yolanda Celbridge | |

## SAMPLERS & COLLECTIONS

| | | |
|---|---|---|
| NEW EROTICA 3 | | |
| NEW EROTICA 5 | | Nov |
| A DOZEN STROKES | Various | |

## NEXUS CLASSICS

*A new imprint dedicated to putting the finest works of erotic fiction back in print*

| | | |
|---|---|---|
| AGONY AUNT | G. C. Scott | |
| THE HANDMAIDENS | Aran Ashe | |
| OBSESSION | Maria del Rey | |
| HIS MISTRESS'S VOICE | G.C. Scott | |
| CITADEL OF SERVITUDE | Aran Ashe | |
| BOUND TO SERVE | Amanda Ware | |
| SISTERHOOD OF THE INSTITUTE | Maria del Rey | |
| A MATTER OF POSSESSION | G.C. Scott | |
| THE PLEASURE PRINCIPLE | Maria del Rey | |
| CONDUCT UNBECOMING | Arabella Knight | |
| CANDY IN CAPTIVITY | Arabella Knight | |
| THE SLAVE OF LIDIR | Aran Ashe | |
| THE DUNGEONS OF LIDIR | Aran Ashe | |
| SERVING TIME | Sarah Veitch | July |
| THE TRAINING GROUNDS | Sarah Veitch | Aug |
| DIFFERENT STROKES | Sarah Veitch | Sept |
| LINGERING LESSONS | Sarah Veitch | Oct |
| EDEN UNVEILED | Maria del Rey | Nov |
| UNDERWORLD | Maria del Rey | Dec |

Please send me the books I have ticked above.

Name ........................................................................................

Address ........................................................................................

........................................................................................

........................................................................................

.......................................... Post code........................

Send to: **Cash Sales, Nexus Books, Thames Wharf Studios, Rainville Road, London W6 9HA**

US customers: for prices and details of how to order books for delivery by mail, call 1-800-805-1083.

Please enclose a cheque or postal order, made payable to **Nexus Books**, to the value of the books you have ordered plus postage and packing costs as follows:

UK and BFPO – £1.00 for the first book, 50p for the second book and 30p for each subsequent book to a maximum of £3.00;

Overseas (including Republic of Ireland) – £2.00 for the first book, £1.00 for the second book and 50p for each subsequent book.

We accept all major credit cards, including VISA, ACCESS/ MASTERCARD, AMEX, DINERS CLUB, SWITCH, SOLO, and DELTA. Please write your card number and expiry date here:

........................................................................................

Please allow up to 28 days for delivery.

**Signature** ........................................................................